THE

MAVEN

KNIGHT

MATTHEW ROMEO

To the muses.

TABLE OF CONTENTS

THE MAVEN KNIGHT 1

Copyright 2

DRAMATIS PERSONAE 7

PROLOGUE: *Order and Chaos* 8

PART ONE 13

CHAPTER 1: *Blind Rage* 14

CHAPTER 2: *Honest Living* 18

CHAPTER 3: *Slugg's* 26

CHAPTER 4: *A Drastic Change* 31

CHAPTER 5: *The Convoy* 40

CHAPTER 6: *Left for Dead* 55

CHAPTER 7: *Tensions Charge* 69

CHAPTER 8: *Roil Surprise* 82

CHAPTER 9: *Underworld* 97

CHAPTER 10: *Pieces of the Puzzle* 108

CHAPTER 11: *Well Below* 118

CHAPTER 12: *Abrax* 133

CHAPTER 13: *Lost Ideals* 151

PART TWO 167

CHAPTER 14: *Re-Questing* 168

CHAPTER 15: *Rules, Forms, and Drawbacks* 174

CHAPTER 16: *The Great Journey* 186

CHAPTER 17: *The Flames* 190

CHAPTER 18: *Crimsons* 198

CHAPTER 19: *The Maven Way*   212

CHAPTER 20: *The Mission*   224

CHAPTER 21: *Z'hart City*   231

CHAPTER 22: *The Merchant and the Blacksmith*   241

CHAPTER 23: *The Puzzle*   251

CHAPTER 24: *Flight Not Fight*   259

CHAPTER 25: *Catacombs*   263

CHAPTER 26: *Old Friends*   274

CHAPTER 27: *The Lady of the Silver Palm*   285

CHAPTER 28: *The Citadel*   296

CHAPTER 29: *Lockdown*   305

PART THREE   313

CHAPTER 30: *Oasis*   314

CHAPTER 31: *A Part of You*   325

CHAPTER 32: *Re-Earning Trust*   332

CHAPTER 33: *Murky Feelings*   341

CHAPTER 34: *The Outlands*   353

CHAPTER 35: *Bonds*   360

CHAPTER 36: *The Itinerant Mind*   370

CHAPTER 37: *Revelations*   381

CHAPTER 38: *Retribution*   391

CHAPTER 39: *Sacrifice*   401

CHAPTER 40: *Hells Break Loose*   408

CHAPTER 41: *A Departing Arrival*   416

CHAPTER 42: *Inspiration*   427

CHAPTER 43: *Remnant Rematch*   432

CHAPTER 44: *At Our Parting* 442

CHAPTER 45: *Light in the Darkness* 448

INDEX 452

ACKNOWLEDGMENTS 460

ABOUT THE AUTHOR 462

DRAMATIS PERSONAE

TÁLIR a salvager

SARINA a brewer

DEVIN a mercenary

VIVÍAN a huntress

VYCK a mercenary

AIDA a scholar and healer

REMUS a former warrior

ABRAX a cave dweller and former warrior

SEPTEM a magic warrior and member of the Remnant Order

CENTUM a magic warrior and leader of the Remnant Order

SAHARI a noble and the nation of Z'hart's regent

LEIR'TAH a Crimson Cross Outlander leader

ROMULUS a former magic warrior and Tálir's father

VIGINTI a member of the Remnant Order

ÁLVIN a salvager and Tálir's best friend

LÁNNA a friend of Tálir

HOLDIN a friend of Tálir

RITA a lower city informant in Z'hart City and friend of Sarina

DANIUL a blacksmith and informant in Z'hart City

PROLOGUE

Centum

Order and Chaos

THE MAVEN GAUNTLET OPENS, and a tongue of blue fire forms in my palm.

Magic energy rushes through my hand with a warm thrum. Azure flames lick the air and send sparks drizzling from my open palm. Merely a small demonstration of my power, out of sake of boredom. It barely takes any concentration these days.

This bronze armor covering my hand is the legacy of the past. One of the last symbols of the old order of this world. After the Ending a thousand years ago, the Old World had been thrown into turmoil; the united nations of the Domain were torn apart. In the millennium that has passed, corruption and stagnation have festered in our great continent of Pan'gea. It is up to me and my Order to reestablish the natural state of the world. A rot must be burned away. Clenching my fist, I silence the fire and continue waiting.

I stand upon the rooftop of an apartment building in the capital city of Z'hart. The land of ore mining and technology, Z'hart holds a certain appeal for those seeking to build a better world. While my Order has been present in all of the three nations for some time, our current efforts have only just entered the perceptions of Z'hart. We have been summoned from the shadows of existence to answer the call of the newest Lady. Our mission is to quell the Insurgent uprisings that have erupted in the capital. But more importantly, our goal is to find the lost heir of the noble House of Z'hart.

Ten stories above ground level, the complex looks out over an austere looking embassy building. Structured like a cathedral, the metal and concrete used in its frame arches to its pointed roof. The massive front doors have been opened and guests spill out into the steps and front courtyard. Colossal windows line the walls, allowing me to see the festivities that occur within.

"I have eyes on the target," says the woman next to me. *Finally.*

Her long range rifle is mounted on the concrete parapets lining the roof. The meter-and-a-half long bowrifle reflects blue light off the burnished metal that coats it. Almost like waves rippling through it, metal pieces on its side shuffle around as the bowrifle primes for fire.

"Is it a clean shot, Viginti?" I address her by her Numeron

title. "I want all evidence to point at our target. The riots will allow us efficient access to what we need."

Viginti nods and adjusts the scope on her bowrifle. She parts her crimson hair and says, "You really think this will work, Suzerain Centum? Rooting out the Insurgents is one thing. But this…"

I fold my arms across my chest; the bronze gauntlets reflect the blue light of a holoprojection above us. I do not like my decisions to be questioned. I am the First Master of our Order, the ultimate wielder of our mythic power. Still, Viginti is one of my most prized pupils, so I'm a bit more willing to indulge her.

"The Lady of the Silver Palm tasked us with rooting out the Insurgent leader," I remind Viginti of the importance of our mission. "We play this right; we kill two birds with one shot. While Sahari isn't to be *officially* elected until tomorrow, staying in her good graces will greatly benefit us. The Order can ask many favors from her, so we must deliver on our promises."

Viginti looks away from the scope and turns her gaze to me. "She agreed to our oversight on military occupation?"

"In a heartbeat," I reply without merriment. "If the rest of this plan falls into place, we'll have the resources to ensure my plans for this nation and finally find Providence. No one in this last millennium has been closer to finding it than we are. Its power will be ours, and we shall fulfill the prophecy of Ymandi'as."

Viginti gives a dark smile as she returns her focus to the scope in her rifle. I activate my helmet, which slithers over my head and face from within my pauldrons. The heads-up-display has been modified and I can magnify my optics to see more detail. I scan the area for a few moments, hoping to see another intended target. And after a moment, I see him.

With his lovely scholar as a companion, he waltzes into the gala though clearly hesitant. Bronze armor covers parts of his body along with a dark jacket that drapes to his knees. Se'bau Remus: a heretic and a traitor to my Order.

I smile in delight. I might be able to kill several birds with one stone this evening. And Remus deserves a far more painful punishment for deserting our Order for his own glory. Death is too quick. I will make him and his little paramour pay for the discord they've caused.

I keep my disdain in check, for I do respect his tenacity. But no one is allowed to search for Providence without my consent. No one.

"Take the shot," I command.

Viginti hesitates for a second before loading the toxic dart into the secondary firing mechanism. Bowrifles generally fire energy bolts that can stun or kill targets. But modified rifles possess liveround
chambers for stealth darts, tracking devices, or even tranquilizers. Since the energy bolts are bright and loud, we've chosen to use a much stealthier method of taking out our target.

Metal *snaps* resound in the air as the rifle primes. Viginti follows the target with the elongated barrel of the weapon for a few seconds. I see her exhale and cease to breathe. For a moment, she almost seems like a frozen mannequin. The air is still.

The shot fires from the silenced barrel of her rifle. Faster than I can follow, the projectile whizzes across the gap and through one of the towering windows of the cathedral. I cannot see if it hits the target, but Viginti reflects an aura of confidence.

"The target has been tagged." Viginti says, standing up and slinging the rifle across her shoulder. "Soon chaos will be ignited."

"And soon…" I say as we prepare to venture over to the embassy cathedral. "It will be our job to establish order."

PART ONE:

Strangers in the Desert

CHAPTER 1

Sarina

Blind Rage

RED IS ALL I SEE as I'm dragged away from the sound of carnage. Like blood spattered all over a blank canvas, it blocks out my sight. I'm in a feral state of panic. I don't know what's happened. I just hear sounds of violence, the smell of smoke, and feel gloved hands dragging me away.

What is this? My mind wanders in a state of primal fear. Thoughts are scattered like embers blown from a fire and into the wind. Stomach is churning. Blood is pumping. Heart is fluttering.

Anger is rising.

The crimson paint fades slightly from the canvas. There's still a red haze over my field of vision, a mist of hate. I see swarms of people fighting with fists, swords, and rifles. The hall is a ruin and fires shine in my eyes like light piercing through water.

I'm in the grand hall of a cathedral-like embassy building. The refined metal supports and beams crisscross high in the rafters before the ceiling arches above. Dark, glossy pieces of ore form like shingles within the vaunted roof. Chandeliers imbued with holographic lights dangle from chains. Within its fifty-meter diameter, along the burnished cream tiles, are elongated tables laden with spilled food and drink.

I think I made those drinks…

Everything is clouded in a crimson mist. Like everything is bloody or on fire, and it stirs the uncontrollable anger within me. I've never been one to act out of hatred, but I feel like an enraged beast. As the moments pass more of my anger builds in frustration. Uncontrollable and hungry for blood, I try to free myself from the clutches of those dragging me. But I can no longer move. My body is numb, and I panic again in confused trepidation.

What in all the Hells is going on?

My mind struggles to think back.

I remember that my name is Sarina. I remember my job as a brewer for the Blue Den bar. I can remember that I had been invited to an embassy gala to serve ale for the ambassadors. And I remember one reason why there's chaos present in this embassy.

There's been an ongoing struggle between the commoners and the royals in the capital of Z'hart City. My homeland has been plagued with a trade war, leaving thousands to starve. O'ran, the nation of the north, raised their taxes on crops while Z'hart raised its value of ore. So I understand some the reasons behind the violence. But I cannot remember how *this* chaos erupted.

My mind starts spinning. I blank on details, and I can't even remember why I'm being dragged away. Why is my vision misted with red? It feels unnatural.

Through the haze, I can vaguely see silver armored Imperial guards firing blasts of energy to stun many. Commoners have rushed into the cathedral and are clawing, beating, and stabbing at many of the nobles. I cannot focus on anyone's face, for they're all silhouetted in red. They are like fiery demons from the pits of Hells.

A table has overturned and commoners scramble to scavenge spilled food. Like barbarians, they cram food into their mouth ravenously. Some even attack those attempting to obtain food like a wolf fending off scavenging foxes.

It's barbaric. A frenzy of which my own rage feeds upon.

But as I'm dragged from the cathedral and outside into a courtyard, my rage subsides. My body feels cooler, like a fever is wearing off. Soon the red begins to turn darker, like shadows obscuring the light. The night air is refreshing, but my eyes start to roll back. I can hear the faint whine of a repulsor engine.

As I'm dragged through a courtyard, I see more chaos through a hazy field of vision. Four figures stand out in the darkness. A stocky man with black hair, a dark-skinned woman, and two individuals wearing full armor. The man is on all fours before the armored people, and he's in pain. I feel a surge of pity for him.

My attention fades. Muffled voices say, "We have her. Get the ship ready and round up some of the others for transport. More orders await at the Pit."

My mind barely comprehends this. Manacles are locked over my hands as the guards carry me. Darkness clouds my vision the way a storm blocks out the sun. The blinding red of rage has passed. But the cold fingers of fear clutch at my heart. Unconsciousness takes me.

CHAPTER 2

Tálir

Honest Living

"I HOPE YOU PLAN on staking a claim on those fuel cylinders, Tálir!" Álvin calls my name from across the service shaft. "They'll pay for a week's worth of rations."

I hold up the small, metal cylinder and unscrew the lid to get a look at its contents. The muddy sight and pungent smell tell me it is definitely old fuel. Whether or not it is worth anything, that I have to find out the hard way. Taking three cylinders and storing them in my satchel, I gingerly walk along the service shaft within the hull of the ship.

A canopy of frayed wires and pipes obscures most of the way, and the air smells like stale lubricants. Sunlight peeks through openings in the hull, and I can hear the innate breeze outside. A few meters ahead of me is Álvin, my friend for many years. His frizzy blonde hair is pulled back into a bun and he sports a raggedy shirt and pants.

It is around midday as I fiddle with a degraded transport sticking out of the desert sand. The old civilizations are certainly generous when it comes to leaving their old toys behind. The one I am currently salvaging seems to be a trading vehicle. It is one of many in this part of the Pyrack desert, but they are also sparse enough to be rare salvage jobs. The big job for the week is to find working parts, fuel, or sheets of bronze, and I intend to find something valuable to pay for some food. Old fuel cells are relatively valuable, but I don't have high hopes for making a fortune.

It is a tough life, salvaging scrap in the Pyrack—but it is an honest life. Work hard and you get to eat; that was the long and short of it.

"What have you gotten a hold of?" I call, my voice echoing in the empty service shaft. "Hopefully something better than that polished sensor last week."

"Hey, to be fair, it wasn't broken until Jáhn got his hands on it," Álvin admits shrewdly. "And I think he'll go for some repulsor energy chambers this time."

"Aren't those radioactive?" I ask with alarm.

"Only if opened," he chuckles nervously.

Typical Álvin, always riding the line between being risky and being stupid. I can't help but smile at his confidence, though. He knows when to gamble, when to take risks, and when to strive for more than his comfort zone.

I'm never really one to take huge risks in my life; and the life I live is a testament to this. But oddly enough, I am content with the grubby work and shabby living conditions. Certainly not happy, but content.

"So how about we split the profits on the servo actuator?" I ask after a moment. "You'll need some help disassembling it."

"What's to stop me from taking all the credit?" Álvin snorts, looking back at me.

I shrug. "The bond of friendship?"

"That's not really doing it for me, Tálir," he snorts a laugh. "How about you buy me a drink at Slugg's?"

I give him a slight nod. "Let's go to work."

The orange sun is setting over the dunes when we finish disassembling the servo actuator. The temperature is dropping and the wind is kicking up flurries of sand. Clambering down from the transport, Álvin and I start our trek back to the village.

It takes almost an hour, but we make it back just in time to catch Jáhn closing the shop for the night. A glorified garage of sorts, Jáhn's parlor is the main hub for work and trade in this part of the Pyrack. Large enough to hold a transport, the stone floor is covered in sand, oil puddles, and spare parts. Chains and cargo racks drape from the dimly lit ceiling, and tables and shelves line the perimeter. The garage owner is locking up his valuable parts into a container when we enter the garage.

"Five minutes till I close for salvage claims," Jáhn grumbles with his back to us. "Make it quick boys."

I go up to him first as he stands and turns towards me. His dark hair has smears of grime while his tan face seems sunburnt. He stands to his full height, which barely surpasses me as he arches a bushy eyebrow.

"Here are some old fuel cylinders from the transport at Site Four," I say, placing the three cylinders on a nearby table.

"The sludge in these things is barely worth an hour's pay, Tálir," Jáhn says, examining the contents. "All it's really good for is fire fuel. So for three, I'll give you five oreings."

"Just five?" I ask with a tinge of disappointment. "I thought they'd be worth at least ten."

Jáhn gives me a shrug. "Normally they'd only be worth three. But since you're a good kid, Tálir, I'm giving you a bit extra."

Taken aback for a moment, I nod in appreciation as he hands me five of the silver coins. I hear Álvin scoff from my flank.

"Do I get some extra, Jáhny?" he asks with a hint of innocence.

Jáhn regards him with scrutiny, likely because he hates nicknames from his underlings. Scratching at his thin, black beard, Jáhn narrows his eyes and snorts.

"Perhaps I would, if you knew how to keep your mouth shut,

Álvin," he grunts, taking the energy chambers for examination. "But since you don't know how to do that, no! You will not get extra."

Álvin's face loses some color, and his expression turns shameful. Jáhn doesn't care, and instead focuses on testing the energy levels of the chambers. I am relieved that he doesn't try to open the chambers for fear of radiation. The chambers start to hum lightly as his tests are completed, and he looks marginally satisfied.

"Ten oreings for these energy chambers," Jáhn says in a monotone, passing the coins to Álvin. "I'll run a full check later tonight. Anything else you boys managed to salvage?"

Retrieving the parts for the servo actuator, we present the various pieces to Jáhn as he quickly starts checking them. After a moment, Jáhn sniffs and walks to retrieve another handful of coins.

"This actually seems operational, so I'll say 'well done'," he says rather reluctantly. "I'll give a total of fifteen for the actuator. Now shoo! I'm closed for the day."

Taking the coins, I give him a smile of appreciation as we exit the garage and travel into the village. The homes are all made of tattered leather and clay, so it isn't a grandiose place but it is home. Spanning a few hundred meters, Erron's Ville is comprised mainly of huts but also various scrap yards, garages, and markets. A small penitentiary is perhaps the only sophisticated structure in the village, and it serves as one of the main ties to the outside world. Monthly transports make quick stops at the markets and the penitentiary between the nation of Z'hart and the salvage Pits deeper in the Pyrack.

The huts are hewn from low quality leather pieces and rusting metal frameworks. This town hasn't really raised any architects or surveyors, so the town is really disorganized. A jagged and incomplete street made of cobblestones weaves through the center of the village. I walk past another garage that looks like an elongated shack with leather sheets draping over its roof. I can see the penitentiary towering over the huts, for it's the only solidly built structure.

Continuing into the village, I am greeted by many of the neighbors including Holdin and his wife Lánna—both of whom I am very fond of. I almost consider them to be my older siblings. Half a decade older than I, Holdin is a beast of a man due to working in labor fields. But he has a heart twice his size. Lánna is almost as tall as me, and she is much lighter skinned than I. One of the many beauties in Erron's Ville.

"Hard day at work?" Holdin grunts as I shake his meaty hand. "Did that old dog pay you right?"

I rock my head from side to side. "He was fair... relatively."

As per usual, I give an oreing to Lánna as she presents me with a loaf of fresh bread. She uses a rare honey glaze during the baking process, and I've since bought one every day. My cooking skills are subpar, perhaps even non-existent. So I always seek the help of others in matters of food.

"Smells exquisite as always, Lánna," I comment with a smile.

Despite some of the hardships, we all manage to find pleasantries within our lives and form tight bonds of solidarity. We are a community after all, so we protect our own. Each of us helps and supports the other in any way we can. Even Jáhn does his small part to provide work to those with a flair for adventure.

Just seeing these two on my way home makes my day that much brighter. And Holdin is always quick to show his affection for his wife. He kisses the side of her head.

"I'm heading to Slugg's tonight, Tálir," Holdin grunts spiritedly. "I'll try not to drink you under the table again."

"If I let you drink me under the table," I retort. "Lánna won't forgive me if your heart attacks you again."

Lánna snuggles close to Holdin as he laughs. I smile in response, but I reflect on the grim irony at our merriment. He survived one, but he certainly wouldn't survive a second. But they both brush off the remark.

"I'll make sure this old oaf gets home in one piece," I say to Lánna, drawing a snort from Holdin.

"I'd certainly appreciate that, Tálir," Lánna says, looking at me with a smile. "See you the same time tomorrow."

After wishing them a good night, I make a quick stop by the market to pick up a block of cheese and fill up my jug of water. With most of my earnings spent, Álvin and I continue walking a few more meters before he stops in front of his small hut.

"So, split the fifteen?" he asks me.

"That's the idea," I reply sardonically, splitting up the coins in my hand. "I'll only take seven, though. You keep the eight."

Álvin adopts a look of surprise, and a faint grin is etched

upon his clean shaven face. "That's mighty generous of you," he chuckles. "What's the catch?"

"You're buying at Slugg's," I reply, pocketing the seven coins. "I'll meet you there in two hours."

Álvin gives me a mocking salute. "Aye, sir," he says before entering his hut.

As the sun starts to set over the horizon, I finish my walk to my home as a cool breeze hits my face. Life is simple, and there is a calming escapism to it that allows me to feel comfortable. Things aren't likely to change very much out here, so I have chosen to make the best of it.

But it is always present in my mind, that glint of a wondrous future.

CHAPTER 3

Tálir

Slugg's

THE TWO HOURS FLY BY after I return to my hut, bathe, and change into less pungent clothes. Simple tunic and pants, for it's just a night out with the guys. Almost a weekly tradition at this point. I comb back my long, auburn hair so that it drapes down my neck. A shave would usually do, but I'm not trying to impress a lady tonight.

With three oreings in my pocket, I head out to the eastern part of the village. Slugg's is exactly what you'd expect in a sand village. An open, outdoor shack with a wooden bar table guarding the liqueurs. About twenty meters in diameter, the outdoor bar is barely covered by a canopy roof that springs from the center. Stools are planted in the ground, but most choose to stand around the bar. A large circular rack sits in the center and hold the booze while several holoprojections emit above it.

Norn, the thick-skinned, middle-aged barkeep is already passing out shares of intoxicants. Gamma pale ales, Blue Den drafts, Bac whiskey, and even O'ranian wine. A small grill and coal oven are also inside for cooking meals. The best way to keep someone drinking is to give them food to go with it. Many are gathered after the work hours and night has fallen. The stars gleam above and a cool breeze wafts by.

I walk up and pat both Holdin and Álvin on their shoulders. I sit between them and Álvin passes me a mug of ale. Holdin's eyes are glued to the holoscreen affixed above the liquor racks.

"To the servo actuators!" Álvin toasts as we clink our mugs and drink. The Gamma ale is light but bitter, burning a bit at the tongue. I can feel it putting a few pounds on me.

"To my wife Lánna, who I'm surprised still loves an oaf like me!" Holdin cheers in a slurred voice.

"To the oaf and the maiden!"

We cheer and drink more, laughing merrily even as the holoscreen displays disturbing news from the north. As I drink my ale, my eyes curiously watch the headline.

Sahari of House Z'hart Ascends Capital Throne. Anniversary of Older Sibling's Disappearance.

Then the headline shifts.

Lady Sahari of Z'hart City Summons Unknown Military Presence.

Pundits are confused about this decision, questioning her first royal decree since her coronation. I've never really thought much about the other nations, since the Pyrack is sort of a realm of its own. Not many Z'hartians travel out here into the wastes, so why bother with their politics?

"Looks like our western neighbors are about to shit their pants," Holdin grunts, scratching his balding head. "A series of riots right before a coronation. Now this? Ha! Sure am glad we live out here away from the politics. No trade war out here."

"We just get the ass-end of civilization," Álvin chuckles, calling a refill of ale. "Drinking piss like this. Right Norn?"

"Frag off!" Norn replies, slightly offended. He ruffles his matted sand-colored hair.

I plant an oreing on the bar table and Norn passes me another ale and a shot of whiskey. We all get pleasantly intoxicated as we discuss current endeavors, social issues, and bitch about work. Trade wars between western Z'hart and northern O'ran, more Outlander raids in the east, and the increased forecast of Roil storms. I'm more curious about Lady Sahari's summoning of extra military forces. She already has the largest army of Imperial soldiers in the three nations. Are they under attack?

Perhaps we'd find out more on the next convoy rotation. It'll be a while, since the Imperial convoy won't make a trip to our village for another two weeks.

"I hear the riots spread all the way to the foreign embassy in the upper districts." Holdin impressively holds his liquor as he drinks another pint. "O'ran might go to war if their ambassadors were harmed. Excitement might befall us, gents! Z'hart will certainly call upon Pyrack settlements, so that means we are up!"

"I don't think Lánna would like you getting eager for battle," I say with a chuckle. Álvin and I start to play a game of chess with the shoddy wooden set atop the bar. The rules at Slugg's dictate loser buys a drink for the winner.

I demonstrate a king gambit. Both king pawns forward for bait. He falls for it, thinking my defense is open. But I move pawns into a wall. Pick off his pawns. He retaliates with rooks. I counter with knights. Our bishops clash. His queen approaches. But mine closes in on his king. He's in checkmate.

It's all about reading the opponent. If they fall for bait, they're hasty in their movements. Álvin groans. It's the second drink he buys for me. I give him a swig of it first, a show of good sport.

"As strategic as you are, Tálir, I'm surprised you aren't running this town," Holdin cheers to me, finishing his final ale. "You're great at making friends! You'd give those fools in Z'hart City a run for their oreings! Ha!"

"I'd rather stay out of trade wars and political maneuverings."

Holdin shrugs before rising from his stool and stumbling into the bar. He hiccups. I laugh and pat him on the back.

"You think you can make it home, old friend?" I ask with a grin.

He pounds his chest. "If a heart attack can't stop me, ale certainly can't!"

Lánna's going to kill me, I laugh to myself.

Holdin stumbles away from the bar as Álvin and I watch more on the holoscreen. Footage shows dozens of rioters arrested and awaiting imprisonment. Casualties are shown. Burn victims, men stunned by bowrifles, and even a young boy killed by a bowrifle bolt to the head. I feel so much pity for that city. They needed a more secure form of stability, someone to keep them safe. Innocents shouldn't be victim to political squabbles.

"More troops and hired militia are making their way into Z'hart City from an unknown source," a male pundit narrates, images flash on screen. *"No one knows where Lady Sahari received these reinforcements. The Council has deliberated on what action to take against these new developments."*

Álvin wobbles to his feet from his stool, and I rise to assist him. "We used to drink waaaayyy much more than this…" He hiccups.

I laugh, my own mind feeling rather sluggish after a few ales and shots of whiskey. It's time to turn in for the night. So I flick my last oreing to Norn as a tip for putting up with our ruckus. Putting Álvin's arm around my shoulder, I help him walk back to his hut. Well, we end up helping each other. Patting him on his shoulder, he stumbles into his hut as I calmly walk towards mine.

It's a decent life I live. Even if it's devoid of adventure and beautiful single women. But my family here keeps me content. I smile and enter my hut for a good night's sleep.

CHAPTER 4

Tálir

A Drastic Change

THE BRONZE METAL has a distinct molten look to it—the esoteric swirls almost remind me of serpent tongues. Each piece is distinctively smooth and sharp. Pyramid designs are etched into the breastplate. The pauldrons almost have a wing-like shape to them while the gauntlets and vambraces seem like tendrils of fire. A dark exosuit underneath it all is woven of a light yet durable fabric.

A bit worn and clearly generations old, the suit of armor drapes over a wooden mannequin near my tattered cot. It sticks out like a sore thumb next to all of my belongings. My stained clothes, old wooden table, stools, and torn carpets make the armor seem divine in comparison.

It stands out and rightly so, for it is the only thing that connects me to my parents. Well, more specifically, to my father. I've never known my mother and my father had died when I was five. He didn't own much, but he left me his hut and the ceremonial armor he'd inherited. It is my most prized possession, the legacy of my father.

Placing what's left of my earnings in a clay jar, I eat a small meal of bread and cheese to sop up some of the alcohol. The buzz starts to wear off. I pack up the leftovers and clean up a bit before I walk over to examine the armor. Almost a nightly tradition in a sense, I try to polish and study it the best I am able to. Bits of technology are incorporated such as wires and compact computers in the bracers. But without a proper power supply, it is useless. Only mild electromagnetic fields are capable of powering it temporarily.

Detaching one of the gauntlets, I note the scale plating that connects the finger joints to the bracer. It is an odd design, yet it seems strangely practical. I yearn to know more about it, where it originated from, and what its true purpose was.

I spend a few minutes polishing the bronze metal when I hear a noise coming from outside my hut, further in the village. A consistent rumbling hum echo through the air, and it is followed by violent gusts of wind. The humming continues, but grows quieter in pitch after a moment—and the breeze calms.

The monthly convoy? I ask myself as the wind continues to blow against the leather flaps covering my doorway. *They're two weeks early.*

However, that isn't the only noise coming from outside.

Shouting erupts, and I hear several panicked screams and the rushing of boots. I can hear tables being overturned, items breakings, and the striking of flesh. A rush of footsteps starts to head my way, and I freeze momentarily in alarm. Sensing potential danger, I rush to grab the wooden quarterstaff near my bed. I barely have a hand on it when someone bursts into my hut.

Álvin stumbles in, his face dripping with perspiration and a panicked look in his eyes. He reeks of sweat and booze.

"Álvin?" I ask in a perturbed voice. "What's going on?"

"Imperials," he wheezes. "Imperials are scouring through the village, invading our huts! They've sacked Jáhn's garage and bolted Norn! They're heading to my quadrant!"

Fear and anger start to boil inside me. Lánna and Holdin's place would be next, followed by Álvin's. Imperials are a dangerous lot, and we know better than to impede their search. But sacking homes, striking fear, and threatening my friends? That, I won't tolerate. I don't care what they are looking for. The Imperials have no right to brutalize our village.

"Stay in here," I say firmly. "I'm going to try and put a stop to this." As fast as I am able, I adorn the armor handed down by my father and it fits snugly to my frame. I strap on the gauntlets, vambraces, greaves, pauldrons, breastplate, and sabatons. I am ready to defend my home.

"Tálir," he says, concern brewing in his panicked eyes. Shorter than I, he knows better than to physically stop me. "Wait—"

I move him out of the way, giving him a stern glance to stay inside. I hear more shouts outside and the clanking of armor. I can always tell the sound of Imperial armor, the racket their metal makes as the pieces clash together. Another woman screams, and I hear the Imperials ransack another hut down the street.

They will not ruin my home. They will not sack our village. They will not hurt anymore of my friends.

Imperials may be royal guards and enforcers of the nation, but they have no right to besiege our village. My mind doesn't even register the consequences of what my actions could bring. I am a burning furnace of anger and justice. And the Imperials shall be my coals.

Rushing out of my hut in full regalia, I run as fast as I can towards the source of the screams and commotions. I can see some small fires burning in the market areas, and the light of the moon creates an etheric white shine on my metal. With my armor shifting together as I run, I stop suddenly after a few meters. I see Holdin's hut.

He and Lánna are dragged from their home by soldiers I've never seen before. Though they wear some variant of Imperial armor, it all seems less pristine and their right arms are covered by a more bronze armor. Four in total, they all brandish meter-long stunpikes. They are careful to hurt, not kill us.

Holdin shouts at them to leave Lánna alone, but they smash a stunpike into his stomach. Even his size and strength can't help him. He convulses and shouts in agony. I know his heart cannot take the electricity seeping into his body. Tears roll down Lánna's face as the soldiers snort in amusement.

"If you had only cooperated, you could've avoided this, peasant!" one says viciously. He strikes him again with the stunpike. Holdin convulses violently, and then his body goes limp. Eyes wide but unmoving. Lánna screams his name.

My anger begins to bubble forth like water boiling over a pot. It can only be managed if the heat is taken away. But the heat of my anger burns all the hotter.

The soldiers see me approaching in my armor and halt abruptly. Even underneath their helms, I can see the looks of disquiet on their faces. But it's almost eerie the way they stare at me, like they're genuinely astonished.

I give them no time to prepare. With my rage and sense of protection fueling me, I charge. The heat within my chest and head prevents any other thought from forming. Logic, reason, and even strategy are subsumed by the blind fury I feel.

My body slams into the nearest soldier—the one who electrocuted Holdin to death. Dazed and on the ground, the Imperial is too slow to react as I roll atop him. I smack the staff over the side of his head.

The element of surprise runs out faster than I anticipated. Like cold water splashing against one's skin, the initial bite of it fades quickly.

A stunpike whips towards my face and I barely raise my staff in time to block it. Vibrations jolt down my arms. Several attacks follow and I sloppily manage to block or dodge them. More out of luck than skill. Attempting to back away, I find the other two soldiers moving to flank me. I'm not fast enough to move out of the trap.

Like pieces on the chess board, they position themselves to eliminate me. My face grows cold as the blood rushes away. Blocking another swing, I try to duck away and into a better position. A stunpike sweeps under and strikes my legs.

A cold numbness hits my legs and they fold underneath me—sending me falling into the sandy cobblestones. On my back, I try desperately to swing the staff and trip one of the soldiers. One plants his pike vertically and blocks it. The sudden force rips the staff from my hand and it spins out of my reach.

Then, the attacks come.

Blow after blow from three stunpikes pummel every inch of my torso. Surprisingly, my father's armor helps ward off some of the effects. But not for long. The soldiers strike me all the harder with the stunpikes. After a moment, everything is icily numb and I'm barely conscious. Squinting my eyes, I see Lánna cradling Holdin's body and watching me in horror.

I failed to save them. Even if she's unharmed, she lost Holdin and I wasn't fast enough to save them. Shame and anger well within me as I look at her.

"Lánna, run!" I manage to shout.

Something strikes me upside my head and darkness washes over my eyes.

I wake suddenly, gasping for breath as my heart begins to pound in anxiety. At first, I notice my hands and legs are bound by cuffs and chains. Then I notice that I've been stripped down to my shirt and pants. No armor or exosuit. Confusion and fear set in.

Where is my father's armor? I ask myself in a panic.

I'm seated against the metal hull of the Imperial transport at the edge of the village. Fires engulf one of the markets and villagers are beaten and bruised in the streets. The screams have died down, but smoke still fills the air. A small crowd of the villagers watches from a distance. I see Lánna and Álvin watching me with solemn expressions, tears are in her eyes while Álvin looks grave. A dozen soldiers start marching up the loading ramp at the tail end of the ship. Two break away and approach me. They reek of snide arrogance.

"You're not Imperials," I grunt. "Why attack us? Why are you using our convoy?"

"We are the new marshals of Z'hart, fool," one says.

"I've met some stupid people in my life, but this takes the cake," one sniggers tapping my side with his boot. "Not only do we have an account of assaulting Z'hart's new militia, but we have one account of possessing illegal arsenals."

"Domain armor and weapons are now illegal for commoners to possess," the other says, planting his stunpike in the sand. "All belongs to the Remnant, and so yours has been confiscated."

My body is tense like the knots in a lengthy rope. I feel my brow furrow, and my eyes pierce into them like a blade. In my twenty years, I have never been so appalled by the thought that owning my father's armor was a crime. What makes it more outrageous is that no one before has tried to claim it as a crime. This new law has only recently been instilled, and I resent it. My father's armor is not illegal; it belongs to me through right of inheritance.

No one can take that away from me. No one *will* take it from me.

"That armor belonged to my father, bastards," I hiss dangerously, my anger returning. "It is mine by inheritance! You have no right to it, just like you had no right to raid our village. You'll pay!"

One of them smacks me in the face with the butt-end of the stunpike, eliciting a grunt of irritation from me. He says in a slimy voice, "We had orders to scour all settlements for Domain technology. And we had a quota to reach. Maybe if you'd come forth earlier, we could've spared the rest of Erron's Ville. Shame."

I look at the others and see their solemn faces of defeat. I feel an echo of shame eating away at my anger. Was this all my fault? Bruises and blood are upon all their faces. I could've saved them from that. I tried to, and I failed.

"Since we're already on our way to the pits," the Imperial says as they both hoist me to my feet. "You can serve a nice long sentence there with the other rabble we have on board. We'll be taking your armor back to Centum when we're done."

They drag me over to the boarding ramp as I hear Álvin shout, "Tálir! No!"

I glance over my shoulder to give a look of assurance before calling back. "Don't worry about me Álvin! Take care of Lánna and the others! I'll be fine."

Álvin gives me a look that shows his disbelief at my last statement, but nods with reluctance. His face contorts in determined anger, and Lánna bows her head in sorrow. I'm touched by their affection, but I know it will be a long time before I'll see them again. And that measure of grief chips away at my heart as if it were being mined like rock.

As the moonlight illuminates the night sky, I'm dragged into the convoy and away from my home. Words can't always describe a change this size.

CHAPTER 5

Sarina

The Convoy

LOW RUMBLES ARISE from the underside of my seat and reverberate around the chamber I sit within. The reverberation is low and resonant, but somehow musical and rhythmical in a certain sense. One moment the rumble is soft and muffled, then another moment it is loud and clear. It feels like I'm sitting above an orchestra composed of only violins or cellos, but they all only played one, resonating note.

The noise arouses me from unconsciousness, and causes me to lift my head. I am disconcerted and frightened as to what has potentially occurred. My ears start ringing as the vibrations resonate within my head, and my mouth is dry from being left agape. A mixture of smells wafts through my nostrils as I slowly awaken—the smell of stale sweat, engine fumes, and spoiling food.

Fear clutches at my chest, and my breathing starts to quicken as I try to figure out what's going on. I am like a trapped animal in a cage. Primal.

Attempting to sit up, I find that something has been placed around my wrists—binding them to whatever I was sitting upon. Even as I open my eyes, a dark shroud clouds my vision—but it slowly begins to dissipate. While startled at the impairment done to my eyes, I am more terrified at how I've awoken in such a debilitated state.

I try to think back. I am having difficulty remembering what had caused me to lose consciousness. A memory flashes by. The brewing of fresh ale. Orchestral music. Elegant food and clothes.

That's it? All I can remember is that I had been making drinks at a fancy dinner? My mind tries more, but then my memory goes blank. No matter how hard I try, I cannot remember what happened past the dinner.

I look up, my eyes fully functional.

I am seated on a metal bench that is as about as comfortable as sitting on a block of ice; my arms cuffed together by a standard restrainer and chained to the floor of the compartment. Due to the nature of this restraint, I'm constantly hunching over and straining my back. Seated to my right and left are a male and a female similarly restrained, but more composed than I. Across the compartment is another metal bench seating three other males and a female.

Everyone is chained to the floor. Distress tugs at me again.

We all sit in what appears to be a detainee cavity of a repulsor convoy, a ship that is bulky by design but sturdy and fortified to prevent escapes. A few florescent lights that cast a golden hue unto everything in sight light the rusted, fluid stained floors of the chamber. Various chains, cables, and wires affix to the ceiling and dangling like vines in a jungle.

Our compartment is about ten meters across and thirty meters long, enough to hold two dozen and not be claustrophobic. While the compartment is generally empty, there are some containers and supply crates strapped to metal racks about three feet above us. First aid kits and small packages of food stuffs are additionally housed in wall mounted cubbies and shelves.

While it seems like our transport has only been travelling for a day, the cargo aboard the ship might last us up to a week. It isn't a comforting sign.

The control bridge is behind a fortified blast door on the right side of the chamber while the boarding ramp is on my left. At the front of the chamber towards the blast boor, a hooded individual is chained to the floor. It is odd at first, but then I realize it is an attempt at solitary confinement.

He is dressed finely as if he is a member of some importance: a black leather jacket that drapes to his knees with a finer tunic and pants. A crimson symbol is embroidered into his jacket, but I can't tell what it is at my angle. A dark hood covers his head, but after a moment he turns just enough to allow a glimpse of his face. He appears to be in his late forties. Average features make up his gaunt face while black hair drapes past his jawline. Emerald eyes are a colorful contrast to the paleness of his skin.

I'm unnerved more by his collected behavior and aloof attitude. Despite being a prisoner, his face is eerily nonchalant.

"Ey!" one of the men sitting across from me shouts to the solitary prisoner. His voice is loudly obnoxious. It's evident that he's been talking for a long time. "C'mon, what's your deal, man? Why are you so special being up there and not with back here with us stately individuals? I'm not going to stop asking."

The prisoner gives him a quick, apathetic glance through his draping black hair. He remains silent, but cocks an eyebrow before looking elsewhere.

I start to glance at the others around me. I first notice the woman sitting on my left. She's rough around the edges, but very attractive. Her olive skin looks odd with her whacky crimson hair held up by a headband. Her violet eyes shine with perturbed entertainment as she looks from me to the boisterous man shouting insults. She attempts to conceal a snicker.

"He's been like this the whole trip," she says to me, glancing at the rambunctious man. "Drove us ballistic the first hour. But it grew on me. I think he likes the sound of his voice."

I feel a slight sense of relief at her friendliness. However it's overshadowed by my apprehension. I don't know who to trust and what to say. Do I tell her who I am? Do I ask if she's a criminal?

It makes little difference at this point. What I need it information. So I choose to accept her friendliness.

"Or he just wants some attention," I reply clandestinely. "I can imagine his attitude is a response for his insecurities."

"I never thought male prisoners could be insecure about themselves," she says softly with a slight smirk. "But then again, I've seen this act before."

She pauses for a moment, and then says, "I'm Vivían, by the way."

I relax somewhat, yet I remain cautious. It can't hurt to reveal a name. I don't need to go into lots of details, so I nod curtly and gesture to myself. "Sarina. I'd shake your hand, but—" I cut off and raise my manacled hands.

Vivían smiles but says nothing more, and instead diverts her attention back to the rambunctious scene before her. It's like she's attending a play.

While a year or two older than I, Vivían seems much more laid back and composed. Even her wardrobe hints at a hedonistic side: tattered tunic which shows her midriff, short trousers, tall sandals, and a russet colored duster.

I'm a stark contrast to Vivían in both appearance and fashion since we seemingly hail from different lifestyles. My beige tunic, fitted trousers, boots, and shoulder-cape clash with her attire. Not that it matters anymore, for my clothes now smell of beer, sweat, and oil.

The boisterous man across from me is still in the heat of his own commentary. I actually believe he likes listening to his own voice.

"Seriously, I'm all for solitary confinement and everything, but why did they pick his ass?" He lets out a scoff and tries to lean back. His lips purse under his dark goatee. "Maybe I want to be in solitary confinement! I was the one who punched that Z'hartian ambassador."

He lowers his head to his manacled hands so his fingers could scratch his black hair. Garbed in an azure tunic and dark pants, he seems to fill out his clothes with muscular weight.

"Oh please, Devin," the man sitting next to him snickers. "You haven't done enough to get locked up in a juvenile detention facility. I think I deserve the honor. I boned that warlord's fortress last month."

Devin, I think to myself and pinning the name to the face. *Let's see if any other names are mentioned.*

The man next to Devin is a wily, blonde haired and oliveskinned man with green eyes. Similarly dressed like Devin, they both seem to be in their mid-twenties and clearly have history. Although, the blonde haired man seems much more boyish.

Devin regards the other man by saying, "It's a shame only you and I find this fishy, Vyck." Devin eyes the rest of us before addressing the longhaired man. "C'mon, man! C'mon! How come you aren't on the bench with us?"

Vyck, I make a mental note. *Three down, four to go.*

"Do you understand what we're saying?" Vyck goads to the solitary prisoner, with no avail.

As Devin and Vyck continue to cajole the anonymous detainee, I begin to observe some of the other prisoners sitting across from me. Aside from Vyck and Devin, there is only one other male and a female cuffed along their bench.

The male is a stocky, dark haired, bearded, and milky-skinned individual who sports a very similar outfit to the furtive prisoner. I'm instantly transfixed by the similarity, and I begin to grow suspicious. The only difference is that he has torn off the sigil on his jacket. Strange.

Whatever the case, I don't think it's a coincidence that the two are wearing identical outfits.

Sitting next to him is an aristocratic, dark-skinned woman with a bald head. She wears a dirtied grey tunic with tan trousers, and the shirt looks like it has burn marks on it. Her face is rather gaunt and bony while her dark skin appears to be thinly stretched over her cheeks. It's a trait that hints she hasn't eaten in some time. She stares intently at the man next to her, whispering to him soothingly. They seem to be the same age, perhaps in their mid-twenties.

It takes a moment, but the man's skin turns even paler and he starts cradling his head. A sickness must be welling within him, for he looks stricken. Yet, he doesn't cough, sneeze, or vomit. He just shakes and grunts.

But as I observe the two and their inaudible conversation, something about them seems familiar. Part of me feels like I've seen them before, but my memory is still foggy. Nevertheless, I concentrate on thinking back.

A muddled image of a banquet makes its way into my head, and it seemingly took place within some sort of cathedral. It must've been a formal festivity, but my mind blanks on any other details. I have some of the puzzle pieces.

I just need to find the rest.

Glancing to my right, I notice the last male sitting a meter from me. He's maybe two years older than I, with shoulder-length auburn hair and bronze skin. His rangy, stubble-coated face and wiry frame tells me he doesn't live in luxury. Tattered clothes smeared with utility stains and his stench of engine fuel says he might be a mechanic. Maybe a salvager.

Yet, the most striking thing that stands out to me is that his hazel eyes reflect a plethora of emotions. Eyes showing anger, confusion, grief, and fear all at the same time. It is beguiling.

I can't help but wonder what is occurring in his mind. Is he feigning it? There is something about him that seems to be hurt, and yet vengeful. His eyes start to dart around as he silently looks at each of us. Hazel finds blue, and his gaze fixes on me.

Instantly, I feel a bit of awkwardness after staring at him so I turn away. Odd, because I've been over my fear of talking to men for some time. But, there is always that awkward feeling I get when someone sees me looking at them. However, he doesn't take it as an offense, but more as an opportunity to say something.

"You know, it's impolite to stare at someone without saying 'hello'," he says in a low voice, his mouth forming a faint grin. Clearly he's trying to use a small façade to hide all that emotion. I'll bite.

"I wasn't staring," I reply shortly, trying to brush it off, "I was just observing you. Along with everyone else. I'm a bit new to this."

His response is raising a dark eyebrow in perturbed interest. His hazel eyes gaze into mine, and we both see hints that we're masquerading.

"Ey, checking us all out are you?" Devin suddenly boasts, turning his attention to me and giving a flirtatious wink. "I'm flattered, m'lady. But I can tell you, I'm more of a catch than the rest of these people, so why bother with them?"

"Please, Devin. We both know that I'm much more good looking," Vyck adds slyly, cocking an eyebrow. "She'd do better to observe my good looks over yours. We'd bone and make prettier babies."

"How about I observe the right to kick your teeth in?" I rebuke with a bit of venom, leaning forward threateningly.

While I'm only eighteen, I know enough about men to tell which ones need lessons in respect.

Devin is not fazed by my attitude, and instead raises his eyebrows and adds, "You're a feisty little one aren't you? Don't worry; I'll go easy on you for your first time."

"Leave her alone. Don't you two have anything better to do than harass a girl?" the dark-skinned woman hisses, giving Devin a scathing glance.

The others freeze for a moment. This is the first time she's apparently uttered anything audible to anyone other than her male companion. I find it perplexing, but I give her a nod of appreciation regardless. Devin and Vyck shrug and continue cajoling the man up front.

Ignoring them, I look at her squarely and give her a halfsmile. "Thanks for that," I say with gratitude. "I'm at a loss as to why you'd help me, not that I'm complaining."

"It's the least I can do," she shrugs with her shoulders. "After what you've been through, I don't mind lending support, Sarina. You had a rough time the other night."

Taken aback momentarily, I adopt a look of wide-eyed astonishment. So something did happen. The night before last. A sense of familiarity clings to my mind. When did I meet her?

"Have we met before?" I ask, leaning back with unease. I mustn't betray my curiosity.

She seems genuinely astounded. "You mean; you don't remember that night?" she asks with raised eyebrows. "You were one of the brewers. Remus and I both ordered drinks from you at the bar."

Remus, I say to myself as I attempt to remember where I'd met them.

"I'm having some… memory issues," I reply with a quizzical look. "What was your name again?"

"Aida," she voices. "We were present when the riots kicked off. You were caught in the middle of it."

Even as she says it, my mind is still groggy and struggling to remember the details of the event. I blink and see fists and blood.

Fire. My hand pressing a man's face away. I inhale with dismay. What happened? If she was there, she can tell me what happened. But that feeling of mistrust grows stronger in me. Like vines growing to obscure a tree.

"I'm sorry, I don't remember anything," I say, shaking my head as if to clear it.

"I can explain more to you when we're in a more civil environment, if you wish." Aida glances at Devin and Vyck. "I don't want the wrong ears listening in."

The vines of distrust are snaking all around the tree. Explain more alone? Wrong ears listening? I'm not ready to trust. Not so suddenly. For all I know, she might be the one responsible. She might not. One thing is certain. This is no coincidence.

"Thanks for the offer," I respond rather coldly. "But, I think I should figure that on my own."

Before Aida can respond to my statement, Devin and Vyck pipe up again with renewed vigor. They glance at the rest of us.

"Well, now that we're getting all cozy, why don't we try and get the fragging Hells out of here?" Devin snorts loudly, eyeing the exit ramp to the compartment. "I don't plan on working in a salvage Pit for the rest of my life."

I'm being shipped off to a Pit? I wonder frantically. *What could have possibly happened that night to cause this?*

Vyck glances over at the man chained at the front of the cabin. "Well, maybe he'll kindly represent all of us," Vyck adopts a smirk on his boyish face. "Don't think we forgot about you, good sir."

The hooded man looks up at us with cold apathy. The look in his eye is both haughty and dangerous. Instantly there is a feeling of icy terror emanating from everyone in the room.

Although his expression is hard to read, his intentions become clear. He straightens his back as if he's about to stand up.

"Oh you won't be forgetting this anytime soon, dear ones," he says in a portentous voice. It resonates throughout the cabin.

Silence elapses for a moment as we sit in unease. Despite the chains binding him to the floor, his dark omnipresence is not contained. In some strange sense, it is almost charismatic.

But that ominous foreboding in his words tells me that something is about to happen to him. About to happen to *us*.

"By the Sage God, he speaks," Vivían comments in genuine astonishment, her eyes are wide with curiosity and trepidation. "Although, I figured your voice would be deeper."

"What in all the Hells are you talking about, man?" Devin addresses the man, his face conceited. "Forgetting what?"

The prisoner cracks his neck with a minor grunt. "Let's just say that this trip here is going to be cut a bit short." His words ooze with chilling aloofness.

In eerie conjunction with his words, there is a flash of ruby light and the cuffs binding him shatter. The remains of metal clank unto the floor. I stare at him incredulously. *How? Is he a fragging magician?* He stands up, stretches, cracks his back, and lowers his hood. His full mess of black hair drapes to his shoulders—and his aloof demeanor shifts to one of purpose.

He starts to walk through the center aisle with stern intent, clearly heading towards the exit ramp at the back of the convoy. His shoes tap against the metal floor. Movements are almost regal, arrogant in a sense. Like he's about to attend an opera.

As he passes us, Devin shows slight fear on his face and asks, "Who in all the Hells are you?"

The man pauses for a brief moment and looks over at Devin, clearly vexed in posture but there is a small hint of eccentricity emanating from him. Perhaps it's genuine or perhaps it's stirred by his own haughtiness that he considered and paused for Devin's question.

I can't see the look on his face, but I'm sure it is one of shrewd confidence as he says, "You can call me Septem. Not that it matters now."

I tilt my head in utter bewilderment at the sound of his name as some others also trade looks of perturbation and slight trepidation. His name is from an older dialect, one that hasn't been used for at least ten Cycles. It is more number than name.

As Septem walks back towards the exit ramp, I remark in a sharp voice, "What in the fragging Hells kind of name is that?"

Septem says nothing as he reaches for the activation switches at the back of the cabin.

"It's not my name," he finally says in a baleful voice, glancing over his shoulder at me. "It's my title."

He then turns his head away and glances coldly at Remus,

who in turn gives him a grim look; the likes of which sends shivers down my spine. The standoff happens for only a few seconds before Septem turns his gaze back towards the opening ramp.

The ramp begins to slide open. Over the metallic clicks and scrapes is a screeching sound as the ramp begins to open and reveal the outside world to us.

We're flying nearly ten meters above golden sand dunes that weave across a vast expanse of land while occasional rock formations dot the terrain. The rock formations seem large enough to support caves or underground crevasses while the dunes vary in height and depth. Golden sunlight reflects off the sand with an almost etheric glow of heat as the gust of the engines kicks up clouds of sand dust.

Septem turns to give us a mocking salute before leaping off the ramp. I'm instantly dumbfounded. *Is he manic?* But a more dreadful fact takes my attention. As the convoy continues to move though, the dunes fail to yield any variation of terrain, which leads me to one stressful conclusion.

We're in the middle of the Pyrack, I think to myself. *Shit.*

The convoy suddenly lurches to its starboard side. An explosion rattles through the air. My head snaps back in whiplash. Seconds later, I feel the ship swiftly descend towards the ground at an incredible speed. Klaxons ring through the chamber as muffled shouting emanates from the cockpit. I feel the ship spiraling downward. Sparks fly from the ceiling lights as they short out, and loose materials start to cascade unto the floor.

Around me, everyone is attempting to brace for impact. Sheer terror is on most of their faces. Except for Vivían. Her eyes gleam madly with excitement and she laughs.

"Ey guys, in case it's unclear," Devin yells over the commotion, clearly bracing himself. "Hang the fragging Hells on to something!"

"No shit!" I call back, attempting to cling to my cuffs as a security measure.

I'm not sure what I'm going to accomplish by holding on to my chains, but in a state of panic, it is all I can think to do. And after another moment, the convoy hits the ground.

CHAPTER 6

Sarina

Left for Dead

EVEN AS I ATTEMPT to brace myself, I feel the ship collide with the ground before it flings all of us towards the front cabin. We all land in various places due to the placement of our chains: the walls, floor, or the opposite bench. I'm thrown to the floor as the back of my head strikes the oxidized iron, driving the breath from me and causing my eyes to lose focus for a moment. While disoriented, I glimpse Devin landing in a similar fashion a few feet next to me; his face contorts as his back hits the flooring.

After hitting the ground, I can feel the vibrations of the convoy skidding through the sandy terrain and crashing into various rock formations. The ship starts to capsize; causing everything to fall towards the starboard side as the convoy turns on itself.

There is chaos. Fear grips my chest and I close my eyes as if to hide from the pandemonium. I can't. My teeth chatter as the ship shakes and turns.

Upon capsizing, all of the crates and packages within the cubbies and shelves cascade from their resting spots and tumble to the now-capsized ceiling. Sparks flash through the air and clouds of sand are kicked up from the impact and pouring into the compartment from the opening. A loose object hurls itself towards me and strikes the left side of my face, driving the breath from me and sending pain into my cheek.

The ship comes to a sudden halt as I reorient myself from the shock of being hit in the face.

All of the loose crates and packages are scattered across the capsized ceiling as piles of golden sand cake the corners and edges of the ground. Floor panels are loose, electrical wires have been strewn about, and sparks frequently flicker from the broken florescent lights. Fluids of various sorts leak from cracks in the hull, and the stench of fried circuitry and burning oil wafts through the air.

The rest of us are all dangling five meters in the air from the capsized benches, our chains still securely bolted to the seats. Part of me laughs at the ridiculous sight. Seven people all hanging down like puppets.

I take a quick look around to see if my fellow prisoners have sustained any injuries. To my disappointment, both Vyck and Devin remain unharmed and are attempting to free themselves from their cuffs. Part of me wishes they had been injured, mainly for the sake of initializing a bit of humility on their parts. Remus has been knocked unconscious by something and a small trickle of blood seeps from under his hairline. Aida is doing her best to get free and tend to him despite her injuries. I admire her priorities.

Vivían is gingerly working to get free since her cuffs managed to cut into her wrists, drawing a fair amount of blood in the process. She pauses to regard me with a pained, yet concerned gaze.

"Hanging in there?" she comments. "Not meaning to spout shitty puns already."

"I was thinking something similar, but I didn't want to steal your thunder," I grunt with a smirk as Vivían reorients her attention.

Turning my head, I notice the young salvager dangling a meter away from me. Unconscious and bleeding from a gash on his forehead. He's barely breathing. I can hear something outside of the ship. Movement. A strange sense of urgency builds within me. I need to get him down. *I* need to get down.

Looking up, I notice the chains holding me are bolted to the floor by only one, rusted screw. It's been loosened by the crash. In my dangling state, I realize that I might break the screw if I put my full weight in momentum down on the chains. A long shot, but it is the best idea I can think of.

Using my legs, I start to swing back and forth before using the downward momentum to yank on the chain. I fail at the first attempt and the screw let out a mere creak as I begin to swing back and forth helplessly. It takes several tries, but eventually I'm able to pull the chain at the right instant that causes the rusted screw to snap with a click. I fall to the ground.

While I land with less grace than I intended, I stumble for a moment as a sharp pain curls up within both of my legs. I shake it off. Immediately, I scour for something to pick the locks on my restraints, eventually coming across some flayed metal wires. Familiar with picking locks, I proceed with relative ease and unlock the cuffs after a moment of tinkering with the locking mechanisms. My chains fall to the ground with several loud clanks. I glance around.

Vyck and Devin have also managed to free themselves and are scouring the dispersed equipment for anything of use. Aida has also succeeded in freeing herself and is attempting to figure out how to free the cataleptic Remus from his chains. Vivían has obtained some of the flayed cables above her and is endeavoring to pick the locks in her manacles. Her high competency causes me to focus on helping the unconscious young salvager.

Still unconscious and bleeding from his forehead, the man hangs from the shackle like a marionette in mid show. I start to fear for him. His breathing stops.

I note that one of the links in his chain is worn and thin, close to snapping in half due to the rust. I realize that a strong tug with enough weight could potentially break it, a much easier way than breaking the screw bolting it to the ceiling.

However, even if I managed to break the chain, his wilted body would crash to the floor and likely cause him more impairment. Part of me wonders why I even care so much for his wellbeing. But I can't just let him die.

The movement outside is growing louder. The others begin to sense it as well. Outlanders? Dune whargs? I've heard stories about shipwrecks being immediately swarmed by those creatures, survivors are ripped to shreds. A howl emanates from beyond the ship.

Panic rushing through my chest, I yank the salvager from his chain and do my best to ease his fall. It's less graceful than I'd hoped. His body tumbles atop mine, and I'm forced to roll him off. Seconds later, I start trying to resuscitate him.

I hear Devin whistle. "Ey, now that's some fierce foreplay if I ever saw. Get him girl!"

"Time to get boned," Vyck adds. I see them staring at the scene out of the corner of my eye.

I do my best to ignore their piggish jeering and continue pressing the salvager's chest. Twenty-nine. Thirty. I breathe twice into his mouth, pinching his nose. Nothing.

C'mon, c'mon! I say to myself, starting the count over again. I get to thirty again and breathe into his mouth.

He spurts up. Coughing and trying to suck in air. His eyes are still closed, but his breathing stabilizes. Adrenaline still fuels me. I hear Devin and Vyck clapping condescendingly.

"Two minutes and he's done?" Devin snorts. "Shit, must've been his first time. Needs to work on lasting longer for our lady here."

With disgust and anger fueling me, I whirl on him and throw my clenched right fist into his jaw. While I don't use all of my strength to hit him, he's still taken aback by the attack and grunts in shock. He takes a step back while Vyck jumps to his defense.

"Go frag yourself," I hiss, entering a defensive stance in the event of a counter attack. "Maybe you'd be more useful if you actually helped instead of standing and scratching your balls."

Devin straightens his posture and stretches his neck, almost like my punch barely fazed him. Something emanates from him though. His broad chest puffs up and his eyebrows raise.

He says nothing in response to my attack, but his eyes reflect a hint of eager surprise. He gives a mischievous smile and starts to say something when Aida shouts, "Knock it off! Something's heading this way!"

Another howl punctuates her sentence, and Devin and I both adopt looks of dread. Our squabble has ended. But now, we need to prepare for whatever is out there. Everyone else has managed to escape their chains and shackles and Remus has regained consciousness.

There is a sickened look of pain on his face, but there is also fear. Howls emits from the desert beyond the hull, barely fifty meters away it seems. We all start to rush to patch wounds and find weapons of any sort. Remus sits with his back against the hull, still in a state of shock.

Devin and Vyck gather their chains, seemingly with the intent to use them as weapons. Crude and impractical, it is better than nothing. I grab a length of metal pipe for protection.

Movement is right outside the hull, making its way towards

the open ramp. Something is growling. Definitely a dune wharg. Before I can consider it further, Devin and Vyck dart past me and head towards the opening of the ship. Instantly I think they're trying to flee, but then I see them take cover behind the parapets flanking the opening. Alarm strikes their faces, and sweat glistens on their pale foreheads.

"It's right outside," Devin warns in a quiet voice, tinged with urgency. "Take cover and remain quiet. I smell wharg fur."

A surge of adrenaline rushes through me, and I dart up to the entrance and take cover next to Vyck. Why did I do this? I'm not much of a fighter. Especially against a beast. But it was all I could think to do. Survive or die.

As I wait there, I perceive a soft patter of footsteps striking the sand outside the convoy and approaching the opening. Whoever it is, they rode the whargs to get here evidently. A wharg snarls angrily. I can hear the snapping of maws.

Could it be a band of mercenaries or Outlanders? I think to myself as a mixture of resentment and alarm goes through me. If indeed it is, we are woefully unprepared to defend ourselves, let alone sneak away or barter with them. The native bands of Outlanders normally keep to themselves, but they are also ruthless when it comes to raiding villages or convoys. My heart pounds in my chest. My body turns cold and my breathing becomes faster.

Someone casually walks through the opening with deliberate footsteps. Yet, his steps are deliberate, concise, and resolute. And it sounds very familiar. A figure appears in my line of vision as the rest of the party tenses in caution upon seeing the intruder.

It's Septem.

Still attired in his long jacket and pants, the only perceptible alterations to Septem are a custom-made, hand and half sword strapped to his back in addition to sporting a few pieces of armor. While I can't view the sword, the armor is of a unique design that I've never seen before.

Almost as if it is a liquid metal, the bronze colored armor hugs his chest firmly and gauntleted hands protrude from the black sleeves. The black leather drapes over the armor like a parted curtain, and the colors accentuate each other in a surprising way.

With his jacket in view, I finally am able to see vividly what the symbol is: an upside-down V overtaking a pyramid all enclosed in an ornate circle. While ominously captivating, I'm struggling to associate which royal house or tribe possesses such a symbol. I'm rather enthralled by it, even more so when I see the same esoteric symbol engraved at the center of his breastplate.

"Well, isn't this a surprise," he comments rather slyly, but with a hint of genuine surprise. His face remains cold. "That was quite a mess of a crash; I was beginning to wonder if anyone made it out alive."

"So you mean the guards didn't make it?" Vivían queries, attempting to divert his attention.

"Some did, but they're dead now. They challenged me and paid the price," Septem replies casually. "No need to thank me. But they were only going to cause more problems." He pauses, then adds in a more resounding voice, "And to Devin, Vyck, and Sarina: those are some terrible hiding spots. A bit cliché, don't you think?"

He doesn't even bother turning his head to address us. He'd figured out where we were before entering the ship. *Dammit!* Devin closes his eyes and heaves a sigh of exasperated defeat as he saunters into Septem's view. Vyck and I follow suite, though we brandish our weapons in a flimsy display of threat.

Septem's cool collectiveness practically shatters our defensive rally. He shows no fear of us, and rightly so. But my mind reels as to why. Why was he here on the transport? Why was it shot down? Only Outlanders are known for attacking convoys. But the evidence points to Septem's involvement with the crash. Septem is definitely not an Outlander, but he also isn't in league with the Imperials. His uniform and arcane crests hint towards his association with something outside public knowledge.

So what is his game plan?

Even as my thoughts reel, Devin takes a threatening step towards Septem; but all the latter does is wave his hands in a dismissive gesture.

"Those *weapons* won't do you any good against bowrifles, Devin," he comments, almost apathetically. "My men have got me covered in the event my reflexes prove lax, which is very unlikely in any case."

As if on cue again, a bowrifle stunbolt strikes the ground inches away from Devin's foot; causing him to jump back in alarm. Scanning the illuminated entry, I note two figures silhouetted several meters away from the opening but I can't distinguish their appearance. The scorching sunlight obscures all but their shadows, and the breeze wafting by makes it seem as if their bodies are almost ethereal.

"What in all the Hells is this, man?" Devin grumbles as he composes himself. "Are you a gang leader? An Outlander? Is that why you escaped, because your thugs shot us down?"

Septem regards him coldly. "My Order is far beyond the pettiness of those vagrants," he says, tilting his chin up with arrogance. "Thugs did shoot us down, but only because it serves my mission. Plans are in motion."

Remus gives Septem a strained look of bewilderment, even though something in his eyes hints at familiarity. Septem's eyes quickly flash at Remus. Clearly the two know each other, that much is obvious. But how do Remus and Septem know one another?

Had they worked together before something untoward had befallen Remus? Or did they simply possess a rivalry like so many did in various professions?

"Alright, you've got my attention. Who are you two?" Vivían asks, noticing the subtle exchange.

Remus lowers his head in a bow as Aida looks at him with a concerned, yet unyielding gaze. It seems as though she is adamant for him to reveal his association with whatever he had been a part of.

Evidently Aida has just as many issues with this past connection as Remus did, which makes me consider how close the two are.

Septem remains emotionless and answers, "All you really need to know is that we used to be… brothers. Not by blood. But my dear Remus here decided that his own personal glory was more important than our Order's mandate."

"If you call it 'mandate'," Aida mutters with a note of derision, her eyes shoot towards Septem.

He ignores her remark and concludes, "These days I no longer have such reservations for brothers, sisters, or friends. They are petty distractions."

"How very wise of you," I retort sarcastically. "But what is this Order you speak of?"

"I've already said too much, Sarina," Septem says silkily with impatience. "If I were to go into details, we'd be here all day. And I certainly don't want to hang around this arid dustbin till sunset. But my Order has been around longer than any other—and is far grander than any of you can imagine, well except for Remus, I suppose."

"And me," Aida comments, narrowing her eyes at him.

"Yes, that too," Septem dismissively replies, barely paying her any attention.

There is a pause in the air that lasts for a few moments. But if it is stirred by tension or fear, I cannot tell. Is he here to kill us and make the crash look like an accident? His nonthreatening demeanor convinces me otherwise, but there is a motive he hasn't disclosed yet.

"So where do we go from here?" Vyck interjects after the moment elapses.

"I left something behind," Septem says drawing his sword in a threatening manner. My heart starts to race. Dread bubbling up. "Move or die."

He walks towards us and we immediately falter in his wake, as do the others. Even if we did attack him from behind, his men outside would shoot us. I don't know what to do. He retrieves something from the front of the compartment—something hidden in a wall panel. I can't see what it is, but he pockets it and makes his way back towards us. He brandishes his sword and we stay in place.

"Are you going to kill us?" Vyck asks, unease in his throat.

"Why would I kill you?" Septem asks, facing us. His arrogance oozes out like filth. "You're already stranded in the Pyrack, far from any hospitable civilization. And I have no use for you, so why waste the effort?"

"You son of a bitch. I'm not going out like that!" Vyck snarls taking a step forward, but stops as Septem holds the sword to Vyck's throat.

"I'm afraid you are," he sneers; his arctic demeanor cuts the air like a blade. "There were plans in store for some of you according to my Order. But I think I'll spare them of your uselessness."

"Why?" I shout, restraining an urge to lunge at him. "Why do this to us? Do you not have the balls to kill us yourself?"

Septem looks directly at me with a look of annoyance. "I like the idea of the desert taking you for its own; it's a lot more poetic than dying by the sword."

"Yup, he's got no balls," Devin retorts.

"You'll be the victim of your own hubris one day, Septem," I spit. "I won't forget this!"

His eyes reflect cold apathy as he remains silent. It seems beneath him to even respond to our taunts. And it makes him all the more detestable. My fear is replaced with a dark wrath, like a shadow growing over a light.

He doesn't bother with any kind of retort, and merely turns quickly on his heels. As he walks towards the exit, he pauses briefly to look at the salvager whom remains unconscious. A deep, seething look of disgust radiates from Septem's eyes as he stares at him. *What in all the Hells is that about?* Does he know him?

I barely get a chance to ponder before his gaze turns to glance at Remus. Septem's eyes fail to yield any kind of emotion as he gazes at Remus for the span of a few seconds.

Remus emotes so much more. Pity, frustration, apprehension, confusion, and even curiosity can be seen within his eyes. It's a whirlpool of expressions, all swirling together like the winds within a storm. What kind of exchange is this? One between old friends or bitter enemies?

"Wrong— Path—" Remus says suddenly even as Septem looks away.

We are all speechless due to the exchange, but more to the fact that it is the first time Remus has said anything on his own. *Wrong path?* I repeat to myself. Is he trying to warn Septem about something? Or is it merely a veiled taunt?

Septem doesn't respond, in a very predictable fashion. But I can see under his jacket and armor that he's tensing up. So he *is* relatively human.

Stepping suddenly, Septem walks out the exit without so much as a second glance towards us. His walk is quick and deliberate; it seems like he is repressing something. Anger? Fear? I can't tell. No doubt it's caused by Remus' comment, but there's something off about the whole exchange. Septem doesn't seem the type to reveal too much about what's going on inside his heart and mind.

After a moment he's gone, and I hear the muffled sound of snarling whargs running off into the distance. The sound continues for a moment, and softens into the distance leaving us within the wastes.

CHAPTER 7

Sarina

Tensions Charge

THERE IS AN AURA of trepidation as we remain motionless and silent for several minutes; clearly all are affected by Septem's actions. I start to wonder if anyone would even come and look for us, despite Septem's claims. Not many people mourn for convicts, except for maybe the slavers we are being delivered to.

"Well I for one don't plan on dying out in this shit way!" Devin declares after a moment. "I'm too young to die!"

He rushes out the exit, but doesn't leave the vicinity of the crash site. From what I can tell, he seems to be searching around the ship for something. Vyck shortly follows suite, though not in as mad of a rush as his partner had been.

"Yeah, I've got so much to live for!" Vyck says as he leaves.

"You're both like twenty-five," I call out to them. "That's not that young."

"We know!" they both shout back in conjunction.

I sniff, both in amusement and irritation. I turn my attention back to the others only to see Remus and Aida collecting what appears to be packs of dry food and medical supplies. Aida looks at Remus after filling a metal box with a dozen packages, concern glinting in her eyes. "You did well, Remus," she says quietly to him. "You don't owe him anything."

Remus returns her gaze with her a look of appreciation but says nothing, continuing to fill another crate with packages. The signs are there. The way the gaze at each other. The soothing whisper of voice Aida gives him. But it's not just intimacy in her eyes, it's also worry.

What is going on with these two? I ask myself. *What could Septem have done to Remus to cause such disdain?*

I'm half tempted to ask as much, but I believe it better to ask at a different time when we aren't trapped in the Pyrack. Plus, I don't want to give too many signs of comfortability. Guard must remain up.

Looking over at Vivían, I'm surprised to see that she's helping the shaggy-haired salvager to his feet. He seems disoriented and groggy. No surprise, since he was flirting with death minutes ago. Once on his feet, he grunts in pain as he caresses his forehead. Blood smears his hand.

"Nice of you to join us," I say with a slight smirk, placing my hands on my hips. "How's the head?"

"A bit fuzzy, and there's this terrible thumping coming from the gash, but otherwise I'll live," he replies in a strained voice, blinking rapidly. "Thanks though."

"Don't mention it," I say, brushing off the remark. "Wouldn't be right to leave you hanging in this mess."

Vivían snorts a laugh. "Heh, hanging," she mutters.

A few moments are spent patching up wounds thanks to Aida. Naturally talented with first aid, she cleans and bandages my cheek, Vivían's wrists, and the salvager's forehead. Shaking his head in discomfort, he grunts, "So what did I miss? You know, aside from the crash."

In a short summary, Vivían and I explain the events following the crash and our encounter with Septem. When we finish our short recap, he looks bewildered for a moment and eyes Remus. Aida currently examines her companion for ailment.

"You think they could both be Outlanders?" he asks after a moment, turning his eyes back to us.

"Hard to say," I shrug. "Septem's tactics and talk of his Order suggests he could be an Outlander. But I think their group is more diverse than a mere clan. More sophisticated based on his armor and weapons."

"Agreed," Vivían nods, crossing her arms. "They don't smell like Outlanders either. It can be very distinct."

"I suppose we might be able to ask Remus once we're in a

more comfortable environment," the salvager voices with a stern look before talking more to himself. "Where would Septem know me from, though?"

As I see him begin to turn away, I ask, "What do we call you?" My voice is more forceful than I intended, more interest in the subtext.

Looking back at me, he arches an eyebrow and adopting a look of vague curiosity. "You can call me Tálir," he replies.

I blink in a confused manner. "Tálir?" I repeat, brushing my hair aside. "You're not from the western regions, are you?"

"I didn't realize Pyrack natives were so distinct," he snorts in surprise. "Nope, I'm from the eastern settlements. But I'm not an Outlander, if that's what you're thinking. I know Z'hart sometimes refers to us as such because we're not 'officially' part of a nation. I'm just a salvager."

I smile faintly, for it's a bit refreshing to meet someone who's just as lost as I am in our predicament. While I should be wary around a settlement foreigner, I still feel some comfort with him. Plus, he seems decent for a desert salvager. Turning my attention to Remus and Aida, I help them pack another case full of supplies before all of us exit the compartment.

Slowly, almost reluctantly, I step out into the golden sunlight as a wave of heat washes over me.

Amongst the irradiate blaze of the sun, the sandy mounds reflect the golden light with such intensity that my eyes grow weak and my skin begins to feel scorched. The occasional draft that whisks by is hot, irritating, and kicks up light filaments of sand. The cloudless sky is almost crystalline blue as the sun reflects through the atmosphere. As far as my eyes can see, only sand and rock are discernible in each direction.

Walking around the tail end of the overturned ship, I'm able to fully detail the remains of the convoy. The impact skid mark is nearly half a kilometer long, the massive whale-shaped convoy lost both its maneuvering fins and the repulsor engines are crumpled like paper. Small fires emanate from the engines, and columns of black smoke billow into the sky as if it's a bonfire. The tarnished, bronze steel of the vessel reflects the beating sun ever more intensely as if it were a gemstone in the sand.

In the distance beyond the wreckage, I can see large rock formations nearly three kilometers away, but nothing beyond that. Just more dunes and sandy plains.

I look back to the debris. Devin and Vyck are ascending out of a blasted hole in the hull. They are close to the cockpit of the ship, but they've seemingly clambered out of some sort of storage room. I surmise it's a storage chamber because they each bear new equipment and weapons along with some supply satchels.

Almost instantaneously, Vivian comments in a jubilant voice, "That could be where they stored my equipment. My bow could still be in there! Joys to the Sage God! Hunting shall resume!"

With renewed potency and a bit of exhilaration, I perk up and follow Vivian. Clambering up the wreckage, we stop short of the hole Vyck and Devin are climbing through and take note of the items sprawled across the hull. The two have been piling up weapons, ammunition, equipment packs, and armor accessories atop the rusted hull of the ship. It's almost like a makeshift black market arms deal.

They also start placing various wineskins and dried food packages atop the hull, to which Aida immediately darts for. She uncorks a wineskin and sniffs its contents—her expression turning to joyous relief.

"Remus, I found it," she says, passing it to him as he eagerly takes a quick gulp. "Hopefully it'll help stave off the effects for now."

I can only assume she's found some form of medication for Remus' illness, whatever it is. I'm still too nervous to ask, however. Still frightful, despite tensions calming a bit.

After scanning through the items, I pick up the only weapon I'm acquainted with: a bowpistol. The bowpistol is almost as long as my forearm, result of an elongated hilt for quick-draws. Dark grey metal coats the weapon, and the mechanisms fire two types of energy bolts: stun and kill. The rest of the equipment is standard survival gear, ammunition, and some light leather greaves and pauldrons.

Pleasantly relieved to acquire suitable forms of protection, I start to equip myself when I catch my reflection in the hull of the ship.

A grimy, tattered, and exhausted face stares back at me. Blue eyes are still emphasized by long lashes and peach skin. My shoulder length, black hair drapes around my round face and is disheveled with sand caked in it.

Something's different though; a newfound determinism is rising inside of me. I'm now ready to undertake my quest. For answers, for justice, for revenge. Strangely though, the idea of retribution is something new to me. And it's a conception that makes me anxious in my core, but it that primal fear also inspires me.

I holster the bowpistol, standing proud upon the hull of the crashed ship. Fear is pumping in my chest, but it's making me stronger. Not weaker.

Vyck and Devin have fully equipped themselves in what appears to be mercenary gear. Thin, violet armor covers their chests, shoulders, and arms while they sport short swords. Remus only possesses a satchel and a rucksack while Aida carries several bags of supplies and a few daggers tucked under her belt. She's both healer and warrior it seems. Vivían also travels light with a small backpack, an energy bow and a recharging pack. While the limbs and grip of the bow are carbon fiber, the bowstring and arrows are made of pure blue plasma when active. A grip is set within the strings for the wielder's safety. The energy deactivates and she collapses the bow mechanism.

I'm most surprised by what Tálir starts to put on, however. Similar to Septem, the same ancient and ceremonial suit of armor covers his entire body except his head. Despite its lack of versatility, the suit possesses an almost artistic nature due to the swirling designs etched into the bronze metal. Each piece almost has a winged or fiery design to it. Even the digits of his fingers are covered by talon-like armor. With a leather satchel draping across his shoulder, Tálir doesn't bother with a weapon and just starts adjusting pieces of the armor.

Is it a coincidence that he has the same armor? Septem did give him a scathing look, but Tálir seems to have never met him. I'm unsure how to feel. Tálir is linked to Septem in some indirect sense, I'm certain of it. My misgiving flares inside my core.

I can't help but be suspicious of the coincidence that both Tálir and Septem wear similar armor. Then again, Remus and Septem know each other and seem to be enemies. I'm completely baffled by this entire scenario, but I'll learn what's going on soon enough.

Aida is the first to break the silence. "What's our game plan now? I'm sensing a hike is in order no matter which direction we go in."

Devin and Vyck both give her perturbed looks, something that hints at what they are about to respond with.

"What in fragging Hells makes you think we plan on going anywhere with you guys?" Devin voices with a bit of incredulity, scratching his goatee. "Vyck and I don't need anyone else slowing us down, and no offense, but you lot aren't cream of the crop. We're going our separate way. Back to Vapor Bay."

"No offense taken," Tálir mutters with a condescending look.

Exasperated, Aida pipes up in an insulted voice, "And why exactly would we slow you down? Are you in some sort of hurry? Aren't you worried about Outlanders?"

"Why does it matter?" Vyck asks in a perturbed voice. "We've known you for just a few hours; I don't give a boning frag where you all choose to go. All of us are innocent, am I right?"

I withhold my response, despite partially agreeing with Devin and Vyck. Sure, it's beneficial to travel in a group, but would we all really work together? I'm already blundering over trust, so how could I cooperate with them? I hate the fear and misgiving, yet I can't shake it.

"Why is it beneficial to travel in a group?" Devin is saying, irritation showing on his face. "It's slower and less organized. We plan on traveling light and quick, because in case you all forgot, we are in the middle of a fragging desert."

"Aw c'mon, do you have no inclination for adventure?" Vivían voices lightly, trying to ease the tension. "We can take more supplies if we travel in a group. Plus, this ship has at least a week's worth of rations stored, and it'll take all of us to carry them."

"I like your spirit, Viv. But, this isn't helping your case," Vyck responds, giving Vivían a wink. "Our plan involves traveling light. We don't need a week's worth of supplies. And this is certainly not an adventure. Are you so desperate for thrills?"

Devin contorts his features in a gesture of irascibility. "I still don't understand why in all the Hells you people give a damn about us. It's not like we're robbing you and leaving you for dead."

"Survival one-oh-one," Vivían retorts, cocking an eyebrow and gives a sly smile. "Strength in numbers. We could have an exciting time together."

Tálir presses a hand to his forehead. "How about we all go our separate ways," he affirms in a commanding voice. "We are wasting time here, and I'm sure I'm not the only one roasting in this heat. I'd like to go home."

"I can concur with that, Tálir," I respond, leaning on one leg and putting a hand on my hip. "Nothing personal, but I don't necessarily fancy travelling with a group of strangers. Prison strangers. So let's not waste any more energy arguing with these two buffoons." I gesture to Devin and Vyck.

Devin looks a bit insulted. Aida and Vivían seem a little surprised, but also disappointed. Like seeing a glimmer of treasure before losing it. I feel some regret even as the words leave my mouth. But I have to stand firm, to keep them at arm's length. They're strangers with their own agendas, and I'm afraid of what I might get caught up in. Plus, the more time we waste, the greater the chance of being spotted by slavers or Outlanders is. I'm ready to go my own way.

But what way is that? Who knows how far away Z'hart City is.

"Listen, m'lady," Devin retorts in a smug tone. "Let the more experienced people chat here for a bit, and then you can mouth off to whichever one of us gives a shit."

"Maybe another punch to the face will make you give a shit," I hiss, standing strait and placing a hand on my bowpistol. Tensions are no longer calm.

A loud laugh escapes him. "If you call that a punch," Devin chuckles condescendingly. "I bet you won't last five minutes out here, seeing as you're a spoiled city girl. How about a first lesson in survival? Don't pick fights you can't win."

"Careful," Aida says dangerously, hand on her dagger.

"Ey! I'm just trying to teach her some respect!"

"Respect? You're less respectful than a wharg in mating season!" I nearly shout.

"That makes no boning sense!"

Tálir plants a foot forward and shouts, "Would you all please just—"

His words are cut short by a soft beeping noise that echoes through the air. The sound is something strange to me. It's repetitive and calming at the same time. Initially, the beeps seem sporadic, but over the course of a few seconds they begin to become repetitive and calculated. More than once the beeps reach a fevered pitch before returning to a normal repetition. The sound doesn't strike me as an alarm, but something more along the lines of something gaining power.

Electrical and energy equipment is commonplace, but the noise seems to echo of the past. I'm at a loss though. None of us have an active energy source to power anything.

The others are perplexed as well, looking around hastily for the source of the noise. From what I can tell, the beeping is as unfamiliar to them as it is to me.

As I listen more intently, I realize the noise is emanating from Tálir, who immediately adopts a tormented look. He fiddles with his right gauntlet. Lifting up a metal plate, he reveals what looks to be a small console housed within the bracer. While small, the instrument features brightly lit screens of data and a holographic display meter.

It is astonishing to see an advanced computer system wired into a suit of armor, mainly since most technology is only used for royals, economic, or military use. I'm mystified by the consoles, for they appear ancient. Worn, cracked screens and older display systems.

I stand close to Tálir. My eyes examine the holographic screens with belied caution. As a red bar starts to gradually fill in the meter, the words above the display merely read: *30% Charge.*

"It's charging," he says in a low monotone, even as apprehension contorts his features.

We pause in confusion. "What do you mean, it's 'charging'?" I ask, tilting my head to get a better look at the computer. "Doesn't it need a power source in order to charge?"

Tálir jumps back suddenly in alarm, almost like a deer catching the scent of a predator. His eyes widen with trepidation, and his body tenses as he snaps the panel back over the computer.

"Gather as much as you can carry," Tálir says in an ominous voice, looking towards the sky. "A Roil is coming."

I know that title all too well, and it signifies one of the greatest and most destructive calamities of our world. Thousands have been subsumed by them. Bodies are left blackened and frozen in whatever terrified pose the victim died in. Roils are the dark storms of unknown origin that plague this world. They strike randomly in Pan'gea and only every month or so.

But as we all stand in terrified silence, I think to myself: *How do we outrun a storm?*

CHAPTER 8

Sarina

Roil Surprise

THE BLAZING GOLDEN SUN beats down upon us even as we stand upon the smoking ruin of the convoy, the metal hull sizzling with absorbed heat. If not for our boots and footwear, the metal would sear the flesh on our soles and burn right to the bone. The occasional breeze that wafts by is hot, irritating, and blowing smog and fumes into our faces. The air is hot and dry, and any source of moisture emanates from the crushed husk of the ship in the form of lubricants and oils. Sparse fires along the ship spew even more heat our way as the wind continues passing by.

As horrid as the setting seems, a surprise is coming our way that will make this putrid scenario seem like a vacation spot. While

I'm unsure how Tálir was able to determine it, a Roil is evidently on its way towards our current location.

I'm accustomed to hearing of Roils and seeing some footage of the aftermath. But I've never seen a storm with my own eyes let alone stood in the path of one. The prospect is ominously foreboding, but a slight tinge of curiosity writhes in me for a split second. My interest is immediately snuffed out by the panicked expressions on my companions' faces as they all scan the sky for signs of the storm.

Roils are composed of trillions of Nanites and the cloud can be visible even if they are kilometers away. While the Nanites individually are the size of ants, a swarm of them produces a cloudlike
storm as they travel with the wind. Old Domain shields and weapons are the only things that can repel them. Since we're nowhere near a city or village, we have no such protection. So Roils can roam free out here.

The Nanites only affect living tissue, so secure buildings or ships can keep inhabitants safe. If the storm is intense enough though, even metal walls can't stop it. With a ruined ship as our shelter, we would be subsumed in seconds.

But as I continue to scan the skyline, I see no trace of a storm let alone a cloud of any sort.

I turn my gaze back to Tálir, who is still tensed with trepidation.

"I don't see anything," I tell him, my face hiding the fear.

"How can you know a Roil is coming if it's nowhere near the vicinity?"

He regards me with an urgent expression. "I'll explain more once we are out of the charge-zone."

"The what?" Aida interjects.

"Later!" Tálir shouts as he jumps into action and starts grabbing supply and ration pouches.

Stunned into silence, the rest of us look at one another for a brief moment of confusion before the pandemonium sets in.

Vyck and Devin dive back into the storage compartment in a mad dash for supplies, while Aida and Remus move towards the front of the ship. Vivían and I stand quietly for a moment and regard each other in abject bewilderment.

Sure, the possibility of a Roil is something to be fearful about, but I'm more concerned with Tálir's intuition. Roils don't follow patterns and can't be predicted like the weather forecast, they just hit randomly. So how can he know?

"I know you've got some trust issues," Vivían says suddenly as she walks by me. "But, why turn away some help? It's not like we've got it out for you or anything, Sarina."

"I don't mean to be abrasive," I retort shrewdly. "It's just hard to make friends under these circumstances. Plus, I'm just looking out for myself. Why is that a problem?"

"Because you deny help from those willing to help you," Vivían says, glancing over her shoulder. "In a hunt, the pack triumphs over the lone wolf."

"I don't need help," I reply quietly.

Before anyone else can say anything, a more intense beeping emanates from Tálir's bracer. I see him freeze in disbelief. Frantically, he pulls open the panel and looks at the display as the beeping reaches a heightened repetition. His eyes widen in terror and his head snaps towards the sky. Footsteps smash along the top of the ship.

Looking up, I glimpse Vyck and Devin hurling themselves from the top of the convoy and nearly fly five meters before hitting the ground. The panicked expressions on their faces, the contortion of their frames, and their panting breaths tells their story.

"Run, you dumb shits!" Vyck nearly screams as he and his partner dart off to the south. "Or you're boned!"

Instantly, I run around the side of the ship to get a look at what they are running from. And what I see makes me wish I'd started running sooner. About four kilometers away, past several sweeping areas of dunes and rocky formations is the storm.

Similar to an incoming sand storm, a cloud of silvery filaments creeps over the dunes in the distance. Occasional tendrils seep out from the cloud as it tramples over the terrain at an impressive speed. An eerie gust of wind picks up, and a distant howl can be heard as the storm spirals towards us. Over the howl of the wind, a creeping hiss emanates from the distance as I see the Roil consume the terrain in its dark silver mist.

Gradually, I adopt a look of alarm and start to back away as the others hastily start running. Dread grips me, preventing movement. I struggle to fight out of it. In my moment of hesitation, I'm the last to turn south and sprint away from the miasma.

I'm not used to running with equipment. The weight presses me down into the sandy terrain with each step. All of the equipment we acquired is a serious hindrance, but I can't slow or stop. The straps and gear smack all over the place as I enter an all-out sprint, my boots digging into the sand with each step.

With the others a few meters in front of me and kicking up sand, I'm forced to squint my eyes to remain stable. Sand blurs my vision. I inhale the filaments and cough. *I can't stop!* The turbulent winds kick up from the storm, creating swirling clouds of sand.

As the howl of the storm grows more audible, I grow more frantic and desperate in my pace as I quicken my stride. I've never been a good long distance runner. Sprinting is my specialty. But the weight keeps me slow. My legs ache, the straps tear into my shoulders, and my breaths are shallow. The hiss grows louder.

I start to sputter in panic. Straining my muscles, I'm able to sprint several meters more before my boot smacks against a protruding rock.

Tumbling forward, my chin is the first to hit the sand as my body follows suite. The breath is driven from my chest, and I inhale a cloud of sand and sputter a cough that sears my lungs. Struggling to reorient myself and spitting out sand, I manage to push myself unto my knees and turn over. I lay dazed in the sand, rooted in place by terror as I see the Roil.

Only a kilometer away from us, the storm consumes the area with the darkness of the cloud. The hiss of the conjured breeze swept up by the storm echoes in my ears as it closes in. The swirling clusters of Nanites form a hand-like shape as they cascade over the landscape and blot out the blistering sunlight.

At the current speed, the Roil will overtake me in a matter of minutes before subsuming the rest of the party. We have no chance of escape. It's too fast. The Roil's hand reaches for me, as terror grips my heart.

Struggling in a panic to get to my feet, the Roil is half a kilometer from me when I feel someone hoist me to my feet.

Turning my head, I see both Vivían and Tálir. They came back for me. And they give me a look that translates into something simple. *Run like all the fragging Hells!*

Particles of sand and rock are gyrating around us as the storm nips at our heels. We are moments away from being interred by the Roil when I see Aida and the others duck into a scabrous rock edifice.

"There's an underground shaft!" she manages to yell before entering the cavern. "Hurry!"

We waste not a moment.

Running as fast as my legs could take, Tálir surrenders the lead and allows Vivían and I to reach the outcropping first. I grind to a brief halt next to the three-meter-tall rock that entombs the cavernous shaft. Four meters wide, I can only guess where the shaft leads to. But I can't stop to think.

Folding my arms, I leap into the hole followed closely by Vivían and Tálir. The tunnel is completely obscured by darkness, leaving me to blindly free fall for a few seconds before the shaft angles into a steep slant. Still in motion, my body slides along the slope, tearing my clothes and abrading my skin. I grunt in pain as I slide along the rock. Minutes pass. Then I'm thrown to the floor made of rock. My breath falters momentarily.

I roll to my back in an attempt to stabilize my breathing. The wheezing subsides. I take several deep breaths and my muscles relax. My head is dazed and a sharp ringing echoes through my ears as my body attempts to recover. Slowly, the dizziness falters and the noise ceases as I inhale deeply.

Through the haze of bodily pain, I hear Tálir and Vivían similarly tumble from the tunnel. Similarly stunned with pain, the two start groaning as they attempted to reorient themselves.

I sit up on the rocky ground, rubbing my head to ensure my focus is true.

While nearly pitch black, the cavern we stumbled upon is lit very dimly by bioluminescent crystals that cast an etheric emerald glow. *Fascinating!* Glowing crystals have never been catalogued in mining operations. All the gems are barely the size of a finger. Some protrude from the rocks like spines while some are imbedded within, providing various intensities of light. While numerous, the crystals only illuminate so much, leaving the darkness to reign supreme.

From what I can see, the cavern is the size of a small

cathedral and produces small ponds as streams of water fall from the arched ceiling. The air smells of sea salt and water vapor, and there's a heaviness as I breathe. The sound of fluttering wings tells me that cavebats dwell within and are disturbed by our sudden entrance.

Upon seeing the metallic ore embedded in the rock, I immediately figure out what we have fallen into.

This is an excavation site and we've just fallen through an access tunnel. What's odd though, is that this doesn't seem to be the work of House Z'hart: the noble family of ore refinements. For several Cycles, Z'hart made its fortune by mining the rich amounts of versatile ore the nation resides upon. Spanning thousands of kilometers, the nation holds access to all caves, tunnels, and mountains producing the ore. It's very valuable, because the other nations have weak and brittle minerals.

As a native to Z'hart, I know this cave is not within their jurisdiction. More, it seems like whoever was mining it abandoned it a long time ago. Most of the machines and constructions within the grotto seem to have been left behind for some time. It's eerie. This was a prime location, so why abandon it?

What's more mysterious are the crystals. These emerald gems have never been catalogued, or Z'hart would make even more of a fortune. This must have been a secret operation.

A few meters ahead of us are Aida, Remus, Devin, and Vyck; the latter two are fervently extracting some of the gems that obtrude from the walls. While honestly I shouldn't be surprised by their behavior, I'm nonetheless stunned at their current priorities.

"Really?" I call out to them, nursing my bruised arms. "This isn't a treasure hunt, you two. I know you're out for profit and all, but don't you have bigger priorities than nicking some crystals?"

"For your information," Devin retorts, hardly glancing at me. "We're collecting these things to help light the way out of here. You're welcome."

I'm flushed with mortification.

"Seriously, Sarina," Vyck adds, "don't assume shit."

As my cheeks burn with embarrassment, I remain silent as I rise to my feet. It's an odd thing to feel guilty for assumptions, but they aren't the types to disprove stereotypes. I've seen their like a hundred times before. My job as a brewer is normally merry work, but I often see the backside of society while living in the poorer districts of Z'hart. Shady individuals at the bar are more inclined to cause trouble, and that perception has stuck with me.

Vivían, Tálir, Aida, and Remus seem to be decent people, yet I feel like keeping them at a distance is a safe move. Trust has the potential to build, but I don't want to place them in harm's way. If I've made enemies in Z'hart, I don't want anyone else to be a casualty—so I need to remain alone.

Is it wrong of me? Perhaps. But after seemingly being drugged, assaulted, then sold like a slave, I believe it wise.

Pivoting slightly, I see that Vivían and Tálir have also recovered from the drop and are on their feet.

"That was exciting," Vivían comments with a half-laugh. "Shall we go again?"

Regarding them, I ask, "Are you two ok?" I ask only as a courtesy, trying not to convey true emotional concern. I hate myself for doing it.

Tálir regards me quizzically. I think he might sense my conflict. "Remind me never to slide down rocks again," Tálir groans, rotating his shoulders in discomfort. "It's not good for my armor."

"Because that's what's important, Tálir," Vivían comments sarcastically, stretching her back. "I'll be sure to save your armor instead of you next time you're in danger."

Tálir gives Vivían a pained smile as he adjusts pieces of his suit with several resounding clicks. She winks at him, and I feel a tinge of jealousy at her comfortability. I can't be mad at her though, she's true to herself. Vivían starts to look around the cave and says, "This doesn't look like a natural formation. Is it just me, or do the walls look unnaturally smooth?"

"It's an excavation chamber for a mining operation," I reply. "House Z'hart usually would be first to stake a claim, but their sigil is nowhere to be found. Odd. Must be an independent site."

The two regard me with dubious looks, their expressions hint of curiosity in addition to their concern.

"You know that from first glance? Are you a miner?" Tálir inquires, folding his arms across his chest. "I pegged you for more of an aristocrat." He gestures to my outfit.

I pause before saying, "I'm a native of Z'hart. Even the lower districts possess some flair for aristocracy. I'm no miner, but I know a bit about the trade."

Tálir drops his suspicious demeanor and considers what I've said. Vivían follows suite, but not nearly as visible as Tálir. Vivían moves around me to examine a protruding crystal.

"Have you ever seen something like this before?" she asks, glancing back at me.

Shaking my head, I say, "No. In all my life, I've never seen these types of gems. More, they seem to be an unnatural type of growth."

Confirming my suspicions, I easily yank a thumb-sized gem from the wall with a small *pop*. It feels warm and static seems to come from it. "It's like we're inside some kind of mound that's producing the gems on a regular basis. This is something more than a simple mine."

Another sense of eerie dread creeps through my body, like a serpent slithering through the grass. I get the feeling that we're not alone in this cave. Something else is down here. *Something* echoes in the air.

We pause as the echo hums through the cave. Chills run up my spine, and I feel cold. Something is definitely in here watching us. Cautiously, we step through the darkness towards the others. Remus is currently squatting, cradling his head as if he's suffered another concussion. Perhaps he did, considering how fast we slid down the tunnel. Aida is frantically searching through one of their satchels before pulling out her wineskin. Uncorking it, she presents it to Remus and he drinks for a moment. After he finishes however, I note that the pungent smell emanating from the skin isn't wine, ale, or water. In fact, the smell is more resembling the stench of motor oil or molten metal.

As Remus hands the wineskin back to Aida, I adopt a look of concern before saying, "That didn't seem like water. Is he ok?"

Aida regards me with a hard look. "He's suffered some—damage in the last few days," she says gravely before gesturing to the skin. "The medication can help him relax somewhat."

We watch them with enigmatic looks. "What happened to him?" Vivían asks with a quizzical look.

Aida scowls. "Now's not the time," she mutters. "Let's focus on getting out of here first." Without another word, she helps Remus get to his feet and starts walking deeper into the cavern towards Devin.

As we approach, I begin to speculate more about what Remus is currently going through. With his evident connection with Septem and the realization of bodily ailments, I can't help but consider if he'd been exposed to experimentation, torture, or something else. I construe that his involvement with Septem had theoretically led to his condition, but beyond that I'm still unsure

From the brief exchange I just saw, I know that Remus' condition doesn't seem natural. Aida essentially confirmed it, and I continue to wonder what happened to him.

We walk several meters through the cavern towards one of the other

tunnels that's obscured by darkness. Near the mouth of the tunnel are Vyck and Devin, both of whom are holding two glass bottles filled with several coin-sized crystals. The emerald jewels cast a substantial amount of light when grouped together, and they almost pulsate with raw energy.

We stop short of the tunnel's entrance. Devin and Vyck toss me and Tálir a gem-filled bottle. "No need to thank us," Devin says smugly. "They should provide you all with enough light to make it out of here."

There's a pause before Vivían asks, "I take it you plan on going somewhere else?"

Vyck regards her with an exasperated look. "We've been over this, Viv. Devin and I are going our separate way, but before we do, we're going to collect some more of the gems in this grotto. They could be worth a fortune topside."

"I'm surprised you all aren't doing the same," Devin adds, brandishing his bottle with swagger.

"There might be larger crystals deeper in the cave that might fetch for a couple thousand oreings," Tálir points out, trying to remain nonchalant.

"What are you saying?" Devin and Vyck say, almost in unison. "What's your game?"

What is his game? Is he trying to rally them? If so, he might actually succeed. He's playing on their desire for reward. Smart. If I were him, I'd adamantly stay away from those two though.

"I'm just saying," he replies, his voice starting to reflect notes of subtle charisma. "Despite my earlier opinions, it seems like we're all stuck together for the time being. It's inevitable. So why don't we make it work for all our benefit. There could be a profit in this for all of us." He words it almost perfectly. *Well played Tálir.*

Vivían grins at him. "A treasure hunt of sorts. We all are heading in the same direction anyways, so what's there to lose?"

"Again with the adventure stuff, Viv," Vyck groans. "Give it a rest."

Devin rolls his eyes and heaves a sigh. "If it'll shut you up, Tálir," Devin huffs. "We'll tag along. But only until we get to the surface."

"I'm not sure if this is a good idea," I say, my demeanor reflecting notes of unease and distrust. I can't shake my feelings of misgiving, no matter his magnetism.

"Aw c'mon, Sarina," Vivían says vigorously, trying to smooth things over. "Tálir and I helped save you from the Roil; you can at least trust us. Don't you want to see how this all plays out?"

Vivían is right about one thing. After saving my life from the Roil, I now find it a bit easier to trust her and Tálir. It was a simple act, but I realize that they were willing to risk their lives even for a stranger. So perhaps I can stick with them, for now. Caution is still present in my heart though.

I sigh reluctantly. "I suppose I can tag along until we reach the surface. After that, I think it's best for me to go on my own."

"For once, we agree on something, m'lady," Devin grunts. "We go catch our big break, reach the surface, and then part ways."

Vyck grunts something about boning in accordance while the others reluctantly nod in agreement.

It's an odd sensation, accepting the help of a group of strangers. We all hailed from very different backgrounds, but we reluctantly unite for the sake of survival. For the sake of escaping this Hellish cavern. Tálir surprised me the most. He seemed so quiet and reluctant when we were on the transport. But here, he demonstrated surprising prowess in rallying us to stick together.

Sure, he played on Devin and Vyck's greed. But it was strategic. The rest of us are tired and afraid. He's providing comforting unity, so it hooks the rest of us. Is he just naturally like this? Tálir's far from perfect, but he has shown captivating initiative in times of crisis.

Lightness returns to me. Perhaps I could let him into this untrusting crypt that is myself. Given time. But who knows what'll happen once we reach the surface.

CHAPTER 9

Tálir

Underworld

THE AIR IS HEAVY.

We are nearly a kilometer beneath the
surface; it almost feels like the world is crushing the air around us. It's
thick, humid, and smells like vaporized salt water. The nature of the
air makes it seem like I can cut through it with a knife.

The channels narrow and grow cylindrical as we traverse with
the bottles of luminescent gems clenched in our hands. Occasional
pools of sweltering water pepper the ground along with thin layers of
spotted fungi and mosses. Our shoes make an echoing *smack* against
the rock, making it seem like we travel within an ethereal realm.

We trek further into the mine tunnels for a few hours, and

everyone is on edge. I walk at the head of the group, holding the glowing bottle high to illuminate the tunnels. I never considered myself to be a successful leader. I've never commanded troops, run businesses, or ruled nations. But I realize that unity is something everyone seeks when survival is on the line. Erron's Ville was the epitome of this sentiment. The village banded together under the guidance of our leader because we wanted to survive and prosper.

I am terrified to lead a group of strangers. Especially when experienced hunters and killers follow me. There's no telling what they might try. Still, there is a fragile truce between the seven of us. And someone needed to voice reason and guidance.

Am I qualified? Hells no, but that won't stop me from trying.

Sarina and Vivían follow close behind me, Remus and Aida have the middle, and Devin and Vyck guard our rear. Conversation is faint between the pairs behind me, and I'm able to gleam some insight into the individuals who travel with me. Aida worries about Remus' ailment and gives him another dose of what seems to be sedatives. Color returns to his face somewhat, but Aida still expresses discomfort over it. Devin and Vyck are discussing how they were nabbed by Imperials for defending themselves from attack.

It might help solidify trust if I can understand a bit more about them. Although, I'm not sure I want to befriend the mercenaries. They are arrogant, misogynistic, and dangerous. It'll take a lot to have conviction in them.

I take a look back at Sarina. She seems just as mistrusting and anxious as I am. A bit of myself is in her, in some sense. But something else is occurring within her mind that she's not letting on. Her eyes reflect hints of sadness, anger, and even betrayal. Her hand is constantly glossing over her bowpistol, as if she's expecting an attack at any moment. A strange sense of protectiveness flickers within me like a spark. I need to be brave. Not just for my sake, but for hers and the others as well.

Perhaps it's some weird sense of solidarity I feel, seeing how afraid she looks. But her eyes flash towards mine, and I see a faint glimmer of fire within. She's definitely not all she seems. And my interest peaks with caution.

Another hour passes as we wind through more caverns and tunnels. It seems endless. I can sense the weariness is taking hold of the others, so I decide to take a break within one of the small grottos that occasionally interrupts the tunnels.

Everyone discards their bags and satchels in a pile and sit, starting to munch on rations. Unlike the previous cave, the small gems protrude from the arched ceiling like stalactites about a dozen meters above us. Like miniature florescent lights, the gems bathe the setting an ambient emerald light along with the crystals we possess.

Devin and Vyck sit a little further away than the rest of us. But Sarina sits relatively close to me. I take a quick swig of water and bite off a bit of jerky from my rations. Conversations are faint between some, but I remain silent for a few moments. I inspect my armor for any damage after taking a tumble through the mine shaft. Scraped and chipped in a few places, it hasn't suffered serious damage. But I'm still shocked that the suit actually began to charge in response to the Roil. A defense mechanism?

Though he told me little of it, my father's one warning about the suit was that it could detect incoming Roils. *Whenever it charges with no source, the Roil shall come*, he said. Today, he was right. But in all my life, I'd never been able to find the right source of energy for the suit. But maybe I was looking in the wrong places.

I notice Sarina taking quick glances at me before returning her gaze to the ground. Like she wants to speak, but can't think of the words. Normally I'd have been flattered by her attention. But her gaze is still troubled, and I feel more concerned about why she feels so. Cursing my feelings of empathy, I attempt to lighten the mood.

"I guess I can be the first to ask," I say. "Are you alright, Sarina?"

Her gaze shifts to me briefly and we make eye contact, but she quickly turns away and remains silent.

"Just trying to make this little trip a bit more pleasant," I shrug, leaning back against the wall.

There is a long pause before Sarina begrudgingly breaks her silence. "So are you going to tell us how you managed to predict the Roil was incoming? Or are we just going to drop that?"

I eye her with a perplexed look and arch an eyebrow. "Even I'm not fully sure about how it works. On a side note, thank you for acknowledging me, Sarina. I feel a bit less embarrassed."

She sniffs in exacerbation. Her thin lips purse in doubt. "Stop dodging," she says, her eyes narrowing. But it's not out of antagonism. "You looked at your gauntlet and knew that the Roil was incoming. That seems rather lucky."

I clear my throat to tell what information I have. Some of the others also turn their attention to me. I flip open the panel and reveal the console in the gauntlet. "This suit was used by the Domain millennia ago. I grew up without anyone to tell me how it properly works. So it is tough to figure out the inner workings." I explain, my voice calm but firm. "And since it's in an inoperable state, it's much more difficult. But my father told me that faint fields of energy might be able to temporarily power the armor."

I speak to everyone and gesture to the bracer computer. "The system in this suit would need to run on a constant stream of energy, and without such a source…" I tap the inert holoscreens. "It's useless. So if an energy source trickled into the suit, the system would start charging as it did earlier. Legends say that some type of energy field builds up within a certain area point before a Roil comes in. Domain shields kept the Roils away from Erron's Ville all my life, so I was never privy to seeing this happen. Until today."

"So what was the charge zone?" Sarina inquires, caressing her round chin.

"The area where the energy field was charging up," I reply, cocking my head. "Think of it like this: Before lightning strikes, the positive ground charge attracts the negative lightning charge and there's a small buildup before the strike occurs. Whatever energy is there before the Roil, I can only assume that it's there as a sort of buildup before the storm hits."

I conclude my explanation, and Sarina looks content with the answers I provide. The others seem satisfied as well, although Devin and Vyck shrug it off as some weird sorcery in the armor. Oddly though, Remus seems to not only accept my answers. He approves of them, like he's grading a test. Is he familiar with the armor?

I can't help but ask, "Remus, do you know about this armor?"

Under his dark beard, I can see him giving me a faint smile. It's not maniacal or sinister. More along the lines of nostalgic, like he's daydreaming about some past glory. "Yes— I— Know—" he struggles to say.

Aida gives him a look of caution, but says nothing. I'm stunned and eager at the same time. With his age and status, he probably knows countless things about the armor. I'm ecstatic. So many questions to ask.

"What can you tell me about it?" I inquire, perhaps more eagerly than I intend. "Who made it? What does it do?"

"Legacy— Of— Knights—" Remus grunts in pain, and then Aida cuts him off.

"You are in no condition to start rambling about that, Remus," she says tenderly. But her voice reflects notes of discipline and she addresses me. "Tálir, he's been through… a lot these last few hours. Ask him about it again when we're under better circumstances. He needs to take it easy."

I'm a bit taken aback by her sudden sternness, but I nod in acceptance. I'm not ready to face the wrath of a woman like her. I'll just have even more questions once Remus' condition stabilizes.

Vivían snorts a laugh at me. "Alright big leader Tálir. If you flinch at her claws, I'll bet you'd shit a pile if you faced an Outlander woman's scorn. Make sure not to anger me too much." She gives me a flirtatious wink.

I can see an indistinct flush of red on Sarina's cheeks. "You're an Outlander?" she asks, turning her head to the side. "I just thought you had a different style of hair and dress than the rest of us."

"My hair has been rather wild lately," she replies, running her fingers through the whacky, crimson mess. "And my clothes are light for hunting. But I'm not an Outlander. Not anymore."

Before Sarina can ask further questions, Devin and Vyck stand to stretch their legs rather loudly. "Ey guys, not that the catching up isn't nice and all," Devin grumbles derisively. "But I plan on getting out of this shithole by the end of the day. Tálir, would you be so kind as to lead the way? Fearless *leader*."

His snide attitude causes my frustration to start bubbling up to the surface. I need to control my temper, though. My last hasty decision resulted in being captured by the new Imperial militia. I mustn't let it slip again.

In unison, the rest of us get to our feet and retrieve our bags and satchels. We exit the grotto and walk for a few minutes, the others falling behind my lead. Part of me can sense that this decision isn't entirely based on my willingness to lead. I'm also the first one to come into harm's way. *Lovely.*

"So how much longer do you think we have, m'lady?" Devin inquires to Sarina from our flank. "After all that talk about being native to Z'hart and shit, I figured you might have some inkling to where we are."

She regards them with scrutiny. "Do I look like a miner to you?" she asks, her face contorting in distaste. "My guess is that there might be a central excavation Well at the end of this tunnel."

Devin tries to glimpse down the tunnel and then looks to Sarina. "You *guess* there's a Well at the end of this?" he queries shrewdly. "I'm filled with confidence right now. Let's just *guess* how to escape a mining tunnel."

"Do you have a better option?" I butt in with a bit of vindictiveness. I halt and wheel around, trying to assert authority. I think it fails.

The two men look hard at me, and I could almost see them resisting the urge to snigger. Under Devin's black goatee, I see him smirking in amusement. What is wrong with these guys? Are they so arrogantly delusional that they can't take anyone seriously?

"Always so quick to side with the city girl, eh Tálir?" Devin says with derision. "Cute. I assume since she was giving mouth-to-mouth earlier, you're trying to… repay the debt."

"Time to get boned!" Vyck snorts. "Don't blame you in the least Tálir."

My cheeks flush with embarrassment, but my expression makes it seem more like indignation. Out of the corner of my eye, I see Sarina giving Devin an arctic glare as she reaches for her boltpistol. Her azure eyes burn into him, like a bolt searing through flesh. *Now there's a fire*, I say to myself.

"What's so wrong about someone stepping in to fend off an asshole?" I ask in return, grinning slightly. "Or are you jealous?"

Devin chokes on his next words and his face loses a bit of color. Behind me, I hear Vivían snort with merriment. I'm shocked, however, when Devin fails to retort and instead adopts a neutral mask.

"How will we know when we've reached the Well?" Devin asks Sarina in a much deeper voice, changing the subject.

She adopts a look of deliberation before saying, "I'm guessing it's the size of a sinkhole, so I doubt we'll miss it. But I'd guess maybe another five kilometers before we get there."

Aida gives a quick glance at Remus before letting out a sigh. "Then let's get to it," she says. "I'd fancy some fresh air right about now."

Nodding, I adjust my satchel and rotate my shoulders to loosen up. Without fanfare, I lead the way through the tunnel. The energized bottle of crystals is pulsating with light in my hand.

The tunnels narrow and quicken once again after walking for several minutes, and the ceiling drops to a meter above our heads. The amount of crystal protrusions also grows smaller. The emerald light shines a bit dimmer. The echo of dripping water can be heard all within the tunnels, the noise reverberates with constant repetition.

We pass under an abrupt slump in the ceiling of the

passageway and I hear Sarina sigh with reluctance before addressing me.

"So your father passed down that armor for inheritance?" she intones. "Forgive me, but how does a simple salvager end up possessing a relic like that?"

I look over my shoulder and acknowledge her shrewd attitude. "Thanks for that, I'm sure my father would've loved a compliment such as that," I say with a derisive tone. It's petty, but I won't allow anyone to talk poorly about my father. "He wasn't always a salvager. He used to be a… well, I actually don't know what he did before coming to Erron's Ville with me. I always assumed he inherited it just like I did."

I slow my pace so that she comes right up next to me. She barely comes up to my shoulder, and yet I feel myself shrinking under her attention. I want to gauge what exactly is going through Sarina's mind. She's reclusive, yet inquisitive all at once. My father once taught me that: *Our minds perpetually suffer the divine state of mania. Fear and joy. Anger and despair. All in an instant. The mind is ill, yet it is healthy.*

I can't help but wonder if this is the case with Sarina. One moment she's like fire, fearful and angry. Then another moment she's like water, calm and quiet. Either way, perhaps this might be a way to let her feel a bit more comfortable.

"You think he stole it, don't you?" I inquire in return, arching an eyebrow playfully.

"Anything's possible," she shrugs mordantly. "Salvagers are

well known for 'claiming what's not theirs'."

I snort in offense. "So you're calling us thieves?"

She adopts a faint grin. "Crafty devils would be an accurate title," she retorts.

I return her remark with a grin. I have no delusions about what I did for a living. Salvaging revolved around taking other people's stuff and selling it. But our targets were always old Domain relics and such. I'm not sure what game she's playing at, but I'll play along. Simply for the sake of keeping her friendly.

"Crafty devils," I repeat sarcastically. My voice turns theatric. "I'm now trying to imagine myself as such. Scouring the night for the perfect prize. Beware children. The crafty devils will steal your toys. I could steal from kids, right?" I gesture to myself.

She sizes me up with a look. "I doubt you'd even feel bad for stealing from kids," she says jokingly, her eyes smile for a brief moment.

I adopt a mockingly flattered look. She says nothing more. For some reason, it feels good to see her smile even if it's at the expense of myself. But a relationship has to be built upon something, and it feels good that we've developed a flicker of one. Where it could end up, I'm not sure—seeing that she wants to go out on her own.

Even though I'm reluctant to keep this group rallied, a small part of me feels enjoyment. It feels empowering. Even if all we have are surface relationships.

CHAPTER 10

Sarina

Pieces of the Puzzle

CHILLS CREEP UP MY SPINE as a cold tingle touches my skin. The gaping maw of the cavern seems as if it is about to swallow us all in its black depths. At points, I can see concentric rings of the glowing crystals spiraling into the tunnels ahead, as if they are trying to hypnotize us.

We've travelled for several hours into the cavern. It's seemingly endless. The lack of sunlight and thick air is putting all of us on edge. So after a time, we take pause for a water break and to rest our legs within another small grotto. There seems to be a pattern in these mines. This grotto is larger than the last, large stalagmites protrude from the ground like spines. Tiny pieces of crystal are imbedded all around the formations—they sparkle like glitter. I sit in solitude.

I enjoy conversing with Tálir to some degree. He has charm and wit, but most of all he has a quiet charisma. He doesn't overexert trying to lead us. I think that's why we follow him. Something still tells me I can't get too close to anyone here. Darkness within my mind prevents me from fully opening up. No matter how much I'd like to.

I look up and see Remus and Aida approaching me—both of whom bear expressions of concern as they sit next to me. The vines have fully entangled the tree, and I grow distant. I let it show, perhaps more than I intend.

"What do you want?" I ask, barely glancing at them.

"Well I was going to bring you up to speed, but seeing as you're so apathetic to our concern, I guess we don't have to say anything," Aida replies with flustered irritation.

I was a bit harsh. Alright, I'll let them in just a bit.

"Is this about the banquet you mentioned?" I inquire as she turns away. They both perk up slightly to my sudden change.

"Yes—" Remus grunts, his mouth seems to struggle forming the word. "Not— Sure— To— Tell— Others—"

"Fair enough," I reply with a shrug. Wariness tugs at me.

"Tell me what you know, then."

Aida takes a deep breath. "We're not exactly sure what started it all," she recounts. "Remus and I were on a mission in Z'hart City's upper district when we received an invitation to a diplomatic gala in the foreign embassy. While suspicious, we reluctantly accepted and came to participate in the festivities at the cathedral. There was a rally of commoners and miners outside protesting, but it wasn't out of hand. We saw you behind one of the bars, pouring and stocking ales.

"Everything was going fine, but I saw something happen to you, Sarina. Many crowded around you and a fight broke out. You were fighting back, but the look in your eyes—it wasn't natural. It was like you were intoxicated by something. Then the entire place erupted in pandemonium as the riots outside turned violent. We tried to help you, but the Imperials stunned you and dragged you off— claiming you started an uprising."

My memory flashes before my eyes. The smell of ale. A burning, feverish rage unnaturally struck me. Pushing the man's face away. Beating him in a frenzy. Fires erupted. Crowds fought. Then blackness.

The puzzle pieces are becoming clearer. But my mind races. How could I have done such a thing? Attacking a man without reason. But then I remembered the fever rage. It was unnatural. *I had been drugged!*

I suppress my growing dread, because I need to know more. "Putting aside the fact that I'd never do that," I say quietly, my face contorted in confusion. "Doesn't it seem a little convenient that the night this happens just so happened to be the same night you two showed up? How do I know you two aren't the ones behind this?"

"We— Victims—" Remus says almost defiantly. He runs his fingers through his black hair.

"You're not wrong to think like that," Aida replies neutrally, sitting down in front of me. Her dark face reflects solemnness. "But if we are behind your drugging, why would we be captured, punished, and shipped off?"

"To keep an eye on me," I affirm forcefully, crossing my arms.

"But being charged with high treason isn't something they'd brand an undercover agent with," Aida comments, nodding to Remus. "Amidst the chaos, many of us are rounded up by Imperials, and taken into custody. You, Remus, myself, and many others are charged with high treason against O'ran and Z'hart."

My heart stops for a moment. I can feel the blood in my veins turning cold, and my breathing slows as I attempt to grasp what I heard. I feel hollow, as if some part of me has suddenly been taken away. Like the caves around us, part of me has been carved away— leaving an empty void.

High treason? I ask myself. Never in a thousand years would I think myself capable of such acts. Yet, I had. And the worst part is that it wasn't the real me who did it. A drug induced rage made me into a tool to do it.

"Remus and I both concur," Aida says after a moment—her fingers touching her smooth chin. "You had to have been given some drug or hallucinogen to provoke you into that behavior and also receive somewhat of a memory wipe. We also agree that it would take some powerful planning and skill to orchestrate something like this."

"What do you mean?" I ask, my voice sounding faint. Remus

squats next to Aida. His long, leather jacket glistens with bright green reflections.

"Aside from the troubling circumstances of the event, we were all quickly taken by the Imperials and shipped off on a prison convoy without even a trial," Aida replies, scratching her bald head. "They then isolate the three of us and ship us to a salvage pit in the Pyrack. Someone wanted us shipped off quickly to a remote salvage pit. And I'm still trying to piece that together."

I say nothing for a moment, my thoughts fixated on what I've done. The guilt. The fear. The anger. A cyclone of emotions goes through me, and I feel sick to my stomach. It is a betrayal the likes which I've never felt before. My home city, where I was born and raised, had deceived me and set me up to be taken advantage of. I want to vomit. I'd been apprehended for committing high treason under the influence of a forced drug, how is that justice?

Fury begins to fill me as I keep trying to process this, and I start to hate those who have done this to me.

"What did they pick you up for?" I ask finally, finding a way to focus on something besides my rage.

She glances at Remus; her expression seems as if she's asking for permission—to which Remus nods in approval. There's a spark between them when their eyes make contact. Aida's thick lips smile momentarily.

"Remus and I have been utilizing various resources to locate a place called Providence," she relays quietly.

"What in all the Hells is Providence?" I ask with a perturbed look on my face.

"Domain—" Remus replies, cocking his head. Though it's dimly lit, I can see his brown eyes reflecting a measure of purpose.

"It's the legendary final fortress of the Domain," Aida clarifies. "Remus and I believe it exists. And our mission in Z'hart was to find resources that would help us locate it."

"That's impossible," I say in disbelief. "If Providence isn't a myth, why hasn't anyone found it in this last millennium?"

"Because it's a place so small that it has taken nine Cycles to even piece together a vague recollection about it," Aida explains. "Many are not even aware of its myth. But there are old societies and historians who believe in these stories. I'm one such scholar."

"So you were a scholar in Z'hart." I say, piecing a bit of her background together. "What was Remus? Your bodyguard?"

"In a manner of speaking," she says. Aida glances at him and places her hand gently on his shoulder. "Remus was part of an old Order, as Septem so kindly revealed. His studies led him to learn of the existence of this Providence myth. It drove him into more research, and that's how he met me."

I feel a bit of weight coming off my shoulders. Learning a bit about their pasts makes them seem less threatening, despite their talk about secret societies and such. But there was still the question as to why they were rounded up with me.

"So how does this play into our arrests?" I ask, resisting the urge to pick at the cut on my cheek.

"Remus' old master, a person by the name of Centum, likely

set us up to attend the banquet," Aida continues, her tone turning dark. She clearly abhors this character. "Centum knew we were there, and knew we were starting to look for Providence. I don't know much about the Order's master, but I do know Centum is possessive over any matter regarding anything Domain related. Obsessed even. Centum captured us and…" Her voice fades for a moment, and Remus pats her hand on his shoulder.

"Punished— Me—" Remus finishes vaguely when Aida won't continue.

So his ailment isn't natural after all. His conditions were unlike anything I've ever seen, even the sedatives look like they barely help him. I want to know more, but I know it's not the right time.

"So Centum is the one who had us all shipped off?" I ask instead. I think I'm finding the final pieces.

"Yes, but I'm baffled as to why Centum's interested in you." Aida quickly makes a placating gesture. "Meaning no offense. But you're just a brewer from Z'hart. Why would they have an interest in shipping you off with us?"

I start to think about it for a long moment, my eyes staring at the rigid rock floor of the cave. I think I know the reason they targeted me. And I'm mystified as to how Centum learned about me. But I'm more concerned with how they've managed to manipulate events in Z'hart.

"Perhaps because I have lots of connections in my line of work," I say, brushing my hair behind an ear. "I hear a lot of underground info while working at the Blue Den. I heard rumors about various cults looking for Domain technology. Could this be the same thing?"

"More— Than— Cult—" Remus retorts with a snort. "Order—"

"You remember what Septem said on the convoy?" Aida asks quietly. "He said that his Order has been around longer than we could imagine. He's right. Remus told me everything, and these people have ties everywhere. They are the masters and the nations are their puppets."

"What do we do then?" I ask, completely unsure of how to face something as grand as this. I feel so small, like an ant among humans.

"We'll figure that out in due time, Sarina." Aida adopts a questioning look. "You can help by telling us why you were at that embassy."

"I was working as a brewer for the Blue Den. An invitation was sent to us, requesting that we provide service to the gala," I recount vaguely, still hesitant to reveal too much about myself. "But you know that."

"A brewer, eh," someone comments from behind me.

I turn to see Vivían coming around one of the stalagmites. She's just come around, so likely she only heard about my job. Still, I'm a bit surprised by her sudden appearance. Flopping down next to me, her expression reflects casualness but also hints at curiosity.

"I took you as more of a bouncer," she says wryly, giving me a grin. "That hot headedness seemed perfect for taking care of drunk pricks."

"I dealt with drunk pricks anyways," I retort lightly. "How long have you been listening?"

"Long enough," Vivían shrugs, leaning back and placing her hands behind her crazy hair. There doesn't seem to be anything nefarious about her. "You were all clearly set up at that banquet, you know?"

"Yes, I'm well aware of that," I affirm darkly. "We just need to figure out who sent the invitation to us all."

"Really, you all accepted these invites without knowing who sent it?" Vivían scoffs, looking to the three of us. Surprise is etched in her flawless features when we don't deny.

"I didn't have any say in the matter," I say quietly. "I did as my barkeep ordered. Plus, it seemed just like any other catering job."

"That's stupid," Vivían says in concern. She seems oddly protective. "Rule number one of survival: Never take anything for what it is. Always remain vigilant."

"That's a tough way to live," I reply. Vivían adjusts the headband just above her forehead. "I don't live in the Outlands."

"Look where that's gotten you," she retorts. Her violet eyes show some measure of resolve. "At least in the Outlands, danger doesn't resort to back stabbings and intrigue. Z'hart seems more dangerous than the Outlands."

"That may be," Aida says as she stands up. "But it looks like the only way to find out what's happening is to return to Z'hart."

She looks directly at me; her dark eyes reflect the gravity of her words. "Only there will we find answers."

I remain silent and reflect on what I've been told. Whoever this Centum character is, he has some nefarious plan revolving around us, Z'hart, and this Providence place.

Reluctance starts to weigh on me again. I know that the only place I will find answers is in Z'hart City itself. I develop an uneasy sensation in my stomach that tells me I might need the others even after we survive the mines.

CHAPTER 11

Sarina

Well Below

IT SEEMS LIKE AN entire day has passed after traversing down the endless mine tunnels. My legs are beginning to tire, my luggage weighs down on my back, and our meals are kept short and simple. The rations provided in the packs are nothing but hard bread, dried meat, and canned beans. Hardly a worthy meal for a fatigued stomach. Nevertheless, what we possess will suffice and there is no use dwelling on the comforts of banquet meals.

The group proceeds at a brisk pace. We're all determined to be rid of the mines and find fresh air. Despite this, I notice that Devin and Vyck are starting to falter in our flank. Their movements are intermittent, they huff their breaths, and their heads are persistently looking back and forth from me to the tunnel.

"You know, looking at me isn't going to make this go faster, right?" I call back to them, my voice echoing in the tunnel.

Devin gives me a scathing glance over. "I'm starting to think you're full of shit, m'lady," he grunts. "We haven't reached the Well, so I don't think it's here."

"What do you want to do, turn around?" Vivían juts in, making a mockery of the idea. "I think I speak for all of us in saying *to all the Hells with that*. We shouldn't be too far."

"And another reassuring statement from the navigation team," Vyck growls in derision. "Let's just keep walking. Hope we don't run out of food or get boned by some cave monsters."

"It's been barely a day," I say aghast. "We have enough food for a couple more."

"Shut up," he spits immaturely.

The trek has put everyone on edge, not just due to the exhaustion and lack of clean air but also because of the lack of substantial sustenance. Survivors we are, but we all share the same hope to eat a hearty meal sooner rather than later. As if to punctuate my point, my stomach growls with exhaustion and I begin to crave for fresh onion stew.

We continue at our pace for nearly another kilometer when I hear the duo halt loudly within the tunnel. We all stop to look at them. The look in Devin's eye is feral, almost insane despite his collected composure and neutral expression. Tálir turns around slightly, but keeps his luminescent bottle held towards the tunnel ahead. We all pause in disconcerted confusion.

"I'm about to lose my shit here, Sarina," Devin says in a desperate voice. "I need to get out of here before I start clawing my way out. The crystals aren't as important as my sanity."

I place a hand on my hip. "We are heading for the exit," I reply insightfully. "You do realize that."

Aida takes a step towards him in a placating manner. "It's just a bit of claustrophobia," she tells him with a soothing gesture. "Just breathe and relax—"

"Breathe what?" Devin snaps. "It's like breathing in steam down here! It's tough to remain calm if there is no air!"

"I think I'm starting to see spots," Vyck says, trying to affirm Devin's argument.

"We're going to die down here!"

As Devin starts to raise his voice, Remus goes into another spasm-type fit. He's holding his head hysterically and rocking his body. Lowering himself, he starts breathing frantically An audible whimper emanates from him, but it doesn't seem to be sprung from anxiety or embarrassment. It's from pain.

Alarmed, Aida drops her equipment satchel and kneels beside him before struggling to retrieve her wineskin. There is a brief pause and I'm able to gaze at Remus and his contorted face. Pale, stricken, and pitiful. He looks almost like a helpless child struggling in pain, and it fills me with both pity and concern.

Over the last several hours, Remus was required to imbibe

the phosphorous antidote three times to keep him stable. His condition is graver than I thought, for he needed the sedatives almost every two hours. My thoughts reel as I try to guess what exactly Centum plagued him with. Trauma? Hematomas? Whatever it is, it's gradually getting worse.

Remus is clawing at his temples, as if to dig the pain out. Sweat begins to glisten on his brow, and his jaw is clenched firmly. It's an excruciating sight to behold, and one that would've prompted me into action if I knew how to help him. Sadly, I have no idea what to do for him.

But even as Aida fumbles through the bag, Devin starts became even more disconcerted and enraged. "He is starting to damage my cool!" Devin nearly screams. "I need to get the fragging Hells out of here, and I'm about to start running without you people!"

"Seriously Devin! You're not helping this situation!" I growl back at him with fists clenched. "We have other problems than your claustrophobia. In case you haven't noticed, Remus is kind of losing it—so I think that takes more precedent than your issues!"

He stares at me with disbelief, and his mouth falls open. "Are you fragging serious?" Devin's eyes are wild. "My issues are just as important as Remus'! I. Need. To. Get. OUT!"

Devin is about to unleash his panicked fury on us when Tálir calls out, "Devin calm yourself! We've reached our destination!"

We all wheel around and see Tálir a few meters down in the tunnel. His luminous bottle illustrates an opening. Almost imperceptibly, Devin darts around us and rushes down the tunnel towards the opening. Evidently Tálir ventured a bit further in the midst of our squabbles, and I'm perplexed as to why he abandoned the scene. Perhaps he realized that the exit was mere meters from us.

Aida stabilizes Remus quickly after letting him drink the sedative. With the pandemonium calming down, the rest of us start to approach the exit. Reaching the exit, I see the tunnel open into a massive open space which is craftily lit by scores of crystals. Finally standing at the tunnel's exit, Tálir holds his radiant bottle high and we are able to glimpse the Well.

It's awe inspiring to witness the enormity of the cylindrical mining shaft that sinks deeper into the earth and rises a kilometer above us. Two hundred meters in diameter, the Well's cylindrical sides are etched with escalating pathways that gyrate around it like a whirlpool. The dark features of the dirt, rock, and ore that make up the Well are impalpably lit by hordes of emerald gems. Stacked in piles, resting in mine carts, or buried in rock, the crystals are numerous. Light is predominant. Deeper into the earth, I can see vague outlines of remaining equipment and construction scaffolds.

Above us, the Well rises into a vaulted ceiling that narrows almost like a cone at its peak. The ceiling is lined with lanterns and other illumination devices, long since deactivated. A small cavity has been etched out on the far right side of the dome, and the last rays of daylight streak through the small opening.

Respite tugs at my features and I can sense the rest of the group unwinding somewhat. After the last few hours, I'm jubilant to see our means of escape. Even if it leads us back to the Pyrack, it'll at least be more capacious and less oppressive. Fresh air, sunlight, and ample space seem like an extravagance after our trek through the mines. However, we still have a bit of a hike ahead of us before we reach the exit.

What surprises me most of all is that the equipment and structures seem to be very, very old. The wood looks worn and dry while rust cakes some of the metal machines. It becomes evident to me that perhaps the Well hasn't been occupied in some time. Perhaps even a few Cycles.

Devin lets out an audible moan of liberation, and his shoulders heave a tremendous weight off of them. "Tálir, you beautiful son of a bitch!" he exclaims with a wide grin. "I think I'd have gone on a murder spree if we'd have been stuck in that tunnel for much longer."

"What the shit?" I snap, aghast.

"That seems a bit—excessive, don't you think, buddy?" Vyck comments with a disconcerted look.

"I was just being honest."

I'm nervous for a moment. Talk of a killing spree makes me a tad uncomfortable. I shake the feeling, however, and we soon start to scout around the rocky outcropping for the best way to reach the top.

A series of old ladders connects the ledge we stand upon to a scaffolding a few hundred meters above us. The ladders creep up the rocky walls like vines. The large scaffolding is built almost like a seaside home, its massive stakes imbedded in the edge of the shaft. A rickety wooden bridge connects the scaffold to a nearby niche that directly leads into the spiral pathway that wind to the top. The bridge is incredibly thin, so we'll need to go single file. It's a moderately clear path, but I can't help but shake a feeling of misgiving. Who knows how old this equipment is.

What if the condition of the bridges and scaffolds is severe, and ends up collapsing under our weight? While my dread is prevalent, I know I'll have to face the obstacles if we're to get out.

"It looks like that pathway is our ticket out," Tálir points out, cautiously. "But judging the conditions of the scaffolds and walkways, we need to be extra careful."

"Yeah, I'm not too keen on those old-ass ladders either," I affirm. "Perhaps we should go one at a time?"

"Pussies," Vivían snorts playfully. "What's life without a little danger?"

"Being able to live," Aida points out dryly.

I point to a spiraling pathway that snakes around the diameter of the Well and culminates at a large extension near the top.

"If we can just make it across that walkway, we won't have to rely too much on the constructed paths," I say. "Doesn't look too difficult."

"See, you say that…" Vyck comments hesitantly as the rest of us reluctantly prepare for the climb.

Tálir has everyone go before him. An odd strategy for someone who wishes to lead. But I soon realize that he's prioritizing us over himself. I rock my head to the side in approval.

Devin goes first. As he makes the first step unto the ladder, it creaks loudly as dust falls from various places. He looks back at us, shrugs aloofly, and resumes cautiously clambering up. The rest of us follow suite, only one person on the ladder at a time. While rickety and unstable, it didn't take long for us to finish the first hurtle in this obstacle course.

Then the process repeats over the course of the next couple ladders as we rise nearly half a kilometer. Reaching the scaffolding, we clamber up one at a time despite the fact that the structure is large enough to hold a dozen men. Stepping unto the dark, worn wood at the top, we pause as Tálir speaks up.

"Follow closely on the bridge in the event anything starts to become more unstable." His voice reflects worry, but he remains steadfast. "If we move light and fast, there might be less risk of it collapsing under our weight."

"Or more of a risk," I comment warily. While he acknowledges my misgivings, we have no time to argue.

Vigilantly, Devin and Vyck take the lead and briskly make their way across the unsteady causeway. Prolonged *squeaks* echo in the cavernous Well as they go across. After a few moments, they make it to the other side.

Remus and Aida go forward, much more cautiously than the other pair. However, their reluctance is met with several *creaks* and *snaps* as their boots touch the aged wood. I can see dust falling from the crevasses in the wood, and the dangerous *snaps* grow more frequent.

"I'll go last," Tálir says with determination. "Get over there as fast as you can."

While I worry for him, I don't hesitate. Vivían and I both go across the walkway, and I can feel each piece of wood vibrate with a grating noise. I can almost sense the nails being pulled from the wood as we step onto the lumber.

We're halfway across and I take a slow step. *Snap*. My foot breaks through one of the boards. Flinching violently, I nearly fling myself backwards in response—stumbling as I retreat. My momentum carries me to the far side of the catwalk and I almost step off. My breath catches in my chest. I glimpse the ominous darkness below me, and it feels like it's trying to consume me.

"Woah—woah!" Aida shouts from the niche at the end of the catwalk. Terrified alarm is in her voice.

Vivían quickly grabs my arm and pulls me back. I regain my balance imperceptibly, and I let out a sigh of relief. Reorienting myself, we hastily make our way to the other side. The tenseness in my body is relieved, muscles are uncoiling.

It's now Tálir's turn. After making only a few steps, something snaps underneath the walkway. There's a prolonged *creak*. The structure shifts downwards slightly, and Tálir freezes and tries to keep his footing. He's petrified. And he looks directly at me in terror.

"RUN!" I yell.

Tálir doesn't hesitate.

As the catwalk continues to break, he races across with a look of frightened determination on his face. His auburn hair blazes around his head. Parts of the walkway starts to fall away as it crumbles, the darkness below subsuming the fragments. His armored boots smack against the collapsing catwalk, and for a moment he's steady. But a meter from us, he stumbles forward and the walkway collapses completely and swings downward—Tálir holding on for dear life.

Dangling from the outcropping, the walkway is supported by one picket and an aged piece of rope. With the age of the picket holding the weight of the remaining walkway, I reckon it will last for maybe a few minutes.

Hurriedly, Vivían and I rush forward and look over the edifice to see Tálir still holding on—his face reflects dumbfounded shock. I lie on the ground and extend my arm as far as it'll go towards him.

"Take my hand!" I call as Vivían prepares to help me hoist him up.

"I would've gone for 'hang on'," Vivían says in a joking manner.

Tálir climbs a bit before grabbing my outstretched arm. The muscles start screaming in pain under his weight. Despite this, I use all of my strength to help him ascend. Vivían grabs his other arm. Even Remus and Aida join to help. It is an odd moment of solidarity, the four of us banding together to help another. It's unusually thrilling, and we heave him unto the outcropping with finality.

As he flops unto the rock, a resounding crack signals the

breaking of the picket—and the walkway falls into the Well. Tálir lays on his back, breathing rapidly as his heart races.

"That was exciting," Vivían comments energetically, getting to her feet. "A solid thrill."

"Not for me," Tálir comments warily, standing up and glancing at all of us. "Thanks for having my back, everyone."

"No thanks to the other two," Aida scoffs. Vyck and Devin are nowhere to be found. "I suppose we shouldn't have expected much from a couple of mercenaries."

"Now we're mercenaries?" a voice calls from higher along the spiral path, moving towards us. "I'll take that as a compliment over being called an Outlander."

Unsurprisingly, Devin and Vyck walk around the bend of the pathway, the latter of which carries an antique chest roughly the width of his torso. While it seems heavy, Vyck's eagerness outshines any strain the chest puts on his arms.

"Was the bridge always like that?" Vyck snorts.

"To the Hells with you guys!" I spit, placing my hands on my hips. I let my disappointment show. "You ditched us!"

"Eyyeah, but we came back," Devin retorts innocently, looking at Vyck. "Show them."

Vyck sits the chest down and lifts the top. He reveals five, polished emerald jewels the size of large onions. A bright glow emits from the crystals, and their polished state seems to enhance their stores of bioluminescent energy. Devin smiles with glee.

"Think of what we could buy with these gorgeous things,"

Devin thinks aloud wishfully. "I could probably buy an apartment complex in Z'hart City with one."

"I think I might capitalize on some ancestral technology," Vyck says, eyeing Tálir. "Tálir is kind of getting me hooked on Domain tech. Plus, I like that shade of bronze over the violet."

"You're taking all five of them?" Vivían inquires, trying to hide her envy.

"Do we look like sticklers to you, Viv?" Vyck responds, somewhat appalled. He gives Vivían a guiltless look. "Devin and I get three and the other two you can divide amongst yourselves. Fair enough?"

"If you're offering," Vivían says lightly. There's a glint in her eye as she looks at Vyck.

"Consider it our way of saying *sorry*—for not looking out for Tálir," Devin says snidely, but there seems to be a sliver of shame in his voice.

I snort in derision. "Just like that we're supposed to be cool?"

"It's not worth fighting over," Tálir admits exhaustively. "Let's just get out of here."

Their sudden disappearance in a crisis vexes me to a degree. But, I honestly should've expected nothing less. They were out for riches, not friendship. I'm surprised, though, that they're willing to share their plunder. Perhaps I've been a bit too harsh on judging them. Only time will tell though.

So in unison, we begin ascending the spiraling walkway as the rays of evening can be seen from the opening. The gyrating pathway is littered with mine carts filled with piles of crystals. Our way is pleasantly illuminated. The snaking walls have smooth curvatures. Our feet step upon smooth rock. To our left is a drop-off leading into the Well's abyss.

Everything progresses smoothly until we reach a cave nearly halfway up. Carved out of the wall next to the pathway, the cave is about ten meters in diameter. Support beams and other pieces of construction help keep it from collapsing. Rigid pieces of rock stick out from its opening, and light barely passes into its darkness. It's a gaping maw. A jangling feeling of foreboding crawls within me as I pause to look. There is something ominous about the cave that catches my attention. Like it isn't meant to be there. More to the point, it seems new—the lumber and metal used for support beams looks fresh. Carvings within the cave hint that it has been excavated within the last decade.

"Sarina," Vivian addresses me with a worried look. "Are you alright? What's wrong?"

It takes me a moment to answer as the others glance at me. "Why would there be a cavern this high up in a mining Well?" I query to the group as they pause to glance at it.

There is a silence of obstinate confusion before Vyck answers, "Maybe because we're in a mine? C'mon, Sarina. Aren't there supposed to be lots of caves?"

"But if the excavation for the Well started from up here, why does this cave look recently excavated?" I ask seriously. "Look at the support beams, too. The metal seems—less ancient."

The air is still for a moment as the group comes to the realization as well. I berate myself for not making the conclusion sooner. Something is wrong, and we might have fallen into a precarious situation.

"Bone me. Is this where I say 'it looks like a trap'?" Vyck asks mordantly, looking alarmed. "Clearly these crystals are slowing our minds to obvious stuff. We should go back."

"You're a moron," I exhale.

He doesn't respond, and there is an arctic pause as a hissing noise emanates from within the cave. It's a soft noise, almost like the wind blowing through a crevasse and whistling by. But its sudden audibility, the way it grows louder, and the intensity of the noise suggests it isn't natural. After a moment the noise stops. I then feel a light breeze derive from within the cavern. A dark sheet blinds us to what resides inside even as the hissing spews from the mouth of the cave like an exhalation.

Due to the unnaturalness of the draught, everyone stiffens and brandishes their weapons. I draw my bowpistol and ready myself for the imminent danger. The draft grows stronger and louder, and I tense my grip around the pistol as the hissing reaches a frenzied pitch. There is a pause. Then a cloud of pale vapor blows out from the mouth of the cave and envelopes us in a cold wisp.

Before any of us can react or hold our breaths, the gas overtakes us and I inhale the odorless mixture. For a moment, it seems to be nothing more than a cloud of water vapor expelled from the cave. Then, something happens.

My body starts to feel lethargic, and my limbs begin to feel icy as numbness starts to creep through them. Dizziness strikes me. Sensation in my fingers is lost, and I drop my bowpistol. A stammering cough escapes me as I try to cover my mouth and nose, even though the damage is already done. The entire group begins coughing vigorously, and I hear metallic weapons striking the rocky ground. I squint my eyes in an attempt to peer through the cloud. Tears well up as I squint. But I can see only silhouettes.

Amid the chaos, I hear someone wheeze, "Whatever— you— do. Don't pass— out—" It's Tálir's voice, but his last words slur from his mouth. Then there's a soft thud.

More thuds occur as the coughing begins to quiet and dissipate. Nearly everyone has fallen to the ground as I try to figure out if they're dead or unconscious. Heart racing, but the cold begins to slow its terrorized beat. Darkness clouds into my vision. My body then falls with a thud.

CHAPTER 12

Sarina

Abrax

THERE IS A WARMTH as I drift out of unconsciousness. In contrast to the cool air, the warmth feels oddly comforting. My body is relaxed. Underneath my eyelids, an orange light seeps through and the smell of smoke and salt wafts in the air. The cackling noise in my ears indicates a fire has been started, but by whom?

Outlanders, perhaps? Or maybe something else that resided in the cave? No matter the case, someone has apparently retrieved me.

I'm sitting upright against a rocky wall, and my head is hanging between my shoulders. As feeling returns to my arms and legs, I notice that they aren't bound by anything. Shifting a little, I bump against another individual, who remains motionless even after I make contact.

Vigilantly, I open my eyes and allow the fog of bleariness wear off. As my vision focuses, I can see a sizable fire crackling in front of me. Cooking above it is a pot of stew and a roasting carcass of what appears to be a cavebat. Its body is the size of a small cat. Instantly my stomach rumbles at the sight of fresh meat, and the smell of mesquite smoke fills the air. Even if it is a roasting rodent.

The fire rests at the center of a domed structure about the size of a large living room, the ground is smooth and burnished. The curving walls are also smooth, like they're carved from marble. A small tunnel is also carved out on the other side of the area, lit by a single torch. I can't see where it leads. Lumber pillars line the walls while beams web across the ceiling. The arched ceiling rises about six meters and a small opening has been carved out of the center. A metal slab hangs from it, indicating it can be closed. Rays of moonlight seep through.

So we've been here for a few hours evidently, I think to myself.

Strangely though, the structure isn't untenanted. Tattered rugs, clay pots, bits of salvaged junk, and a massive chest are in the room. With the addition of the fire pit, I conclude that someone has resided here for some time.

Leaned up along the wall on both sides of me, the group also struggles to regain consciousness as several groans fill the air. Directly flanking me is Vivian and Remus, the latter of who is baulking in discomfort.

Everyone is still in their gear and armor while our weapons are laid out in front of them. I notice my bowpistol and pouches have been placed by my feet. Whoever had found us didn't seem interested in our belongings, which bewilders me.

While wary of our surroundings, I still shuffle forward and say aloud, "So much for not passing out."

"I don't know what you're talking about," I hear Vyck groan cynically. "Something hit me." He puts a thin hand to his forehead and then cracks his back.

"Was it a brain?" I ask mockingly, stretching my arms. I pull my bowpistol closer to my side.

"Let's not start shit now," Aida calls out. Quickly she stands and rushes over to Remus. She checks his vitals, and then shows relief. "I'd like to figure out where in all the Hells we are."

"Whoever took us in," Tálir grunts, "they mustn't mind letting us keep our things. I'd bet my ass it's not slavers." He shakes his head as if to clear it, sending his long hair into a frenzy.

"An odd thing to bet," Vivían comments in a flirting manner. Her eyes track him for a second. "I might take that."

I shake off the burning in my cheeks. Devin and Tálir stand and stretch their legs. Vivían picks up her energy bow and activates the blue strings. Vyck unsheathes a dagger, but his eyes are on the cooking food. Rising to one knee, I take hold of my bowpistol and glance around the cavern. Or whatever this place is.

"Why do you think they let us keep our stuff?" I ask aloud, my eyebrows furrowing.

"Because it's your stuff, not mine," a basso voice answers me. Heads snap around to look for the source of the voice, our faces stricken. Like deer, we've caught the scent of a predator.

From within the small tunnel across from us, a man comes out from the shadows. It's like he materialized from the darkness. His footsteps are heavy, and there's something weighing him down. As he moves closer, the flames illuminate his appearance with a fiery tint.

He's an older man roughly in his late seventies, dark-skinned, tall and sinewy with long white hair pulled into a ponytail. His face is thin and angular, his nose is set between dark eyes, and his lips are obscured by a scraggly silver beard. Exhaustion rings his eyes, and I can see the toll of time on his features.

But his attire sends chills down my spine. Identical to Tálir, the man wears the same ceremonial bronze armor across his chest, hands, forearms, and over his legs. The suit is far more aged than Tálir's, and various dents and scrapes hint that the metal has seen some action. The winged edges of the gauntlets and pauldrons are dull and chipped. Underneath the armor and exosuit, the man sports a sage trench coat with simple a tunic and trousers. Bronze metal covers his boots.

Clenched in his hands are glass vials containing salts, spices, and herbs. I surmise that he has a storage pantry further in the cave, but there's only one way he gets these supplies out here. By raiding convoys.

I jump to my feet with the bowpistol in hand, and I raise it towards him. I don't care that he left us untied and fully armed. This man gassed us. And with his current living situation, who knows what drives him. It could be madness, or it could be not. I won't be unprepared again.

Tálir and Devin take more aggressive stances as the man approaches. Devin draws his short sword. Vyck already has his dagger ready to throw. Vivían goes on one knee and strings a plasma arrow.

The old man doesn't flinch; much less acknowledge the weapons aiming for him. He kneels in front of the fire and begins dropping sprinkling the spices into the pot of stew. His eyes barely look at us. His aloofness is jarring.

"Excuse me sir," Tálir says with caution. Hints of a sloppy martial pose can be seen in his features. "If you don't mind me asking: who in all the Hells are you? Why did you gas us? And… are you cooking food for all of us?" A growl from his stomach punctuates this.

The man holds up a hand but fails to look at Tálir. "Three things, lad." His voice is grating and raspy. I can tell he's a smoker of greenweed. "One: don't use that tone with me. Two: the gas was merely a defense mechanism. And three: I suppose I can share."

Devin and Vyck glance at one another in disbelief. "You gassed us? That feat doesn't exactly inspire me to feel safe here," Devin comments, raising his blade slightly. "Give me a reason why we shouldn't kill you?"

The old man pauses for a moment before glancing up at us;

his eyes shine with cool confidence and blatant irritation. "I made you supper," he says flatly.

Vivian sniffs in amusement. I blink with confusion. The others seem just as perplexed. My guard is up, but there's something about him that doesn't seem entirely threatening. Sure, he looks dangerous. But he has no weapons, and no indication of wanting to harm us. He's just cooking a late dinner.

Devin is unconvinced, however, and brandishes his sword. "Not a good enough answer, old timer," he replies before advancing around the fire pit.

The old man's eyes track Devin as he moves around the fire with his sword held to the side. Meters away from him, Devin raises the sword in an attempt to split the old man's head in half. And yet, the old man remains motionless as if he's watching a child throw a tantrum.

Concerned for both of their safety, I yell out, "Devin, wait!"

But it's too late.

As Devin swings the sword down, the old man raises his left hand and points his fingers at his assailant's chest. There's a cackle of noise as five, emerald beams of energy spring from his fingertips.

I'm dumbstruck.

The event is torn straight out of a fairy tale of wizards and magic. The beams speed through the air and strike Devin in the center of his breastplate. The impact of the beams drives the breath from him. His body is flung several meters, and he crashes into the wall. His thin armor sends sparks as it brushes against the rock. The sword falls from his hands. Crumpling to the ground, Devin is motionless but moaning in pain.

There's an arctic pause, and then Vyck snarls like a beast and throws his dagger towards the old man's face. Vivían fires an energy arrow that whisks through the air. In a blur of motion, the old man raises his right arm and locks it at ninety degrees. After a millisecond, a circular, emerald energy shield forms and blocks each projectile—deflecting them.

Stunned into silence, I watch the shield dissipate and the old man points his fingers at both Vivían and Vyck. The same emerald beams erupt from his fingertips and strike the pair. Similarly interred like Devin, the two crumple backwards and remain motionless even as they grunt in discomfort.

I'm rooted on the spot. Wondrous caution freezes my body. What exactly just happened? I have no idea. I aim my bowpistol in a defensive manner. While he acted only in defense, his dexterity and supernatural retribution invokes high levels of caution in me. How is he able to harness pure energy with a flick of his fingers? And since when have such feats ever been possible?

A moment of silence elapses as Tálir and I stare intensely at the old man. There's a stillness in the air. His eyes dart to Tálir, whom immediately holds up his hands in an innocent gesture. The old man sizes Tálir up with a look.

"Wait, wait, wait!" he sputters, taking a step back. "Let's talk about this. We don't have to—"

A single torrent of energy hits Tálir in the torso, causing him to choke on his words and tumble backwards. I regard Tálir for a moment as he rolls on the ground. He lets loose an audible moan. The old man quirks an amused grin as he lowers his hands.

"Stop moaning, laddies. You'll be fine," he huffs with a condescending look. "It'll wear off in a few minutes. Perhaps you shouldn't be so keen to attack someone who offers food."

The altercation lasted for barely a minute and yet, the old man had subdued more than half of the group and hadn't even gotten to his feet. *Badass*, I say to myself. Caution still snakes through me upon seeing his handiwork. Half the group is down, and the old man didn't even get to his feet. I keep my bowpistol aimed at him, but I don't fire. My curiosity is what stays my hand.

The old man looks at me with his aged dark eyes, notes of appreciation can be seen in his irises. He inclines his head slightly, a gesture of respect for not shooting him. I think he can sense my deliberations. Something else is in his look, however.

He turns his head to look at Aida and Remus. Aida is chilled by what had happened, but doesn't leave Remus' side. Inside I chuckle at her priorities. She's not interested in fighting, just ensuring Remus is safe.

"I gave him a dose of the sedatives," the old man says after a moment, eyeing Remus. "I hope you know that he has maybe a month left before the affliction consumes him. You're going to need a lot more sedatives if you want him to last."

Aida's thick lips part in awe, and she looks from Remus to the man and back again. "How do you know about his condition?"

she asks in disbelief.

The old man picks up a wooden spoon and starts tenderly stirring the stew. "I'm old and I know things," he says wryly. He sprinkles some herbs into the soup then looks back at her. "When his spasms came, I searched your belongings for anything that could've been used for treatment. I can only assume that you're this gaggle's medic, based on the contents you carried."

"How long have we been here?" I ask, scanning him.

He locks eyes with me. "Just under three hours," he admits. "I'd hoped you'd all take the opportunity to sleep until morning, but I misjudged your tenacity."

The four who'd been zapped by the energy gradually start to recover and push themselves off of the ground, their faces grimacing. "Ow," Tálir strains to say, getting to one knee. "What in all the Hells was that for?"

"It amused me," the old man mumbles wryly. "Humiliating the alpha male is always fun."

"Let me rephrase that: what was that stuff you shot at us?" Tálir voices indignantly, endeavoring to stand. "Magic?"

The old man lets out a chuckle and stops stirring the stew. "In a matter of speaking. But I'm surprised you don't know the full implications of your armor, Tálir. I suppose you wear it merely for show, rather than for its substance."

Wait what?

No one speaks for the long moment. I'm thunderstruck that he knows Tálir by name. But Tálir evidently doesn't know this man.

So how did he know? Tálir's tan face adopts a cautiously curious look, his hazel eyes reflect some measure of wonder.

"How do you know my name?" Tálir asks quietly, his eyes reflecting misgiving.

"I know all of your names," the elder man grunts, surveying us. "I've been monitoring you all for some time."

"Hold on, wait a second!" Vyck blurts out before standing up. "How long have you been watching us? Days, weeks, months, years?" His voice becomes nervous, and his green eyes widen.

The old man looks at him questioningly. "No, only since you entered the caves you imbecile." Irritated frustration shows in his eyes.

"Oh… See I thought—"

"Just shut up, you dumb idiot!" Devin snaps, shooting Vyck a look.

The old man gives a lethargic look and holds up his hands in a placating manner. Devin and Vyck flinch with alarm even as the old man keeps his palms open in a gesture of friendliness.

"I'm not psychic," he says dryly. "I installed proximity monitors within the Well and surrounding tunnels during my years of residing here. You are all also fairly loud."

Now it all makes sense. The feeling we were being watched in the tunnels. That was merely the proximity monitors.

My mind jumps to another revelation. "You're the one who created this cave," I deduce, staring at him intently. "You must've excavated this place long after the Well was unearthed."

The old man nods with vague appraisal. "Very good, Sarina. Although I figured that was obvious. This place was once a great harvester for the gems you've seen. This is one of many special mounds throughout the land that produce them naturally. Ore, minerals, and other materials were mined by the Domain in the years before their downfall. But after the Ending, it has long been unknown to the populace. It took a little research, but I found it after some time. And it serves as a nice incognito home."

"In the years you've resided here, no one has stumbled upon this place?" I ask, lowering the boltpistol. "It's hard to believe we're the only ones who've found this place."

He rocks his head. "Some have found this place, you're right about that. But it normally just takes a hearty meal and some shiny valuables to keep a mouth shut."

Devin snorts. "That sounds way too easy."

The man doesn't respond, but instead starts to portion the stew into eight separate wooden bowls before retrieving the roasted bat. Slicing the carcass delicately with a serrated knife, he places thin slabs of meat into the separate bowls before gesturing for us to take them.

"Cavebat stew." He says, taking his own bowl. "It's not much, but it's heartier than the junk you've been eating."

"It could be poisoned," Vyck comments warily.

The old man looks at him askance; his eyes are full of condescension. "If it's poisoned, then I suppose I'm a dead man," he says, eating a spoonful.

Although Vyck has a point, I consider the logistics of it and it doesn't add up. It's a suspicious scenario. The proximity sensors, the gassing, and then taking us into his home. But my gut tells me that there's nothing to fear.

"Why would he poison us after gassing us?" I ask Vyck. He scratches at his shaggy, blonde hair in thought. "If he wanted us dead, he could've killed us while we were unconscious."

Vyck shuffles in discomfort. "Maybe he's playing some sick game."

Everybody sighs with exasperation. I wait until everyone has recovered before cautiously retrieving a bowl of stew. Despite being wary of danger, my stomach's fatigue overrules everything else. I start to eat. My taste buds rejoice at the flavor of the stew, and my whole body relaxes in rejuvenation. The meat is tender and packed with flavor while the hot soup fills my stomach. I eat joyfully.

Tálir is next to do so, but his eyes still examine the old man's armor. Everyone else reluctantly follows suite. Vyck starts examining the bowl and spoon for dangers before sniffing the stew. I snort in wry amusement at his attempts to be cautious. Everyone eats in silence, for it is the heartiest meal we've had all day. Eating scraps of rations was a bit of a strain on a stomach. The fire cackles before me, and I see the embers floating through the open roof.

When everyone is finished, we sit comfortably with full stomachs.

Our guards seem to remain up, however. The old man notices this, and addresses us all.

"If you're still angry about the gassing, just put yourselves in my shoes," he says, standing up with great effort. "Alone in a massive, dark cave with plenty of creatures prowling around. I don't like anything sneaking up on me."

"No, instead you just sneak up on us when we're trying to escape," Tálir voices sardonically. "I think that's what we're all bitter about. If you were monitoring us, you knew we were just trying to leave."

The old man regards him. "Your supply rations," he grunts, gesturing to our bags. "How long do you think those will last you? A few days?"

"Three to be exact," Tálir replies, his eyes narrowing in suspicion. "What's your point?"

"The nearest civilization is a week away." The elder man scratches at his silver beard. "Erron's Ville is two thousand kilometers to the northeast. Z'hart is two point five thousand kilometers to the north. And you'll need to prepare for the activity of Roils since they are increasing exponentially."

Two thousand kilometers? That seems nigh impossible to travel in. With the desert conditions, dwindling supplies, and threat of Roils, I don't know how I could make it home. But, why would the Roils be increasing in activity?

"What do you mean?" I ask, leaning forward. I draw my legs to my chest.

"You all just escaped one of the fastest Roils in living memory," the old man says, pausing and facing us squarely. "If it wasn't for Tálir's equipment, you'd probably be dead. It's not the first one I've seen. When I… acquired some supplies from a downed convoy two months back, a Roil chased me back home. It spawned out of nowhere, and spread to my area within minutes. Less than a month after, I heard a faster and longer Roil pass overhead. They're no longer monthly storms. One could find you on your journey north."

There is a pause that lingers in the air like mist. If what he said is true, there's no way for us to make it to any shielded settlement in time if another Roil hits again. Are we going to be trapped in this mine shaft? My chest feels the heavy weight of dread pulling it down. But within that dread lurks something else. Resolve. I resolve to uncover the truth about what happened to me, and Z'hart is the only place I'll find answers.

Roil or no, I won't let anything stop me from hindering my progress for justice. Like the Roil earlier today, I won't let the fear consume me.

"Is there no way for us to escape or outmaneuver these storms?" I ask the old man. A surprised look is etched on his dark face. "A way to stop them altogether?"

"There are some ways," he says, placing his hands behind his back. "Abandoned shelters and caves dot the area between here and civilization. One has to know where to look. But there's no permanent way to stop them unless you believe in legends."

"Legends?" Tálir inquires, cocking his head slightly in wonder. "Legends of what?"

The old man doesn't respond at first, instead electing to pull a pipe out of his coat. In the other pocket was a small vial of dark green leaves known as greenweed. He packs his pipe with a few of the herbs and lights it, pale smoke blowing from his nose.

"So many legends and so little time," he says, his voice is raspy as he smokes. "I'll have to keep this simple. It is said that during the fall of the Domain, weapons were used to eradicate sections of Pan'gea. With no continents to flee to, our ancestors were unable to hide from the destructive forces. Legends say that one such weapon was the Roils, and that during the Ending, the source of this weapon was lost. So it continues to activate and spread these storms across the lands.

"Over the Cycles, we've developed some methods of defending against them. Reverse engineering Domain shields can deflect the small storms, but I sense that these ones are weaker than what came before. Our current defenses won't be effective against a *true* Roil. If they aren't shut down at their source, the world may be doomed to a second Ending."

I reflect on the gravity of this. Deep down, I sense that he's right, and that things will only get worse if no one steps up to fight the real fight. But I'm no fighter, and I never will be. This task should be left to someone who can battle for the good of all. The only thing I want to do is to solve the mystery of the banquet.

Before I can say anything, Remus speaks up for the first time in hours. "Way— To— Stop— It—" he says in response to the old man's tale. "Find— Providence—"

Everyone stares at Remus in unreserved incredulity. I know his mission is to find the mythic location, but then I realize something. This Providence place could be the key to saving the world from the Roils. *That's* why he seems so determined to find this place. Things are starting to make more sense.

"What is Providence, Remus?" Tálir asks before I can say anything.

Remus gives Aida a look, for he knows he's unable to properly convey his descriptions. "Providence is said to be the last bastion of the Domain. Their final stronghold before the Ending. Some say it holds the source of their knowledge. But many believe it to be the source of a weapon of mass destruction. It's hard to tell. The legends aren't exactly forthcoming."

"Providence is a myth, long forgotten by the world, Remus," the old man grouses with a bit of melancholy. "Trust me—many have tried to find it. But all have failed. Miserably."

There is some deep-rooted regret emanating from the old man, and his dark eyes reflect mournful loss. He starts to avert his gaze back to the fire pit, orange light dancing in his eyes.

"Only fanatics truly believe it exists, and are crazy enough to look for it," he finishes.

"Not— Fanatic—" Remus says, making a placating gesture. "Find— Providence— Save— World—"

"That sounds like a massive undertaking." Devin snorts,

sitting back against the wall. "A bit too grandiose for my tastes."

His words are selfish, but there's some truth in them. If any of us are to undertake this task, our personal goals will be thrown to the wind. I can't risk following a quest when I need to find answers.

"You might actually be right, Devin," I say reluctantly, hating the words. "This notion seems more attuned to true heroes. I'm not sure any of us qualify."

"Bone that, I'm hero-type!" Vyck butts in, his face flushed with indignity.

Remus' eyes find mine, and a novel is written in the look he gives me. All of his dreams, hopes, and aspirations are bound by this mission he has. But he also recognizes that he can't do it alone, even with Aida's help. He understands my priorities, but I think he wants me to look at the bigger picture. I give him a look of pity, but I stand firm.

Remus in turn looks at Aida, and she conveys his words. "Will any of you help us once we leave this place?"

"You're asking us now?" Devin scoffs. "Why not bring this shit up earlier?"

"You didn't ask," she replies simply. "We know it's a lot to ask from a group of strangers. But this is the world we're talking about. All of you will be affected by this sooner or later. But we can stop it! We can—"

The old man holds up his hand and cuts her off. I can see exhaustion tugging at his features.

"Let's finish this discussion in the morning," the old man says before yawning. Seeing his bleariness, I'm suddenly starting to feel tired as well. "Just a few hours out. Get a bit of rest, think about this more, have something to eat, and then you laddies can discuss this predicament further."

"Cutting right to the chase," I sniff. "Who are you anyways?"
"I'm just an old hermit who spends way too much time cooking," he says with droll humor, turning his back to me. "But you can call me Abrax."

CHAPTER 13

Tálir

Lost Ideals

LIGHT FROM THE EARLY morning sun passes through the roof while we recuperate within Abrax's lair. I'm glad everyone decided to rest before continuing the discussion. The elderly man had rolled out several, straw-stuffed mattresses for us to rest upon while he went deeper into his home for sleep. Our cots line the perimeter of the fire pit, and everyone stripped their equipment before resting. The fire crackles in front of me, and the rays of morning seep in through the opened crevasse meters above us. I hear a light breeze over the sparking fire, along with the snores of Devin and Vyck.

I sit up with my knees drawn to my chest, and I gaze into the fire in a sleep-like trance. I've removed my pieces of armor and set them next to my cot—the bronze armor looks burnished in the orange glow.

I'd slept for an hour, but restlessness and agitation roused me from slumber. So I turn to my thoughts for comfort while the others sleep, and I try to grasp the events of the night even as the bruise on my chest throbs.

Abrax had demonstrated powers currently beyond our skill levels. The magical energy harnessed by his armor seemed impossible. Yet, he did it. Even despite its age and state of incompletion, Abrax's armor channeled magic effortlessly. It took four of us out in the span of mere seconds. Jealousy crawls within my chest. I've never been able to channel any sort of energy through my armor. And I think I've figured out why.

My father told me that the armor needs to be powered by something small and sustainable. Batteries, ion charges, and even ship energy cells never worked when I tried. But after finding this place, seeing the pulsating emerald gems, and watching Abrax channel his magic, I make the deduction.

These crystals are the mystical power sources of the armor, I conclude to myself.

Initially, I dismissed the idea for its absurdity. How could a gem power a suit of armor and give it magical powers? But the more I think about it, the more it seems plausible. When we first noticed them, the crystals seemed to have a deposited energy within them. That energy can likely be harnessed through some means. The armor has to be the true conduit, just like the gems are the true power source. One can't be fully used without the other.

Quietly, I shuffle through the bits of the suit and obtain my right gauntlet. The rigid and ceremonial design practically blends in with the firelight. I fit my hand and arm into the gauntlet, flexing my fingers through the individual digit plates. This time, however, I examine it more closely than I've ever done. There has to be some mechanism that loads the crystals.

I discover a small, flat button imbedded in one of the symbols underneath the bracer. In all my years, I haven't even come close to seeing this mechanism. Perhaps because I wasn't looking for it in the past. I press it, and a small chamber about the length and width of a thumb opens. The interior is indeed some sort of conduit that can channel a solid energy source.

Quietly, I retrieve the glass bottle full of gems and pour out one of the ingots before placing it in the chamber. It fits perfectly as I close the contraption. For a moment, nothing happens.

The terminal in the wrist hums to life, and the metal vibrates as the energy courses through it. I can feel the power of the gauntlet as it charges up, and the vibration begins creeping towards my outstretched fingertips. I open up the terminal and a small dial reads *50% Charge*. And it keeps increasing. As the sensation reaches its pitch, my eyes widen in surprise as I whisper, "Oh shit."

My hastiness has definitely gotten the better of me again.

Emerald streams of energy erupt from my fingertips with a quiet *hiss* and soar towards the ceiling. The sizzling power blasts through the open canopy and into the air above. It even looks like they'll go into the sky itself.

But I can't control it. It's still channeling energy. Panicking, I scramble to deactivate the glove, but the streams continue to fountain from my fingers. In a flash of motion, I hit the button under the bracer and the chamber springs open. The crystal is ejected, and the streams stop imperceptibly. I let out a sigh of relief, but I notice something odd. The ejected shard looks dimmer; its pulsating light seems weaker than before. I deduce that there's only a finite amount of energy within these gems. The armor can actually drain them of power. Fascinating.

I look around with slight trepidation. The event had been inaudible to the group. They still sleep as if nothing happened, aside from Devin's snores growing louder. Relieved that I didn't draw any attention, I relax somewhat. That'd be a tough scenario to explain to them.

"Maybe you should try that outside next time," a voice says, causing me to flinch with a start. It's Abrax.

The old man enters the firelight once again with a basket of eggs and pair of freshly killed serpents. Their limp bodies are as thick as my forearm and a meter in length. Their yellow and black scales look glossy in the light, and their mouths hang open helplessly.

Abrax regards the creatures. "They make a fine replacement for bacon. It's almost time for breakfast, and I see you're working on an alarm clock."

I take off the gauntlet and set it down with visible unease. "What is this thing?" I ask with a look of shock. "It's been mine for almost fifteen years, and I've never seen it do that!"

Abrax chuckles lightly. "Romulus never had the gall to teach you? I'm surprised he stayed true to his vow."

My eyes dart to the old man. "You knew my father?"

"Almost everyone in our Order knew him," Abrax says rather fondly. "Romulus was largely liked by everyone too. Well… apart from Septem and a few others."

My mind instantly sparks. "Wait, you know Septem too?"

Abrax looks at me darkly. "Aye, lad. Septem is a tough son of a bitch. Very powerful, very calculated. Dozens have met their end at his cold blade. He's a man who despises the bonds of relationships. Hells, even when Romulus tried to act brotherly towards him, nothing but a bitter rivalry grew from it."

That explains it. The others told me Septem recognized me on the ship. Now, I understand why he looked at me with disdain. He knew I was the son of Romulus. My fists clench, and I feel my own enmity forming against Septem as well.

Abrax sighs and switches gears, "But alas, he was a good man, Romulus. A bit dim at times, but he had more sense than I. How is he?"

The question stings at my heart like a needle pricking a finger. "He died. Almost fifteen years ago."

To my surprise, Abrax's eyes adopt a look of sorrow. He bows his head. "It's been two decades since I last saw him. I'm sorry, lad. Truly."

I shake off the heartache, focusing on a lingering question. "What was his vow?"

Abrax faintly grins through his thick beard. "He vowed to never have anything to do with magic again. For he wanted his son to grow up safe and without it."

Glancing at the armor, I ask more to myself, "Father—what did you leave me with?"

Abrax kneels down and sits the dead snakes on the ground. Pulling a knife from his belt, he starts to cut meat slabs with finesse. "Stability," he says simply, barely looking up at me. "That right there is one of the tools used by the ancients to establish order. This armor was the pinnacle of their science, but the power within the gems allowed them to become much more."

"I always assumed our ancestors were explorers, diplomats, and scientists. Not warriors," I intone, sitting cross-legged. "These suits make it seem like they were sorcerers, and their technology must've been godlike to withstand the test of time."

Abrax looks up at me with a grave look on his face. "You'd do well not to venerate the past, lad. Many alive today have obsessed over the Domain and this Providence place. And they've forgotten what it means to be vicarious. For greed is the death of empathy."

I glance over everyone in the group, my eyes falling on Devin and Vyck. *Greed is the death of empathy*. The words repeat in my head. I know those two have actively stated their self-centered goals and independence. But there seems to be some shred of decency in both.

Despite their claims, they've stuck around us longer than I would've thought possible. They were even willing to follow my lead, though reluctant as it was.

"Are you trying to make an analogy to those two?" I ask, nodding my head towards them.

Abrax's dark face hints at curiosity, despite his hard creases of age. "Perhaps," he says mildly. "Is it an inaccurate analogy?"

I rock my head to the side and adopt a look of uncertainty. "They haven't necessarily disproven that statement about greed. But they haven't lost all empathy. If I'm to have any success at leading them out of here, I have to believe in each of them. Despite what uncertainties there may be."

The old man gives me faint approval as he places a frying pan on a rack above the fire. "That's a wise statement. But it's also a naïve statement. They're not the only ones capable of greed, lad. The others, and especially yourself, are susceptible as well."

I scoff at his statement. I grew up in a life of hard work, honesty, and compassion. There's no way I'd ever give into the claws of greed. But I remain silent for a moment, a more important question lingering in my mind.

"How does it work?" I ask suddenly, nodding my head to the bronze metal. "The armor. I get that the chambers can harness energy within the crystals. But the energy itself seems… something else entirely."

"It's a form of magic," Abrax grunts, flexing his fingers. The digits in his gauntlet glove show a faint glow of emerald. "While there is a science to the magic of the stones and armor, there are mystical properties that even I don't understand. All you need to know is that the gems are full of a form of magic energy that can be channeled into Maven armor. It takes practice, but one can master how to control the energy properly—if they have all the tools."

Now there's a title I've never heard before regarding our ancestors of old. The Domain is a comprehensive title, but this is something different.

"Mavens," I say with a tinge of eagerness. "That's their name, isn't it? Those who came before."

The old man nods his head, but his face remains blank. "One of the names of those who came before. Our ancestors were divided into many names and cultures. But the Maven Knights were the marshals of that society."

I pause to reflect on the information, only to think of a new question entirely.

"Would you teach me how to use it?" I ask after a moment, looking down at the pieces of my armor. "Could I learn how to use the armor like a Maven once did?" I pause. "Like my father did."

Abrax looks into the fire with a solemn expression. "Those days are long behind me. After my last se'bau, I realized I'm not exactly a great teacher. More along the lines of a crazy coot who shouts out riddles and stories."

"Your last what?"

"Se'bau," he grunts, shaking his head as if to clear it. "That's what novices are called in Maven training, and we adopted most of their traditions. And my last se'bau was—"

He looks away from the flames in what seems to be shame. But he doesn't finish his line of thought. Part of me is curious as to what transpired between Abrax and his former apprentice, but it's not my place to ask. I want to learn about my armor's heritage, and what it might mean to possess it. Why my father had it, and why he passed it along to me. I'm not sure where I could find someone else to teach me about the armor. Abrax is the only opportunity right now, and I won't let it slip away.

The sky is becoming brighter, and I realize I only have maybe a few minutes to convince him before the group awakens.

"Haven't you ever had an ideal, Abrax?" I inquire, looking into the cackling flames.

"Are we really having this talk?" the old man growls in annoyance. "I've met too many dreamy-eyed hopefuls in my lifetime and I grow tired of their speeches about 'I had a dream to become this'."

"I've merely wanted to understand why my father left me this armor," I continue through clenched teeth. "It's the only thing I can call my own, and I deserve to know what it is. Haven't you ever wanted something like that?"

His dark eyes peer intensely at me before his focus shifts to the carcasses strewn before him. He says nothing for a moment, taking his time slicing more slabs from another serpent. After the first few slices, he sticks the knife deep in the flesh of the carcass in a burst of irritation.

"Yeah," he grunts, his eyes reflect a measure of melancholy. "I wanted something like that when I was young and stupid. But like all things you want, they end up slipping through your fingers. What you laddies fail to see is that what you want and what you need are two very different things. You say you want to learn about the Maven armor, but do you need to? I wanted to find Providence, but did I need to?"

"Of course you need to," a voice says tiredly.

I flinch in surprise as I notice Sarina has woken up. By the looks of it, she's been up for a few minutes. Her black hair hangs like curtains over her eyes. She yawns and stretches. Some of the others are starting to shuffle as well.

"When you want to do something, you should go for it out of necessity." Her voice is oddly thoughtful, and she combs her hair back with her fingers. "I have a need to find answers, so I will follow through with it. What does it say about your conviction if you choose not to follow your decisions?"

"It's not a matter of lacking conviction, Sarina," Abrax sighs with a hint of depressed exasperation. "It's a matter of strength in character. If you lack the proper will to strive for it, you'll fall flat on your face. As I did."

"What do you mean?" she asks as she pulls her knees up to her chest.

The old man looks gravely at us. "A story for another time, all you need to know is that I gave up my dream many years ago."

◆ ◆ ◆

My companions are all awakened by the increased conversations and the smell of eggs and grilled serpent. Vyck and Devin begin a series of martial stretches and poses upon waking up, no doubt to attune their senses. As we prepare to eat, faint conversation grows as some discuss the events of the previous day while others voice concerns for the future.

I, however, am starting to focus on two things in the future. Learning about the Maven Knights and finding a way to stop the Roils. If what Abrax and Remus say is true, the Roils could consume everything if they aren't stopped. Everyone in Erron's Ville, everyone in the nations, will soon suffer.

If Remus is right, Providence might be the key to not only stopping the Roils, but possibly discovering more about my armor. It's foolhardy, but it seems like an opportunity that only comes about once in a lifetime. I need to take the chance. But I know I can't do it alone.

"While it's certainly been lovely traveling with you shits," Devin says, setting his plate down. "Vyck and I ought to part ways now that we're almost out of the caves. You shits are alright, but it's probably for the best that we all part ways. We've got supplies to acquire and gems to spend."

I grin at them. This might be my chance. A way to initiate the quest. And a way to keep them around. "We haven't even discussed the opportunity of treasure hunting yet." I keep my voice casual and vague.

All attention snaps to me. Vyck's eyes flash a malicious shade of eagerness. He tries to hide it, but I can read him better than he thinks. If treasure and reward is what fuels these guys, perhaps all they need is a bit more incentive. With their skills as mercenaries, we might need them.

"Say what now?" Vyck asks, his voice failing to be nonchalant.

I sit up straight, keeping my confidence apparent but in check. "Last night, Aida and Remus told us all about the opportunity to find a lost relic of the Domain. Now, I'm not a very learned man. But I'm willing to bet that all kinds of riches and artifacts might wait for plunder at an undiscovered location. Especially if it's a hidden repository."

Vyck is already sold. His green eyes reflect his willingness to go on an expedition, despite the perils. His greed sometimes trumps his logic, just like my anger trumps mine.

"Ey, don't start with that shit again," Devin says. He notices Vyck's reaction as well and rolls his blue eyes. "What reason would we have for trying to find this… Providence?"

It's at this point Aida recognizes the game I'm playing. And I can see a faint smirk spreading over her thick lips. "For starters," she says, joining the game. "Artifacts that are millennia old would be housed in there, and would probably fetch more than those crystals. Some say there's a data mainframe that holds histories dating back a millennium to the Old World. There might even be actual treasure.

You'd make a fortune."

"Isn't it a bit insensitive to play the reward card?" Devin asks, insulted. His face scrunches with indignity. "What are we? Mercenaries?"

"That's exactly what you are." Sarina points out rather taciturnly, taking a bite of the serpent meat. "I don't think I've met anyone who'd pass up a treasure hunt. Especially you two."

I sniffle a laugh as Vyck and Devin both take offense. "Who says we'd want to go just for the treasure?" Devin retorts with a tinge of sincerity.

"Mercenary or no," I say loudly to maintain focus. "Wouldn't this be more worthwhile than a life of freelance? Do you really want to wander aimlessly forever? That doesn't seem like a life with guaranteed luxury."

The two say nothing for a long moment. To my surprise, their expressions reflect serious thought. Even if they aren't just out for the money, they also recognize this once in a lifetime opportunity. The chance to make a difference.

"I know I'm going to regret this," Devin sighs. His fingers run through his black hair. "But if we do this, we're not soldiers. We're not bound by oath or honor or etcetera. We go when we want. We leave when we want. Clear?"

"Are you sure, Devin?" Vyck asks, even though his eyes scream with fervor. "What if it's a fluke?"

"It may be," Devin replies quietly back to him. He pats his partner on the shoulder. "But the reward outweighs the costs, for now. Plus, it might do us some good to uncover old Domain relics. Hells, we could become wealthy museum owners in our retirement."

"I'm in too," Vivían pipes up. Her red hair is disheveled, but she still radiates beauty despite it. Her duster is rolled up beside her, and her shirt certainly accentuates her features. "I've been dying for some action lately, and this seems like a great opportunity."

"We were already going," Aida says as she pats Remus on the shoulder. She sniffs happily. "Copycats. We're in too."

A strange energy comes into my chest, and I feel like I can do anything. My heart races, and I get the sense that this is what charisma feels like. Being able to show strength of conviction, and uniting others. Even if our personalities clashed, or our goals weren't synonymous. But my high is evened out when I look at Sarina. I grow nervous about asking her, especially after what she's been through.

"Sarina?" My voice is quiet, but not lacking certainty. I have to remain strong for this to work, but stay compassionate. "I know it's not on your priority list, but will you join us? We could use someone like you."

Sarina looks at me earnestly before saying, "I'm not sure if I'd be of much use. I can't fight, I can't hunt, and I can't navigate. Plus, I've got a lot of ordeals to sort out on my own. Might not be worth it to have me tag along."

"But you know Z'hart," Vivían says rather plainly. "You know its people. If we ever needed help from within their cities, you'd know exactly who to contact. In my book, that's just as important as being able to hunt."

Vivían is right. Sarina probably knows lots of people in the lower reaches of Z'hart. People that might provide information or supplies, and wouldn't charge outrageous prices. But there's something else I see that makes Sarina important.

She has a hidden magnetism about her. The others will listen to her. Especially when we were in the tunnels and Well. They've shown trust in her judgment, and it will likely carry over in the future.

"Sarina," Aida says after a moment. "I know what you're looking for, and I know we'll find the right answers if we do this together. You don't have to do this alone."

"Bring— Assholes— Justice—" Remus grunts with a cunning smirk.

Vyck snorts a laugh as Sarina looks at Remus with a weak smile. "Alright, I'm in."

"If I might interject…" Abrax says suddenly, his voice suppressing irritation. Our heads turn to regard the old man who sits cross-legged. His silver-haired head is bowed.

I can sense an aura of misgiving from him. "There's three things. One: You all won't make it a week out there without supplies and a guide," he continues. His tone is begrudging, and he cracks his knuckles. "Two: The only supplier-guide around these parts is me. And three: You're going to need this supplier-guide's help if you'll have any luck. Providence may be a myth, but I'm not about to let you all spend your lives for nothing."

"So you do care about the ideals of young people," I say with a smirk.

Abrax stares at me incredulously. He wrinkles his nose. "Also four: I really hate you young people."

The final knell has sounded. Our journey is greenlit; the fates have been decided. Dreams of adventure I'd had in Erron's Ville are coming true. The chance to live for more than I've been given. To seize what destiny offers. While I know it'll be dangerous, a spark of adventurousness has formed within me. And it is not going to be extinguished.

Above us, I can see the rays of the morning sun fully in the sky. Sweltering tendrils streak into the starry atmosphere and the azure skyline is cloudless. It is a new day. A new beginning.

PART TWO:

Seeking Truths

CHAPTER 14

Sarina

Re-Questing

THE DAY IS CALM and bright as we trek across the barren wastelands that stretch before us. The sky is clear, the sun is bright, and the air is more brisk and cool than the previous day. Underneath my feet, the sandy dunes give way to my boots as I trudge in front of the party with Abrax and Tálir. While both seem encumbered by their armor and survival gear, they walk with a brisk pace. It's even more surprising seeing Abrax keep pace despite his age. Sweat glistens upon his dark forehead, and he wears a light cloak over his attire. Likely to keep the armor cooler. Tálir does the same, but is noticeably more uncomfortable.

The rest of my companions follow behind us. If they're the

sheep, we're the shepherds. It's still odd, their regarding of me as important. I don't see how they view me as such.

A small repulsorcart floats at the center of our group as we walk. The size of a table, the hovering container is one of Abrax's latest finds after ransacking a convoy. Packed inside it like a chest are containers of food, medical supplies, water cartons, and a few metal cases. Also stored inside is our chest of polished crystals, packs of food rations, and ammunition. Tálir pulls the cart via chain with ease. Everything has happened so quickly. I'm still reeling over the events. A day ago, the seven of us had chanced upon meeting and settled on a tentative truce for survival. Now, here we are—a band of companions off to find Providence. Off to save the world.

My mission hasn't taken the back burner yet, however. No matter how distracting this quest may be, my goal to uncover the truth of the banquet is still prevalent. Memory flashes are still vague. I can remember everything up to the point of serving ale at the gala. Then, it's like a mirror shattering before me. Pieces are everywhere.

So I'll work with my companions. Assist this quest, accept their company, and try to save the world. But if the moment arises, I'm not sure if I'd be strong enough to resist finishing *my* mission. It's horribly selfish of me, and my gut turns to knots as I think about it. However, I can't fix this world if I'm broken as well.

The dunes give way to several rock edifices after the first couple hours of our journey. We're able to find some semblance of shade and cover as Abrax keeps an eye out for any signs of a Roil. Like spiny trees, the brown and grey rocks jag upwards. Small nooks are hollowed out within their bases, and we use them for shelter against the sun. The sand underneath is cooler, but firmer against our feet. Patches of brown weeds dot the ground. The edifices rise above us like the canopy of a forest.

Water is passed around from the canisters. Devin leans against the rock wall, chewing on some jerky while Vyck sits in the sand. Aida gives Remus a dose of sedatives. Tálir shakes sand off of his cloak while Abrax starts up a small holoprojector detailing a map.

It's fascinating to see the amount of supplies and technology the old man had been able to steal from Imperial convoys. He says that it was a *tax on the greedy*, and that they had more supplies than they needed. The chip-like projector sends a three-dimensional image above it, detailing the Pyrack desert and the nation of Z'hart. A red dot near the northern quadrant of the desert indicates where we are.

"Gather around laddies. Shit's about to get important and I don't want to repeat myself," Abrax grunts to everyone. We do as he says and he gestures to the holoprojection. "So our journey at this point is threefold. One: We travel north for another three days in the Pyrack at a brisk pace. I sure as Hells don't need my skin looking any more like leather."

The image magnifies and shows the northern reaches of the Pyrack. East of us by about eight hundred kilometers is Tálir's home, Erron's Ville. I can almost see his hazel eyes gleam with hope at the sight of it. I think Abrax does too, and he decides to put it to rest.

"Erron's Ville is too far out of the way, lad." Abrax's voice is sympathetic, but stern. Tálir's shoulders sink somewhat in defeat.

"I'm sorry, but it doesn't serve our journey to go there."

Tálir's face shows disappointment, even a sense of nostalgia. I can't blame him at all. Home has a certain call to it. But Abrax points to a mountainous region that spans along the border of the Pyrack and Z'hart.

"Two: The Flames of Z'hart will be our direct access into the nation after the three day hike," he says as the image scrolls to detail the northern nation. Then it hits me.

We're going to the capital: Z'hart City, I say to myself. A dark enthusiasm forms in me, and I realize that perhaps my mission might become more prominent than I thought.

"And three: Z'hart City is another three days from the border," he continues as the holoprojection enhances the image of the capital city. "That is where we must go. For supplies, money, and some navigation tools. I also don't fancy walking for the duration of this… quest."

"Perhaps we can pick up some repulsorbikes." Vivían intones with a bit of excitement. Her cheeks are sunburned.

The others show similar enthusiasm for this decision, despite the trek ahead. Abrax nods as he turns off the holoprojector.

"Then what?" Tálir asks, his disappointment still present but fading. "Where do we go after Z'hart City?"

Aida chimes in while Remus shivers from the sedatives. "Then we head east. To the land of Asi." Her voice points it out like it's obvious.

Abrax paces around the cart, regarding her with a nod. "Very good, Aida." He then turns back to Tálir and me. "The legends are vast, but they all hint that Providence lies deep within the jungle wilderness of the eastern Outlands—beyond the Raged Rapids of Asi. Even in nine Cycles, those jungles have remained untouched by exploration. Or at least, *survived* exploration."

"Why not use an airship to fly over the jungle?" I ask, crossing my arms.

Aida and Abrax both look at me like parents when a child asks about monsters. "Believe me, Providence would've been found Cycles ago if it were that easy," Abrax retorts, caressing his beard.

"After this past millennium, the jungles have likely grown over the fortress itself," Aida points out leaning on the cart slightly. "It's been six Cycles since we retrofitted Domain tech for flight capabilities. But in those Cycles, nothing was found from above."

I'm still having a hard time believing that in all these Cycles, no one has ever come close to finding Providence. It all seems like a matter of convenience. But then, perhaps that's why it's known as a legend. Because no one *can* find it. Even Devin, Vyck, and Vivían show signs of similar skepticism after the exposition.

Abrax stops next to the cart before lighting his pipe. "I can guess what some of you are thinking, right now. How can we find this place if no one in a millennium has?" He takes a drag from his pipe, and then says, "But what you have that makes this different is experience, resources, and a guide. Decades ago I failed to find it, and I don't have much faith that we'll find it this time. But there's something in Z'hart City that can help. The Tome."

Tálir flashes Abrax an intrigued look. "A map," he says. "A map that can lead us there."

"More like comprehensive puzzle pieces," the old man affirms, smoke blowing from his nostrils. "We get to Z'hart City. Find supplies and transportation. And I'll find this Tome where it's said to be hidden."

"This thing is hidden too?" Tálir comments with cynicism. "Fragging Hells, we've got our work cut out for us. How do we find it?"

Abrax grins devilishly and inhales one last drag of greenweed. In his dark eyes, I can see the light of adventurousness being rekindled. He has hope, more so than he did in the last decades. "All in due time, lad."

CHAPTER 15

Tálir

Rules, Forms, and Drawbacks

IT IS LATE IN the afternoon on our first day trekking into the desert, nearly a week until we reach civilization. The hot sun is getting low in the sky, and the scorching heat of the day is swept away by winds. Night is approaching, and so does the cooler weather. Streams of sand are blown away from the tops of the dunes, and a persistent howl echoes across the terrain.

With the evening approaching, we decide to make camp within a dried up ravine. A series of shallow caves have formed within the maroon walls of the gorge. The caves aren't incredibly large, but they're deep enough in the event we need shelter from a Roil.

The repulsorcart is deactivated, and the supply container sits on the bare ground. Cots, sheets, stored foods, and other materials are unpacked. Vivian starts a fire while the others dress into more casual nightwear. Devin takes a whetstone and sharpens his shortsword. Sarina reviews some of the charts stored within the holoprojector along with Aida.

As the sun sets we eat a portioned meal of soups, dried meats, and hard bread. It's a quick meal, but everyone gobbles their food before preparing to rest until sunrise.

On my cot and chewing a slab of jerky, I see Abrax approach me from the corner of my eye.

"You, come with me," he says impatiently. He moves to the edge of the cavern, a satchel draped over his shoulder. "Keep your armor on and bring a cartridge of crystals."

"Cartridge of crystals?" I ask after swallowing a bite of dried meat.

He gestures to one of the metal cases within the cart. "Open one of those up and grab a cartridge. We have work to do."

A bit wary of his intentions, I cautiously get up and chew the last bite of jerky. Approaching the cart, I open the metal case and unveil nearly three dozen cartridges the size of a bowrifle magazine. Picking one up, I can deduce by its weight that nearly thirty crystal ingots are within. Abrax is certainly not unprepared when it comes to having ample energy for his armor. He won't run out anytime soon.

I place the magazine in my belt as I approach the cavern's entrance. The others are bewildered as to what's going on. "This is between me and him," Abrax says to everyone. His eyes glance at Remus for a moment, but says nothing more.

Abrax starts walking back into the gulch and gestures for me to follow him. "What's this about, Abrax?" I ask as I follow him. "Is something wrong?"

"It's about time someone shows you how to operate the armor," the old man says, heading north. Sand crunches under his boots. "Properly, anyways."

"So you mean, you're actually going to teach me?" I ask with a growing excitement, delight glowing in my eyes. "What happened to 'those days are behind me'?"

"They are," he growls. "But what good will it do if we have two Knight suits, but only one is used? It's a waste having a useless set or armor."

Without another word, we hike through the sand and gravel in the ravine. My legs are sore from the day, but my determinism pushes me forward. It's time to learn about my inheritance.

We walk for almost a half hour towards the top of the gorge where dry bushes and grasses form. The wind blows by, tossing my hair into a frenzy. The sun is practically gone and the moon lights up the night sky. Stars dot the inky blackness of space.

We settle near the edge of the plateau watching over the inner ravine. I can see the firelight in our cave half a kilometer away. It's almost like seeing a candle pulsate with light from within a dark room.

Setting up a pile of twigs and weeds, the old man snaps his fingers and a small stream emits from his index finger. The magic strikes the twigs and a fire starts. I smile eagerly at the display. Abrax sets his bag down and starts unpacking some tools and pieces of metal. Is he planning to perform maintenance on my armor? But my armor hasn't taken any serious damage.

I look closer at what he's doing. Bronze metal pieces are fused together by the tools he uses. He's building something.

"So," Abrax says after a moment, his back to me as he keeps tinkering with the metal. "How much did your father teach you about the armor?"

"He never really taught me anything apart from the Roil warning." I rub my chin as I think back with melancholy. "He died when I was five, and the armor was just there for me to inherit. It was the only thing I had to remember him by, so I kept it safe for his memory."

My eyes start to itch as I think back. My father was a good man, a goofball at times and a bit reckless, but I loved him dearly. Despite the lack of books, he recited countless stories and songs before bed. With his death and the absence of a mother, I chose to fixate on the one thing he left me: the armor. It helped sooth my grief, believing his spirit was somewhere in the metal. Foolish thoughts of a child.

"Romulus always was a stubborn fool. I still can't believe he never showed you its true power. But, today's as good a day as any," Abrax says, finally turning to me. I stare in awe at what he holds.

It's a helmet. The bronze metal forms smoothly over the back and top of the head piece. A small spike protrudes from the forehead. Rigid wing shapes jut out from the sides, where my ears will be. A transparent visor comes down over the location of the eyes while a jaw-plate emblazoned with symbols finishes the faceplate. My heart races with ecstatic excitement. *My armor is about to be completed!*

The old man sees my exhilaration and rolls his eyes, but not out of annoyance. A faint grin can be seen under his beard. Time slows as he walks towards me and places the helmet on my head. It fits perfectly, and I oddly feel whole. Plates shift down over my throat and neck, connecting the helmet to the armor.

A holographic heads-up-display lines the transparent visor, showing several different readouts. *Armor Integrity: 87%. Output Charge: 0%. Kryo Charge: 0%.* What is this kryo charge?

"Abrax, this is incredible!" I say, my voice sounding metallic. "But what does it mean by eighty-seven percent armor integrity? And zero percent kryo charge?"

He starts examining my armor. "Well, your armor isn't exactly meant for your size," he says. "It's meant for Romulus. I'll get to the other part in a second."

The old man picks up some sort of high-tech wrench and asks me to perform various martial poses. The tool whirls as it connects and loosens various joints, plates, and pieces in the armor. It's tedious work, but the armor feels like it's becoming less like something I wear. More like it's a part of me. It feels lighter, more fluid, and easy to move.

Abrax sets the wrench down and examines his handiwork, scratching his beard. His eyes show some measure of satisfaction, and he grabs my left forearm. I watch him press in a small plate right above the top side of my wrist, and the helmet miraculously retracts. It folds away into the pauldrons of the armor, leaving my face unprotected.

"Just in case you ever need a clearer line of sight," he points out. "Your armor is now fully synched to your body, and with that comes safeguards. It's programmed so that only you can do anything with it. Activating it, using it, and even undressing it. It will only permit the wearer to do such things. Of course, there are ways for someone to get it off in the event of an emergency… but it's a complicated process. Now take two gems out of the cartridge."

I do as he instructs, opening the metal magazine which reveals thirty polished, marble-like gems. Their irradiate glow is intense, like staring into molten lava. Abrax takes one and places it into his right gauntlet.

"The first lesson I will teach you is the importance of the kryos," Abrax says, sparking emerald energy from his fingertips. He starts to pace around the fire, his boots kick up dirt.

"*Kryo* is the Maven title for these gems, so you'd be wise to refer to them as such." Abrax forms a faint flame of emerald energy in his palm. "But the kryo is the heart of the armor. Without it, the armor is lifeless. As you've noted, the HUD shows that your kryo charge is at zero. However, you don't always have to use the helmet to be aware of your output. The terminal in the wrist does the exact same thing.

"Now, the kryos are a very... particular type of magical energy. So, there are three rules you must be aware of. The First Rule is that the kryo gem has a finite amount of energy. You've seen how their light dims when used, so they must be used wisely. The Second Rule is that magic energy can only be safely harnessed by Maven armor or weapons. Maven kryo Forms are an extension of this rule—the magic has very specific outputs. The Third Rule—and this is by far the most important—is to never use a kryo without a conduit. Raw kryo power is uncontrollable, unpredictable, and lethal... so never, *ever* use them without the armor."

He adopts a martial pose and extends his arm and fingers. He lets loose a torrent of five energy streams from his fingers. "This is Form One: Stream. The energy must flow within you like a stream of water and out your fingertips."

Pivoting to another pose, Abrax bends his knees and locks his elbow at ninety degrees. A domed shield of light energy forms atop his arm and shields his torso. "This is Form Two: Shield," he says. "For your defense to be strong, your body and footing must equally be strong. If not, you and your energy will crumble."

Spryer than I would've anticipated, Abrax spins with his leg arcing like a martial kick. He performs a backward swing with his right arm, and an energy disk the size of his hand spins through the air. It hits the opposing canyon wall in a shower of sparks and he continues, "This is Form Three: Discus. Your body must be agile and flexible to throw and dodge these. They can come in many shapes. From disks to orbs of fire."

Like a dance, he shifts his legs into a wide stance. Extending his right arm, his palm opens and fires a solid beam of sage energy. It thunders through the air and into the night sky. I'm seeing a pattern to these motions. "This is Form Four: Blaze. As the final Form, it must be used in last resort, for its destruction will blaze through anything. This is a lethal Form, so it must be used carefully."

I'm entranced by what I've seen. Each Form is built atop the other, each movement complimented the other. It is graceful and deadly. The area seems to calm after Abrax relaxes his posture, and he ejects the kryo from his gauntlet. I'm amazed, for the amount of energy he used had completely drained the gem.

"It will be some time before you master all of these Forms," Abrax says, taking a few steps away from me. He crosses his arms. "Now, load a kryo and attempt Form One."

I take a deep breath. *No pressure, right?* I open the chamber on my right gauntlet and place the kryo within. Warmth radiates from it. I can feel the suit begin to vibrate as the energy courses within. It's an exhilarating sensation. A little heartbeat is within the armor as if it's alive. I press the button on my left wrist, and the helmet covers my face. It's less like armor now, and more like a living thing.

With the new upgrades, I can practically feel the energy as if it's within my own skin. Like liquid fire in my veins, I feel so powerful. It's invigorating. But despite the buildup of energy, nothing happens. I extend my fingers, but nothing is channeled.

"One question," I say after a moment of attempting. "How exactly do I *channel* the energy?"

Abrax heaves a sigh of annoyance. "Don't overthink it, lad. Just think about what you want to do."

"What in all the Hells does that even mean?" I snap, looking at my armored arms in confusion. Moonlight reflects off of the bronze metal.

The old man sits cross-legged on the plateau while my back faces the gorge below. He watches me curiously. "Focus your mind and body," Abrax says. "If you keep your intentions simple and precise, the armor will channel exactly what you want it to. You are linked to the armor. To the energy. Just focus and it will obey your command if you are disciplined enough."

I pause and reflect. "Well I guess that makes some sense. Being a sorcerer would take a lot of mental clarity."

The old man snorts in derision, his silver hair seems to absorb the moon's color. "Don't think too much about it, lad. Just focus on releasing the energy."

I huff a few breaths in nervousness. Closing my eyes, I try to focus on letting the energy flow into my right hand. I think of nothing else. Slowly, I feel the heat of the energy flow from my forearm and into my palm. I breathe slowly, and I can feel that it's about to happen. The energy is at a crescendo.

An image flashes through my eyelids. I see my father wearing the armor and looking at me through his helmet. He looks disappointed. Then, I see Sarina with her back turned to me…

I gasp and open my eyes. A blinding flash of emerald erupts from my hand, and I feel myself being hurled backwards into the sand. I slide to the edge of the plateau, and my heart stops for a moment. I'm inches away from falling off. An emerald haze forms over my field of vision for a moment. My arm feels numb.

That's probably not supposed to happen, I say to myself in shame. I need to seriously mind where my thoughts go if I'm to succeed at this.

Abrax snorts in merriment as I groan and sit up—sand falls from my armor and my head is spinning. He stands and hovers over me. "Not bad for a first attempt. But it looks like you've got some focusing problems to get over."

He extends a hand and helps me get to my feet. The look on his face isn't disappointment, it's understanding. It quickly vanishes as he starts to say, "This will be our system every morning and every night. For one hour, we will practice until you focus properly and learn the Forms. We'll need them when we reach Z'hart."

I'm prepared to ask why, but he stands back and folds his arms across his chest. "We still have thirty more minutes, lad. Try again."

It's going to be a long night, I sigh to myself.

It certainly turns out to be. The last half hour drags on as I try to channel the energy. I don't improve spectacularly. My energy streams are flimsy and weak. The same distraction plagues my mind. Father. Sarina. Why do I keep thinking about them?

When we finish the session, we make our way back into the gorge and to the campsite. On our way, Abrax gives a vague grunt of approval as he smokes some greenweed.

"There's one more basic thing you must know about this power," he croaks. "There is a slight drawback. Kryo magic has a way of affecting a person's mind."

Alarm snakes through me like an eel swimming through water.

"What do you mean they affect a person's mind?"

Puffs of smoke leave his nostrils. "It's nothing terribly dangerous. They're mild hallucinations, strange dreams, and such. Perhaps you've seen some already."

Nodding in hesitation, I say, "I saw my father in the armor. And then I saw Sarina."

He pats my shoulder and regards me seriously. "Keep note of what you see. Flashes they may be, but there's something to them. Messages of a sort. It could be a glimpse into the past, a premonition, or a manifestation of your fears."

Regarding the anxious look on my face, he grumbles, "This is the cost of this power, lad. Either take it or leave it. But the visions will come randomly with continued exposure to the magic. Don't fret, they haven't killed me yet."

There's little comfort to his words, but this is a drawback I must unwittingly accept. I want this power, so I must accept the cost. Even if it terrifies me.

We reach the camp quickly as the wind picks up. The others

are fast asleep. I undress the armor without hindrance, just like he said.

But as I prepare for bed, Abrax hisses at me, "Always eject the kryos before you sleep. It might inadvertently charge a blast while we rest. Even magic residue in the conduits could go off if triggered. Safety first, lad."

So many rules! I roll my eyes at the absurdity, but I do as he commands. Ejecting the kryo, I notice that the gem has barely been drained of any energy. So I store it back in the cartridge before flopping unto my cot. But even as I close my eyes, I see the same image of my father garbed in the armor. The look on his face makes me feel hollow, and I hold back tears upon seeing his displeasure. But why? Is his spirit angry that I've decided to follow in his footsteps? Or is it something else?

Trying to shake it off, I see the second image. Sarina's back is to me, and I feel an ocean of separation. A premonition? Or are these images just manifested feelings buried within my subconscious? The openness between Sarina expands infinitely until she's a tiny spot in my vision, and then there's darkness.

CHAPTER 16

Tálir

The Great Journey

THE PYRACK IS A BRUTAL, uncompromising adversary. If it isn't sand storms or sheer heat, the perpetual thirst always gnaws at me. Sand sticks to my face, hair, clothes, and armor. A sunburn stings under my eyes and on my cheeks. Sweat glistens on my face and soaks my shirt. We all smell rancid.

Hiking over sand is an arduous task, since my feet have no solid base to step. My calves are sore from the travel, my armor and cargo bearing down on me. I'm forced to wrap a light cloak around my body everyday so the armor stays cool.

We trek for what seems like an eternity through the desert,

rationing our water carefully. I'm still baffled by our willing cooperation to travel en company. Everyone was willing to follow my lead in the caves, and again on our new quest. Some are reluctant, I know that much. Devin and Vyck definitely have feelings of resentment about this. Sarina has warmed up to me and Vivían, but I sense that she's still guarding a part of herself. I can't blame her, but it's still a bit frustrating.

The strange visions I had the previous day still linger in my mind. And I start to wonder if it's symbolic of Sarina's current personality. Closed off to the rest of us, but almost within reach.

I want to know everything about her. Not just the quiet, cautious person she is pretending to be, but the real Sarina. The struggle to keep my feelings in check is constant. I try to fight it, seeing as I've only known her for a few days. After she saved my life in the mines and on the convoy, I can't help but feel extremely grateful to her. But I resolve to not entirely focus on her.

The others are growing on me as well. Remus normally keeps to himself and stays quiet, except in matters of importance. While it's a bit odd, by no means does he hamper our journey. In fact, he's always the first packed and ready before the morning hike. Aida is also pleasant when it comes to making sure our health stays strong. Vivían is quite the character. Bare bones and snarky, her enthusiasm and charisma has enthralled me. She's a huge flirt with me, Devin, and Vyck. Despite this, she and Vyck can be seen chatting by themselves during our hikes. She laughs at him a lot, but he simply keeps talking and smiles with her.

After just a few days, here we are. A band of strangers bonding together. It's almost a bit surreal at times. But our shared experience in the convoy, mines, and desert sprouts strong friendships.

Sessions continue with Abrax twice a day. One in the morning and one at night. It's an arduous process, but I have to trust in Abrax's gruff wisdom. I still struggle with Form I. My body is always too tense or my mind is always wandering out of focus. The old man's patience wears thin, but he remains steadfast in the lesson. I must flow like a river if the energy is to properly stream through me.

Days pass by as our system repeats. Wake up, train, eat, travel, make camp, eat, train, and then rest. The three days begin to blur together. The Pyrack's dunes vary from crescent shapes to rippled waves like an ocean. So far, no Roils have been detected. Lucky for us. More importantly, the training makes some improvement. I begin to recognize a way to channel the magic, keeping my focus on the feat itself rather than on the energy. It's still a weak *Output Charge at 3%*, but it's better than nothing.

My body eases up and the Form feels like a dance as I adopt the poses to channel the Stream. The energy fountains from my fingertips during practice, but their energy level would barely stun a cat. So I train. Hard. Abrax says that I'll need some mastery of the Forms before we arrive at the capital of Z'hart. His reasons are still unclear, but I can sense that danger likely awaits us there.

Rounding out the third day, the dunes make way for more

varying geographical features. Outcrops of grey bedrock, dry soils that smear brown and maroon, and more flora such as weathered trees and wildflowers. We rest within a series of boulder formations that look as if they're piled up towards the higher ground. The smooth rocks are pale and creased with wavelike erosions.

From our camp on the third night, I can see the outline of the jagged mountains and ravines that bordered Z'hart. Peaks rise moderately high in the night sky, and I can almost see the varying terrain ahead of us. The Flames are just a few kilometers away, and we'll be through by the following evening. But as I gaze out and see the small mountains, firelight can be seen near one of the peaks.

We won't be alone when we reach the Flames.

CHAPTER 17

Sarina

The Flames

THE HEEL OF MY BOOT crunches against the thin, tan colored grasses. The golden sands have been replaced with orange and violet wildflowers, russet dirt, and patches of bronzed grass. Sloping on both sides of us are rock walls hewn from pale stone, nooks and crevasses snake within their bases. Small mountains fill our view ahead, their bases grassy and colorful. The gorges that run between them seem to be carved out for the single purpose of navigational ease.

While a bit narrow, the gorge twists in odd ways as the rocky foundations skewer out from the landscape. Bedrock juts out in different shapes that seem similar to the tendrils of a fire, and the heat from the sun adds to the illusion. Most rise to be about a fifty meters while withered trees grow from their sides.

Water is scarce, but a slim creek stretches along the crevasse of the largest ravine, where plenty of edible plants and animals await. We all tire from the ration foods. It doesn't take long for Vivían to subdue a sizable kodragon with her bow, and Abrax is quick to store the dog-sized reptile for our next meal. I'm rather astonished at their skills in the realm of survival—Vivían with hunting and Abrax with his finesse at cooking fresh kills. I hope to learn more about it one day.

In fact, I'm starting to find myself even more interested with the others than I thought I would. Vivían's background in hunting, archery, and survival in the Outlands is fascinating to me. Growing up within a city with constant shelter makes her life seem even more adventurous. The same thing could be said about Tálir and his upbringing as a salvager in the Pyrack. Only twenty, he had been forced to work for his survival since he was a boy. Scavenging old parts without a family in the desert was no way for a child to grow up, yet he did so. But it's not just that.

Abrax has been taking Tálir off to train every morning and evening since we'd left the mines. I can see them occasionally, sending out bursts of magical energy. It's captivating in a sense, seeing the power of magic. Tálir's enthusiasm has enhanced his charismatic personality, and I can see him accepting leadership more and more. Yet, there's still that deep rooted sadness within him about being taken from his home. And I pity him.

Remus and Aida are also on decent terms with me, but they won't go into any more details about the riots. Like me, they probably want to wait until Z'hart City before we make any more discoveries. Devin and Vyck, on the other hand, are always a handful. Constantly jeering, sardonic, and acting like misogynistic bigots. Vyck isn't *as* bad, since he's definitely taking a liking to Vivían. But Devin is just so frustrating sometimes that it makes my blood boil.

Our journey takes us deep within the Flames, and the ground and surrounding bedrock begin to take more fiery colors. Blazing orange, bright red, and even spots of light gold. We clamber over mounds of rigid stones between each of the gorges. But I slowly begin to notice something.

Faint smoke columns can be seen near the higher mountains, and the strange feeling returns. The feeling like we're being watched and followed. More than once, I see shadowy movement upon the walls of the gorges. But my eyes never land on anything. Still, there's no doubt that someone is following our journey.

We pass by a plethora of wildflowers, cacti, and tumbleweeds as our journey continues into the Flames. Clouds start to spot the blue sky and occasionally blot out the sun for a few minutes. The distinct smell of the wildflowers causes me to sneeze a few times. Paranoia still grips me even as we venture, but it doesn't seem like danger is predominant yet.

Clambering up to higher ground on some of the bedrock outcroppings, we take a break for lunch at the top of the gorge. Another valley is below us, though much dryer and barren of plant life. The kodragon makes an interesting meal for the midday—its flesh is tough and almost devoid of taste. But, it is the only animal sizeable enough to feed the entire group.

During the break, everyone begins checking their equipment and weapons. I sit a distance away on an elevated outcropping, not feeling entirely social at the moment. It's comical in some sense, watching them. Like they're afraid their stuff is going to disappear or fall apart from neglect. Every day Devin sharpens his blade, even when he don't use it. Is it just a nervous habit?

Conforming slightly, I pull my bowpistol from its holster and start examining its features. *Nope, it's still intact*, I tell myself. The bolt magazine is still in there, the trigger isn't jammed, and the barrel seems fine. Nothing too special about it.

Abrax sits next to me suddenly, and I flinch in surprise. Already puffing out columns of smoke like a chimney, the old man grunts in amusement. He's aware of my feelings, and I think he likes to prod at them.

"The good old weapon examination time," he says gruffly. A cough escapes him. "Trying to conform are we? You don't look like you care too much about your weapon of choice."

I place the weapon flat on my palm, balancing it. "It's not that I don't like it," I explain. "It's just that, everyone else seems to have some sort of connection with their weapons or tools. Vivian and her bow. Devin and his sword. Aida with her medicines. You and Tálir with your armor."

I holster the bowpistol, my face reflecting some measure of displeasure. I cross my arms and continue, "I need something that fits me. Sure, the pistol is adequate. But it's not my preferable choice."

Abrax says nothing as I look into his leathery face, his eyes seem extremely tired. He stands and goes to retrieve something from the cart. Something he stored in one of his metal cases. He returns and sits next to me again and hands me something.

A thin, brass bar the length of a flute is in his hands. Made from a copper-colored metal, the rod is about half a meter and has a serrated spear tip fashioned to its head. It's like a half spear.

"Try this out," he says, placing it into my hands. It's heavier than I thought it'd be. "A relic I picked up decades ago. The spear of a Maven Knight."

I practically smack my head, not realizing the obvious similarity to the metal of the weapon and armor. Thrilling heat rises in my chest. Abrax is giving me a weapon used by the Domain, and I feel the gravity of what I've been given.

Grasping it gently, I feel the chill of the cool steel. The bronze metal is etched with symbols and esoteric markings from those long dead. Some images have been carved into its hilt, but they seem incomplete and jumbled. Abrax notices my confusion, stands in front of me, and presses down upon a metallic symbol near the blade.

The steel bar expands with a snap, lengthening to its full size of two meters. I watch in awe. My open mouth forms a smile, and I realize how unique this weapon really is. Fully extended, the shaft details many carvings of stars, the moon, and fire. The shapes of the crystals are also etched into the metal. A theme of light in the darkness seems present.

I stand and feel the balance of the weapon. How my body moves with it, and how heavy it will be when I strike. I'm honored to receive such a gift, and I can feel Abrax growing on me a bit. The others watch me briefly in surprise, but continue their own work.

"Abrax, this is incredible." I say, flourishing the spear delicately. "I don't know what to say. Thank you."

The old man snorts, and I see him grin indistinctly under his beard. He nods his head and puffs out more smoke. "Carry it well, Sarina. For that weapon has more legendary heritage than you can possibly imagine. Just don't cut yourself with it."

As I make a few motions with the spear, I notice that he doesn't leave—his eyes look disturbed. While I stand and get used to the weapon, I ask him, "Is something wrong?"

He shifts his weight upon the outcropping upon which we stand. The sage trench coattails are crumpled under his rear. "I'm curious about something." Abrax says, leaning forward with his pipe still clenched in his teeth. "Aida told me about what happened to you in Z'hart City. Can I ask, are you going to venture out alone to find answers when we get there?"

I stop my motions in shock, and I look back at him with befuddlement. What suddenly spurred this on? While I've been a little reclusive, I haven't shown any such signs since we started our journey. Does he really think I'm *that* self-centered? I'm a little offended.

"Why exactly is it your concern if I do?" I retort, firing right back at him. "What brought this on all of a sudden?"

Abrax snorts with a bit of respect to my backtalk. I think he rather enjoys someone to verbally spar with him. He leans back somewhat. "I know it will be tempting for you to seek out what you've lost, Sarina. I wouldn't entirely blame you if you did. But consider this: You'll only find pain and anger if you find those answers. There might be a terrible cost to your story, and it may end up being too much for you to pay. Is it really worth it to find something like that?"

My hands clench around the cold metal, my knuckles turn white from the anger that presses into them. My lips form a thin line, and I can feel my nostrils flare.

"Of course it is!" I hiss, trying to control the amplification of my voice. I don't want to draw the attention of the others.

"I don't plan on abandoning anyone," I continue, my anger expelling out like steam in a vent. "But I won't let what happened to me go without justice! If I get a chance to piece together what happened that night, I'm going to take it. I don't care what path it leads to! Abandoning the group has nothing to do with it!"

The old man watches me with serious apprehension imprinted upon his dark face. Dark eyes practically stare into my soul as if the Sage God himself watches me. "This is my warning to you, Sarina," he says quietly. "Secrets always come at a cost."

I turn away and say nothing to the old man. My anger buffets. What does he know? He hasn't been drugged, assaulted, and shipped off like a common thug. *He'll never know how I feel,* none of them will! The warning still rings in my head, and I hate hearing it. I *will* find the answers I seek, and they can't stop me.

"I'm still keeping the spear even if I think you're wrong." I seethe softly.

He sniffs. "I'd be disappointed if you didn't."

CHAPTER 18

Sarina

Crimsons

FIERY SUNLIGHT FADES in the sky as we approach the tail end of the winding ravines. In the morning, we'll be free of the Flames and traversing within the nation of Z'hart. I'll be that much closer to home. To answers.

Our camp is set up within the gorge, flanked by concave walls that can provide us shelter. Russet gravel coats the ground and dusty bushes dot the landscape. Stars begin to wink in the fading sunlight, and the sky is torn between fiery orange and blackened blue. We space ourselves out since there's ample space. Upon finishing one final meal for the day, Abrax and Tálir wander off for their usual evening tutelage while the rest of us start preparing for rest. I sit next to the campfire with my new spear in hand, and I contemplate what Abrax told me about finding answers.

There might be a terrible darkness to your story, he had said. Every terrible story has this attribute, and most stories in life are going to be dark. But my goal is to overcome that darkness even as I feel it creeping within me. Around me. There's a semblance of loneliness in feeling such pessimism. Like no one will ever understand or help.

That's why it's my duty to uncover the hidden details of my tale. No one else can do it. And I hate the fact that Abrax is trying to dissuade me from it. Ever since the convoy, I've felt like there's a piece of me that's been lost. Broken. Z'hart City is the only place where I might be able to piece myself back together. To feel whole once more. But the old man thinks that it'll lead me down a dark path. I don't care, because darkness will always be present no matter what I do.

The key is to find the light within that darkness.

A noise snaps me out of my musings. I hear the sound of movement scuttling across the rock walls around us. At first, I think it's Abrax and Tálir returning from their tutelage—but the movements suggest that there's more than two people. Soft pattering of boots echo into the ravine, and I can see trickles of dirt and rock falling into the gorge.

I remember the smoke columns earlier in the day. The shadows watching us during the trek. The stealthy trackers are moving closer.

Immediately a sense of alarm goes through me and I stand up

suddenly, scanning the ravine. Sand and dirt under my boot crunches as I move and unholster my bowpistol. The spear is collapsed within my left hand, but ready to be drawn. Vivían too, is alerted to the sound but rises slowly and draws her energy bow with silent lethality. The azure energy hums as an arrow forms from the device.

"They're already alerted to you; you know?" Devin voices softly. He stands easily and unsheathes his shortsword. Battle readiness is on his face.

"What do you mean?" I reply quietly with a tinge of anger. "We haven't done anything—"

"He's right, Sarina," Vivían confirms as she pivots. "You weren't exactly graceful in showing your alertness. They're likely changing tactics as we speak."

"Frag off!"

Almost imperceptibly, the others follow suite and retrieve their weapons even as the footsteps grow louder. The sound of movement is directed towards the rock wall on our right flank and everyone's attention is diverted to the twenty-meter cliff-face. There's barely enough light to see. The movement stops, and a moment of pause elapses as I aim my bowpistol for whatever is approaching.

But nothing happens, at least for a moment.

"GET DOWN!" Devin shouts from behind me before I hear two bodies slam against the ground.

Instinctively I do so, and a millisecond later a bowrifle energy bolt whizzes past my scalp and strikes the wall in front of me. The red energy smashes into the rock and showers sparks. I roll out of the way as I hear several more bolts strike the ground all around us—and the various dodges my companions employ. When the first volley ends, a chorus of shouting emanates from behind us and I scramble to my feet. I glimpse the assailants.

Twelve figures are perched upon the ledge overlooking the ravine. Smoking bowrifles in hand. All are garbed in brown and crimson dust robes, black gloves, cargo pants, and tan boots. Their faces are obscured by cloth masks that cover their lower faces while dark goggles hide their eyes. Each individual sports long, unkempt blonde hair that is twisted into dreadlocks. This is my first encounter with an Outland tribe.

They let their weapons cool down before unleashing the rest of their clips. Red energy bolts hail into the ravine as we scatter and use various boulders for cover. I fire blindly at them, the bowpistol recoils ferociously. Their bolts smack into the stone with loud *clacks*, and I see bits of rock being chipped away. The volley ends when their weapons overheat and the magazines are dry. But strangely, they don't reload.

"Iri'tah! Usta pin na confit!" Vivían shouts. Despite being aware of her Outland experience, I'm still surprised at her Outspeak dialect.

The Outlanders seemingly disregard her words. "O'rah tah!" they shout in unison, tossing their bowrifles aside before clambering down the ledge towards us. "O'rah tah!"

Vivían rocks her head and lets out a sigh. "Alright. Let's go! I've been itching for a scrap!" she says with a confident smirk. A look in her violet eyes says something different.

She fires the energy arrow. Blue light whisks through the air and strikes one of the Outlanders in the head. The body smacks against the ground from the fall. Vivían fires another arrow that burns through the leg of another. The Outlanders reach the ground level at an incredible speed and charge at us, barely giving Vivían enough time to draw another arrow.

One of the Outlanders lunges at her with his drawn sword. I steady my bowpistol and prepare to fire. It's set to kill. I try to aim for the man's head. But I'm too slow. Instantly, a dagger strikes him in the throat and blood spurts from the impact as he crumples a meter from Vivían.

"You need to be faster than that, Sarina!" Vyck shouts as he tosses another dagger at one of the assailants. The Outlander ducks and the blade flings past him.

Instinctively, I point the bowpistol at the attacker and pull the trigger. A crimson bolt speeds through the air and hits his torso. I catch him in the ribcage. The man collapses on all fours; the cauterized wound still bleeds indistinctly. He spits up blood. Vyck takes a quick look at me and draws his shortsword. He looks impressed.

"Nice shot!" he shouts with a tinge of smugness before rushing another attacker.

"You're welcome!" I shout in response, firing a few more shots. Lack of light impedes my aim. I miss my targets and the pistol overheats. Tossing it away, I expand the spear with a metallic *snap*.

Let's do this, I say to myself as a rush of adrenaline runs through me.

The remaining attackers branch off into groups to take on various individuals. Five converge on Devin and Vyck while another four head towards the rest of us. Vivían and I both step forward to cover Remus and Aida as the first of the assailants brandishes his sword and swings at me.

I've never dueled anyone before, but I won't let that stop me. I center my gravity and focus my attention. At the last second, I parry the blade with the shaft of my spear—sending a vibration through my arms and into my core. Digging my feet into the ground, I hold my ground and push against the Outlander with my entire body weight. He recoils somewhat. I take a few steps back. With some distance between us, I ready the spear and begin jabbing the spear at him. I want to keep him on edge and at a distance. With some space between us, I begin to formulate a strategy.

My mind is in a state of tranquil focus. My body reacts almost naturally in response to the danger. Time seems to slow down, and the area around me blurs as my attention centers on my opponent. If I keep my center, it's less likely that I'll be caught off guard. With my legs spread and knees bent, I continue to stab at my opponent. Then, my strategy comes to fruition.

After a lengthy jab, the attacker bats the spear to his side with a grunt and lunges. He thinks I've left him an opening. *Good.* With the momentum generated from his blow, I twist to my left and the spear's tip goes into a blinding arc. I whirl around and swing the spear with all my might. The motion is too fast for the man to react, and the tip of the spear cleanly cuts into his throat. Blood leaks from the wound like water leaking from a cracked mug. A gurgling sound emanates from his mouth as he drops his sword. Collapsing to the ground, his hands flail to try and staunch the bleeding.

A sense of foreboding jangles up my spine as I glimpse his body, and coldness starts to creep into my heart. The heat of battle fades somewhat. I've ended this man's life. He's slowly bleeding to death. A dark pit forms in my chest. It's like another part of me has been chipped away.

Mustering all my courage and strength, I jam the tip of the spear into the man's heart. There's a wet crunch. His body goes limp, and he's out of misery.

My head snaps to see Devin and Vyck cleanly cut down two of their attackers before twisting their blades into defensive parries. Vivían is down on one knee and fires another arrow into the left goggle of another. Sparks and drops of blood explode from the impact. Despite her glee, there seems to be some portentous disturbance to her eyes as she fires another blue arrow.

Impressively, I see Aida keeping an attacker away from Remus who had been knocked to the ground. He fumbles while looking for a weapon. Aida uses twin daggers in a blinding dance that both blocks attacks and opens cuts on her opponent's wrists and thighs. Remus finds my discarded bowpistol and struggles to reload it.

A yell snaps my attention elsewhere. Another Outlander

charges at me, his face unreadable by the mask and goggles. I'm too slow in my reaction time. Using two hands, the attacker bashes my spear with his sword. The metal slips through my fingers and it flies from my hands. Defenseless, I attempt to retreat even as the man raises his sword to deliver the final blow as he chants: "O'rah tah!"

I brace for the pain even as the same feeling of tranquil aversion envelopes me.

I hear an electric *crack*. He halts imperceptibly. And sparks flying from his back. An energy bolt hit him. The Outlander moans in pain and drops his sword. A second bolt explodes on the back of his head, burning a hole into his brain. Crunching against the gravel, his body topples over and I glimpse my savior.

It's Remus.

Down on one knee and with my bowpistol raised in his right hand, he gives me a nod of reassurance. A look of comradery emanates from him. A reciprocal nod escapes me. I'm still in awe at his sudden initiative and concise deadliness, two characteristics I thought I'd never see. He certainly isn't helpless.

Energy bolts fire from the pistol as he tries to assist the others. I snatch up my spear. I see Devin and Vyck have dispatched their opponents and are now battling two Outlanders from the second group. Aida moves gracefully as she battles her last opponent. Neither Remus nor Vivían have clear shots, so they hold.

Weaving to doge a wide swing, Aida spins her body and stabs one of her daggers into the calf of the Outlander. He yelps with pain and falters. Aida takes the opening. Delivering a martial kick to his other leg, the man falls backwards and Aida practically flips over him. The last dagger is flung into the forehead of the Outlander.

Vyck slays his opponent with ease, but Devin's seems to be more than a match for him. Their one-handed styles mirror each other. But Devin starts to get overconfident, and I can see huge holes in his defense. He's leaving himself wide open. A moment later, I'm proven right.

At the height of a two-handed swing, Devin lunges at his attacker. And he's too slow in reacting to the assailant's dodge. The Outlander spins and delivers a kick to Devin's stomach—driving the breath from him. His body smacks against the dirt, and his blade slips away. Vyck's too far away to reach him in time. The Outlander raises his sword to deliver the coup de grace. *I have to act now!*

A fiery determinism ignites within me like embers setting fire to a dry bush. I pull the spear back, aiming the tip at the Outlander's masked face. I exhale and hold. The target is in sight. And with a yell, I toss the spear as hard as I can. Seamlessly it soars through the air like one of Vivían's arrows. It flies…

And I miss. Spectacularly.

The weapon spins inches from the man's face and collides into the ravine wall. Sparks and chips of rock fly everywhere. A sharp *clank* echoes. The assailant pauses, looks at the spear, and then looks over at me with his head slightly cocked. Underneath his goggles, I suspect he's giving me a look of amused condescension.

"Fragging Hells," I mutter bitterly.

I berate myself for acting impetuously. However, my

performance did distract the attacker for the right amount of time. Before he even turns his head back to Devin, the tip of Vyck's shortsword is flung into the Outlander's chest. Right through the heart. He dies immediately even as his body is sent flying backwards.

The commotion dies down, and I can feel tension leaving my body. Shouting stops, blades no longer clash, and dust clouds linger from excessive movement. My heart beats at a normal pace, and my fear for the others recedes. There is a still quiet even as we stare at those fallen. We have won.

◆ ◆ ◆

All is quiet at first. But then I hear panting breaths, groans of pain, and clanking of weapons. Blood thunders in my head. My breaths feel shallow. Adrenaline rush?

"A worthy scrap!" she comments, rising from her knee. "That was fun."

"Seems like you all aren't worthless in a fight after all." Devin grunts as Vyck helps him to his feet. He cradles his stomach. "And that was a great throw, Sarina—really spectacular."

"To the Hells with you, asshole!" I sneer through clenched teeth, approaching the others. Remus stands and hands me back my pistol. He grins at me.

Vyck snickers. "In all seriousness, it was a good distraction. Nice work."

I'm not sure if he's being serious or denigrating, but I yield and accept his gratitude. I snort a laugh upon thinking of the ridiculous sight it must've been.

"It was my first time throwing a spear. Like a fifty-fifty shot of hitting."

Devin picks up his sword and my spear, walking over and handing the latter to me with slight gratitude.

"Ey, I'm not complaining," he says as I take my weapon. Genuine gratitude shines in his blue eyes.

I sniff in an amused way. I look around at our handiwork. Twelve bodies are scattered around the gorge and within our camp. Their frizzy hair wisps in the wind, and flies already begin buzzing around the corpses. The last rays of the sun cast a blazing haze over the puddles of blood. It smells like death.

"Who are they?" Aida asks as she pulls her daggers from the fallen Outlander. "I didn't think Outlanders ventured this close to a nation."

Vivían plugs a cable up to her bow and links it to her battery pack. Something still reflects in her eyes, and I think I know why. They were familiar to her.

"They're members of the Crimson Cross." she says, revealing a symbol on the jacket of a fallen warrior. A blood red cross engulfed in golden flames within a silver triangle.

"A prominent tribe in the eastern Outlands," she continues. "Fervent worshipers of the Cross Way, the clan symbol and title reflect their devotion to immolation and crucifixion. 'Yielding to the flame', as they call it. The battle chant they called out holds some similar meaning."

"You got that just by their outfits and behavior, Viv?" Vyck inquires, scratching his head. He gazes at her intently.

"You could say something like that," she replies, her voice actually tinged with abhorrence. "I was raised a Crimson. I hunted as a Crimson. But I refused to murder as a Crimson. That's the long and short of it, Vyck. I'll say nothing more."

Vyck is taken aback somewhat, but he nods genuinely— eliciting a smile from her. Now it makes sense. The red in her hair didn't seem natural, but now I understand it's dyed. Vivían had forsaken her natural blonde hair when she left the Crimsons. An act of defiance.

I see Aida and Remus approaching the corpses, removing the goggles, and closing eyelids. A respectful gesture. One of which I feel compelled to do, at least to the man whose life I took.

I approach the body of the man I killed, and squat next to the stinking corpse. I remove the black goggles and see cold, brown eyes staring up at me. Chills run along my spine as I stare death in the face. Respectfully, I close his eyes. But then, something grabs my attention.

A leather pouch is affixed to his belt. Seemingly common at first, my interest peaks when I see a symbol etched within the leather. Upside down V outlining a pyramid all within a circle. *The same as Septem's!* Whatever is in this pouch, it has to be involved with the Order Septem mentioned. Heading to this mysterious Centum character, perhaps.

I have to look. My determined curiosity gets the better of me. I slowly open the pouch. A holoprojector and a handwritten letter are inside. My eyes dart back to the others, and they haven't noticed me. I'm tempted to share my discovery with them, but I stop and think back. If Abrax wants to prevent me from digging into things, what if the others start to as well?

With the involvement of this Centum person, I need to piece together their reasoning for shipping me off. Perhaps these documents can help prove it, perhaps not. But I'm going to need to know a lot more about these people and their connections. Abrax and Aida sure as Hells won't go into extreme detail, so I'll do it on my own.

Surreptitiously pocketing the letter and device in my belt pouch, I stand and look to my companions. I see some of the others moving the corpses into a singular spot away from the camp. A fire starts to immolate the bodies. Following suite, I pull the body as best I can to the burning corpses. Vivían makes a few silent gestures to honor the fallen.

"Any sign of Tálir or Abrax?" I ask when the work is done. "We could've used some of those magic powers."

Devin shakes his head. "Haven't seen the wizards since they left," he grunts irritably. "They're probably too far to have gotten here in time anyways. Shame. I would've enjoyed seeing what all that training amounts to."

I nod my head in agreement. Seeing the raw power of their magic would've been enough to scare them off without a fight. If only.

"So what did you say to them earlier, Vivían? Before they attacked." I ask.

Her olive face adopts a disappointed look. "I told them that we weren't a threat," she replies. "I incorrectly assumed that my knowledge of Outspeak would seem friendly. Guess I don't know them as well as I thought."

I run my fingers through my hair. "Any reason why Crimsons would be venturing into Z'hart?" I ask Vivían.

Her red hair is unkempt from the fight, and she looks a bit wired. "They were definitely a scouting party. Perhaps even messengers. But I honestly can't say. The tribe normally sticks to the east, although the camp constantly moves. Did you find anything that says otherwise, Sarina?"

All of their eyes are suddenly upon me, and each carries a crushing weight. It's like all of them are bearing down upon my very soul. All of the Hells and the Sage God bear witness to this judgment, and I feel so empty. Terrible, even.

"No."

Another piece of me feels like it's chipped away. This time, for lying to those who are becoming more than companions. They're becoming friends.

CHAPTER 19

Tálir

The Maven Way

NIGHT HAS FALLEN.

Abrax has taken me to the top of the highest plateau to train without drawing attention from the ravines below us. The plateau is large enough to obscure our session from any prying eyes. The uneven, maroon stone beneath my feet reflects the silvery glow from the moon in the early night sky, and a cool breeze howls past us. From our altitude, the night sky is cloudless. The stars above glitter like windblown embers across the atmosphere as the planet rotates through the darkness.

Almost an hour ago, I thought I heard bowrifle fire coming from further in the Flames. But the noise didn't last long enough for

Abrax and I to determine if it was anything substantial. I hope it wasn't.

A small fire crackles nearby and the old man is perched atop one of the protruding boulders. Normally, he participates in the exercises. But tonight, he watches.

"Focus and flow," I repeat Abrax's words from moments ago. "Focus! And flow!"

In the days that have followed since Abrax first demonstrated the suit's power, I've progressed slowly. The movements are simple and I've mastered the basic footwork and poses that string together each Form. But, the focus of drawing the right amount of energy is… difficult. It's like trying to focus on a singular memory for several minutes at a time. The world around me is full of distractions that easily pull away that specific focus.

Stream is the most basic Form and I've managed to gain a partial grip on it. Each Form has its own individual set of rules as well. Abrax informed me that as the initial Form, Stream's versatility is quite limited. A basic attack, Stream will stun and push living beings but nothing beyond that. At full *25%*, it can spark fires or serve as a small energy source. If I'm fast enough, Stream can deflect Discus, but it has no effect on any other Form.

Planting my feet shoulder-width apart, I extend my right arm and keep my left tucked close my ribcage. Summoning the energy within the gauntlet, I focus on bringing it to my fingertips. Warm vibrations run down my forearm and my fingers begin to feel static. This is the easy part. Now, I have to concentrate on what I want it to do.

Imagining the five individual torrents in great detail, I attempt to release the energy in my fingertips. My HUD reads *Output Charge: 15%* as the Stream activates and flows from me. Five emerald energy beams emit with a low *hiss* and soar into the open air. Holding the position and output, I try to enhance my concentration to make the torrents more intense.

But the difficulty increases. Abrax told me I have to eliminate distractions to intensify the magic. Sweat trickles into my eyes. I'm distracted by the bowrifle fire I thought I heard and my attention immediately snaps out of focus. The Stream fizzles out, and I'm left panting in frustration. I'm barely able to hold the Stream, so how will I possibly be able to harness the other three Forms?

The old man heaves a sigh of exasperation and points his index finger at me—releasing a tangle of emerald energy that speeds towards my torso. Instinctively, I spin to the side and the Stream flickers past. Testing my reflexes has become commonplace in our training. Abrax wants to test my footing and awareness under duress.

Alright then, I think as I accept the challenge. More Stream blasts spring from his fingers and I begin to dodge. An added benefit to Maven armor is that it can enhance one's reflexes and movements if properly attuned. It's also more durable against non-magic attacks. Now that it's fitted to me, the armor assists my body in becoming physically responsive.

I move left, leaping into a dodge-roll and using the momentum to close the gap. Abrax blasts at my feet, hoping to catch me in mid stride. Twisting once more, I practically cyclone in the air even with the weight of the armor. My movements are used to it now.

I'm meters from him as I get my footing. Calling on the energy in my right gauntlet, I prepare to counterattack to finish the trial. But I'm too slow. A Stream hits me right in the chest and I'm thrown backwards.

While on a low level, the energy still courses through my veins with an electric fury and neutralizes my motor functions seconds before my brain even registers the itching numbness. It lasts for a few seconds, but it's enough to send me tumbling for almost a meter—my teeth grinding away as the pain wells up.

Dammit! I think to myself sardonically. *He's still too damn fast.*

"You get too easily sidetracked, lad," Abrax says, grunting in amusement. "Kryo magic won't obey you if your mind is always running amuck."

I bite back my frustration. How can I be expected to harness the energy when life itself is distracting?

"Why is this so damned complicated?" I curse, still on my knees. My long hair is like curtains around my face. I'm too shameful to even look at Abrax. "Why can't I fragging focus?"

I glance up and see him shuffling through a pile of loose stones. "Because you're allowing distractions to block your focus," he says, picking up one of the rocks. "If stones fall into a river, the flow becomes altered and perhaps even blocked. If unblocked, the river flows naturally without impediment. Your focus must flow without distractions."

He starts casually tossing the stone up and catching it within his palm. "Try a new target. Focus the energy and hit the rock," the old man says rather haughtily.

Taking a deep breath, I relax somewhat and fixate on the rock. It goes up and down as he casually tosses it. I try my best to think only about the stone. Thoughts are blocked out. Energy starts to build within my arm again. Watching the stone rise and fall, I feel my mind ease and the charge starts to increase further. Reaching *15%*, I smirk with confidence and try to unleash the energy. The distractions don't fade, however.

I consider the bowrifles sounds from earlier. Fear grips me as I imagine a hole burned in Sarina's stomach. *No!*

A flimsy beam leaves my index finger and vaporizes inches from the stone. Swearing at my incompetency, I stomp in agitation. Abrax sighs with disappointment. In a blur of motion, he throws the stone high into the air before blasting it in mid-air with his left hand.

"The miracles of focusing, wouldn't you say?" he says rather smugly.

"Because that's just so fragging simple, Abrax!" I snarl irreverently, retracting the helmet to show my frustration. "Maybe next time I should just stare at it until it explodes. Would that be enough fragging focus for you?"

He regards me stonily. "One: Don't use that tone with me. Two: You're too distracted by events outside this session. And three: You're your own worst enemy, you know that?" Abrax says with a note of disappointment. "The fact that you have such little faith in yourself is going to hinder your ability to properly focus. It's like I'm teaching Romulus all over again."

"I have plenty of faith in myself, thank you," I retort in an attempt to show confidence when in reality I'm utterly unsure of myself. "And don't speak poorly about my father."

Abrax lets loose an irritated sigh. "Look Tálir, if you had faith in yourself you'd know the right median of concentration necessary for the magic. There's no shame in it. Every Maven Knight started out where you are right now. You need to get past your own doubts and fears if you're ever going to learn. Listen to what I'm saying!"

I scowl at him. He's perched upon that boulder like some sort of judgmental deity. His bronze armor even looks cleaner than usual. "You're not my father; and you'll never come close to him. What makes you think you can lecture me about my doubts and my failures?"

"Because, you are the one who requested that I teach you. Remember?" Abrax mutters simply, crossing his arms as a disappointed look etches across his dark brow. "So I hold the authority of instructor while you hold no authority as pupil. That's the way this works, se'bau."

I look away from him and towards the rocky mesas that surround us, an ethereal reflection of the moonlight shines from the rocks. I want nothing more than to master the abilities and to learn about the history behind it. I'm willing to carry the responsibilities of the Maven legacy, but how arduous will that process be? I might have bitten off more than I can chew.

My resolve holds though. I won't give up just after a couple days of failure. I want to become a master with these abilities, and I won't let any deterrent stop me. Perhaps, that's part of the lesson he's trying to teach me. Perseverance.

"I'll take your lesson to heart, Suzerain," I say respectfully, addressing him by the Maven title of *master*. Speaking the title induces an interesting reaction within his eyes. For a brief moment, his eyes light up in delight.

Abrax grunts and arises from his perch. Predictably, he lights his greenweed pipe and takes some drags before saying, "Just focus your attention on something other than fear or doubt. Fear, anger, and doubt are chaotic emotions. They are like forest fires and can blaze uninhibited for long times, causing irreparable damage. Do not let chaotic emotions rule you, for the Maven way is order." There's a pause before he continues, "From the lessons I've given you, can you tell me why the armor is used mainly for defensive countermeasures?"

I consider his question and think back to both early training lessons and common histories. Abrax had told me in our second session that a few hundred years before the Ending, the Maven Knights were formed. With technology at its peak and the new discovery of the kryo gems, a caste of marshals was formed to unite the nations of the Old World. It was the single greatest act of unity in that bygone world. Nations pooled their resources and their recruits to form the Maven Knights, the marshals of law and order.

A hundred years later, the enemies of order began fracturing both the Domain and the Mavens. Doctrine and discipline prevented the Knights from mobilizing into a full army. Application of the armor was meant to keep the peace, not to escalate the conflict. But this was also their failure. They failed to stop chaos because of misguidance to their principles. So Abrax's question isn't just about the armor itself, it's about the history of it.

"Maven culture dictates that combat application of the armor is only used in dire situations," I paraphrase, touching my chin. "The armor must be shown to all to establish order, but only used to quell the danger of chaos. They failed to do this in the years before the Ending."

Abrax grins thinly. He paces around the mesa, and I see the various terrains beyond. By morning, we'll reach the grassy plains beyond the Flames. Sparse clusters of trees and plant life are within those plains as far as I can see

"Good. You are taking something away from this after all, Tálir," the old man mutters sardonically as he looks to the night sky. "The Maven Knights of old became too prideful in their disciplines when the true threat of chaos was presented. The Ones of Aster, a corrupted sub-sect of Knights, knew of this weakness and so they used it against their counterparts. Their downfall was of their own making. What you must take away from this is that any weakness can be used against you. The Mavens forgot what it meant to ensure order, and so chaos met no resistance."

Sitting down upon the rocky edifice, I prepare for the history lecture Abrax is famous for. Our sessions normally start with practicing Form I before moving into some of the cultural lessons. It's all been fascinating to hear, but I'm uncertain of how Abrax knows so much about them. The culture has been supposedly dead for ten Cycles.

"How could they let that happen?" I inquire as the old man pauses. "They were the marshals against chaos, so why would they just sit back and let it happen?"

Abrax scratches at his long, silver hair. "A good question, lad." He puffs smoke, his face reflecting some manner of disenchanted pain. "Order and chaos exist in symbiosis: one cannot exist without the other. I believe some of the Knights considered this, and wanted there to be a reason for establishing order."

I look at him intensely as the moonlight illuminates him. "So they conspired to let it happen." I conclude as a dark horror builds up in me. "If there's no chaos, how can there be order? But if a crisis unfolds and is unchecked, they'd be the bringers of order once again."

The wind wisps by and blows my hair into a wavy mess. It extinguishes Abrax's pipe, and he shows a bit of annoyance.

"Very good," he says with indistinct acclaim. "The Ones of Aster had corrupted many within the Maven Knights, leading them to believe their sense of order was nothing but stagnation. Chaos was the natural order of the world, they believed. But it wasn't a full out war between the Ones of Aster that brought the Mavens to extinction. As our histories might have you believe."

"What do you mean?"

He places his pipe in his trench coat and stands so that the moon is directly above him. I almost snort. It's like he understands the effect of the dramatic lighting.

"It was civil war that caused the Mavens to collapse," Abrax says. I pay close attention as he grasps his arms behind his back. There's always a hidden meaning in these lectures.

"Younger Knights, those with more devotion to their creed of order, rebelled," the old man narrates as if he had been there in those years. "Se'baus fought Suzerains and obliterated many of their old fortresses and training grounds. Millions died. The younger Knights even sought to stop the Ones of Aster on their own. But the conflict merely ended with the utter annihilation of the Mavens. The conflict of ideologies erupted this civil war, and it turned them into the very things they fought against. They lost their true focus."

There it is. He ties the history neatly into the lesson of the day. I praise him slightly for his consistency.

Abrax approaches me with a questioning look upon his face. His lips are a thin line under his beard before he asks, "Do you understand the importance of guided focus now, Tálir?"

I regard him without expression. It's a bit frustrating, having him hammer home this concept of focus. But I realize the deeper implications of it. The Mavens fell because of misguided focus, and the same could happen to me if I let it.

"Focus keeps our true goals in sight," I say in a reflecting manner. "My focus needs to be true if I'm to remain guided. It makes sense."

The old man gives no expression, but he nods in approval before he examining his right gauntlet. "Misguided focus is what led to the extinction of our culture. Distractions, doubt, fear, and corruption dug in like parasites and turned them against one another. You must be better than that, lad. I must as well. Despite the Ending, the Mavens are slowly returning. But only in the shadow of the Ones of Aster. So our focus must remain strong against the many enemies we'll face."

I gulp at this undertaking. *The many enemies we'll face?* I repeat. This is more dangerous than I thought. With awkward unease, I comment, "Now I'm not so sure I want this responsibility."

"Be serious, dammit!" Abrax snaps, furrowing his brow. "You don't have a choice in any case; you have a heritage that will attract the same enemies even if you discard the armor."

"My father," I piece together, caution snaking through me. "What in all the Hells happened, Abrax? What did he do?"

The old man looks at me indifferently, and he strokes his tangled beard. "That's a story for another time, lad," Abrax says quietly, turning and approaching his perch. "Our current lesson stands: Focus and flow."

Picking up another stone, he tosses it in the air a couple times before calling, "Focus true!"

He hurls the stone at my face. My mind goes blank and my attention turns into a haze around the stone spiraling towards me. Almost moving in slow motion, the stone rotates towards me as I raise my hand. Energy springs from my fingers towards the stone. It hits! The helmet isn't even activated to assist me. Although the blast hits the stone, the energy isn't strong enough to halt its trajectory—and it hits me in the forehead.

Grunting in pain, I hear a soft clap emanate from Abrax before he says, "Some progress. A bit better. There's hope for you yet, se'bau."

CHAPTER 20

Tálir

The Mission

FREEDOM RISES IN ME as we journey out of the Flames—a
weight lifts from our shoulders both physically and metaphorically.
There had been a sense of claustrophobia in the Flames. The gorges
constantly surrounded by high walls while the ravines themselves
narrowed. Even the air seemed thicker in comparison to our newest
environment.

Grassy savannas and rolling plains are filled with tall weeds
that flow with the wind. Wildflowers clumped near sections of
colorful bushes in the patches of lemon, red oat, and star grasses.
Palm and acacia trees sprout from the damp soil, their canopies
nearly twice the size of their thin trunks. The savannas stretch

hundreds of kilometers as we enter the nation of Z'hart. Water springs and oases dot the plains as various long-necked quadrupeds flock together. The creatures are large enough to carry a few hundred pounds' worth of meat and bone, much more appetizing than the kodragon.

However, the creatures are rather skittish and bound across the plains faster than we can devise a plan to hunt them. Still, I'm absolutely ecstatic about seeing new variations of terrain after living in the desert my whole life. The Flames provided some small samples of new terrain, but it was still a part of the desert. Here though, grass is all kinds of colors and the trees aren't lifeless. Flowers are supple and healthy, and the breeze carries a sweet smell through the air. It's miraculous to behold.

This is my first time traveling anywhere near an established nation. I rarely ever wandered out of a few kilometers from Erron's Ville. I'm growing slightly more nervous as we approach a place so lively and full of danger. I'm also apprehensive because I've barely started on the Shield Form. My Stream Form is becoming adequate, but I'm still in the beginning tiers of Maven training. And Abrax wants me ready for something. I'm glad no one notices my anxiety as I pull the repulsorcart.

Another three days pass as we venture north, and I can vaguely sense a shift in the weather. The air is cooler and the sun isn't as intense. Clouds more frequently block out the sun and provide shade to the world. It's mid-afternoon on the third day when we hike over a massive hillside. Taller than any dune in the Pyrack, this beast of a hill takes almost twenty minutes to hike over. But when we reach the top, that's when I see a truly magnificent sight.

Kilometers in the distance are a vast expanse of charcoal mountains. The jagged mounds of rock and ore are punctuated by sharp peaks which rise into the thin clouds above. The mountains overlook a rather plain landscape of tan grass and sporadic acacia trees. A massive lake rests near the western side of the mountain range. Carved out from the center of the mountains and expanding into the plains before us, is the capital of Z'hart City.

Nearly twelve kilometers in diameter, the city is consolidated within high walls. The parapets seem to be a combination of modern technology and Domain materials. Repulsor vehicles buzz in and around the city like bees around a hive. Steel structures line the inner districts of the city; skyscrapers sport flashy holoprojections and advertisements. Smaller apartment complexes, workshops, landing platforms, and factories make up the outer districts. At the center of the city is a grand cathedral flanked by a number of sentry towers and nobility suites. Azure banners drape from each tower while a massive violet curtain hangs from the parapets of the cathedral. Each banner bears the crest of House Z'hart: a black oreing within an open, silver palm.

"Ah, the grandiose capital of harvesting and shipping turd ore," Vyck comments as we pause to observe the landscape. "Seems just like yesterday that we were here getting our asses boned by those silver-armored pricks."

"Now I know why Z'hart is always in a food crisis," I say.

"There are no farms."

"Not many farmers or fishermen here, Tálir," Devin affirms. "The rainy season also prevents adequate harvests. O'ran has always been much better at food harvesting than these people. Block headed miners."

Sarina sniffs with derision, eliciting a quick response from Devin. "Meaning no offense to you, m'lady," he says trying to placate. It's peculiar seeing Devin trying to mind his comments with Sarina.

Her expression eases as she steps forward. "There's some measure of food industry here. But the ore within the mountains is what Z'hart prizes on harvesting. Why farm when you can pay others to do it for you?"

Vyck's expression turned to vague acceptance as he comments, "Well, when you put it that way…"

I let the cart rest at the center of our group atop the hillside before stepping forward. "We've got a lot of ground to cover during our time here," I say. I turn and face everyone, and their eyes watch me. "We're going to need rations, survival gear, oreings, and a few repulsorbikes. Abrax and I also need to search for this Tome device to help us get to Providence."

My eyes find Sarina and I address her, "Sarina. You know the lower connections within this city. Where might we be able to acquire everything?"

She gives me a slight nod for acknowledging her expertise. Her blue eyes reflect pondering thought before she says, "Most of what we need can be purchased within the outskirts of the city itself." She points and we all look.

Bordering outside the perimeter of the walls are hundreds of smaller, shabbier looking buildings. Shacks, garages, shops, and food vendors can be seen even at our distance. It all looks substantially shady, but I trust in Sarina's judgment.

"Repulsorbikes normally go for a thousand oreings a piece," she continues. "We'll need to find a merchant to sell our treasure gems to and seriously haggle a price. But other than that, everything else should be easy to get without even going into the city."

Her voice betrays some sense of longing, like she's disappointed we may not enter the city. Saddened that she can't return to her *true* home. However, Abrax chimes in and says, "You all may not have to enter the city, but Tálir and I will have to. The location of the Tome can only be accessed through the city. And we may need someone else to accompany us."

"Sarina knows the city best; she can accompany us into the city," I comment and nod to her, eliciting a weak smile from her. Perhaps this can be her chance to see her true home. And gain some answers to her past.

Abrax's voice is stern and uncompromising. "No. There's a chance she could attract unwarranted attention in the city. She must stay in the outskirts."

"Don't tell me what I can and can't do, old man!" Sarina spits. "I know the districts! I can help—"

"The answer is no!" Abrax asserts loudly, his voice echoing

atop the hillside. We shrink in response to his authority. "You'll be safer with the others. However, I wouldn't mind having someone with combat experience tag along."

While I'm expecting Vivían to jump at the chance at danger, it's a surprise when Devin speaks up. He takes a step forward and says, "Speaking as an individual with said experience, I'll volunteer to go with the wizards. Are you expecting trouble?"

"It's best to be prepared," Abrax says cryptically.

"You're sure about this, Devin?" I ask giving him a look of concern.

"Who do you think I am? Of course I'm sure."

I look to Abrax who in turn gives a nod of satisfaction. While not my first pick, I accept Devin's expertise and willingness to accompany our mission. I sense that he isn't bluffing about his experience, and that leads me to trust him.

"Welcome to the mission, Devin," I say, clapping him on his armored shoulder. He cocks an eyebrow, but doesn't dismiss my gesture.

I address the others. "So here's the plan: Abrax, Devin, and I will head into the city and locate this Tome device. The rest of you will stick to the outskirts and round up the equipment for the quest. Is everyone in agreement?"

Their heads nod in approval even as Vivían comments, "Dammit. You guys get the exciting part of the mission while we get to go shopping."

Abrax approaches the cart, shuffles through one of his metal cases, and retrieves two wristbands. Each has a metal chip at the center of the band. He hands one to Aida and one to Sarina.

"Use these comlinks to contact us if anything goes wrong," he says before gesturing to himself. "Their signal is linked to each of our helmets. We'll also give updates on our progress. Press the red button to talk."

The signal is linked to my helmet as well? Interesting. I can only guess that Abrax meddled with it when he first constructed it for me. The two regard the comlinks quizzically as they strap them to their wrists. We all glance at one another as a pause hangs in the air. Like they're waiting for a cue.

I speak up once again. "We have our missions. Let's try not to get into any more precarious situations, eh?"

Their nods and grins signal the start of our missions.

CHAPTER 21

Tálir

Z'hart City

BARELY AN HOUR PASSES before Abrax, Devin, and I draw nearer to the gates of the city. The others split from us almost immediately when we entered the outskirts. Hundreds if not thousands occupy the shacks, garages, and kiosks bordering the walls of the grand city. Despite my faith in my companions, I still feel a tinge of worry even after we separated. I don't want anything untoward to happen to any of them.

We pass along dirt streets while most of the shacks and kiosks were made of cheaper metals, wood, and brick. None rise above three stories, and shoddy holoprojectors display flickering images on their roofs or balconies. The static projections show broadcasts detailing the inflated prices of food, increased military traffic, and Insurgent violence. The commoners and impoverished reside in this part of Z'hart City, and their clothing matches the ragged state of their society. Despite having grown up in similar conditions, I nonetheless feel a degree of pity for those who trot shoeless through the dirt streets.

The streets wind around for nearly half a kilometer as we pass various shabby homes, dumpsters overflowing with garbage, and garages stinking of oil and lubricants. Heads constantly turn to watch us pass by. Their expressions range from awe to disdain. Abrax and I still wear our cloaks now to prevent drawing attention. Yet, it's like they can almost see through them. The stench of rotting food and body odor hangs in the air like an invisible mist.

I try to divert my attention from the miserable lifestyles I see here. Abrax walks ahead of me while Devin follows alongside me.

"We are nearing the gates," Abrax says over his shoulder, gingerly taking a kryo from his pouch and placing it into the battery chamber on his right bracer. "Follow my lead, and don't do anything suspicious."

Devin snorts as we push through a group of commoners. "Please, this isn't my first time infiltrating a city."

"Infiltrating? I guess we can add that to the infinite skills you have," I reply sardonically. Devin shrugs innocently. "And Abrax, I think our magic is less common in cities than in the outskirts. Don't you think it'll attract attention?"

The old man looks back at me with a slight grin on his face.

"Just follow my lead."

Though confused, I brush it off. I trust in his ability to get us in. Still, I can't help but feel everyone's eyes watching us. Pushing through a crowd of merchants, we enter an open courtyard situated in front of the ten-meter-high gates. The walls and fortifications are made of an amalgamation of technology, giving it a silver and pale shade. The gates, however, are carved out of the dark ore the mountain provides. The twin doors are sleek, burnished, and engraved in sigils that represent old forms of spiritual protection from the Sage God. The doors are a stark contrast to the metallic walls; the silver metal has been worn and washed over the centuries.

Since the Arc is the most common religion, it makes sense to see holy symbols of the Sage God engraved in the ore for security. Father taught me to obey the Arc and avoid retribution in the Hells, but I've never really delved too much into its worship. Perhaps one day I will.

As we walk across the cobblestone courtyard, I spot four guards perched in front of the gate—bowrifles clutched in their hands. But as we get closer, I'm able to vividly see the details of their armor and gear.

They're wearing pieces of Maven armor.

Astonishment and anger wash over me all at once. Only their right arms and shoulders are covered by the Maven armor. The rest of their attire is of the same silver material the Imperials wear. Spiked helmets that seem almost avian obscure their faces. I've seen this style before. During the raid on Erron's Ville, the soldiers wore the same armor type. These must be the foreign soldiers Lady Sahari summoned weeks ago. Stoppering my bubbling hate as one corks a bottle of wine; I realize I mustn't draw their unwanted attention.

We approach the gates and two of the guards spot us, their grip tenses on the bowrifles. They move to intercept us when we're a few meters from the dark gates.

Devin casually stops as they approach and opens his hands in a friendly gesture. "Ey good day, boys," he says in an innocent voice. "It's great to be home! Been away from this place for almost five years."

The guards brandish their weapons and stop a meter from Devin. "State your business within the capital," one of them commands. "Or else be on your way."

"No worries, gents. I'm just stopping by to visit my parents with my companions here," Devin lies through his teeth and gestures to us. I look at him with bewilderment. "I'm Devin of the lower House Nova. My family's words are: Reap what you sow."

The guards pause in confusion for a moment. I think all of us do. What's Devin playing at? Will family mottos really get us into the city?

A bowrifle primes for fire, and the guards aim directly at Devin as one growls, "House Nova's words are: Reap what you *mine*. Liar."

Oh shit! I think as I try to scramble a plan together. The bowrifles begin to hum and I can see the faint tinge of red within their barrels. They're set to kill.

The old man steps forward however, and the guards pause in confusion. Their rifles are aimed at him, but he stops purposefully.

"One hundred and one oreings pay," Abrax says in a commanding voice, as he raises his right arm showcasing the Maven gauntlet. A tangle of emerald fire sparks in his palm.

I look at him in confusion for an instant, but my attention diverts when the guards immediately lower their weapons and bow slightly.

"Apologies, Suzerain!" one of the guards says. He makes a fist with his right hand and presses it to his chest. "We were unaware of your presence here. I presume you've just arrived from the Himal temple?"

"In a manner of speaking. I'm here on a mission with my se'bau and another... prospective student," Abrax replies authoritatively. He glances at Devin with irritation. "This lad needs some serious conditioning to fix his petulant tongue. Trying to make a mockery of House Nova. All brawn and no brains."

Devin's goatee-covered mouth hangs open in both shock and embarrassment. His eyes are full of shame, but I can see hints of a boiling rage that he's struggling to keep in check.

"What is your mission, Suzerain?" the same guard asks respectfully. I can tell he's quick to try and not upset a Suzerain.

"Classified," Abrax replies sternly. Some of the other guards turn their heads to one another. Confusion emanates from under their helms. "By authority of Suzerain, I request to enter the capital so that I may accomplish my mission. I will personally check in with the higher members of the Order once I'm satisfied."

The guard bows. "Of course, Suzerain. I'll alert Centum of your arrival…"

"That will not be necessary." Abrax commands, his voice reflecting hints of staged anger.

"But—"

"Must I repeat myself, soldier?" The old man's voice practically carries through the streets, drawing the attention of others. I shrink beneath such authority. "I will alert Centum myself on my own time. Now, open the gate."

In a fluster, the guard bows yet again and yells, "Open the gate!"

"Much obliged," Abrax nods courteously. "As you were, gentlemen."

A long, strenuous creak emanates from the twin doors as they slowly start opening. The ore reflects the varying rays of sunlight like water. The doors open only slightly however, enough for the three of us to get in. Moving forward with Devin and Abrax, the guards begin to close ranks as we enter the small opening between the gates.

My eyes open wide at the sight of the city.

Pristinely forged ore metal has been fashioned into the towering structures that border the marketplace. Half a kilometer, the crescent shaped market holds hundreds upon its burnished cobblestones. Kiosks and shacks of a finer quality pepper the streets, sheets of vibrant violets and blues drape from their roofs. The smell of fresh fruits and roasting meats wafts through the air as the noisy bustle of a hundred voices echoes through the streets.

Beyond the market, towering skyscrapers nearly twenty stories high overlook the districts. Dark ore is used in their framework, but varying colors of maroon and violet are used in the concrete and other materials. Cleaner holoprojections light up billboards near the roofs of the structures. Repulsor vehicles whine through the air above, sending currents from their engines.

More to my astonishment, the city itself seems to be made of concentric rings of avenues such as the one we entered. In the distance, I can see a more elevated level of apartments and buildings of a grander nature. At the highest point of the city, punctuated at the center of the mountainside, is the royal cathedral. While nearly a kilometer away, I can see the austere and angular architecture—and the violet banners of House Z'hart.

Magnificent, I think to myself as a small grin etched in the corners of my mouth. Never in my life did I think I'd see a sight like this.

But even as I bask in awe of the city, I hear the gates close behind us. I notice the attention of some curious individuals is upon us. Our cloaks and Devin's mercenary armor draw a bit of attention.

"Come," Abrax whispers to the both of us. He starts to gently push through the crowd.

Devin and I follow Abrax for a few yards into the marketplace, avoiding curious bystanders and patrols as we move into the crowd. It's a frustrating endeavor, but we quickly break free before veering off into an alleyway between the apartment skyscrapers. The alley is narrow and packed with piles of trash, spoiling food, and clumps of feces—the sweet smell of the market is drowned out by the stench.

Out of public sight, Abrax sheds himself of his cloak. I do the same, even though I'm still a bit nervous about losing our cover. Devin suddenly whirls on Abrax, the look in his eye is almost feral. Like it was in the mines.

"The fragging Hells was that?" he asks angrily, trying to keep his voice down. "All brawn and no brains? You can burn in the Hells, old man!"

Abrax adopts a look of mild innocence. "How else would we have gotten past the gate guards, hot shot? They were about to shoot us thanks to your little slip up. I just saved us a substantial amount of time and energy at the small expense of your dignity."

"Frag off!" Devin looks at me for support. "C'mon, Tálir. You thought it was a good idea, right?"

I hold up my hands in a gesture of uncertainty. "It started out as a good idea," I try to compromise. "But, I suppose that's why we're all here. To get each other's backs even if we slip up."

Devin's face takes on a bit of color as he spits, "Fragging teacher's pet."

I chuckle lightly. Looking further down the alley, I see a maze of interconnected paths through the various buildings. They intersect and fork off based on the design of the buildings. More garbage, scrap piles, and scurrying rodents can be seen along the stained stone paths. Clouds start to gather over the sunlight, casting a dim grey light over the area. It feels like it's going to rain.

"So where do we go from here?" I ask Abrax as I lean against the side of the structure. "It looks like we'll need to navigate the alleys to wherever this place is. Can't risk being seen by other guards."

Abrax gives an uncanny grin as he strokes his beard. "You're right, lad," he says. "How do you two feel about dark, dank tunnels?" I frown. "I'm not exactly a fan." I admit, glancing down at my breastplate with concern. "I'd like to keep this armor relatively clean."

"Likewise," Devin concurs, placing a hand on his burnished chest piece. "I rather like the shine it's attained."

"Stop being a bunch of pansies," Abrax voices in a disgruntled tone, walking past Devin. "Consider this the first trial of our quest: we need to venture into the underground catacombs. From there, we should be able to find the entrance to wherever the Tome resides."

Devin and I glance at each other with mild trepidation. Not just concerning our armor, but because of how Abrax knows about this place. Perhaps I haven't realized just how knowledgeable the old man is until now. And the thought is quite alarming. What else does he know about?

"If you knew the Tome existed here, why didn't you uncover its location on your first quest for Providence?" I ask, folding my arms over my chest.

Abrax brushes some dirt from his trench coat before saying,

"What makes you think I didn't?" he asks in kind. "I failed last time because I was young, stupid, and alone. That's why I need your help. One cannot find the Tome alone."

I hesitate briefly. But I sigh with a reluctant acceptance before saying, "Where do we start?"

"Fragging Hells," Devin huffs as he looks at his shiny, violet armor.

CHAPTER 22

Sarina

The Merchant and the Blacksmith

THE STENCH OF SPOILING FOOD fills my nostrils, and the air seems hot and heavy as crowds snake by the markets. Mud cakes my boots and I roll up my sleeves to let my arms cool a bit. There are fewer of us, but it's no less difficult trying to navigate the various shops and shacks for supplies.

A patrol of new militia soldiers march through what passes as the street, their incomplete Imperial uniforms seem ridiculous. Bronze pauldrons, vambraces, and gauntlets are on their right arms while silver armor covers the rest. Remus said this lower class militia has been provided by Centum, but I'm at a loss as to why their suits are incomplete. One would think Centum is a person of perfection and strict adherence to whatever doctrine they have. Incomplete ceremonial armor of the Mavens should've seemed detrimental to Centum's beliefs.

But then again, Centum seems to be a person who sows the seeds of chaos before order. A person who wants to tear everything down before rebuilding it. Tear a girl down.

It has been a few hours since Abrax, Tálir, and Vyck set about their mission to obtain the Tome. I grow faintly eager to start searching for answers now that Abrax is gone. He's no longer watching over my shoulder, and I want to find out what happened. However, I remain with the others because they have no knowledge about the capital and outskirts. I cannot ditch them when they have no idea where to go.

"I was told I'd get six thousand for one of these!" Vyck barks as he haggles with a merchant. "If you're gonna haggle on price, you need to start near four thousand."

An antiques merchant of small stature, outlandish garb, and frizzy hair has accepted our bargain for the last polished kryo. We stand within the open threshold to his shop, which is a large metal shack full of items many would pay a great deal for. Intricate foreign rugs sweep across the dirt floor while marble statues flank us.

Aida and Remus are next to me and placing several bags and cases of supplies into the cart behind me. Vivian is across the street from us, using some of our earnings to purchase more rations and clothes. If we spend our kryo earnings right, we'll be able to purchase four repulsorbikes with the rest. My only hope is for Vyck to not scare away every merchant with his haggling.

"Four thousand," the light-skinned merchant says with a heavy northern accent. "You'll find that these gems are not as valuable as they used to be. Over saturation, in a sense."

"Five thousand!" Vyck growls firmly. "Or at least four point five, with a store discount."

"Do I look that desperate to you?" the merchant hisses.

"It'd be an improvement!"

The haggling is getting us nowhere, and my impatience starts to rise. The faster we accomplish our tasks, the quicker it'll be for us to begin uncovering the secrets of the riots.

"Four— Two—" Remus butts in as much as he can. His condition prevents him from speaking properly yet again.

"Four point two?" Vyck exclaims, aghast. "That's not a trade, that's boning theft."

"Information—" he says, ignoring Vyck. "Trade— Info—"

The merchant's bushy eyebrows rise into his matted hair, and his eyes reflect reluctant interest.

"Information." he repeats, stroking the tangled hair on his chin. "I'm not the informative type, unless you know the proper payment."

Remus snorts in wry amusement. "Twenty— Four— Oreings— Spent—" he says quietly, but a grin forms on his mouth.

What does that mean? Twenty-four oreings spent. Then it clicks in my head. It's a code.

Aida, in turn, presses her left index finger to her forehead in a show of some secret gesture. The merchant's face remains neutral, but he nods with approval. He then shows them a tattoo on his left wrist: two black swords crossed in front of a red triangle. I grow wary after realizing what's taking place. The merchant, Remus, and Aida are Insurgents.

The underworld band of liberators has been working to prevent the capital's ruling class from hoarding food and wealth. Noble bandits, as the common folk call them. Insurgents are still invisible to the ruling systems, but seen by those who know how to look. I know from experience that most merchants in Z'hart City's outskirts would be sympathetic to Insurgents. Although I don't dismiss their cause for equality and distribution of wealth, I don't agree with their means.

Riots, bombings, and clandestine works in the underworld have a certain negative connotation. While I still hold Remus and Aida as friends, I instantly grow suspicious of their goals. Are they liberators? Or are they just terrorists?

"I only have so much, frítolö," the merchant says as he puts his index finger on his forehead in a sign of solidarity. "What would you like to know?"

"Embassy— Riots—" Remus says simply, gesturing for Vyck to give the man the gem.

"How did Centum get influence in this city," Aida asks in kind. "They had to know someone high up to pull off that little stunt."

I stand rooted in place. If the Insurgents have qualms with

Centum, then perhaps our interests align. The merchant hands over three bags of oreings to Vyck who begrudgingly accepts them. Taking the payment as his sign to duck out for a moment, he heads towards one of the bike garages.

"Only whispers are circulating," the merchant says quietly, placing the gem into a small box. "Something about rooting out the leader of the Insurgents. Evidently invitations were sent to potential suspects in order to narrow down a selection."

"Did they find him?" Aida asks with apprehension.

The merchant shakes his head. "No, we all received his encrypted messages yesterday regarding our new orders. But it's not who was invited that has gotten our attention. It's who sent the invitations."

"Who?" Remus manages to grunt. He glances back at me and he knows my interest is snared.

"From what I've heard," the merchant looks around surreptitiously, "someone within the Citadel of Z'hart City made that order."

Someone within? I ask myself. *That means Centum might have the ear of a noble, or even the Council itself.*

"That's all I know," the merchant says with unease. "Daniul the blacksmith might know more, frítolös."

Walking us out of his shop, he follows us out into the street as commoners pass by. He gestures further down the avenue towards one of the light columns of smoke.

Remus gives him a slight bow. "My— Thanks—"

"Frítolö," Aida finishes as we all turn away and head to our next target. The Insurgents might be my key to figuring out what exactly Centum is up to.

◆ ◆ ◆

Vivían chooses to go with us as she concludes her business in the shops. Placing the new supplies and four new bowpistols in the repulsorcart, we navigate through the crowds of commoners. It takes only a few minutes, but we soon reach the low-roofed shack that houses a massive furnace and anvil. Heat radiates from within along with the smell of smoke and coal. The pinging of metal and the hissing of steaming water reverberates inside. A metal table laden with a display of crafted items for purchase blocks the entrance to the shop.

Behind the table is a broad man in a tattered, soot smeared apron. His tangled grey beard has bits of ember and charcoal stuck within, and his arms are nearly stained black. In his gloved hands, he polishes a thin dagger that looks esoteric by design.

"Daniul?" Aida asks as we stop in front of the kiosk. His beady eyes glance at us for a moment before snapping back to focus on his craft. Blacksmiths are usually the quiet type, since most of their attention focuses on their abilities. The blade in his hands glimmers like molten silver.

"There's a three-day wait," he grunts, his thick accented voice sounding hoarse. "I've got eight bloody orders left before I can do anything for yeh. Unless yeh want something in stock."

"Not— Buying—" Remus says, drawing a bitter look from Daniul. His round face seems offended by Remus' answer. He doesn't seem to be desperate for work.

"What's wrong with yeh?" the blacksmith mutters. "Speech impediment?"

"Trauma—" he replies simply. Remus ruffles up his dark hair in a nervous habit.

"Right," Daniul snorts, placing the blade on the wooden table. "Well if yer not here to buy anything, what in all the bloody Hells do yeh want?"

Remus tilts his head slightly before repeating the same coded phrase used by members of the Insurgents. Daniul nods his balding head in reverence. However, he seems unnerved by Vivían and me.

"You can trust them," Aida says in response to his skepticism. "Frítolö."

Finger to forehead, she proves her loyalty and seemingly vouches for Vivían and me. Daniul is nonetheless incredulous about this, but I see his shoulders relax somewhat.

"Very well, frítolös," Daniul grunts, placing both hands on the table. "How may I assist yeh?"

We all close in on the table to prevent the wrong ears from listening. "Banquet— Riots—" Remus repeats, scratching at his beard.

"The antiques merchant said you might know about who sent invitations for the banquet," Aida says. She puts her hands on her hips. "Do you know who might've sent them?"

Daniul sniffs. "Well he's wrong. I don't have no idea about the bloody invitations. But, I do have a custom order that was placed by someone within the Citadel."

"What?" I blurt out, trying to keep my voice down. "What was it?"

"I received it about two weeks ago," he says, twirling his tangled beard. "A... representative from the Citadel placed an order for custom darts. Stealth military grade."

"That's a unique order," I comment with unease. I fold my arms with cold inquisitiveness. "What makes yours so special?"

Daniul walks into his shop, retrieves a small box, and returns to place it atop the table. Opening it, he reveals six needle-like darts about two inches long. Their pointed tips are so sharp that they almost seem the width of a hair, and violet feathers poke from the butt-ends.

"Oho hello, little pricks! I'm surprised these aren't illegal," Vivían says in a slightly giddy voice. "How did you manage to file the tips to this level?"

"Trade secret," Daniul says with a bit of pride. He crosses his meaty arms and adopts a bewildered look. "The odd thing was, the order called for seven, but only one of the bloody things was picked up."

"Only one?" Aida asks in alarm. She leans unto the table, hands flat on its surface. "You're telling me the buyer was so confident that they only needed one shot?"

Daniul shrugs his broad shoulders. "I thought it was mad too."

That's when it clicks. Centum acquired only one untraceable dart to deliver whatever toxin had been used on me. These darts are a way for me to prove what happened.

"Can I examine one?" I ask slyly, placing an oreing on the table. "I'm considering purchasing the rest."

"Certainly," Daniul replies pleasantly, handing me one of the darts. He pockets the coin. "I'd also appreciate some referrals as well."

My eyes examine the dart as I start pacing back and forth, my expression arctic yet nonchalant. I gently tap my index finger to its tip and feel nothing. No wonder why I hadn't detected it. The more I look at it, the more I'm filled determination to begin my final search for truth. I only need a few more pieces of this puzzle. *I'm so close!*

My eyes dart up to look at everyone. My heart starts pounding with anxiety as I think about what I need to do.

"Who in all the Hells could pull off that kind of luck?" Vivian inquires curiously with a tinge dread. "One dart for a job is taking a damn solid gamble."

"Viginti—" Remus grunts quietly.

Everyone turns their attention to Remus as he picks up another dart for examination. All their eyes are focused on him. But mine are watchful of the others, even as they grow distant.

After a moment, I'm far away from them and under the cover of a hooded robe. The crowd obscures me even as I back away. My bowpistol and comlink had been set upon the cart as I snuck away. Only the spear accompanies me for protection.

Growing farther apart from them, I also feel my heart slowly becoming more distant. Like it's a small boat far out from shore, visible but untouchable. This will hurt them, my abandoning of their trust and protection. But it hurts me even more having to do it. I value them, but I realize that only my methods will solve this puzzle.

Just as Remus hands a small envelope to the blacksmith, Vivian realizes I'm gone and calls for me. Distress is on her face. Now I fully sneak away, blending in with the crowd and following the winding paths of the streets.

I'm alone now, in this sea of people. Alone and on a mission, even as they still call my name.

"Sarina!"

CHAPTER 23

Sarina

The Puzzle

"YOU SHOULDN'T BE HERE," the older woman says to me as I adjust the cowl covering my head.

She's right, of course.

I know traveling anywhere in the city unrecognized is a fool's gambit, and there's a chance an enemy might've already spotted me. I berate myself for diverting from the group, and I know there will be consequences.

But I need more answers, and the only way I'll figure out the truth is to ask my associates from the city. Living in the lower reaches of Z'hart City helped me get acquainted with a number of informants and spies. So I trust them a lot more than Remus and his spies for the Insurgents.

Shame wells up inside my chest, making it seem like I'm crumbling apart. They are my friends and I should've trusted them to help me. But, this is my battle to fight alone. I need to solve who purchased the illegally modified darts. That can help me prove if this Centum was really behind it all along.

I stand inside the threshold of a small vending kiosk that the old woman owns, where she supplies exotic works of art and pottery. She makes meager earnings, but her products fetch the attention of foreigners and more aristocratic residents of Z'hart City. The kiosk is about twelve meters in diameter and tall enough for the both of us to seek shelter under. Leather strips drape over the metal frame of the entrance. They provide less security than I hoped, but it's conspicuous enough for me.

The cobblestone floor is caked in mud, and the only furniture she possesses are a rusted metal table, antique chairs, and a storage crate. Daylight seeps through the fractured steel roof, and a rectangular service window flanks my right side.

"Well I'm already here so there's no turning back, Rita," I reply before looking out the window at a group of peasant boys running in the street. "But I'll make this quick: what do you know of the embassy riots last week?"

The old woman's wrinkled face contorts in distaste, and her blue eyes reflect a suppressed anger. Despite her age, Rita is one of my best informants in the lower side of the city and she's well known for being able to blend in. Her ragged clothes, her unkempt greying black hair, and her grumpy demeanor usually fails to attract attention.

"This city is now swarming with usurpers and murderers," the old woman growls with a hooded gaze. "These new militia guards patrol our streets, spies are keeping track of everything, and new minerals are being harvested in the depths of the mountain. Some whisper of a foreign organization infiltrating this city."

My face turns grim. "I've already deduced that, Rita. Can you give me a name? A person? Anything."

The elder woman stands from her chair and approaches the kiosk table where antiques are placed in view for purchase.

"Sarina, my dear," she says before shuffling through some of her jumbled belongings. "Whatever this organization is, it doesn't leave much behind—let alone leave names or people. But there was a transmission I intercepted the night of the riots."

Rita pulls out a hololetter chip and hands it to me as another meandering group of boys runs by the window. I take the device and activate it within my palm. Instead of a map, the hololetter displays a short paragraph that's peculiar in both substance and articulation.

Seriously adapt regiment introduction near autumn. Have all soldiers begun entry education? Never forget our unwavering need, Dentum. Interestingly, Wilem insists living lavishly. Everyone needs simple upper regiment education here.

Ensure rituals, eliminate xenophobic insurgents, live eternal.
— Octus

"Baffling is it not?" Rita says after I take a moment to read the transmission. "The vernacular in this message is unlike anything I've ever seen, but there's no doubt that whomever wrote this did not want it falling into the wrong hands."

"What makes you say that?"

"Because it's encoded with a secret message," Rita says, pointing to various letters in the display. "It took some time, but I figured out the coded message in the first letter of each word."

Looking closely, I see Rita's finger point out the hidden message within the message. My eyes widen in apprehension as I read:

Sarina has been found. I will ensure her exile.

"What does this mean?" I ask, my body turning cold with fear. "Ensure my exile? This has to be the person who took me out at the banquet, but it didn't leave an order to kill me. Just to ensure my exile."

Rita gives a worried grunt as she sits in the wooden chair across from me. "It seems like whoever this is or who they work for only intended to capture you. You would be more valuable alive than dead. But exile is a strange word for that. It almost seems like they wanted to get you away from public eye, but also make it seem like you accepted that choice."

I consider it for an instance. "Perhaps they wanted me to feel alone so I'd tag along with anyone who'd show an interest in me."

My fear leads to suspicion. I think about Remus and Aida,

both of whom had been eager to gain my companionship before the crash. Maybe they are the ones behind my abduction and I'd merely played into their game by travelling with them. But then a thought enters my head.

They held no qualms about me returning to Z'hart, I calculate. *Granted, I'm not inside the city, but I'm still back in public eye. If they wanted me to be in exile, they wouldn't have let me come this close to civilization. It can't be them.*

"Maybe," Rita affirms, setting her elbows on the table. "Maybe someone wanted to meet you out there… or maybe you were intended for another destination. Or perhaps exile is just a fancy term for saying that they needed to ensure your capture. Organizations have their own vernacular."

A puzzle piece suddenly clicks into my brain. "The armor worn by the new militia," I say darkly. "Do they have any weird symbols or markings on them?"

"They do," she replies warily, arching an eyebrow at me. She steeples her withering fingers in front of her face.

"An upside down V overtaking a pyramid?"

"That's exactly—" Rita says in astonishment before cutting herself off. "Where else have you seen it?"

I think I'm starting to see every puzzle piece clicking into place. Someone in Z'hart City's Citadel had tasked Centum's Order to weed out members of the Insurgents. With newly armed militia and stealth weapons, they performed a hit on the embassy gala. Then they started sending prisoners to the salvage pits in the Pyrack with

Septem as an escort. However, that doesn't explain two crucial facts.

First, why did Septem have the convoy shot down? If he was ordered to escort us or ensure my exile, why did he disobey that command and leave us? I remember the holoprojection I acquired from the Crimson. Perhaps that may have some more answers.

Second, I'm not a member of the Insurgents. Why did Centum target me? Unless... *No, it's not possible.* They couldn't have found out. There's got to be more to this mystery than I thought.

I look out the window as my thoughts reel. I see the degraded shacks and garages that line the upper streets of the outskirts. The walls guarding the city can be seen over the roofs of the shacks and the early evening sun is shrouded by rain clouds.

"A man named Septem wore the exact same armor, and was seemingly escorting us into the Pyrack," I recount, my eyes narrowing in suspicion. "Though he left us to die, I can imagine he might've been there to escort me to my intended destination."

Rita pauses with a disturbed look on her face. "How did you deduce that?"

"His name wasn't really a name," I say, remembering his smug, gaunt face. "It was his designation. Just like the names on the letter: Octus and Dentum. They seem similar to that form of title."

The older woman touches her chin, and I hear more children running and playing in the street. "This is a dangerous game, Sarina," she says after a moment. "But you need to be more careful than ever if you are to solve it. These people have gone to great lengths to find you and capture you, and it's doubtful they're just going to give up.

You know why you're important to them!"

"What?" I ask in astonishment, my body turning numb with fear.

Rita's eyes stare into mine. She's reading every expression and emotion that runs through me. She's always been a great informant, but I never thought she'd dig into my life.

"Sarina, my dear," Rita says in a hushed voice. Her nervousness is growing along with mine. "I've known for a while what you really are. So don't come asking me why these people have an interest in you. Because you know *exactly* why!"

I stare at her in disbelief, my mouth hangs open slightly. "How did you know?"

The old woman shakes her head, letting the grimy mess hanging over her face. "That's not important, Sarina. And we will solve this new mystery soon enough. But you cannot linger here! Return to your companions and leave Z'hart City as fast as you can."

"But—"

Rita raises a hand to cut me off, and she storms to the window in a fury. Nearly flinging herself out the window, she places both hands on the windowsill and sticks her head out.

"Get out of here you little snakes!" she bellows, flailing her arms at something I can't see. "Go on!"

From over her hunched back, I see the same group of young peasant boys scatter into the street in flight from her wrath.

Not peasants, I realize. *Spies.*

I freeze in utter panic as the boys run off, and Rita whirls from the window with fiery determinism in her eyes. Slamming her hand down, Rita deactivates the hololetter chip and jams it into my hand.

"Flee!" she hisses. "NOW!"

"But what about you?" I protest. My heart is racing in my chest for fear of what might happen to Rita. "Those boys saw you with me. They'll be after you as well!"

"I have my ways, Sarina," she replies with a raised eyebrow. "You know my resources. One last thing: This Order isn't aware of your knowledge, and it has given you an edge. Don't lose it!"

Nearly shoving me out of the kiosk, Rita gives me one last look of reassurance before turning away to fetch something underneath the table. I know better than to disobey her. But I give her a nod of gratitude before I flee into the unknown future ahead.

CHAPTER 24

Sarina

Flight Not Fight

I PRACTICALLY TUMBLE OUT from under the leather door strips and into the dusty street. The long cloak wraps around my frame and drags behind my legs slightly. I'm still unused to the weight of the heavy fabric. So I stumble momentarily and hit a garbage barrel, knocking its contents over. Bystanders gasp and pause as they note the ruckus, and I halt only for a moment to get clear bearings on where I stand.

There is a pause, but only for a moment. A primal fear takes hold of me, and I panic from not knowing where to go. It's like some ethereal force has rooted me on the spot. The world around me is spinning at a pace I can't keep up with.

Inhaling through my nostrils, I breathe. Slowly. I'm trying to focus my attention through the anxiety. I slip the hololetter chip into my boot. Taking off at a brisk pace, I break through the crowd and raise the hood of my robe. My direction shifts towards the lower market areas. Back towards the others—to safety.

I wander around the crowded area for some time. A feeling jangles up my spine, and I can sense that I'm being followed. I try not to seem elusive. Praying to the Sage God, I attempt to sneak into another tattered shack.

"There she is!" someone yells from behind me.

I take a quick glance over my shoulder and see two militia guards brandishing bowrifles and running through the crowd. Even though they are yards away, I can see the blue haze of their barrels as they're set to stun. *Oh shit!* In mid stride they stop and aim their weapons at me. I stumble forward as I break into a sprint. Trampling through the dirt, I feel a light gust fly by my left side—and I see two energy bolts strike the wall of a shack.

Sparks fountain as the stunbolts hit the steel. My heart skips a beat as I hear the *pang* of the blasts. *They're firing at me! Shit, shit, shit!* They must have orders to bring me alive to whoever commands them.

I keep my pace and refuse to look back as bystanders shout and scream because of the weapon discharges. My cloak flaps in the air as I flee down the streets, dodging and weaving as I attempt to lose my pursuers. My boots kick up clouds of dirt.

I try to lose them. A kiosk centered between two shacks is

coming up, and I can see through the booth to the other side of the street. An obstacle for the guards. Leaping over the kiosk's table, I push past the vendor and sprint through his tattered shack. I hear the guards fumble and slam into the table, shouting and cursing. I'm already on the other side of the shack and into an opposing street. More guards see that I'm in flight, and thus pursue with their weapons primed.

As fast as I can, I break through another crowd and enter an alleyway across the street. Despite the cloak, I'm able to leap over piles of trash and containers. At one point, I manage to use my motion to bounce off of a large refuse container. Flying a meter through the air, I land and roll to keep my momentum. Back on two feet, I sprint into another section of the outskirts.

I glance back and see the guards are still on me. I hear bowrifles fire. I swerve to my left and hear the bolts whizz past and hit another metal shack. Sparks shower me.

Anxiety begins to well up within me. My heart is racing even as I push through crowds of onlookers. My breaths are shallow. I attempt to lose the guards again by leaping over a merchant's table, but my cloak snags on its corner.

The metal table is yanked forward and spills all of its contents as I practically flip backwards. *No, no, no!* Despite the merchant's cries of confusion, I slip out of my cloak and reorient myself. The two guards are mere yards away. Ditching the cloak, I choose to worry about escaping rather than my recognition.

Pushing myself from the mess, I retreat from the guards even as they paused briefly. *I think they saw my face.* It doesn't matter, for they still pursue a second later.

The stress is starting to get to me. Not just from the physical activity. My chest feels compressed, my head feels light, and legs ache. I'm barely breathing through the anxiety. But I press on into the street, dodging and weaving through crowds. More bolts whizz by and hit the ground near my feet.

I can see an alley ahead, one that only one person at a time could fit through. *This is my escape! I can lose them in there!* My legs sear in pain as I run towards the alley. Almost there.

Five Imperials on patrol push through the crowd ahead. Noticing the commotion and my flight from the militia, they halt and fan out. They move in front of the alley as the militia behind me cover my flank. *Oh shit!* The bowrifles ahead fire their blue energy even as the Imperials faintly realize whom they've shot at.

Two bolts hit me directly in the chest and a numbing sensation erupts from the impact spots. Electric energy flows through my body and I go rigid. My already racing heart feels like it's going to explode. Air catches in my lungs, and I can't even scream. My limbs jerk uncontrollably, my mouth is left agape, and I feel myself slipping into the cold embrace of unconsciousness.

Before I do, the pain stops and I hazily see the Imperials standing over me. They see my face and I hear one's muffled voice say, "Is that who I think it is? Oh shit! Get a stretcherpod and get her to the suite! She'll want to see her!" With a groan, I black out.

CHAPTER 25

Tálir

Catacombs

A PERSISTENT ECHO is present in the darkness.

It springs from the whistling of a breeze, the sporadic drops of leaking water, and the scurrying of rodents. The perpetual reverberations echo through the narrow tunnels of the sewer systems. The horrid stench of excrement and rotten food hangs in the air. Our boots hit the flooded floors of the hollowed metal tunnel, and the only illumination is the emerald glow of a fiery orb in Abrax's palm. Even the pulsating energy creates a distinctive hum throughout the tunnel. And within those echoes rests the most primal fear a man can feel: the fear of the dark.

We had ventured into the lowest levels of the city through a sewer passage outside the marketplace. Thanks to Abrax's uncanny knowledge of the city, we managed to remain undetected as we ventured forth. I know that his wisdom as a Suzerain provides him with unfathomable insight, but I'm still a bit surprised.

We've both activated our helmets, but we possess no night vision capabilities. So the kryos help illuminate the way. The last we've heard from the others is that Sarina has gone missing. Fear grips me. I know what she's doing.

It took us an hour to find the entrance to this series of sewer lines, then another hour gingerly traversing the tunnels. Occasionally I can hear muffled voices from the surface through the ceiling of the tunnel. It's an eerie feeling. A sensation creeps into my spine telling me that we're not the only ones down here. While the tunnel is compact and narrow, I can still envision possible ambush scenarios. I remain on guard.

We pass by another metal ladder that ascends into the districts above. The emerald light glistens off of the curved walls of the tunnel. The metal is stained and smeared with grime. Reflections can be seen in the water below as well. Our boots sink into the water, causing it to slosh all around. Directly behind me, Devin gives an audible shudder as he pivots to watch our flank.

"Why in all the Hells did we chose this way to get to the catacombs?" he asks in an irritated tone. "Isn't there a better lit, less grimy route we could've taken?"

"The common routes caved in more than five Cycles ago," Abrax sighs, barely looking over his shoulder. "The Order has since believed the catacombs inaccessible, so they no longer bury their dead here. Even the Tome was forgotten over the Cycles. But, all it took was time and research for me to find this route."

A thought enters my mind. "So your old Order knows about this place?" I ask with unease.

Abrax snorts with amusement. "Not in the slightest," he grunts. "I reported my finds to no one. This place has long been forgotten to them."

"If you say so," Devin sighs with a tinge of skepticism. I can see the misgiving on his face. "How much further then?"

"Twenty meters," the old man replies.

Even as he says it, I can see a faint light at the end of the tunnel—and a large chamber beyond. Relief tugs at my stomach. The claustrophobia fades and the air almost feels lighter, despite the stink. As water sloshes against our boots, we trudge through the muck and towards the light. The dark metal of the tunnels gives way to foundations of stone, and the ground is no longer flooded with water.

As we enter the chamber, I notice the source of the pallid light. A shifting orb of golden light hangs in thin air within the domed crest of the room. *A holoprojection!* I think to myself. A very ancient one seemingly kept active over the course of the Cycles. Symbols and abstract images can be seen swirling within the light. I have yet to find the source of the image, however.

My gaze shifts to the chamber itself. The room spans a diameter of forty meters and raises about twelve into the arched ceiling. The entire room is carved out of ancient looking tan bedrock, esoteric symbols and numerals are painted in red across the walls. The colors have faded after the passage of time.

The smooth walls only span a few meters before the massive cubby-like catacombs begin to line the perimeter of the room. Within each open tomb lays the skeletal remains of various men and women. Clearly this chamber is meant for lower class brothers and sisters of the Maven Order. The sight of the dusty, cobweb-covered skeletons causes me to gulp in anxiety. Although they are mere remains, I can still feel as if their presences remain. The black sockets of the skulls stare at various places: the ceiling or walls of their tombs, or outwards to us. Blank smiles are frozen in the skulls.

At the far end of the chamber is a massive slab of burnished ore nearly ten meters in diameter. The dark material is tinted with bright reflections due to the golden light. Runes have been carved into it, adding to its ancient nature.

Underneath the runes are two pale crystals constructed within the ore itself. The size of pears, the white gems sparkle in response to the lights. On the stone floor a few meters away from the slab are two square blocks about a meter in diameter. Protruding only by an inch, it looks like the blocks are meant to serve as a contraption. Possibly to open the door itself.

"This is where I failed last time," Abrax says as he approaches the circular slab of ore. "Two must be present if the door is to open."

I move across the dirt covered floor, my boots crunch against the filaments. I'm still surprised at the spaciousness of the catacombs even though it's meant for lower castes. I stand next to the old man whom begins to recite the inscriptions on the slab.

"The knowledge of two passes into the chamber beyond," Abrax says. Though, it's more by memory than direct translation.

He steps upon the protruding block on the right hand side of the room. Looking back at me, he gestures for me to stand upon the left one. I obey, and take a small step unto the square. With my weight fully on it, I feel it slowly slide into the ground as a metallic click emanates from under us. The unlocking mechanism has started to activate.

Abrax addresses me with determination, "This is the tricky part, Tálir. We have to simultaneously direct a Stream into both crystals imbedded in the ore."

My energy will focus to the left while his focuses to the right. And with the requirement of two distributions of weight, I now realize why he failed last time.

Taking in a deep breath, I nod to Abrax through my helmet before looking directly at the crystal ahead. It's a near flawless gem as I look at it through the HUD. With a kryo already situated in my right gauntlet, I watch as Abrax reloads his with a fresh source of energy. He places the used on in his ammo pouch.

Kryo Charge: 100% says the display in the helmet. Devin stands on my left and watches. *No distractions*, I tell myself. We both point our right-hand fingers at our respective crystals.

"Three. Two. One!"

I focus my energy as much as I can, the HUD indicates a *15%*

output. Bright beams shoot from my fingers and strike the crystal with a light *ping*. After a few seconds, I start seeing the gems gradually turn a faint emerald. Abrax's is rapidly turning into a glowing shard of light while mine barely radiates.

"Come on, lad!" he strains as he focuses his energy. "Give it more juice! It needs to be glowing like mine if the door is to open!"

I growl in strained frustration as I concentrate harder and harder. I can feel veins in my temples throbbing, and my face is flushed. I fixate on the crystal.

19%.

That's it! I keep my eyes on the gem, my gaze burns into it like the energy. *20%.* A haze forms over my field of vision, only the crystal remains. *22%.* I feel beads of sweat forming on my forehead. *25%!*

The crystal starts to pulsate and glow with emerald light, and I can almost hear the energy ringing inside of it. A *hiss* emanates from the slab of ore, and we cease our energy output. I relax and let the blood flow out of my head. I feel dizzy. But Abrax's armored hand pats me on the back in praise. Even Devin smacks me on the left shoulder.

Mechanical snaps and the hissing of old hydraulics resound within the chamber. The immense ore slab shifts backwards, sinking into the wall. After a moment, the slab rolls to the side and rests inside a massive nook in the wall. There's darkness in the room beyond.

"Nothing ventured…" Devin says quietly in astonishment.

I grin from within my helmet. "Nothing gained."

I can barely see the massive chamber lies beyond the great ore gate that had barred entry. Light from our current chamber barely pierces into the darkness. With fresh kryo energy, Abrax generates another fireball in his palm. We enter the chamber.

Within the sage light, I can see that the room seems to be smaller than the last. I see no ceiling, only blackness. Cautiously, we stride further in.

"Ey," Devin says as he wanders a few meters away from us. "There seems to be an activation panel over here. Give me the light."

Abrax follows Devin over to the left side of the chamber. Through the barely lit darkness, I can see a small panel with two switches built into it. Caution snakes through me. It could be a trap. But I'm not fast enough to protest.

Devin immediately activates one of the switches and the area floods with light. Similar to the previous chamber, a holoprojection forms at the top of an arched ceiling. This image is different, however. The blue light forms a symbol that rotates in mid-air: A shield imprinted with a pyramid underneath an eye. *Fascinating.*

I turn to see the entire chamber unveiled by the azure light source. Abrax extinguishes his flame and begins to wander about the new catacomb chamber. Smaller than the last, this room is only about twenty-five meters around. The floor is made of smooth marble, and the walls are sandstone. Along the walls, rows of closed crypts jut out slightly from their resting places. The dark granite used for their construction is glossy and smooth. Seemingly divided into sections, I see labels for *Centums*, *Suzerains*, and *Se'baus* over their respective categories.

At the farthest end of the room is another door. It's is made of solid gold with esoteric markings swirling around similarly to my armor. Words are engraved into the gold, but their dialect is unknown to me. Two small dials are built into the center of the door, and it looks as if something is to be placed within them. Like locks missing keys. This must be the vault for the Tome.

Abrax steps forward in the sapphire light and retracts his helmet. Slowly, he begins mouthing the words as he reads.

"One looks up," he recites. "One hands down. The heart pumps blood. The key unlocks the door."

I pause in confusion, reciting the lines over in my head. "One looks up?" I ask aloud, scratching my head. "It's a riddle… that much is obvious. But which part are we supposed to answer?"

Abrax walks forward and moves his hand over one of the dials. Dust falls from the surface. "Whatever the answer is, it probably needs to be a tangible key for us to put in these dials." The old man looks closer at the contraptions.

"I thought you said you knew what's down here!" Devin protests. He looks utterly stumped by the riddle.

Abrax looks over his shoulder and gives him a frown. "Didn't I just say that I'd only ever been in the first chamber? I don't think anyone has been in this room for almost eight Cycles."

Devin throws his hands up but says nothing. We pace around for what seems like hours. Each of us considers the riddle, and the possible answers. But we can't think of anything. Abrax and I try using our energy again to open it, but that strategy doesn't work a second time. Devin even tries to pick the locking mechanism in the vault's door. Nothing is working.

Pacing around, the riddle repeats over and over in my head. *One looks up, one hands down.* One that looks up could mean anything. However, I consider the riddle more. A person looks up while another hands down. A child and a parent? No that's too easy. A soldier and a general? No...

Perhaps a student and teacher? I ponder the thought. One looks up for knowledge might be a novice or student. The teacher hands down knowledge and experience.

I look around the chamber and see the deliberate separation of the Suzerains and se'baus. Yes, a Suzerain hands down experience and teaching to a se'bau. That part of the riddle makes sense. But the heart and key riddles are still perplexing.

Kneeling next to a tomb marked *Amycus of O'ran: Cycle 3*, I run my hand gently over the burnished stone. For some reason, the stone is all I think about—all I focus on. It's a moment of enchantment as I ponder in thought. My hand feels warm.

A *hiss* suddenly emanates from the tomb and I jerk my hand

away. The dark granite begins to shift away into a pocket above the tomb—revealing what rests within. The skeletal and armor remains of Amycus lies a meter from my face.

"What in the Hells are you doing?" Abrax demands, clearly unnerved by what I've done.

"I didn't do anything!" I protest, my eyes still glued to the corpse. "I just touched the tomb and it magically opened…"

My voice trails off as I see something clutched in the skeleton's hands. Folded over his chest with the palms open, Amycus' hands cup what appears to be a kryo gem. But this one is different. The size of a fingernail, the kryo pulsates with a dark ruby shade.

I stare at the pulsating kryo for a moment as my thoughts reel. While I'm transfixed at the different color, I start to realize that this might be a clue. Amycus had died as a se'bau, and the riddle states that one looks up while one hands down. So perhaps Amycus and his Suzerain are parts of the riddle.

I gently take the tiny kryo from Amycus' tomb and turn to Abrax. "I think this is one of the clues we're looking for," I say.

The old man's eyes widen with curiosity. "The heart pumps blood," he recites as he gestures to the kryo. "The key opens the door."

"The heart of the armor," I deduce with a wide grin. "This is the key."

"One of the keys," Abrax affirms as he examines the kryo in my hand. "The vault requires two of these to open."

"If this one was found in the tomb of a se'bau," I deduce, "perhaps the other lies in a Suzerain's tomb."

I gesture to the tomb of Amycus. "He was a se'bau in Cycle Three," I look over to the Suzerain tombs. "His Suzerain must also be from that time."

Abrax nods his head as we both start to examine each of the tombs and the names engraved. Minutes drag by as we search for a Suzerain of Cycle 3. It almost seems hopeless in this mass of honeycomb-like tombs. But then, I spot something.

Nera of Z'hart: Cycle 3.

Promptly I activate it—and as the tomb opens I see the ancient remains of a Maven woman. Clutched over her heart like Amycus, is another ruby kryo. I sigh with relief.

We have our keys.

Venturing to the end of the chamber, Abrax and I simultaneously place the ruby shards of energy into the dials. They click into place and the dials start rotating slowly. Another great *hiss* springs from the vault's golden door, and mechanical *snaps* echo in the chamber. My heart pounds in my chest. The excitement grips me. I can see Devin and Abrax similarly enthralled by the moment.

The vault's door opens and reveals a nook carved out of the dark ore native to Z'hart. And laden upon a metal pedestal within the nook, is the Tome.

CHAPTER 26

Tálir

Old Friends

A PYRAMID-LIKE DEVICE sits upon the metal pedestal; its sides are hewn from both bronze and gold. Carved into each of its sides are runes encircling the symbol of an eye. The size of an apple, the device sits upon the pedestal—waiting to be claimed over the Cycles. We've found the Tome.

Cautiously, Abrax moves forward to retrieve the Tome from its pedestal. We're both still wary of booby-traps. Yet, the old man meets no resistance as he picks up the device. He holds it in his palm for a long moment, amazed that he's found this legendary item. His eyes almost seem watery for a moment.

"Devin," Abrax says, turning towards us. I retract my helmet to show my delight. "Your bag, please."

Devin takes off his light satchel and hands it over to Abrax. The old man gingerly places the Tome inside the bag before handing it to me. "Guard this at all costs, Tálir," he says with a hint of melodrama.

I give him a nod and sling the satchel over my shoulder as we prepare to leave. As we exit the vault chamber and into the secondary catacombs, all seems well for our excursion.

Something moves within the shadows of the tunnel ahead. I can hear footsteps and the clanking of armor. Even with the entire chamber before us, I can see someone approaching us from within the tunnel. *Have we been followed?* Abrax and I prepare our armor for defensive countermeasures. Devin does the same, drawing his shortsword and dagger. The helmets within our Maven suits are still retracted when a voice echoes from the darkness.

"Impressive, Abrax," the voice says with a cold haughtiness. "Even after all these years, you figured it out. Well done."

The voice is cool, collected, and arrogant. It's as if whoever it is addresses us like we are children caught misbehaving. Then I sense the familiarity of the voice. The tinge of arrogance, the collected vernacular, and the ominous presence. I've heard it before, if only briefly.

There's no way... I think.

Out from the shadowy tunnel, flanked by four Imperial guards, Septem enters the catacombs.

♦ ♦ ♦

"Ey fancy seeing you here, pal!" Devin jeers, clearly restraining the urge to lunge at our visitor. Hatred stains his eyes.

The Imperials flanking Septem stiffen in response to Devin. They raise their bowrifles slightly, but Septem waves them down with a collective gesture. Unlike the guards at the gate, these Imperials don't sport the Maven armor over their arms. They are dressed in the traditional silver armor that covers their torsos, arms, legs, and faces. Violet capes are clipped to their shoulders.

Septem has barely changed since last I saw him, when he leaped out of the convoy before the crash. But I detest him all the more, for he now sports Maven armor as well. While incomplete, his look sort of reminds me of Abrax's. Only his forearms, calves, chest, and shoulders wear the bronze metal. And the dark leather jacket that drapes to his knees matches his curtain-like hair.

I can see his conceited demeanor etched in his posture. "I'm surprised you all survived the Roil that hit after I left," he responds taciturnly. "I can assume Abrax here helped with that. Normally I'd be impressed with such tenacity. But then, a dog has just as much willpower to survive."

Devin takes a threatening step forward, but Abrax holds up an arm to keep him back. The golden light shines brightly between the standoff. If they open fire on us, we have no cover in the empty chamber. Just Abrax's Shield Form. We'll need strategy to get out of here.

I try to keep him talking so I can formulate a plan. "How did you find this place, Septem?" I ask, his green eyes dart to me. "How did you even know we were here?"

His pale face shows no measure of emotion, but he snorts in amusement. "Abrax isn't the only one who's been tirelessly researching about this place," Septem says, taking a step forward. "He passed along a bit of his enthusiasm when he taught me years ago. As for how I knew you were here, well… let's just say that I have a lot of resources in this city. But let's not waste our time with how I found you. How about we focus on what's going to happen next?"

I look and see Abrax regarding Septem with an odd expression. It's a mixture of both pride and disgust, like he's both proud and ashamed. Then it clicks.

"Septem was your last se'bau, Abrax," I conclude with a bit of apprehensive shock. "The one that failed you."

Septem sniffs with revulsion, and I see his eyes narrow slightly. Abrax scratches at his beard and responds, "While Spud here was *one* of the many students I taught, he wasn't my true se'bau. That role was given to someone who was much, much worse than he."

Devin snorts a laugh. "Spud?" he asks, twirling his sword casually.

"He was a late bloomer."

"I can see your time in exile hasn't improved your maturity, old man," Septem says dangerously. He's clearly vexed by the title, but he hides it well. "Perhaps that's why you weren't fit to lead the

Remnant. You prized compassion, and compassion is for those too weak to make the hard choices."

The old man's silver eyebrows rise into his forehead. "Oho. Someone's balls finally dropped," he says in a mocking way. "But that's where you're wrong, Spud. Compassion, loyalty, and friendship are what truly make Maven Knights. You never did adhere to that simple, humbling philosophy."

Septem takes another step into the chamber as the Imperials spread out a bit more. I can now see the sword strapped to his back. His fingers seem to be itching for it. But he refrains. I still cannot find a strategy to escape and I'm starting to swell in resentment. Septem is too hard to read. He shows no emotion, he seems composed, and I'm sure even my speed won't drop him. Dammit.

"All those things you just spoke of are nothing but childish delusions," Septem glowers. "What truly makes a Maven Knight is the ability to do what's necessary. To sacrifice such unnecessary delusions."

"Sounds like someone has never been loved," I point out. Both kryos have been loaded and I feel the power of my suit.

Septem barely acknowledges me. I boil with frustration at his arrogant demeanor. A desire to showcase my power starts to rise in my chest. I want to strike that smug look off of his face. I keep it at bay, barely.

"As much as I love catching up, Abrax, I trust you know why I'm here," Septem says as his hands still twitch for the sword. The Imperials aim their bowrifles at us, and I can see the red hue within the barrels. "You've done a brilliant job of getting the Tome for me. No one else in the Remnant believed me when I wanted to find this place. Fate has an interesting sense of humor. Now, hand it over."

His voice turns dangerous and I hear the metallic *clicks* as the bowrifles prime. The Imperials spread out within the chamber in a classic attempt to flank our sides. Keeping my mind on strategy, I think of a feint we can employ. If we drive towards their center, they'll close ranks in an attempt to box us in. They'll likely focus on Abrax due to his mastery and they won't consider me too much of a threat. If they focus on the queen, the knight and bishop can pick them off. I can use their targeting focus against them. A simple game of chess.

I take a few steps forward, but I don't attack just yet. I want to goad them into a fight. "See that's all well and good, Septem…" I say, bouncing a bit of arrogance back at him. "But finders keepers. And from what I've heard, you're not man enough to back up your words. So why don't *you* back down. Lest I show you what it truly means to be a Maven Knight."

"Don't be a fool, Tálir!" Abrax hisses. I glance back to him and give him a wink, telling him to trust me. I turn back and grin at Septem.

His gaunt face leans back in and icy, nonchalant way. I see his lip faintly curl into a snarl. He's disgusted by my words. Perfect. I've got him hooked.

"You are a child playing with toys, Tálir," Septem sneers, cracking his left knuckle. "It's a shame Romulus couldn't have taught you earlier how to use a Maven's armor. But then, your father always was a spineless little worm."

There's an arctic pause. My patience has run out.

Rage stains my eyes and fuels my impulses. I forget about strategy. My fury guides my actions. Snapping my right arm forward, I unleash scorching tangles of emerald energy that hurl towards Septem's face. I smirk maliciously, not just for realizing my speed at attacking but for seeing the slow reaction time of my opponent. However, he seems unfazed by my attack and merely arches an eyebrow.

Something creeps up in my chest, warning me of my mistake. And I soon find out why.

In a blur, Septem unsheathes the sword strapped to his back and slashes it through the air—practically batting my energy away. His blade suddenly erupts crimson flames as it repels my attack in a shower of sparks. As the sparks fade, he twirls the sword and the magic flames continue to envelope the blade. *He's using ruby kryos!* With my mouth agape, I finally note the strange design of his weapon. The hilt and scabbard are made of the same bronze metal as our armor, and I can see hints of esoteric wiring and chambers in its design.

His sword has been forged with Maven technology. Capable of harnessing kryo magic just like our suits did. A legendary relic.

Alright, I think with mild trepidation. *That's new.*

"Dammit, Tálir!" Abrax shouts in disappointment. He immediately activates his helmet, generates a Shield, and rushes in front of me. "You thundering dumbass!"

His Shield forms like a large umbrella before us, covering both Devin and me. Bowrifle fire soon hails from the four Imperials; the red energy bolts whiz towards us. I snap out of my hate-filled trance, realizing the mistake I'd made. The guards have us pinned even as Septem charges forward. The queen moves while the knights and bishops cover. He played me just like I had tried to play him. *Sly bastard!*

Swinging his sword down like an axe, Septem bashes the fiery blade against Abrax's Shield. I can almost see the energy field crack from the impact. Abrax winces as he tries to focus. I'm stunned at the power Septem has at his disposal. He bashes against the Shield again and it cracks even further.

I struggle to think of a strategy. Abrax's Shield cannot hold back the bowrifle fire and Septem's sword for much longer. Septem's face is still eerily collected even as he swings his blade. But I see something behind him. Two of the Imperials are letting their rifles cool down. I look at Devin and he knows my plan.

As Septem prepares for another blow, Devin and I both roll out from under the Shield's protection. My helmet forms around my face. I channel a *25%* charge and fire a Stream upon one of the Imperials. Devin simultaneously throws one of his daggers. Both soldiers are caught unawares by the surprise counterattack. The Stream blasts the guard nearest to me backwards into the stone wall while a dagger slices into the jugular of the other.

Abrax's Shield crumbles. I blast another Stream at Septem as

Devin tackles the old man to the ground, escaping the fire of energy bolts. My magic causes Septem to block it with his blade, taking a few steps back. Emerald and ruby sparks fountain.

Focusing as much as I can, I fling myself between the Imperials and my companions. Bending my right arm at ninety degrees, I focus on one singular thought: a Shield. A gasp escapes me as a *30%* output suddenly generates a thin Shield between me and the Imperials. Their bowrifle bolts pound against my energy, but only for a moment.

Their rifles soon overheat—and they curse even as we act upon their weakness. My Shield crumbles like a pane of glass. Devin tosses another dagger into the throat of an Imperial as Abrax unleashes a Stream powerful enough to knock out the final guard. The odds are back in our favor. I smirk with sadistic delight. My animal instincts have taken over in the heat of battle.

Septem still blocks the exit. He flourishes his blazing sword with haughtiness. Widening his stance, Septem seems like he's ready to take on all three of us. He's that sure of himself? There's only one way to find out.

Abrax and I both start to unleash Stream attacks as Devin charges in with his sword held high. Using the sword, Septem fiercely blocks every surge of energy we send his way. A crimson Shield forms upon his left wrist as Devin closes in. I'm staggered. Septem uses the Shield to parry our magic while implementing his sword to block Devin.

Septem parries a few blows from Devin before using the

Shield to bash him away. My dark haired companion is flung meters away; ruby energy sears his breastplate. I feel so much lesser seeing the power demonstrated by a foe. Not only do I learn about different shades of kryos, but the enhanced power they give to just one man. He's holding the three of us at bay like it's nothing.

20% output. My Stream attacks are useless—even Abrax's energy cannot pierce the ruby Shield. My HUD reads *Output Charge: 5%*, so I quickly reload two fresh kryos into my gauntlets. But Septem uses this delay against me.

Dissipating his Shield, he blasts Abrax away with magic emanating from his palm. In the same motion, he twirls his sword and swings it like a bat towards me. A ruby wave of magic catches me in the chest and I'm flung backwards.

With a *crunch*, I smack against the rock wall—my vision falters from the impact. A burning sensation emanates from my chest and I can smell roasting metal.

Muffled shouts are drowned out by the ringing in my ears. Spots appear in my vision. I try to move. Yet, my limbs barely move. *There's no way!* My armor seems to be locked in certain areas, making my movements sluggish. I struggle to stand, but end up falling forward to the ground. Septem had used magic to lock up my armor.

This can't be happening, I think in a panic. *This is pathetic!*

Tilting my head up, I can see through my visor that Septem is approaching me. Ruby fire swirls around the blade as he flourishes it. I close my eyes, preparing for the pain. For the darkness of death. We can't beat him. We've lost.

Something explodes. My eyes snap open and I see emerald fire in the spot where Septem had been. I scan the room and find that he's been blasted into the far side away from the exit. Practically wedged in, Septem struggles to free himself from being imbedded in the stone wall. Abrax walks into my view and sends another Stream at Septem. Energy pours from both of his hands—pummeling our opponent for continuous seconds.

Devin rushes over to me and hoists me up from the ground, his legs falter under my weight. Abrax assists him after a moment. Limping away, I see Abrax unleash a final Stream attack to push Septem deeper into the wall. Stone crumbles around him as he's pinned and stunned. Yet, we still retreat.

"Why are we leaving him?" I protest as we enter the dark tunnels. My arms are around both of their shoulders as my body hangs limp. "Let's kill him while we have the chance!"

"No," Abrax says firmly, retracting his helmet. There is a deep pain in his voice that echoes in the tunnels. "We need to go! More Imperials are likely coming. While he may be a bastard, I owe him mercy. As an old friend."

CHAPTER 27

Sarina

The Lady of the Silver Palm

MY EYES SNAP OPEN. I wake suddenly to find myself comfortably sprawled on a pristine couch near the edge of a large, oval-shaped room. Stately and elegant, the curved walls are painted with shades of violet and silver. Multicolored carpets line the floors, their designs foreign and abstract. More lavish couches and chairs line the perimeter and twin chestnut doors close over the exit. A silver armored Imperial is perched by the door in a nonthreatening way. My collapsed spear rests on a table near him. It isn't a prison cell as I'd expected. The guards have placed me here for care rather than imprisonment. I'm not sure which one is worse.

Sitting up, I note an elongated antique table and chairs situated in the center of the room. Various foods and drinks are laden upon the table, and the smell of roasted beef fills my nostrils. The Imperial notices my activity but does nothing, merely nodding through his helm. A faint breeze touches my neck. I turn and see a veranda that opens to show the city several stories below us. Night has fallen and a rain storm has kicked up.

I know exactly where I am. *The Citadel,* I say to myself as apprehension crawls in my chest. *The estate tower of House Z'hart.*

The Imperial activates a comlink on his wrist. His voice is quiet, but I can hear him say, "She's awake if you wish to see her."

Someone is waiting to see me. My mind instantly jumps to Centum. If Centum has indeed infiltrated the Citadel, then perhaps their Order wanted me alive. I'm still afraid of the implications. I need to escape.

Before I can think about it further, the doors swing open and a figure rushes into the chamber. The lone figure is a young woman. Gowned in an indigo, silk gown and decorative pauldrons, she walks with dignified grace. Her long, dark hair is in a ceremonial bun. Eagerness tugs at her peach-colored face.

She rushes over without any warning. Excited relief is in her blue eyes. I attempt to stand, but she nearly tackles me with a hug. She's overjoyed. I'm unsure how to respond at the moment, for I'm in a bit of shock. Releasing me, she takes a step back and clasps her hands in excitement.

"Sarina!" she says with a smile. Her eyes are rimmed with

tears. "My dear sister! Welcome home."

"Sahari," I say quietly, trying to suppress my nostalgic feelings. "You're looking well. Aside from the fact that it also looks like you've been enjoying our stores of O'ranian wine."

Sahari lets loose a chuckle. She certainly has missed my droll humor. "Well, as the Lady of Z'hart, I should be allowed to enjoy the perks that come with my position," she says sweetly, brushing loose hair out of her eyes. "But now that you've returned, you should be the one to enjoy all of this privilege."

"I never really wanted to," I reply dryly, pursing my lips. "Too much politics. And I've never liked the taste of wine. I prefer keeping a clear mind."

Sahari smiles and gestures for me to join her at the table. I reluctantly ready myself and follow her. We sit opposite each other. Unease is still trapped within my stomach, even after seeing my sister. I should feel safe, welcome. Yet, I feel the jadedness of what's happened since last we saw each other. It's been a long year.

"I suppose my mind does get a little silly after drinking," Sahari says, pouring herself a goblet of wine. "But I did turn sixteen last week, so by Z'hart's standards I'm an adult. But don't you think it's a bit ironic that you don't like wine, and yet, you chose to work in a bar?"

I laugh faintly. "I suppose it was, but it was more about the service than my wellbeing," I retort before my tone turns sly. "Did father not teach you the same lesson before he died? Nothing is inherited, only earned."

Sahari looks a bit concerned at my reference. "He didn't tell me anything, really," she says rather indifferently. "You are the firstborn, so the pressure and lessons fell unto you. That pressure only found its way to me when you disappeared last year. Part of me understands why you chose to leave. When father died…"

"Don't presume to understand why I left, Sahari," I reply rather coldly. She looks a bit frightened by my response and I regret being so taciturn with her. Letting my aggression fade a bit, I take a few bites from the roast placed in front of me. It's been so long since I've tasted broiled meat spiced with garnishes.

Sahari relaxes somewhat and sips more of her wine. Her thin fingers wrap delicately around the goblet. She's always been a gentle soul, even if a bit ditsy. But fear starts to writhe within me.

"Sahari," I say after a moment. "How exactly did you find me?"

"I've been searching for you since the day you left," Sahari replies, taking a sip of wine and regarding me a genuine look. "My resources were limited since I wasn't of age to take the throne, so I had to rely on word of mouth. But despite all my searching, only my new associates were able to find you. And within only a week after I sought them out!"

There it is. My dread starts to become more and more tangible.

But I need her to keep talking. I have to finish the puzzle.

"I guess you're not as clever as you say you are, Sahari." I say with a grin. "It took you a year to find me while I was in the same city." My tone turns serious. "Who might these *associates* of yours be?"

She lowers the goblet and gives me a look of cautious concern. "That's what you want to ask me after all this time? Come on, Sarina. Let's catch up like normal sisters. We can deal with other political matters later on."

"Sahari," I say darkly, my voice uncompromising. "Who are they?"

"They're called the Remnant," she replies aloofly, waving her hand as if to brush it off. "Not many are aware, but the Remnant has existed as a secret society for the last millennium. Old family records instructed me on how to summon them and they said they'd help find you as well as eradicate the Insurgent terrorists in this city. I figured it wasn't that big of a deal allowing military access to help stabilize this city."

I look into her blue eyes. While she wears the guise of regent, I still see the foolish child she's always been. Acting impulsively and without thinking of consequences. A family trait of ours, but I've always thought I'd been the more skeptical child. She let her desperation to find me cloud her judgment.

"You're already a foolish ruler of Z'hart, Sahari," I say, pressing my hands to the table. "You've compromised our nation's security and infrastructure just to find me. These people have their own agenda and you played right into it! Don't you see that?"

Sahari looks appalled by my answer. "They just wanted all access to old Domain artifacts and technology," Sahari defends, her tone becoming irritated. "But look what they gave us! Extra militia to bring peace, a reduction in Insurgent activity, and returning the firstborn heiress of House Z'hart home!"

"Being kidnapped and shipped off to the Pyrack is a funny way of bringing me home," I hiss, my temper rising. "Or did your new friends forget to mention that?"

Sahari's eyes express true shock before she adopts a look of grave concern. "Wait what? You were shipped off to the Pyrack? When? Centum said they'd only managed to locate you a few hours ago!"

I gulp in unease. If what Sahari is saying was true, the Remnant still holds her ear. Centum can whisper any lies into my sister's ear. That means that they hold enough of her trust to feed her any information and gain whatever favors they want. I begin to think of the dangerous implications of this. Centum holds the keys to Z'hart's infrastructure. Political favors, dictating laws, distributing money, strengthening our army… Centum nearly has control of this entire nation because of Sahari's foolishness. Militia guards who aren't native to the nation are a dangerous proposition, for their loyalty isn't to the Lady of the Silver Palm.

I think a coup is almost upon us. Upon my naïve little sister. Sahari has bargained with the entire nation to find me, but at what cost? There's no safe endgame for her if she placed her rule in the hands of the Remnant.

The puzzle has formed. With Sahari's trust, the Remnant was able to increase military activity and begin campaigns against Insurgents. Centum took me out of the picture when no one realized

I still resided in Z'hart City. If I had been discovered, the people would've had me elected and Centum's influence could've faded. Now, they're formulating a way to take the capital from Sahari. They must have wanted me alive and under watch in the Pyrack as an insurance policy.

Yet, why did they send me out there? Why not keep me imprisoned here? There's still something here that doesn't make sense.

"Sahari!" I exclaim, leaning forward. The Imperial guard twitches nervously. "Please listen to me. You mustn't trust any of what these people have to say. They found me last week at the embassy gala. I was drugged and shipped off to the Pyrack while they used the riots to weed out Insurgents. They had forged invitations sent from the Citadel, commissioned illegal toxic darts, and issued coded commands to capture me!"

Sahari's lips part in confusion. Although she's sincere, I can see misgiving on her face. I'm not sure if she fully believes me. "That's a... lengthy accusation. Why would they do this? Their Order believes in the preservation of order and peace."

I hear thunder outside. "I don't know what their final goal is," I say. "But they've got enough influence in this city to stage a coup, Sahari. They could take this city and you'd have no power to stop them. You—"

Her hand raises to cut me off. The misgiving on her face has deepened. Sahari says nothing for a long moment, her expression conveying an array of complex emotions as she struggles with what to believe. She's always very emotionally expressive while I choose to be more reserved, a way of balancing each other out. She was raised with little to no restriction while I was brought up to be a responsible ruling Lady. That is a part of myself I've never accepted. I want freedom, but evidently Sahari wants responsibility. An ironic reversal that I'd never thought possible.

"My coronation was a little over a week ago, Sarina," she says in a very calculating manner. Her compassion has faded. "If I'm to establish any credibility as the Lady of the Silver Palm, I have to uphold political bargains I have struck. Even if there is something dubious about them. Politically, they've placed themselves in favor of the Council—and I can't just back out of this deal. They could retract all of what they have done. Still, I won't ignore your story, Sarina. Centum will be summoned here to answer your allegations."

No! I can't risk Centum discovering what I've learned. They'll kill us all if we directly interfere with their plans.

"You can't be serious," I protest. I can feel beads of sweat on my forehead. "Sahari, you mustn't—"

"Enough!" Sahari interrupts with a stern voice. "Sarina, I want to believe you. Truly, I do. But you've been through a lot these last few hours. Stunbolts can have nasty side effects. Even if your story is true, I have to consider the political ramifications first. Despite what you think, father did teach me one thing: A ruler never goes back on their word."

She addresses the Imperial who stands near the door. "Inform the Remnant that I request Centum's presence immediately.

I also wish for a doctor to see to my sister's health."

"No," I say flatly, causing the Imperial to halt in mild confusion. "Centum mustn't find out what I know. Not until we figure out what their end plan is. I have to leave."

Sahari's azure eyes shine with defeated disappointment, and she lets out a soft sigh. I know my story must seem a bit manic. Especially considering the circumstances of my discovery. Yet in this instance, Sahari is electing to act like a ruler should. Perhaps my words about being a foolish leader sank in. But this is not when I need her to be a wise ruler. She can be wise when it comes to solving the predicament Centum has placed her in. Right now, I need her to be a *sister*.

However, I cannot risk being captured by Centum again. My awareness of their conspiracy mustn't be discovered until we have a solution to deal with them. Sahari's life will be at stake if my knowledge is unveiled. So it is my job to protect her as I continue my efforts to bring Centum to justice.

"I've tried to play nice here, Sarina." Sahari says suddenly in a dangerous voice. "I have your best interests at heart, but I suppose tough love is the only way to get through to you." She sternly addresses the Imperial. "You will escort Lady Sarina to the healing rooms. I will seek out Centum and we shall join you there shortly."

That's my cue to leave.

He takes a step in my direction. I'm already on my feet and positioning myself behind my chair. I duck behind the wooden seat just as the guard instinctively fires his bowrifle. The stunblot smacks against the back of the chair with a *thud*. My makeshift shield works.

With my adrenaline fueling me, I twist around and fling the chair at the guard with all my might before sprinting to the doorway. A loud *smack* and a grunt of pain indicate the chair has made its mark. I snatch up my spear from the table as I pass. A meter from the door, Sahari attempts to stand and stall my exit but is too slow. I shove her back into her seat.

As fast as I can, I retrieve the hololetter from my boot and cram it into her hand. "First letter of each word," I say in a rush. "If they still hunt me, they have no insurance if they kill you. Stay safe, solve this conspiracy. I love you."

Before she can react, I flash her a look of genuine compassion—a way of saying farewell. Then, I make a break for it. Nearly crashing through the doors and into the stone-carved corridors of the estate's tower. I find the exit stairway and start running down.

The staircase is very spacious; the dark rock that's been carved out is painted a variety of shades to provide diversity. Torches and lamps line the walls to provide a fiery light in the spiraling staircase. My boots trample unto each step as I race down, hearing distinct shouts from above. It takes several minutes to descend the tower, but when I reach the antechamber connecting the tower to the Citadel, I know exactly where to go.

As I begin my retreat, I remind myself of my mission. To flee and have Centum's forces hunt me for as long as I can. The Remnant needs me, so their efforts will focus on *me*. That will keep Sahari safe.

At least, I hope it does.

CHAPTER 28

Sarina

The Citadel

I CAN HEAR THE CITADEL begin to bustle with activity as shouts from Imperials and rushing footsteps reverberate in every hallway. I start to guess which exits they are going to start quarantining: the atriums, the dungeons, the sewers, and even the throne room.

Quite obviously, I'm familiar with the Citadel and the various lockdown procedures that the guards implement. For once, I feel like I'm ahead of the curve. No longer waiting for help. No longer unsure of what to do. Still, our welcome in Z'hart City has worn out and I need to regroup with the others. I will need them in the missions to come.

If my suspicions are correct, the guards are going to section off the escape routes they think I'll take. So the sewers are out of my initial plan.

But the unlikely escape locations will be unguarded. Such as their own barracks. An emergency shaft leads through the mountain, connecting the barracks to the city itself. Easy for the Imperials to respond to crises. I'm not entirely sure if the barracks will be empty. However, I'm certain the majority of the Imperial guards are on their way to secure the dungeons. Most common break-ins or break-outs involve the sewers and lower regions of the Citadel, so I plan to make an unorthodox escape.

Cautiously navigating through the wide, carpeted corridors of the estate of Z'hart, I make my way closer to the inner sanctum that separates the various estates. The left side walls are lined with towering windows that show the night sky shrouded in a rain storm. Lightning flashes illuminate the halls. Portraits and art line the right side, depicting historical events or past lords and ladies of the various houses.

Taking a right at an intersection in the hallway, I sneak several meters down the corridor that connects to the inner sanctum on the left side and the barracks on the right. Minutes later, I approach the massive entrance to the barracks—the oak doors have been left open by the rush of guards.

Furtively, I enter and note the burnished cobblestone floors and the angular architecture of the complex. The first rooms in the complex are merely filled with desks, lockers, and crates for supplies and items. Entering a cross-shaped room, I note the empty weapon racks and lockers and deduce I'm in the armory. My grip tightens around my collapsed spear. I press onward.

Following the corridors within the barracks, I enter the primary training grounds. The circular center chamber is nearly fifty meters in diameter and nearly just as tall. Targets, straw dummies, weighted objects, and obstacles litter the grounds. Unlike the cobblestone floors of the inner rooms, the training center is covered in mud, soil, and patches of grass. Imported, of course, but nonetheless a pleasant contrast to the bleak grayness of the chamber.

A rack of wooden training bokkens is situated on the far side of the room. While lacking lethality, the bokken training swords are used for effective sparring sessions. A few training bowrifles and bo staffs are also situated upon racks in the chamber.

I move further into the combat arena and finally find the emergency access tunnel. Nearly twelve meters in diameter, the tunnel has already been opened. The passageway snakes from the mountain all the way to the Merchant District, so my escape will be nicely streamlined. I move towards the door.

"Halt right there!" someone calls from behind me.

I turn to see an Imperial standing a few meters from me; a bowrifle is clenched in hand and pointing at me. But his sloppy stance and the slight quivering of the bowrifle tells me that something is off about him. Looking closely, I realize that the guard is a young man. Likely in his early twenties, he has a slender frame and silver Imperial armor that seems oversized on him. Shaggy blonde hair can be seen under his helmet and his clean shaven face peeks out from under the facial mask.

This has to be a new recruit. Likely commissioned by the guild recently to add to the Citadel's security. And it's clear that he has been left behind to do grunt work in the barracks.

I realize there might still be a way to escape without drawing too much attention. Maybe I can play on his hesitancy, even convince him to let me go.

"Don't move!" he says, his voice strong but lacking certainty. "You're the fugitive, Lady Sarina, aren't you?"

"That's perceptive of you," I reply, remaining still but keeping the spear tight in my hand. "What's this about?"

"It's not my job to ask questions, My Lady," he says sternly, taking a step forward. "Lady Sahari's advisor Centum wishes for you to be escorted back to the estate, so I need you to come quietly. Lady Sahari has only recently informed the Citadel of your escape."

I suppress a grin. *She's already starting to play the game*, I think to myself. Sahari is letting Centum focus all attention to recapturing me.

"Do you think I'm a fugitive?" I ask him as he starts to approach. Metal restrainers are clenched in one of his hands.

"It's not my job to ask questions," he says. His tone is less stern. "The fact that you're fleeing from our custody seems to point that you might be a tad guilty. But that's a bit above my pay grade."

"Ah, it's above your pay grade," I say rather disgustedly. "What if I said I need to leave the Citadel? It's a mission to keep the current Lady of Z'hart safe. Is it above your pay grade to obey an heiress of Z'hart?"

"All the Hells, is this what every arrest is going to be like?" he sighs to himself. "Of all the people I get—"

I see his posture relax and I take that as an opportunity. Adrenaline starts fueling my motions and my mind relaxes as my body takes over. In a blur, I extend my spear and use the butt-end to knock the bowrifle from his hands. He lets out a surprised grunt as I follow up by sweeping the metal shaft behind his legs. The Imperial falls flat on his back. Spinning the spear in my hands, I stand above him with the spear tip pointed at his throat. Apprehensively, he raises his hands in a gesture of surrender.

"Did I happen to mention I'm terrible at this job?" he comments with a nervous laugh.

"Clearly," I say lightly, but keeping an intense look and a firm hand. "I'd have thought the regiment would've knocked you into shape."

"I thought so too," he replies. His mouth forms an innocent smile. "I guess they're in the mindset of quantity over quality."

"What's your name?" I ask, keeping the spear firmly pointed at him.

"Marek," he replies nervously. "You're not going to kill me, are you?"

I regard him quizzically. "What kind of heiress kills her own guards?" I retort gesturing to the spear. "But I'll have you know this: I'm letting you go because I need you to protect my sister. I believe a coup is rising and that her new advisor is behind it."

A frown forms on his mouth. I can feel his misgiving even though I can't see his full face. "So you think that by sparing me I'll believe you?" he asks dryly. "It's not nearly as simple as—"

With a loud *crack*, I smack the metal shaft across his head and his words catch in his mouth. His body goes limp and his mouth falls open as he's knocked out.

"Perhaps not," I say to his unconscious body. "But maybe it might make you rethink this arrest."

I collapse my spear and tuck it under my belt. Kneeling, I pick up his bowrifle and prime the weapon for stunning countermeasures. Hurriedly, I move towards the passageway at the back of the room.

It takes nearly half an hour, but it's easy to navigate the pathways that lead into the Merchant District. Hollowed into the side of the mountain, the access tunnel connects right into an abandoned building in the third alley ring of the district. I have to admit, it's a crafty way for the Imperials to stealthily get to the city without going through Citadel checkpoints.

Warily making my way through the building, I see no indication of Imperials so I head for the nearest alleyway. Rain soaks me within seconds. Lightning flashes and thunder rolls. Blue light from holoprojections above illuminates the darkness of the alley. Trash, dung piles, and rodent carcasses litter the cobblestone alley between the abandoned building and an apartment complex. It reeks of decadence.

With the bowrifle at the ready, I start a light sprint into the alley. Like running into a waterfall, the rain pummels against my hair and face. After several meters, the path forks and branches off into more alleys between various buildings. Navigating through the maze, I make my way down through the third ring of the district and enter the second.

It's down another long alleyway that I hear shouts and the clanking of armor from the adjacent backstreet. While separated by the structure, I can hear a few individuals hurrying towards an intersection ahead of me. Strangely though, the voices seem familiar.

Hurrying down the alley, I approach the intersection guardedly before looking around the corner at the source. Devin, Abrax, and Tálir are rushing through the alleyway, covered in smudge and grime. A burned slash goes across Tálir's chest and his helmet hasn't retracted. By his sluggish state and seeing Abrax aid him, I surmise that his armor has been disabled. But by what?

"Of all the days to take a kryo hit, this was the worst, Tálir!" Abrax yells as he's seemingly helping Tálir jog through the pathway.

"I thought I had him," he says timidly in response. His voice echoes mechanically from under the helmet.

Relieved to see them, I step out from behind the wall and into their alley. Practically skidding to a halt, the three react defensively.

"SHIT!" Devin shouts in alarm. But upon seeing me, he's

quick to compose himself. "Oh, it's just you, m'lady."

Tálir's helmeted head cocks to one side. "What in the Hells are you doing here, Sarina?" Tálir asks angrily, but with a tinge of concern.

"Long story," I reply simply. I rest the bowrifle on my shoulder and size them up. "You guys look like you've seen better days."

"Less talk, more running!" Abrax grunts in apprehension. Though tough as nails, he's also wary of pursuit. "We need to get to the gates before they—"

"There they are!" someone shouts down the alley behind them.

Four Imperial guards are rushing towards us nearly twenty meters away. Their bowrifles are brandished and ready to fire as they sprint—their boots making a clanking sound in the alley. Two more enter from an intersection to join the quartet. They all pause within fifteen meters and aim their rifles at us. I can tell they've spotted me, so I begin to back away in apprehension.

"Take Lady Sarina into protective custody!" one of the Imperials shouts. "Do what you will with the others."

The words seem to echo within the alley. Rain pours from the gutters above us. *There goes my cover.*

Tálir and Devin give me quick dumbfounded looks as we all break into a sprint away from the guards. Abrax uses his magic to shield us from a hail of bolts as we retreat.

"Lady Sarina?" Tálir repeats in bewilderment.

I look at him through his helmet visor and see the astonishment in his eyes. "Like I said," I huff as we exit the alley into the market square. "It's a long story."

CHAPTER 29

Tálir

Lockdown

LADY SARINA! I try to convince myself. *Sarina is a royal of Z'hart.*

"Follow me!" Sarina shouts, leaping over some storage crates with ease. "I know a way for us to bypass the gates."

My armor is still in a state of sluggishness after Septem's attack, but it no longer slows me as I run through the streets of Z'hart. After encountering Sarina in the back alley, we hastily made our way back to the outer quarter of the city. The six Imperials are hot on our tail though, likely drawn by Sarina's escape from the Citadel. We could've fought them, but we'd lose our chance at escape. The capital is being locked down even as we speak and more Imperials are flocking to the chase. Centum is aware of our presence.

Following Abrax and Sarina, I leap over the same crates as Devin follows behind me. We dodge through the small crowds, weaving and shoving our way to the gates. The wind has picked up and is blowing curtains of rain into our faces. My visor is shrouded with droplets. Stunbolts whiz past us and hit the metal of surrounding buildings. Devin ducks his head as he runs.

I turn slightly as I run, attempting to unleash a Stream at the assailants. However, merely a flash of sparks erupts from my fingertips and I can feel the suit struggling to channel the energy. How's it possible for the ruby kryo blast to cripple my armor for so long?

Sarina, now alongside me, wheels around and quickly fires a few shots from her bowrifle. She doesn't check to see if they make their mark, but I hear a *thud* and a shout of pain seconds later. Weaving around and over various repulsorcarts, crates, and vending tables, we break through the merchant quarter and come upon the colossal gates of the city.

The massive ore doors have been tightly closed in response to our flight. Looking back, I see a small battalion of Imperials charging after us. Nearly twenty of them. I start to panic. How are we going to escape? Sarina, however, doesn't stop her pace and instead darts past the rest of us.

"Follow me!" she says determinedly.

We obey, and she leads us in quick flight along the perimeter of the wall as the guards atop attempt to aim at us. I glance up in apprehension and see rain and stunbolts precipitating from above.

They fire blindly at us as Abrax generates a domed Shield above us like an umbrella—vaporizing the bolts.

After running for several long minutes, Sarina halts in front of a protruding stone slab in the side of the fortification. Practically slamming her fist into it, the slab retracts and a small, stone door slides open. A passage is carved through the wall.

"Ey, how'd you know it'd do that?" Devin calls as he rushes into the tunnel.

"Being a royal earns you some escape secrets," she replies simply.

No one presses the matter as we hastily go through the escape tunnel and exit on the opposite side of the wall. Keeping us shielded, Abrax waits for Sarina to close the tunnel to prevent the Imperials from following. Bowrifle bolts hail from atop the wall as we abscond into the outskirts. Commoners flee around us. Sprinting as hard as I can, we enter the market square of the outskirts and manage to find cover from the surrounding shacks. However, we still aren't fast enough.

A patrol of six militia soldiers spread out in formation to block us from going further down the street. We halt abruptly as the guards ready their bowrifles. Sarina and I turn around to see three more approach us from behind. With the shacks flanking us, we have no escape.

Abrax reloads his gauntlets and generates balls of green fire within his palms. "Let us pass," he says simply, his voice flat and threatening.

"Oh of course, be my guest," one of them scoffs sardonically. "You fooled us once, former Suzerain, but not twice. Now stand down."

"I don't want to hurt you," Abrax says as he steps forward. The guards aim their weapons.

"Sarina," I whisper, leaning towards her slightly. "How long will it take for the rest of the Imperials to get here?"

She looks at me from the corner of her eye. Her rifle is aimed at the three guards on our flank. "Seven, maybe eight minutes," she replies quietly before refocusing on the Imperials. "Depends on how motivated they are to find someone."

"Even with Abrax," I say nervously. "I doubt we'd be able to take them all on without getting hit by a bolt. We could really use a distraction right about now."

In conjunction with my words, one of the guards is struck with an energy arrow and flung backwards. The other two guards jump in response and falter for a second—but it's all we need.

A stunbolt from Sarina's bowrifle strikes another one of the militia guards—sending him into a spasm. As fast as I can, I focus my energy to *19%* and manage to send a tangle of energy from my right hand. The Stream catches the last guard in the stomach and flings him backwards into a wooden crate. A relieved huff escapes me. *Power's back!*

Wheeling around, I see several things happening at once. Abrax has generated a larger discus Shield to block an incoming salvo of bowrifle bolts. Devin prepares to fling anther dagger. I hear the whine of a repulsor engine as I see Vyck, Aida, and Remus practically crash into the militia with their repulsorbikes. The shark-looking bike smashes into three of them. Those left standing divert their attention to their new assailants and prepare to fire a volley at them.

Abrax takes the opportunity to dissipate the Shield and unleash various blasts of energy that fell two more of the guards. The three knocked over by Vyck's bike slowly rise and start firing, not even paying attention to their weapon modes. Blue and red bolts fly in all directions. In a panic, I generate a flimsy Shield to block those heading my way. Bolts pound against the Shield as I strain to focus. My heart stops as I see a red bolt speeding towards Sarina.

I'm still too sluggish to intercept the bolt, but I try nonetheless. Through the energy, I see Devin push Sarina to the ground as the red bolt grazes the right side of his face. Sparks fly and I see the flesh cauterize over his right eye. He yelps in pain and falls to the ground. I can see Vyck fighting furiously to come to the aid of his friend. Energy still whizzes in the air as Remus and Aida dispatch two more guards.

My Shield is weak but I stand to guard Sarina and Devin as Vyck rushes towards us. Abrax reloads his gauntlets. The last guard takes advantage of this.

Aiming swiftly, he fires two lethal bowrifle shots directly at Abrax. The bolts pierce directly through his breastplate covering the right side of his ribcage. I hear the energy sear flesh and bone as he gasps for breath and falls to one knee.

My heart stops for a split second, and I feel a cold sensation of dread as my Shield crumbles.

"ABRAX!" I shout, rushing to his side as I hear another energy arrow strike the final guard.

Still on one knee and his head bowed low, I hear him struggling to breathe as he clutches the cauterized armor. Despite the heat of the energy, blood still dribbles from under his palm.

"This is not how I expected today to go," he grunts through clenched teeth.

His breaths are rapid. I place my hand on his back and kneel down next to him. A wet cough escapes him. His armored hand presses against the wound, trying to prevent blood from leaking.

I look up and see Vivían clambering down from a rooftop some thirty meters away while Remus and Aida rush to our aid. Pulling out some healing cream and a vial of painkiller, Aida attends to Abrax quickly. Vyck is at Devin's side and starts examining his friend's injury. Remus helps me lift Abrax to his feet, frightened concern on his face.

"I hope these bikes are in good shape to make a quick escape!" I call over to Vyck.

"No, we've just spent nearly five grand on some boning rust buckets!" he shouts back as he helps Devin to his feet. "Of course they're ready for that!"

"Make haste!" I hear Vivían call urgently. "We need to get out of here!"

Nearly half a kilometer away, I can see the gates to the city open. Clanking armor echoes within the streets. The Imperials are hot on our tail. We've got maybe four minutes before they're upon us. I can feel my heart pumping with apprehension.

In our current state, there's no way we can fight off anymore pursuers. We have to leave now.

While sluggish, I help carry Abrax a few yards to where the repuslorbikes had crashed into the militia. Three meters long, the slender bikes hover a meter off the ground. Two directional steering vanes protrude from the front half a meter on two outriggers. Finlike flaps protrude from their rears. The leather seats are designed to hold two. Four bikes and exactly two to ride on each.

Everyone begins clambering unto their bikes as Vyck attaches our repulsorcart to the back of his. Vyck, Aida, Vivían, and I elect to drive while the others sit passenger. The old man strains and sits upon the passenger seat of my bike.

"Abrax," I say with distress as I mount the bike. "Are you going to be ok?"

He shoots me an insulted look. "It's going to take more than a few bowrifle bolts to keep me from getting to Providence."

I give him a respectful nod. He's got a lot of fight left in him despite being shot. Relief tugs at me, but only for a moment. Even as we board our bikes, I see a small squad of Imperials rushing down the street. They're about a hundred meters from us. We're out of time.

Everyone's heads snap towards the source of the Imperials. Our repulsorbikes whine as the engines power up. The Imperials are in range. Some stop and take aim.

"Let's get the fragging Hells out of here!" Vyck exclaims, jerking the handlebar on his bike. The bike rotates in place before zipping off towards the outer perimeter of the outskirts.

He doesn't need to tell me twice.

We all accelerate and twist our bikes around towards the exit of the outskirts. Rain pummels against my face as we speed away from the Imperials. Blue stunbolts zip past us as the first wave of Imperials fire upon us. My heart is pounding in my chest.

The metal shacks are a blur as we race through the main street of the outskirts. Commoners scream and dodge out of the way. The bowrifle fire has ceased. Our repulsorbikes break free of the structures and into the open plains surrounding the capital. Lightning splits through the cloudy sky. Our bikes veer east and our current speed puts us nearly a kilometer away within a few minutes. Water dribbles from the metal hulls of the bikes as we pierce through the storm.

While I'm sure the Imperials are mobilizing to pursue us with their own vehicles, I get a feeling it won't be anytime soon. Only a small squad had spotted us, and it'll take time for their superiors to mobilize a hunt. By then, we'll have some measure of distance on them.

But in light of recent news, I fear that the Imperials aren't the only problems we'll need to deal with. Our quest has just begun, but there's an overshadowing issue that needs to be addressed.

PART THREE:

Unity

CHAPTER 30

Sarina

Oasis

OUR BIKES ARE STILL GOING after riding through the night
and away from danger. The storm has subsided, but thin clouds still
obscure the early morning light. The sand kicked up by the engines
sends clouds of filaments into the air behind us, practically masking
our escape from those far away.

The sun is barely over the clouded horizon when we finally
pause to let the engines cool. Our bikes are parked around a small
oasis—the small sanctuary is bordered by a few palm trees and
smooth boulders. The freshwater pond at the center is barely twenty
meters in diameter, but it's enough to quench our thirsts. The more
natural resources we find, the longer our supplies will last.

I fill my container to the brim and casually rest near the shore of the pond next to a palm tree. My hair is still damp and matted because of the rain. My spear and bowpistol are strapped to the saddle of the bike. Yet, I feel like I should still cling to them in preparation for another attack.

We rest for what seems like an hour and everyone is silent— either due to shock or frustration, I can't tell. Devin's injuries have been treated and he's recovering swiftly. A gauze patch covers his right eye. Abrax is still incapacitated from the bowrifle bolts, but his condition is being treated by Aida. Despite the wounds being cauterized and cleaned, Aida took charge of ensuring his hydration and properly healing the burns. I'm relieved to see that he's going to be alright.

No one had died due to my mistakes. And that raised a new level of comfort in me. Abrax had warned me about secrets having a cost, but thankfully the cost hadn't been someone's life. Being a fugitive from my own home isn't a terrible penance. Still, I get the feeling that my actions will have some harsher ramifications sooner or later. I can only hope that the others don't have to pay it.

But now, I owe the others a lot for saving my skin during the escape. That feeling of gratitude begins to shake off some of the misgivings I've had about the group. Trust begins to return through the vines of skepticism. And I feel like they deserve to know why I did what I did.

I owe them answers. Why I hid my identity and why I had been abducted in the first place. Shame and fear had prevented me from telling them my heritage before now. All because I've never fully accepted my role in Z'hart City. I've always been unsure about having that kind of power in the first place. More to the point, I'm afraid of that power and what it might do to myself and those around me. I don't want people to see me as a divine figure who holds absolute authority—I just want to be seen as a regular person. Responsibility is something I've always ran from and it stirs a great shame in me.

I've felt the gravity of my inheritance weighing down on me ever since I was a girl—and I hate it. I loathe it. I want nothing more than to escape that crushing destiny and forge my own. But perhaps that's why I had been afraid to tell them the truth. Because I'm afraid of myself.

Breaking me out of my thoughts, Devin approaches and looks down at me as I remain seated. His expression is neutral, but there's an icy feeling emanating from him—and his good eye reflects some measure of restrained anger.

"Ey," he says rather plainly. "You're not too shaken up about all that excitement are you, your highness?"

I regard him quizzically before saying, "I'm doing better." I rotate to face him, still unsure what he's playing at. "It's not every day you find out that you've been set up as a pawn in someone's plot to overthrow a nation. Or that your own sister is in grave danger for wanting to find you. But I think I'll be alright."

"Good. Good." he replies neutrally, scratching his head. "Then I don't feel too bad about this."

In a blur of motion, Devin slams his fist into the tree behind me and curses at the top of his lungs. His large, muscular form towers over me as I shrink in sudden fear. With his fist still against the tree, he bears down on me as if to keep me trapped. Devin wants me to realize that he's not messing around. And I believe him.

"What the fragging Hells are you doing?" Vivían shouts as she scrambles to get up—the rest of the group follows suite.

"So let's get something strait, *m'lady*," Devin growls, his mouth twisting into a snarl under his goatee. "I think you owe us some fragging answers for the shit that just happened back there! We almost died! And for what? What the Hells are you involved with?"

Before I can get in another word, energy suddenly strikes him in his side. He's flung a few meters from me as I recoil—sand spewing everywhere. My head snaps to see Tálir standing with his hand outstretched—steam billowing from his fingertips. The look in his eyes is protective and dangerous.

"Back off, Devin!" he calls defensively. "Pick on someone your own size."

Oh no, I say to myself. *This is going to get messy.*

Before I can even react, I see Devin spring to his feet. A feral look is on his face and he snarls before charging at Tálir. "Put the toys away and let's see how great a fighter you really are, pussy!"

Tálir's eyes narrow to slits as he charges as well. Everyone is in pause, unsure what to do. The two men collide with an impact that nearly dents their armor. Devin is heavier than Tálir and his weight allows him to successfully tackle his opponent. Sand kicks up as they wrestle for control on the ground. Devin lands a punch to Tálir's left eye, bruising it.

Growling like an animal, Tálir elbows Devin in the jaw and causes him to falter back. A punch to the nose follows up his attack. Blood seeps from Devin's nostrils. He tackles Tálir again, but this time Devin pins his arms. Two punches are delivered to Tálir's face. Another follows. Devin won't stop. His good eye is filled with rage and I fear he might beat Tálir to death.

"Stop!" I scream, rushing in to interfere.

Devin gets in one more punch to Tálir's face before another magic blast hits him in the chest. But it didn't emanate from Tálir. I look and see Abrax weakly hobbling over to us, his right arm is wrapped in a sling. Likely to prevent him from using his right side muscles too much.

"ENOUGH!" he shouts as Tálir arises and prepares to lunge at Devin.

Using his left hand, he fires another burst of energy at his own student. The magic hits Tálir in the back and drives him into the sand face first. Both men have been stunned. Everyone is silent.

Devin arises to one knee, clearly shaking off the effects of the magic blast. "We have been travelling with the missing heiress of Z'hart," he says weakly. "Doesn't anyone else find it alarming that she never told us? Now look! She's on the run again from Imperials and they'll be looking for her tirelessly! She's put us all in danger!"

"This quest was already dangerous, you big dumb idiot!" I say aggressively. "You can't entirely blame me for that. With the convoy, the Roil, and all else—we've already been running from peril."

Vyck walks over to aid his partner. "Sarina, he has a point," Vyck says warily, giving me a look of mistrust. "That's a pretty big secret to keep from your companions. We were all convicts, sure. But whatever you're mixed up in is way above all of our heads."

Vivían steps close to me. Protectiveness is in her violet eyes. "Sarina didn't know who to trust!" she says. "She was smart not to reveal her identity to total strangers!"

I can feel the division forming. The group is beginning to fracture. My thoughts fracture as I try to convey why I did what I did. From the beginning, never directly asked me about my past so I merely lied by omission. However, I know they all deserve answers.

"Sarina doesn't have to justify herself to you, Devin," Tálir growls as he rises to one knee. The skin around his left eye is purple and bruised. "As a princess, I'm sure she had a noble reason for keeping her secret."

"I don't need you to speak for me, Tálir," I say perhaps more coldly than I intended. "You don't know anything about me." His hazel eyes meet mine and I can see some sense of shameful scorn from him.

I'll always value his support, but right now it is my duty to come forth. Not his. So I stand firm and bury my remorse for calling him out. His gaze lowers and I can feel his disheartened consternation.

"I am Sarina of House Z'hart," I say definitively, keeping my head held high. "I am the firstborn daughter of Shiko, the last Lord of the Silver Palm, and the heiress to his throne. As you can all guess, I ran from my responsibilities as the future ruler in favor of freedom. Not exactly a noble reason. But I was happy. I flourished in the bowels of the capital before I was abducted during those riots. I learned that Centum wanted me in captivity as an insurance policy as the Remnant begins their coup for the throne."

"So when you abandoned us…" Aida says with hidden misgiving. "You chose to seek out the answers on your own? Why not let us help you?"

Abrax gives me a look of disappointment. I can hear his words echo. *You'll only find pain and anger.* He was right. I found nothing but more darkness unfolding upon reaching my answers. I still don't have the full story. But I will not back down. I can't.

"Because this was my battle to fight," I say defiantly, stepping forward. I'm at the center, surrounded by them. I pivot to look at each of them.

"It wasn't your battle," I continue. "So I took it upon myself to fight it alone. You all didn't owe me anything."

Remus adopts a concerned look but remains silent. Aida speaks for him, "We wanted to know about what happened that night just as much as you!" She reflects vexation and her dark eyes seem outraged. "The Remnant didn't just target you! All of us were captured that night!"

Vyck nods his head and affirms, "Imperials took us in just for defending ourselves. Sure, we were dangerously lethal. But they attacked us first just because we were in the vicinity."

To my surprise, even Vivían agrees with them. "They arrested me for trying to help some kids flee the carnage. I hate to admit it, but they're right. You weren't the only one they unjustly took that night."

But her attitude still remains protective of me as she addresses Abrax. "What do you think, old man?"

Abrax stares at me weakly before saying, "I already had a feeling who Sarina was. Therefore, I'm not too cut up about it. She had ample reason for concealing her identity."

"What?" the others say simultaneously. I'm not entirely surprised; Abrax always seemed to treat me differently than the others.

"How in all the Hells did you figure that out about her?" Tálir demands angrily. "And why didn't you tell us?"

Abrax shrugs his good shoulder. "I'm old and I know things," he says gruffly. "Her posture, her bearing, the news of her first disappearance over a year ago… Things started to add up. You all were just too oblivious to catch it. As for why I didn't share, it wasn't my place to tell you of her identity. It was her responsibility."

"That still doesn't excuse her from seeking out answers on her own," Aida demands, her fists clenched. "We *all* deserve to know why we were captured! Remus and I were at that gala too!"

"Wait, if you were running from your title as Z'hart's heiress," Vivían points out, "why did you attend a party full of nobles?"

Blushing from indignation and embarrassment, I reply, "The

public only saw me on rare occasions. Since I was mainly brewing ale behind the bar, I hoped no one would recognize me."

"That's stupid," Vivían comments. "What kind of person would —"

"Act recklessly?" Aida points out.

Tálir scoffs as he fumes with animosity while I see Devin scowl. Everything seems as if it's ripping apart. I can feel an emptiness starting to form in my stomach. Not because they are wrong, but because they're right. My actions have been selfish and stupid. I should've realized we all had been affected by the riots. Even Tálir had been a casualty. But what they don't understand is that *I* had been the true causality. The linchpin for the events. All because I had been irresponsible. So I had felt it was *my* job alone to undo the damage I'd caused.

"The only difference is…" I say as my frustration starts to rise. "The Remnant started all of this because of me. If I hadn't been on the run, none of you would've been victims of the riots. It's my fault, so I need to be the one to fix it! None of you are royalty, so you cannot understand where I'm coming from!"

Their eyes stare into my soul. No one says anything and I feel a chill run down my spine. I can see the resentment in their eyes. Swearing under my breath, I realize I shouldn't have elevated myself with that declaration. It makes it seem like they're beneath me even though they're not. I feel hollow, like my words are rotting me from the core.

"Ah yes," Devin sneers; his eye reflects betrayal. "Because

how could we, a simple band of outlaws, ever be considered in the same breath as the heiress of Z'hart. Pardon me, your highness. We're mere peasants beneath your gaze."

"That's not what I—"

"Save it, Sarina," Devin interrupts coldly. "We may be just commoners to you. But we at least tried to help you. We tried to be equals."

Vyck says nothing as he stands next to Devin. Vivían's face reflects worry even as Vyck gives her a sympathetic shrug.

"I knew it was fragging stupid to go on this quest," Devin continues, turning his back to me. "Well… You can count us out. We're done."

The pair begins to walk off into the distance. My chest feels heavy; the sense of loss is starting to spread more. Everyone else also begins to depart silently. Vivían and Remus are the only ones to offer some measure of comfort. They give me looks of understanding, but say nothing.

Tálir's look is the one that makes me feel truly empty. After everything I'd said, he looks at me with a measure of dark defeat— like I've shattered a piece of his heart. Perhaps I did, inadvertently. He stands and says nothing, electing to wander off like the others. Only Abrax remains.

I turn to face him as he leans against the palm tree. His face is haggard and tired. "It's like I said, Sarina," he comments rather dryly. "You'd only find pain and anger if you chose this path."

Indignation boils inside of me. I give him a hooded gaze, my eyes piercing into his. "You of all people should understand why I did this," I hiss quietly. "The high supreme Maven master. I figured you'd understand the sacrifice I was trying to make!"

Abrax's face scrunches as he leans away from the tree and starts limping back to his cot. "Did you sacrifice for them?" he asks cryptically. "Or where you sacrificing for yourself?"

CHAPTER 31

Sarina

A Part of You

THRUST. THRUST. JAB. SWIPE. *Parry. Jab. Swipe. Parry.*

Sweat drips down my face as I pivot and move, swigging and jabbing my spear at unseen enemies. The morning is still early, but it's humid and warm—likely attributed to the nearby oases. Silver clouds obscure the sun. It has been a while since I've been alone, not surrounded by anyone. It's relaxing in a sense, to collect my thoughts as I train.

Thrust. Jab. Swipe. Flourish. Thrust. Parry.

Along the sandy bank of an oasis, I take dance-like steps along its perimeter as I practice. Dunes of pale sand rise along my flanks and a small swamp lies nearly a kilometer to the east. Flies swarm around me even as I continue to move.

I kick up sand as I continue to pivot and my arms begin to grow tired. Some of the others are napping after riding all night. I've chosen to remain awake and train with the spear. It's my weapon of choice after all, so I have elected to master its use. Besides, my last few fights hadn't gone exactly swimmingly. Far from our campsite, I train to become comfortable with the spear's weight and length. Only garbed in a sleeveless tunic, short pants, and boots, I press my routine be without concern of cleanliness.

Thrust. Thrust. Parry. Swipe. Flourish. Spin. Jab. Thrust.

I can still hear Abrax's words echo in my mind. Had I sacrificed for selfish reasons back in Z'hart City? Perhaps he had been right. My motives were purely based around finding answers to *my* problems, not the group's. Shame contorts the features in my face as I make an emotional thrust forward.

All this time, I thought I had been trying to protect the group by fighting alone. But in reality, I had only been concerned with myself. They wanted to be there with me, to solve this alongside me. But my lack of trust and irresponsibility got the better of me. What a shocker.

"You're holding the spear incorrectly," someone says from behind me.

My head snaps around in alarm. Abrax is sitting meters away along the shore of the oasis. He's stripped of his armor and only wears a loose tunic and tattered pants. Using his good arm, he starts to gingerly soak a rag before scrubbing parts of his skin. While initially surprised, I realize I shouldn't be shocked that he knew exactly where to find me. I don't reply for a moment, turning away to continue my routine.

"I doesn't take a genius to know how to hold a spear, Abrax," I reply as I thrust. "I just have a sloppy form, that's all."

"Your sloppiness is a symptom of not holding the spear correctly," he responds critically. "I'm not talking about hand placement. I'm referring to the way you're treating the weapon."

I thrust the spear angrily in front of myself before turning to face him. "And how exactly am I treating it?" I ask in frustration.

His dark face regards me enquiringly. "You're using it like a weapon," he recites calmly. "When you need to use it as an extension of your own body. Let your body move with it. Treat it as an extension of your arms… and allow your body flow with it. Your weapon needs heart, which is what the wielder must provide."

My eyebrows raise in surprise. There's some sense to his words. I almost feel the cold detachment of the spear even as I grip it. While I don't want to prove Abrax right about something again, I'm nonetheless curious to see if his tips hold merit.

Relaxing my grip slightly, I spread my legs farther apart to prepare my stance. Breathing precisely, I imagine the spear being an extension of my arms—a deadly third appendage. With a quick pivot, I thrust the spear forward with a precise force behind it. Almost like the weapon is full of energy. It feels natural, almost easy as I start my exercises again.

A surge of adrenaline kicks in. And with another pivot, I

flourish the spear and throw it like a javelin. With a crunch, the spear strikes the stalk of a palm tree nearly ten meters away—the shaft wobbling as it pierces into the bark.

A slow clap emanates from Abrax. "Not bad," he comments. "Not bad at all."

"It was a lucky shot, Abrax," I reply with a bit of shock. "There's no way I'd be able to pick up that little trick just like that."

"Give yourself some credit," he says with a huff. "You looked less like a belligerent drunkard. But yes, you're right. It'll take much more time and effort to be proficiently good at that skill. But I've got the feeling you'll have plenty of time to practice on this little quest of ours."

"If there even is a quest," I mutter, remembering that Devin wants to leave.

Wiping some sweat from my face, I walk over to the tree and start to wrench my spear from the trunk. The damn thing is imbedded pretty well.

"What do you want, Abrax?" I strain, tugging the spear. "I can only assume you're up to something."

"One: that's an absurd assumption," he says sardonically. "Two: I was actually just coming to wash a little bit. Had no idea you were over here."

I pause and wait, but he says nothing more. *Odd.* "No three?" I ask in surprise. "You're always quick to point out three things, old man. It's kind of what you're known for."

"I'm stumped on a number three, Sarina," he snorts, wiping

off dirt flecked over his forearms. "However, I can guess that you're still upset about earlier."

"I'm not upset!" I snap, finally heaving the spear from the trunk. "I'm just pissed off that no one understands my reasons for being secretive. And for acting independent."

I take a few steps back and collapse the spear. Turning, I face the old man squarely as he sits next to the glimmering pool of water. Grey light from the clouds shimmers off of its surface. He splashes the cool water on his bearded face.

"Sarina, think of a wolf that leaves its pack," Abrax says. His eyes track the sloshing water. "It's dangerous enough on its own to hunt and kill. Large enough to fend off enemies its own size. It may even be successful at remaining as the lone hunter for a time. But, say that wolf needs to fend off a bear in order to eat. The wolf is alone, outmatched, and desperate. The bear is stronger, larger, and used to hunting alone. Do you think the lone wolf could survive?"

I snort in derision. *Always the cryptic.* I kneel along the bank of the oasis and splash some water into my face as I consider his metaphor. No, the lone wolf couldn't survive against the bear alone. But what Abrax misconstrued is that the wolf is smart enough *not* to fight the bear.

"The wolf wouldn't fight the bear," I say after a moment. My eyes fixate on the water. "It would bide its time. Have patience. And wait for an opening to get food."

The old man snorts as he dips his long, silver hair into the water. A small cube of soap is in his hands as he cleans out the tangled mess.

"Only if the wolf isn't desperate."

I regard him stonily; my anger is still present. "What's your point, old man?"

Abrax pauses before rising from the shore. His silver hair is matted and dripping with water. "My point is," he says as he faces me squarely. "Wolves hunt in packs for a reason. Individually they can only accomplish so much. But together, if the pack is strong, they can triumph over anything. Even if one believes it's better suited being alone."

I look at him askance. "We're not wolves, Abrax," I say, tracing my fingers over the spear. "We came together out of necessity, not by being raised together. How was I supposed to trust them when we'd barely known each other for two weeks?"

Abrax scratches his beard. His voice is gravelly when he says, "Sometimes you just have to have faith."

I snort. "It's hard to have faith in anyone when you've been victimized by a city you trusted," I reply harshly. "It was my city. My home. And yet, I still wasn't safe from danger. How can someone have faith when the world is full of so much darkness?"

The old man remains still and looks off into the water. His expression reflects hollow loss. "I know more about losing faith in this world than you think," he says finally, his tone somber. "After seeing your own students and peers turn on you, steal everything you created, and destroy all that you love—it's difficult to have faith in anything. The Sage God isn't going to be happy with me when I keel over."

I run my fingers through my hair and look at the ground. I don't want to meet his gaze. "So you know why I had problems with trusting them," I say. "The fear that the moment you open up; you'll just get hurt all over again. And if someone is dragged down with me next time, I'd never be able to forgive myself. So in answer to your question: Yes, I did sacrifice for myself. But it was a self-sacrifice. I went alone to protect them, because they didn't deserve to be dragged down with me."

Wind whistles by as the old man approaches me. He says nothing, but his eyes are full of something I thought I'd never see. Understanding. He places his good hand upon my shoulder. Despite everything that had happened, everything that had been said, he shows me compassion. It's unconditional, like a true friend.

"If you really do care about them, then you know what you need to do," Abrax says with a look that seems reassuring. "Even if you're unsure, they deserve your trust. For they have given you theirs."

"I'll try. But, I doubt all of this will get fixed overnight," I say, looking away from him.

"Neither does mastering a spear," the old man says. A silver eyebrow cocks in amusement.

CHAPTER 32

Sarina

Re-Earning Trust

I FIND DEVIN AND VYCK TOGETHER, as usual. Sometimes I wonder if they're actually inseparable twins. One seemingly doesn't exist without the other, and sometimes they seem more than brothers. Like a bickering old married couple. It's a kind of adorable.

They're performing some repairs on a repulsorbike. Oil stains and grease are smeared across their gloves, forearms, and shirts. Dressed down from their armor, they seem surprisingly relaxed and aloof. Tools spot the ground and an oasis bastion lies a few meters from them. Some supply packs and armor containers are next to the bike. They really are going to leave.

Clouds are in the sky and I can feel another rain storm is

coming. I approach the pair from behind; Devin is practically underneath one of the bikes. A metallic clicking and snapping sound emanates from underneath.

"Looks like the turbine fan needs to be tightened," he says to Vyck. "Hand me the twenty-two socket."

Vyck does so, but he sees me out of the corner of his eye. His face is neutral, but I can see faint hints of mistrust in his green eyes. Sand and grease are caked in his blonde hair.

"We've got company," he says quietly. He smacks Devin on the leg.

Devin practically hits his head when coming up from underneath the bike. His dark hair and goatee are similarly disheveled by the repairs. The bandage covering his right eye has brown oil stains on it. His left eye finds me, and I can see the coldness of his detachment. It's an icy anger he holds against me. In many ways, it makes me feel guiltier for ignoring his deeds. But it's better than a fiery one.

"Hey," I say. My voice is nervous, but my resolve holds.

Vyck looks from Devin to me with unease. Clearly he's not as angry about the situation as his partner, but he's just as wary.

"What do you want?" Devin asks, his voice taciturn. I can hear the notes of resentment buried in the context. He sits up, but doesn't look me in the eye—electing to focus on the bike repairs.

"What are you doing?" I ask, eyeing their bags and equipment.

"Like I said, we have no desire to stick around," Devin says gruffly. "This little group of ours has fractured thanks to you. I don't want to journey with people who don't trust one another."

Vyck looks at me and adds, "We just need to prep the bike for a long haul."

Our squabble had had more of an effect than I thought. I have to show them I mean to give them trust. Surprisingly, I don't want to lose them.

"How's the bike looking?" I ask Devin, trying to remain calmly neutral. I don't want to cut right to the chase just yet. Hopefully my interest will rouse him.

"Looks like a bike," he says shortly. I hear the clicking of a socket wrench.

My impatience starts to rise. I glower. "Really? How obvious, pretty sure I could've deduced that. Not that difficult."

The tension is like a wall of ice between us, cold and solid. Picking at it isn't going to cause it to fade, so it needs to be melted.

Devin stands and turns to face me. "Ey, congratulations. You can figure out sarcasm. Too bad you can't figure out how to properly appreciate sacrifices people make for you." He spits in the sand.

My hand clenches around my collapsed spear, and I give him a hooded glare. I feel a burning heat rising from my stomach, and I almost shout in anger. Not because he's wrong, but because he's right.

I didn't appreciate the fact that he took a bolt for me. Or the fact that Tálir defended me from Devin's wrath. I hadn't even appreciated that some of the others didn't care about my identity. It's only because I lied about it that they grew upset. They merely wanted for me to trust them. Their loyalty is valuable beyond measure, and I deserve to repay it. And the shame builds within the anger, like a mixing of chemicals.

"You're right," I say as my body shakes with both irritation and indignity. "I haven't shown adequate appreciation for you not completely acting like a dick. But a week ago you barely wanted anything to do with us. So why do you care now?"

Devin opens his mouth as if to say something but stops. He looks away; his lower jaw protrudes a little bit as his irritation shows even more. His shoulders are tense, and I can detect a faint sense emotional frustration. Wait…

Vyck pipes up before I can consider it further. "Sarina, give us a little bit of credit. We're not complete douches all of the time. We chose to trust everyone when we decided to join this quest, but you didn't."

Devin looks back at me, his eye still reflecting malice. "In comparison to the future ruler of Z'hart, how could we ever be considered in her notice? We're just mercenaries out for treasure. What does our loyalty matter? I can see how that can be beneath a royal."

His words hurt, yet I can see they're sprung from bitter immaturity. Devin is upset that I haven't flaunted myself to him for taking the bolt to his face. Normally I'd find it repulsive and juvenile. But the bandage covering his eye does remind me of the sacrifice he made. His willingness to trust me.

Still, I have to approach this tactfully. So I fight it back. "Devin, one decent deed doesn't completely make up for the amount of time you've been an asshole," I say as my temper recedes. "However, you are right. I haven't shown you true appreciation for getting that pretty face of yours all banged up."

I snort playfully. Devin is taken aback slightly. Even Vyck adopts a look of surprise.

"I don't have much to offer you, seeing as I'm an exiled heiress," I continue, folding my arms over my chest. I need to assert both compassion and authority. "But, we need you on this quest. If you leave now, you risk running into Outlanders or Imperial forces. I'm asking you to stay."

Vyck looks off into the distance, and I know he's waiting on his partner's response. Rarely did he act before his friend. Devin's arctic look relinquishes slightly, but he remains stubborn.

"Give us one good reason to stay," Devin says harshly. His emotions are in check, but I can still sense his pain.

I look at both of them before turning away a bit. "I don't have any one reason for you to stay," I say calmly. "But know that, after everything that's happened… I'm sorry. For lying and not trusting any of you. Know that if you stay, you all will have my undivided trust. It's not much, but it's all I can offer you."

I say nothing more as I leave them to their repairs. The offer must be left to sink in. It's now up to them to leave or stay. My first show of trust.

I find the pair at the far end of our campsite; the swamp overlooks them in the distance. Vivian walks by as I approach, and I place a hand upon her slender shoulder as I pass. Our eyes lock, and she sees the gratitude within my eyes. Vivian smiles and nods before continuing on. Aida has just given Remus a dose of sedatives before she starts inventorying her supplies. I don't think they're about to abandon the group, but I know they have deep misgivings. All because of my inability to confide in them.

Aida glances at me as I approach, and I can still see some scrupulousness in her dark eyes. I'm relieved that she's not as angry as Devin was about my decisions, but I still want to win her trust back. After all, she had been one of the first people to show me compassion in the convoy.

"Aida," I say, not wishing to stall like I did with Devin. She knows why I'm here. "I cannot fully regret what I did back in Z'hart City. My incursion allowed me to glimpse what's really going on involving all of us. I have to believe there was some benefit in what I did."

Aida arches an eyebrow and Remus looks puzzled. Though befuddled, Aida responds, "That's... not exactly an optimal apology for—"

I hold up a finger. "However," I continue. "You were right. I should've involved you and the others. I should've trusted you all and your willingness to help. I can't take back what I did, but perhaps there's something I can do now to show you my trust."

From within my pocket, I pull out the tiny holoprojector and letter I acquired days ago in the Flames. In the days that've passed, I nearly forgot all about it. I took it because of its link to the Remnant, and the possibility of connecting to the riots. I can't remember why I hadn't viewed it earlier, but perhaps because I subconsciously knew I'd need it later. Fate has a funny way of guiding us.

Stunned for a moment, Aida stands with a cautious look upon her face. Approaching her, I extend my hand and offer her the device and letter. Taking them, she hesitates for a moment.

"What are these?" she asks, examining the items.

"I pulled them off the body of one of the Crimsons," I explain. "The pouch they were inside bore the insignia of the Remnant. So he must've been delivering these to someone associated with them."

Opening the letter, Aida's eyes fly over the parchment she unfolds. After a moment, she says, "All this says is: 'Leir'tah, open discretely.'"

She flips the paper around and shows me the insignia of the Remnant sealed where a signature might be. So this message was being delivered *from* the Remnant. But to whom? What is a Leir'tah? Aida activates the holoprojector and a three-dimensional image of a man generates above the chip. The holoprojection is shrouded though, the body and face of the person is concealed by shadowy blue.

"The Remnant is unaware of this transmission, Leir'tah," the garbled

voice emanates from the image. A filter is used to disguise whoever sent this. *"By now you've realized my attempts to unite the Outland clans under my name. Many have risen to join my cause, for they see the coming darkness spread by Centum. The Crimsons have not. Your emissaries gave me your answer to my request to join the unification. You are unwise to oppose me, fearless Leri'tah. Rest assured, if you continue to resist us, we will destroy your clan. This is your last chance to join us."*

The transmission ends abruptly and the figure fades. I scratch my head in confusion. Aida and Remus are silent, but their faces are astonished at this new puzzle piece. Aida replays the message.

What is going on? Whoever sent this is no friend of the Remnant, yet they intended for it to remain in secret. The Remnant is unaware of the dealings this person has been doing. It even seems like this person wants to stop Centum's plan from coming to fruition. But there are still so many questions. Uniting the Outlanders, stopping Centum's darkness, and the Crimsons failing to yield. I see there's much more conflict brewing than I originally thought.

Aida examines the image one last time before deactivating it. She puts a finger to her chin in thought before saying, "Every time we think we're close to finding the answer, some new wildcard gets thrown our way."

"Wildcard—" Remus grunts in amusement. I think he likes the use of the word. "Outlander— Army—"

I cross my arms and consider his statement. The message did mention something about uniting the Outland clans. But I've never thought the Outlanders were numerous enough to form an army.

Aida regards me warily, her thick lips purse. "So what does this mean, Sarina?" she asks, trying to figure out why I confided in them. "Why show this to us?"

I place my hands on my hips. My left hand brushes against the spear clipped to my belt. "You've both been set on helping me since the day we met," I say. "I haven't exactly shown you the gratitude you deserve. I had a hard time believing that you genuinely cared about what happened to me. I suppose you could consider that holoprojector as something of an olive branch."

Remus smiles thinly under his beard. His eyes beam with admiration and acceptance. If there's one thing I can take away from him, it's that he's loyal no matter what. He didn't care that I'd abused their trust, he's just happy to see my willingness to finally trust them.

Aida remains stern for a time. Her eyes are skeptical, and she cocks her head with dubiousness. "I find it hard to believe someone can have a change of heart so quickly," she says.

She locks glances with Remus for a moment before looking directly into mine. Suspicion fades and she smiles lightly. "But, I'm a forgiving person. Just, try not to doubt our intentions, will you? We *want* to help."

"Oh, you can definitely count on me wanting your help. I'm going to need it."

Almost naturally, we embrace simultaneously. She pats my back and I smile. It seems so easy. Just a few words and a gesture of trust place me back in their graces. But, I suppose that's what friends do. Trust unconditionally.

CHAPTER 33

Tálir

Murky Feelings

I DON'T NEED YOU to defend me, Tálir, the words echo. I still feel the bruise pulsing on my left eye.

Something is different about my focus today. It's more potent and more precise. Perhaps due to the intense anger I feel. My attention has focused on nothing but my frustration towards Sarina since Abrax and I started practicing this morning. The old man does a variant of one handed exercises to keep himself limber—though he refrains from actually using magic. While our kryo ammunitions are still adequate, Abrax wants to start conserving until we encounter another kryo mound. But who knows when we'll find one.

There's a *snap*, and I reload my right gauntlet. Using several stances, I accustom myself to the Shield Form while instinctively learning to alternate which gauntlet the magic generates from. A combination of left arm Shield and right arm Stream works into the exercise. Outputs for the Shield vary from *30%* to *40%*. Streams are now consistently holding at *25%*, and I berate myself for ever thinking it was hard.

More intense Shield applications involve using the Form as a melee weapon. My kryo output would need to remain at *50%* for that to work, however. Abrax recited the rules of Form II almost an hour ago. Shield can only block Stream and mundane weapons, it cannot be thrown as a large Discus, and it's the second fastest Form to drain kryos. I suppose magic flaming swords can be blocked to some degree as well, but I don't push that subject.

A haze forms over my field of vision as I concentrate on the magic. Intense heat burns in my head and chest. I channel it into each move, and the release it brings is satisfying. Yet, something seems off to the energy and I can't place my finger on it. I reload the kryo in my left gauntlet. Forceful steps resound in the muddy water of the swamp, and I think Abrax finally takes note.

"Lad, this entire swamp is getting hotter with all that anger boiling within you," he comments dryly. "What's the problem?"

The tense silence that follows is only interrupted by the screeches of avians and the croaking of toads. I look over at him askance—my body tense with frustration.

I say nothing but I continue to fume with animosity. Not just towards Sarina's impudence, but to Abrax's admission to knowing who Sarina was all along. I stare at the murky ground, my eyes full of resentment.

My silence is cut short by the sudden impact of a Stream blast that emits from the old man's fingertips. Even without the helmet, he's able to flawlessly channel the stun blast at *25%*.

And it hurts.

I'm instantly thrown from my feet and sent sailing two meters before landing in the murky waters. Mud splashes over my helmet and chest as I make impact. A stinging sensation emanates from within my chest. I can feel my pride taking a beating as well. My head sits up from the mud and I see Abrax rise from his perch.

"You're pathetic, Tálir," Abrax scoffs as he scratches his beard. "You're sulking like a child because she hurt your pride. If you possessed even a shred of discipline, you'd get past this easily and focus on your training. But instead, you keep your head in your ass, and let has-beens like me and Spud kick your ass into the muck. You could've bested him if you were *smart* about it. But no, your brashness got in the way. If I hadn't been there, he would've fried your sorry ass and left your corpse to rot in those catacombs."

I sit up and wipe the mud from my visor. While he can't see my face, I'm sure he can sense my humiliation. Because he's right.

After weeks of training, I have yet to channel at *100%* output. Let alone master any part of the final Forms. Due to these failures, I had almost been killed by Septem as well. Despite how confident I am with my abilities, Abrax and Septem have showed me just how inferior I am. I feel humiliated, helpless as I sit in the mud. Stinging pain still wells in my chest. But through the pain, I feel the heat of my anger slowly working in my chest—and it begins pumping into my veins like fire.

The fury stems from more than just the pain. It's spurred by degradation and inadequacy. How can I continue to let the old man get the better of me if I'm to master the suit? How can I possibly live up to my father's legacy? And the answer is a simple one.

Shaking off the effects of the Stream, I get to my feet as quickly as I can. The sound of sloshing water echoes through the trees. Mud is flecked all across my armor, and swamp water casually drips from various parts of my body.

Abrax regards me stonily, and sizes me up with a look as if he's analyzing what I'm about to do.

"If you want to live up to the Maven legacy, you've got to learn that nothing ever comes from acting out of hotheadedness or foolish pride," he says. "Those from my old Order know more about the armor and kryos than you can hope to perceive, and if you pick irrational fights you'll lose. Brashness leads to failure. You. Will. Lose."

Under the helmet, I flash a cold look at Abrax. Snapping my right arm forward, I release a retaliatory Stream towards his head. The five emerald beams fountain from my fingertips and hurl towards the old man's face at an incredible speed. Unsurprisingly, he tilts his head slightly and the bolts strike the tree behind him. Faster than I anticipated, he sends another blast my way as he slowly begins to advance on me. There's calm focus in his eyes.

Dodging the blast by sidestepping away, I reload my gauntlet and try to focus my suit's energy to *50%*. I want to test myself through experience, not regimented training. The only way I'll learn is to test myself against an opponent.

Abrax is an effective teacher, but he has failed to be a true mentor. A Suzerain is supposed to test their se'bau in more ways than one. The old man's style has been practice, listen, lecture, and then practice. It's too repetitive. His lessons are controlled, regimented, and stagnant. I desire more challenge than just *focusing harder*.

So if he won't take up the task, I'll have to force him to.

Using both hands, I send two Streams towards Abrax—my feet splashing against water and mud as I pivot. In response, Abrax forms a Shield about three meters in diameter over his left arm. The Streams collide with the Shield with a loud *bang* and send spouts of emerald sparks—illuminating the area briefly with an eerie glow. Abrax doesn't pause, and continues to gingerly advance as I continue to evade him around the perimeter of our training area.

Minding my past mistakes, I choose to think strategically. The frustration is still present, but it doesn't inhibit my mind. I have to show him that I'm not just brash during a fight. Minding my kryo usage, I keep sending short and controlled Streams at him for any sign of weakness.

Then, I spot one.

Abrax is so focused on advancing that he's forgotten how taxing the Shield is without reloading. A large reservoir has been built up in that section of his armor. The right amount of magic could overload the system and disable the Shield, for a short time. All I need to do is focus on a more intense Form. The Discus.

My HUD reads *Kryo Charge: 57%* while the output is currently *36%*. I strain my focus, letting my building anger climb. I release a Stream. The beams arc in the air and slam into the Shield, but only cause a shower of sparks to erupt. I curse in irritation. Still, the blast is strong enough to stop him in mid stride for a few seconds—buying me time.

It needs more intensity, I tell myself. My face burns with vexation as I concentrate to focus the intensity to *39%* before releasing the energy. Still nothing.

43% before unleashing another tangle of emerald fire. Nothing.

C'mon, I say to myself. *C'mon!*

Abrax is barely three meters from me and about to ram me head on with the Shield as my anger takes hold. Veins in my temple throb and my face burns. My eyes widen and I let out a savage yell as I suddenly focus the charge to *50%*. Without thinking, I fling my right arm forward like I'm throwing a ball. Materializing in my hand is a rotating disk of energy that hurls towards Abrax. My mouth is agape.

The resulting impact of the Discus generates a green flash that lingers in my vision for a few seconds. As it wears off, I see the results of my attack. Almost as if it's made of solid material, the energy Shield cracks and shatters like a pane of glass.

Silence elapses for a brief moment. My heart jumps in

excitement. Satisfaction then creeps up in me as I see Abrax frozen in astonishment, but it's short lived. With the last bit his kryo can provide, he flicks his index finger and sends a Stream speeding towards my helmeted face. There's a flash of light and then all goes dark.

◆ ◆ ◆

There's a disappointed look on his face as an emerald haze surrounds him. Father stares towards me, his helmet retracted. His dark eyes are solemn and his auburn hair is tied in a knot. From under his beard, I see him frown. It's the same as before.

"What?" I plead, my voice echoing. "Father what have I done to displease you?"

Silence punctuates my words. I move towards him, and his eyes stare ahead. But there's... something else. Stepping to the side, I realize his eyes don't follow me. He's not looking at me after all.

Slowly, I turn around to see what he's looking at. Some distance away from me stands a tall figure. Garbed in full, dazzling Maven armor, the figure he stares at wears a long, golden cape. I begin to step towards the figure, but it vanishes in a wisp of green vapor.

Darkness descends over my eyes.

◆ ◆ ◆

"That seems a bit… extreme. Wouldn't you say?" someone asks as I slowly regain consciousness.

The kryo vision replays in the back of my mind, but I force myself to ignore it… for now. I can feel a burning right behind my forehead—a hangover from the Hells. Even my eyes throb as I attempt to open them.

I'm propped up against what feels like a rotting tree trunk, my rear seated on some leather padding. I also notice that someone has retracted my helmet, for a breeze touches my cheek. As my eyes open, I see Sarina seated close to me while Abrax stands a meter away—his left hand on his hip. He bears a look of wry amusement as Sarina looks at him with perturbation. *What is she doing here?*

"Trial by fire," he says to her. "It's what he seemingly wanted. That's how any of us truly learn any hard lesson. Besides, brash actions only lead to half-victories in the best case. He just ended up with the worst case."

"I thought this was just about using the suit," Sarina replies quickly. "This sounds more like indoctrination."

"Yeah, it does," I grumble as I sit up straighter.

Their heads snap to look at me. Sarina flashes a faint smirk while Abrax looks stern. "I'm convinced that you like taking these beatings, Tálir," he says in a mocking voice. "You keep picking fights you can't win, and you take the hits every time. If you keep this up, you'll get yourself killed. A Maven Knight uses collected focus, not furious concentration."

"Is that concern I hear in your voice, old man?" I retort,

rubbing my head. "I'm touched. But you saw that! Using that bit of heated focus allowed me to use the Discus Form!"

"You used your rage for concentration, not the calm focus of a Maven," Abrax says dangerously. "Yes, that kind of power can grant you brief surges of power. But that's all they are. Brief!"

I glower. "But it worked!" I say even as his dark face contorts in concern. "I broke your Shield like it was nothing! You should be proud!"

"I want you to learn. Not just about how to be a Maven, but also how to act like one." The old man says with a pained voice. "Being hotheaded won't help you if you want to be one. Using an emotional focus is not how a Maven channels their magic."

"You're just as hotheaded as I am, Abrax!" I say, leaning forward and scowling at him. "You can't really preach to me when you have the same faults."

I can see solemnity in his features. I think this might be the first time I've been able to strike an effective blow against him. But it doesn't ring with victory.

"You're right," he nods rather gravely, closing his eyes. "But I'm telling you this because I don't want you to follow my path. I failed not just the Maven legacy, but myself as well. I fell from grace with such finality; I never thought I'd be able to atone for my failure. But if I can properly show someone what it means to inherit that legacy, then maybe I'll find some redemption."

His sincerity takes me by surprise, and I feel rather shameful for challenging him.

Speechless, I reflect on the gravity of Abrax's sudden explanation. I'm *his* legacy. His last chance to redeem himself in his own eyes for failing the Maven Knights. My anger suddenly turns to pity as I look at him. He's chosen me as a successor of sorts—an heir to his myth. A true se'bau. I feel both honored and dreadful, for he's putting a lot of faith in me.

I know I can't disappoint him; I can't let his faith be for nothing. But am I ready? Certainly not, but I know I have to try. A surge of inspired determinism hits me, and I realize what is required of me.

I have to train harder than anyone he's ever seen if I'm to honor his legacy as a Maven, I think. *I owe him that.*

A moment passes when I don't say anything. Avians chirp while toads croak, filling the air with a soft chorus. The sun has come out and it's bright against the cloudless sky above the fog and trees.

"I had no idea you took this that seriously, Abrax," I say sincerely. "If it's that important to you, I'll train diligently until I surpass any others you've trained. I will be your true se'bau. And I won't fail you."

The old man looks surprised, like he's never been taken so seriously before in his life. For a split second, I see a faint grin and his eyes light up with pride. Then it's gone.

"You're not getting off the hook after that little speech, Tálir," he grumbles in his usual demeanor. "So don't try that emotional focus shit again."

Reluctantly, I nod. I'll do my best, but I'm unsure of how well

I can keep my emotions in check. Punctuating my point, I look at Sarina and a churning storm of anger forms in my stomach. My left eye is still bruised from Devin's assault.

So I struggle to remain objective. "What, do you like seeing me get my ass kicked?" I ask coldly, mirroring her tone from earlier. "I suppose that's fair entertainment for someone like you."

She frowns. "You're always the one picking fights you can't win," she says with concern. "I didn't ask you to fight Devin. But, I want you to know that I do appreciate what you did. I know I haven't been the most empathetic and trusting person—"

"That's the understatement of understatements," I snort, earning a quick glare from her.

"But…" she says through gritted teeth. "I shouldn't have turned on you for trying to protect me. I'm going to make this right, and I've promised the same thing to the others. So, can you forgive me for the way I acted, Tálir?"

Silence strangles my voice box for a moment. I don't sense any deception from her. Her blue eyes shine with empathy for the first time, and I'm stunned to see a different side of her. A side that shows empathy and compassion. I feel both relieved and happy to see her open up, even if only for a brief moment. Even in spite of all we've been through, a part of me feels unconditionally compassionate for her.

My anger subsides and is replaced by a warm sense of happiness. It's strange, having my emotions calmed by someone like Sarina. But perhaps that's why she's important to me. Why I feel unconditionally supportive. She can keep me focused.

I look into her blue eyes. "So… You've gone around apologizing like this to everyone?" I ask with a smirk.

Sarina rocks her head. "More or less," she replies returning the grin.

"Well, that seems a bit unnecessarily excessive."

We all leave the swamp and head back to the campsite nearly a kilometer away. It's around midday when we convene with the others. And to my surprise, everyone is there waiting for us. Devin, while harboring some resentment, has elected to stay. Vyck always goes where his friend is, so he stays too. Vivían is certainly pleased with this outcome.

"So…" Aida says once everyone has congregated. "Let's get this quest underway."

CHAPTER 34

Sarina

The Outlands

ANOTHER NIGHT PASSES AS we recuperate from the escape. The next morning, everyone packs their gear and prepares the bikes for our trip. Fuel will be acquired within villages dotting the east.

Before we leave though, Abrax has everyone gather around the repulsorcart. The old man gestures for Tálir to retrieve the Tome from his satchel. In an excited hurry, Tálir thrusts his hand into the satchel and pulls out the device—holding it out for all to see in his palm. A small, bronze pyramid.

"It's time for us to see what we acquired in Z'hart City," the old man says. "Let's see what the Tome has to offer us."

Everyone is excited and my heart races. This technology

hasn't been activated in almost a millennium, and it fills me with anticipation as I wait. The Tome is our map, our true guide.

Abrax presses a finger to the bronze metal. Upon activating the device, the three sides of the pyramid split open and reveal a tiny, glowing orb the color of sapphires. The light shines brightly and begins to pulsate with a low hum. Gradually it grows larger in size until it reaches the width of an apple.

All of us are in awe as a faint image forms within the glowing depths of the orb. The image is cloudy, but gains form over the span of a few seconds. My eyes narrow as I stare intensely at it.

The image of a lone willow tree resting in an on open grove of pine trees is shown to us. The willow tree looks ancient and almost magical as it rests within the depths of the forest. The image lasts for a moment, and then the orb dissipates in a mist of crystal blue as the pyramid closes shut. The Tome remains inert in Tálir's palm for several moments as we wait for something else to happen. Nothing does.

That's it? I ask myself. *We only get an image of a willow tree?*

Tálir scratches his head while examining the device in his hand, slowly pacing in circles. Devin touches his bearded chin and also begins shuffling about. Vyck looks completely befuddled.

"So," Vyck says in a prolonged way. "Am I the only one thinking that this Tome is completely boning us?"

"Shut up," Devin sighs.

"So all we have to go by is an image of a willow tree?" I ask, wiping beads of sweat from my forehead. "The Mavens sure were thorough when it came to keeping this place secret. Hells, I'm not even sure if *they* knew how to find it."

Everyone begins spouting out their own theories regarding the Tome's image. Tálir says Providence could be under the tree while Devin believes it's nothing but a distraction. Aida comments that it could be a marker, but how would we find it? Even Vyck comments that finding a sole willow is next to impossible.

But then, Vivían chimes in, "I might have a solution to this." Everyone quiets as she continues, "Willow trees are only native in the far eastern Outlands, near the Marün Canyons that border the land of Asi. Many of these trees can be found near the Night Sea."

"She's right," Abrax affirms, rubbing his beard. "Our path already lies in the east. So our search for this willow tree can also begin there."

I regard him with mild hesitation. "That'll be like finding an oreing in a rockslide. Who knows how long that search could take."

"It might not be as difficult as we think," Tálir suddenly says.

Everyone looks at him. For the last few minutes, he's been fiddling with the Tome with no imperceptible progress. Pacing in all directions with nothing of note happening. But as he moves the device in the direction of the east, glowing blue lines light up along the sides of the Tome.

"A— Beacon—" Remus grunts with a wide smile on his bearded face.

"Of course!" Abrax exclaims more joyfully than I expected. "The Tome is meant to guide us along the path. I thought it was just part of the legend, but…"

"It will literally light our way," I conclude with a smirk. "Nice job, Tálir!"

He gives me an earnest smile before saying, "We have our guide. We've got our supplies. I never thought I'd be saying this, but, let's go find Providence."

I turn to Vivían and ask, "How long will it take us to get to the Night Sea?"

She runs a hand over her wild, crimson hair before replying, "Two, maybe three weeks. Even with the bikes, we have a lot of ground to cover in the east. The land is winding and unpredictable. We must stay on the lookout for Crimsons. They tend to roam within those canyons. So, we must travel carefully. Otherwise, let's mount up and go for a ride." She winks at Vyck.

Tálir grins and nods. "We have no time to waste then."

Standing firmly in front of our repulsorbikes, I lift my head up confidently. "Let's go save the world."

The quest for Providence has begun. A week passes as we continue to the eastern border of Z'hart. The terrain is more versatile than it was in the south. Oases, savannas, marshes, and ravines make up the countryside. We cover incredible distance on our bikes, nearly five hundred kilometers per day. Still, Pan'gea is a massive continent and we've barely covered a quarter of it. Yet, our quest requires us to press on and in a timely fashion. We have to finish this before Centum's plans come to fruition. Adding to our flight, Vivían reports that something is pursuing us into the east. A menace that seems a day behind us.

It's a race to the finish.

Our journey takes us beyond many places I only dreamed of as a girl. From the swamp, we make our way into the great Gold Plains that mark the eastern border of Z'hart. The Gold Plains are massively expansive, ranging for miles and miles. The sand colored grasses bend in the wind, and waves of antelope flock frequently. We start keeping a close eye out for packs of whargs. One day as we're travelling through the savannah, Vivían starts teaching me how to hunt. A skill I've always wanted to learn, but wasn't exceptionally gifted at. The first time, I mistakenly move upwind and my scent scares the animals off. The second time, I'm not quiet enough.

Still, there's still some measure of triumph when I cripple one of the quadrupeds. My bowpistol doesn't have much range, but the bolts are powerful. As Vivían finishes the kill, she drains a cup full of the animal's blood.

"Your first kill in the hunt," she says, passing the cup to me. "This will mark you as a hunter."

I'll never forget the warm taste of blood.

After two days traversing through the savanna, we pass by a small village named Gillan Towne. Aida, Devin, and Remus spend some of our earnings on rations, fuel, and supplies before we continue into the wilderness. I elect to stay out of public eye, just in case anyone identifies me.

Upon leaving Gillan Towne, we finally enter the lands beyond the three nations. The Outlands.

My hunting skills improve as the days go on, and so does my relationship with the group. Tensions ease and there are less confrontations since danger hasn't presented itself. Stress has begun to wear off, but we remain vigilant. We know we're being hunted, but we accept the challenge.

Devin's rage has mellowed, although we still hold a tentative relationship with one another. Even after my apology and willingness to trust him, he still remains obstinate. As the days go on, I behave a little more empathetic to him just to ease the tension. Devin resists for a time, but I think he's starting to calm as well. Only time will tell.

Tálir's training grows more frequent and more intense as we travel. The closer we get to Providence, the more rigorous the sessions get. For the first time since we met him, Abrax allows me to peek in on their sessions. I think Abrax likes keeping me around for the lessons. I'm a necessary distraction for Tálir, and a way to keep him focused without emotional compromise.

I can now see the bond that exists between Tálir and me. Not that it hadn't already been there, but we can now approach each other as our true selves. He never backs down because of my status as a regent, and I have the utmost respect for that. He accepts me for who I am, not what I am.

It's a fascinating ordeal to watch the legacy of the Mavens. Their combat, philosophy, and culture seem both enigmatic and familiar. Abrax even helps me learn more about the use of the Maven spear he passed to me.

I have grown with it, and recognize that it's no longer just a weapon. So I name it *Silverlight*, and it is part of me.

Two weeks pass after our escape in Z'hart City, and I can't shake my longing for home. I miss my sister and I constantly worry about her safety. She's surrounded by people who seek to overthrow her, and it makes this journey all the more burdensome. But until we find Providence and find a way to stop our enemies, I cannot go home. I have to believe that evading Centum will keep Sahari safe. Until we succeed, I am a queen without a nation.

I am exile.

CHAPTER 35

Sarina

Bonds

IN A BASIC SENSE, you need a firm posture when shooting a bowpistol," Vivían says as we ride together on the repulsorbike. "You've got to lock your arms and keep one foot planted behind you for support. Pistols have a wild drawback, so they need a steady hand and an accurate eye."

Sitting in the passenger seat behind her, I have on hand on Vivían's hip just to keep myself safe on the bike. Her crimson hair still whips in the breeze despite being held up by the headband. She occasionally takes her eyes off the road in front of us to glance at me while we talk.

"What if I need to get a precise hit?" I respond, examining

the pistol in my holster. "Like a knee or an eye?"

"Trust your eye?" she shrugs simply. "Don't think too much about it."

She and I share a laugh, and I feel a sense of relief upon realizing our comfortability. Conversations are always enlightening when they involve Vivían. As a former Outlander, Vivían holds no inhibitions since she grew up in a life of adventure. She believes in being true to oneself and to always seize opportunities. She's certainly true to herself, and I admire it.

Two weeks have passed since we'd traversed through the marshes in the north-eastern reaches of Z'hart. While we only view the maps sporadically, I'm starting to figure out where we are in Pan'gea. If we turn our direction completely north at this point, we'll eventually enter the nation of O'ran.

By the end of the day, we'll reach the shores of the Night Sea that spans nearly a hundred kilometers in diameter. Somewhere in that area we will find the willow that marks a guidance point to Providence.

No sign of any Crimsons… so far.

"I once felled a desert wyrm the size of ten men with four plasma arrows to its skull," Vivían recounts gleefully, breaking my thoughts. "That beast was one tough son of a bitch. Scales so thick it was almost like steel plating. But the skin under their eyes is thinner. So, I aimed quick and put two arrows under each eye and into its skull. Ah, what a feast that was!"

"Two under each eye?" I ask in disbelief. "How did you

manage not to miss?"

Vivían looks over her shoulder at me and smiles. She points to her left eye. I take her meaning, and it forces a laugh out of me. For the first time in a while, I feel like I can be myself.

Around midday, we stop to let the repulsorbike engines cool. Everyone takes the time to eat, drink, and change or wash their clothes. I currently wear tan pants, brown boots, and sleeveless shirt. While I acquired several outfits in Z'hart City, I nonetheless choose to wash some of my old clothes. Most of the others wade into the creek to wash off, but I remain on the banks—an old *habit* of mine. Kneeling cautiously by the creek with a cube of soap, I begin scrubbing the grime and stink out of my tunics and trousers. I finish after a few minutes and place them near one of our heat generators to dry. I can already smell the creek water in the fabric.

The air is cool in the shade of the ravine despite being midday. I hear the sound of the rushing water even over the conversations in the group. For the first time in weeks, I feel relaxed. Inhaling deeply and closing my eyes for a moment, I soak in my relaxation. It seems silly, but I almost feel like a child enjoying playtime in the outdoors.

Once everyone has finished with their tasks, we begin prepping the bikes for further ventures. The pairings for the repulsorbikes are switched as we continue into the ravine, however. Vivían is eager to sit with Vyck for a little while. Devin rides with Abrax. Coincidently, I'm paired with Tálir on his bike and I feel a faint surge of excitement. We haven't talked one-on-one all day. So this seems like prime opportunity.

My arms wrap around his armored torso as the bikes ride smoothly through the marshy ravine. We travel slowly due to the winding paths and narrow space. It's just fast enough for a breeze to blow throughout the air.

Following the creek, the bikes hover about a meter above the long grasses and muddy areas. Rotting carcasses of various animals are half buried in the mud. Flies buzz around and toads croak from within the grasses.

The bikes make a sharp turn, and I hold on to Tálir all the more tightly. It takes me a second to realize that I hold on for a fraction longer than necessary. Even Tálir notices; his head turns around slightly in surprise. Embarrassed, I immediately ease my grip.

"Didn't realize you were that eager to feel me up, Sarina," Tálir chuckles as he refocuses on driving.

I hit him lightly in his ribs. "Don't flatter yourself," I say playfully. "Though, you're not as muscular as some of the other men I've… felt up."

He says nothing, and I think I detect a hint of jealousy emanating from him. His head turns slightly towards Devin, but doesn't linger. Despite not seeing his face, I can see his shoulders tense. I grin deviously.

"Well…" he says quietly. "I'm sorry I'm not up to par with those other beefcakes you've felt up. My diet for twenty years only consisted of bread, water, and some dried meats you know."

I pat him on his armored stomach in a spirited manner. "Well you turned out alright," I reply flippantly. "I imagine the Pyrack was very good at conditioning someone like you. It's an impressive feat, being able to survive out there."

Tálir looks over his shoulder briefly as we enter a smooth patch within the ravine. "Sarina, I've been wondering about something," he says inquisitively.

"Shoot."

"Why did you run from being the queen of Z'hart?" Tálir asks genuinely.

His question fills me with some measure of apprehensive curiosity. No one has ever asked me why I'd chosen to abandon my inheritance. I'm both thrilled and scared to answer his query. I've convinced myself of my reasons, but I've never had to tell someone else.

"I guess because I was scared," I answer as I consider extrapolating. "How could someone at the age of seventeen ever hope to rule a nation?"

"But look at all the power you'd have," Tálir says with vigor. "All the luxury and wealth you'd have as a ruler. As someone who grew up with scraps and salvage, you have no idea what I'd do to have a life like that."

The bikes pass underneath a natural bridge eroded from the rocks around us. The terrain becomes more arboreal; the grass turns to a shade of gold.

"Sure there's the luxury," I affirm as my arms stay firmly wrapped around him. "But there's the responsibility. Imagine that you'd have to not only abide by every law in your nation, but you'd have to uphold them as well. You also cannot venture where you please without constant supervision. And most times, you must marry for powerful alliances instead of love."

He glances back and our eyes meet as I conclude, "Tell me, Tálir. Does that sound as grand as you thought?"

Tálir doesn't respond for a few moments. The bikes move into a single file as we pass through a small cave that marks the exit of the ravine. We're now in an open field of teal grasses, wildflower bushes, and sporadic trees. Our bikes pick up speed now that we've exited the ravines.

I can sense an aura of misgiving coming from Tálir, but he also doesn't want to show aggression. "I suspect the cons out weight the pros on that one," he says after a moment. "But why did you forsake everything? You could've taken some of your riches and lived a comfortable life elsewhere. Instead of working in the lower reaches of Z'hart City."

"That would seem like the operative course of action," I admit. "But my father taught me a very important lesson before he died. True royalty is not inherited, it is earned. It's part of our nation's interpretation in the faith of the Arc. They say that the Sage God blesses acts of honesty and integrity, so Z'hart thrives on earning their luxury."

Tálir glances back at me again, his wavy, brown hair flows in the wind. "That reminds me of a lesson I learned growing up in the Pyrack. Work hard and you get to eat."

I nod and give him a faint smile. "I wanted to know what it was like to live off the bare essentials. To work for my earnings, and to spend them frugally. Learning to brew ale was exciting and different. I fancied the rougher clothes of a brewer as opposed to the regalia of a noble. I've never had too much direct faith in the Arc myself. But in a way, I wanted to see if honest work was worthy of the Sage God's blessings. While it was for my own selfish reasons, I did learn more about the common life than I ever could have in the Citadel."

"That right there is why I think you'd make an excellent ruler, Sarina," Tálir says, taking his right hand off the handlebar and pats the top of my knee gently. My heart beats rapidly.

It lasts for a moment, and then he hurriedly places his hand back atop the handlebar. "But I suppose that's what makes us different," he says. "Our upbringings taught us to value that which we don't have."

I look off into the sky as we ride over the plains. The blue sky is nearly packed with white clouds and the sun beams from above. "Yet, we may not be as different as you think, Tálir," I say soothingly.

As we ride over the top of one of the hills, I see something I thought I'd never see in all my life. The Night Sea.

Spanning for countless kilometers, the Night Sea passes far into the horizon while varying terrain elements dot its perimeter. Canyons, forests, and even light variations of bamboo jungles. Despite the awe I feel, the unnatural color of the Night Sea ebbs the euphoria I feel. The murky waters glow bright with neon algae and the sands of the surrounding beaches are black. It's an eerie thing to lay eyes upon, despite its enigmatic appearance.

We ride for about another kilometer, turning slightly north in order to go around the body of water. It doesn't take long for us to find our target, though. In a grove surrounded by oaks and pine trees, it sticks out like a sore thumb.

We've found the willow tree. The trunk and branches are slender and pliant, forking like a lightning bolt. Its leaves are elongated and serrated.

Our repulsorbikes slow as we approach it. Planted within a small clearing within the trees, the willow almost has its own patch upon which it grows. Evening light penetrates through the surrounding trees and illuminates the willow's branches and leaves. As we all disembark our bikes for a break, Tálir and I approach the willow tree at the center of the grove. The Tome in Tálir's hand glows all the more brightly as we stop a few meters from the tree. I hear a slight hum.

"This thing is vibrating," Tálir says in astonishment.

I look closely and see the device wobbling rapidly. Another sound catches my interest: a slight chirping originates from the tree. Scanning it fervently, I search for any sign of where the noise could be coming from. We both prowl around the willow, listening intently as the chirping gets louder. It reaches a fevered pitch, and then I see it.

Embedded within the pale bark of the tree is a small, cubelike protrusion. Looking at it more closely, I see esoteric lines etched into the protrusion that faintly glow blue. Carefully, I grasp the cube and with a light tug, I pull it from the tree. Surprisingly, cool metal meets my fingers and I examine the azure lines along the pale surface of the cube. *It's another device!*

Tálir hovers close to me with the pyramid in hand. Both objects hum and chirp in an almost musical symphony. Almost in synchronization, Tálir and I both activate the devices and each opens to reveal several new images. The pyramid shows a canyon beyond the forest while the cube reveals a temple-like structure beyond the same canyons.

"It's not just a guide," Tálir says in awe, his hazel eyes widen. "It's—"

"A puzzle," we both say simultaneously. Our eyes meet and we both smile.

"The pyramid Tome led us to the tree," I say after a moment. "Now the cube Tome shows us our next target."

"And the pyramid is showing us how to get there from here," Tálir concludes as the devices deactivate.

"How much you want to bet the next Tome is a sphere?" I ask devilishly, using my hand to brush my hair behind an ear.

Tálir makes an absurd gesture of doubt. "Bet you it's not."

"You're on," I wink.

We both turn to see the others all crowding around us with

curious expressions on their faces. Abrax a few meters from us with a wide grin on his face. "One beacon down it seems," he grunts with a sly smile. "And I believe you two know where the next one is."

The old man points towards the far side of the Night Sea. Despite its breadth, I can faintly see the terrain east of the sea. A massive canyon that spans into the far reaches of the world beyond—the rocks are the color of deep burgundy. I hold up the cube Tome in the direction of the canyons, and imperceptibly it starts to glow.

"The Marün Canyons," Vivían says in revelation.

Abrax nods. "We are on the right track, laddies," he says with a hint of glee.

I smile back, and I can sense determination rising within the group… and in myself. For it's not the discovery of the new Tome that makes me feel this way. It's Abrax's sudden confidence that truly pushes me to believe that we can succeed. Even if it is just a simple beacon, I have a hint of faith that we'll find our way easily.

CHAPTER 36

Tálir

The Itinerant Mind

I FEEL CLEAR.

It has been a while since I've felt this way, and it's difficult to describe. It's as if I've resurfaced from underwater, breathing fresh air and escaping the pressure of the sea. I'm no longer drowning, I'm floating.

A few days after passing the willow tree, we had continued venturing north in order to avoid the Night Sea. After those days, we managed to reach the Marün Canyons that span for six hundred kilometers into the east. It will take us almost three days before we clear these monstrous crags. But the silver lining is that another Tome is supposed to reside not far from these canyons.

Based on what Vivían said, the temple might be located in one of the Outlander territories. Which means that after the Marün Canyons, we'll begin entering the land of Asi: the true home of the Outlander clans.

It's early in the morning as my training continues while Abrax and Sarina observe my progression. Abrax thinks it'll be helpful for someone else to distract me as I attempt to focus. While Sarina observes merely out of curiosity, I believe Abrax is aware of her influence on me. I have to remain much more vigilant in my focus with her there. Yet, there's also strength to her presence like she's making sure I don't pass into emotional focus.

In the weeks that have passed since the battle in the swamp, my sessions with Abrax seem different. Not in just what I'm learning, but because of our newfound respect for one another. It seems easier to absorb the lessons taught by someone I respect as a teacher. He no longer teaches as a drill sergeant, but as a peer.

Away from the group, I practice in one of the smaller ravines that branch off in the crags. A muddy pond is nearby and patches of dried grass litter the sandy ground. The ravine walls barely exceed ten meters, so it's easy for us to climb in and out. Moving freely, my armored boots step from the dry ground and into the muddy water.

Abrax and I are sparring again. Except this time, we're not at each other's throats. Learning through experience is his new method of instruction. Sarina sits off to the side atop a large outcropping, sharpening her spear.

Focusing on objects or fixed positions in my surroundings is a way I concentrate my magic output. Drawing my attention to a patch of grass, a sinewy tree, or a crack in the ravine wall helps most of the time. But the tiniest distraction can break my focus. It's the most exasperating aspect of this power. With Sarina's added presence, my distractions have increased tenfold despite the new adrenaline I get with her around.

Discus has been consistent and yet a struggle. Remaining above *50% Output Charge* has been a constant battle particularly because the magic must be harnessed, contained, and then thrown. It's easy to lose focus once the energy has formed into a disk or orb—leading it to dissipate. Trying the Blaze Form is going to be an even more arduous task.

Movement for Form III is relatively simple since all it really requires is a throwing motion. Forward, sideways, underhand, and back-handed swings each generate the magic. Usually, I prefer sideways throwing. Appearing as emerald fireballs, the Discus impacts the rocky ravine wall. Scorching green flames gyrate around the impact spot as it dissipates.

"One: Discus can cause more serious injuries like burns or even broken bones," Abrax is saying as he uses Stream to quickly deflect another Discus I hurl at him. "It's not lethal, however. Two: Discus can only be deflected by another Discus... or a quick Stream. And three: As you've probably noticed, Discus does not stop until it hits something. Once released, there's no altering its trajectory unless you hit it with something."

"How can Stream deflect it but Shield can't?" I call, ducking under a Discus thrown in retaliation.

Abrax shrugs slightly. "Stream doesn't actively deflect Discus. It just nudges its trajectory enough to send it elsewhere. It's more along the lines of redirecting."

My HUD indicates a *68% Output Charge* as I strain to focus. I try to keep my head clear. But another vision flashes before my eyes. It's one of the earlier ones. Sarina in a vast blackness, meters away from me. Her back is turned to me, but she begins to slowly turn around. I see her face, and her eyes are grey. Blinded. Fear grips me as I snap out of the vision.

The Discus soars from my hand and towards the old man, but he sidesteps from it. I'm too slow to react to his counter. A Stream hits me directly in the chest and I'm flung backwards into the mud.

I swear under my breath. Not just from the damned sting of the energy, but my constant struggle to maintain focus. *Why is this so damn hard?*

"You know," Abrax says, pacing behind me as Sarina sits up straight in interest. She refrains from laughing at my failure. "Most of the Suzerains believe that all se'baus are victims of the Itinerant Mind. Your mind is never at rest, and emotions cloud everything."

"Itinerant Mind?" I repeat, retracting my helmet. "That sounds like some philosophy for monks or—"

"Or ancient warriors?" Sarina comments, extending her spear and examining it. "It's not like you're learning the culture behind said warriors."

"Thanks for the clarification, Sarina," I retort snidely, sitting up in the muddy water. "I'm just curious as to why a warrior culture needs to apply philosophy to their methods."

Abrax approaches me and extends his left hand. Grasping it, he raises me out of the muck. "It's an ideal that dates back to the early eons of the Old World," Abrax says as we walk out of the water. "Warriors of old were always strong in their hearts and minds when it came to battle and discipline. They believed that a human mind naturally wanders in thought, emotion, and memory. True focus came from having a calm mind. An Itinerant Mind prevents this."

I wipe some mud off my pauldrons and look at the old man's dark face. "How can anyone have a calm mind when there's so much activity everywhere?" I ask with a note of frustration. "My mind and heart are always going to be full of emotion. I can't change that."

Abrax scratches at his beard, which needs some measure of trimming now. Wiry strands of silver hair poke out from the tangled mess.

"A Maven knows their heart," he says cryptically.

My face contorts in bewilderment. "What do you mean?" I ask, glancing down at my armor. "A Maven knows their heart?"

"If one knows their mind and their heart, they can find true serenity," Abrax affirms. "If you are one with your mind and heart, you will have no inhibitions. This requires no distractions. No anger, sadness, fear, or happiness. You must be empty to find that level of peace."

He puts his hand on my shoulder. "Forget about all distractions," the old man says calmly. "Just breathe. Focus on that."

Slowly, he walks a few meters in front of me and reloads his gauntlets for another sparring match. I do the same, but I pause after placing fresh kryo shards into my gauntlets.

I marinate on his lesson for a moment, calming myself in the process. I try to clear my mind of all the things around me. Instead, I listen to the running water, the insects chirping, and the whistle of the wind. Breathing slowly, I listen to the armor—the low hum that vibrates in my chest and the faint cackle of energy.

The heat within the armor feels like it's sinking into my bones; the metal is almost like a second skin. I can feel the magic running like water through it, and the humming fluctuates as I focus on it. Slowly, I start reaching my arm out and think about nothing except the energy.

I feel nothing. I think about nothing. It's just me and the armor.

There's a rush of energy, stronger than anything I've felt before. My heart pounds slowly but firmly, and I hear it echo within my mind. I open my eyes, and focus my attention solely on the old man in front of me. Like blood in my veins, I let the energy naturally flow towards my palm.

Activating my helmet, the HUD reads a *75%* charge and climbing. Yet, I contain my excitement. I keep my attention on the energy surging within my armored hand. I feel nothing as I extend my palm and unleash the energy.

Though weak, a Blaze erupts from my palm and speeds towards Abrax. Surprise is etched in the old man's features as he employs a Shield to block the attack. However, he underestimates the strength of my Blaze.

Shattering like glass, his Shield crumbles upon being hit. I cease the output so that the energy doesn't strike Abrax. My goal has been reached.

Sarina starts clapping slowly from her perch as Abrax recovers from the blast. He gives me a nod of pleased approval. "Congratulations Tálir," he says. "You've learned the four Forms of a Maven Knight."

The early morning sun peeks out over the walls of the canyons as my session comes to a close. I feel proud. I've learned the four Forms of kryo magic, even if I haven't fully mastered them yet. Something tells me my training is still far from completion, but I savor my triumph nonetheless.

As the three of us prepare to return to the others, something dawns on me. In the swamp, Abrax had mentioned that those from his Order knew far more about Maven culture than I did. And I wish to know why. Who are these people?

"Abrax," I say suddenly, drawing the attention of my two companions.

"What's wrong, Tálir?" he replies, grasping his arms behind

his back.

I look at Sarina who still perches upon the boulder a few meters from us. Almost like she knows what I'm thinking, she nods her head. And I know why. This is the same Order that kidnapped her and wishes to take control of her nation. Of course she'll want to know.

"I think it's about time you explained what your Order is, Abrax," I say, adjusting my bracer. The look on his dark face sours. But he knows it's time. "You and Remus were both a part of it, and now they're our most prominent threat. You told me they know much more about Maven training than I ever will. So, we need to understand what they're about if we're to beat them."

The old man wipes sweat from his dark face, and he lets out a sigh. Not from exasperation, but more along the lines of melancholy. Sarina collapses her spear and sits up straight. She brushes her hair from her eyes, interest evident on her peach-colored face.

Abrax doesn't respond at first. Taking out his pipe, he packs it and lights it. He takes a few puffs of greenweed before speaking.

"Are you sure you want to know, Tálir?" he asks, a look of warning is in his eyes.

I fold my arms across my chest and adopt a stern look. I demonstrate my resolve, and I won't back down. Abrax respects this.

He inhales deeply; his pipe lets up a column of smoke. "The Remnant Order is the furtive society that has been training many in the old ways of the Maven Knights. Other magic practitioners have been rumored to exist in more recent Cycles, but the Remnant is the oldest. Established a Cycle after the Ending, the Remnant has been trying to rebuild the Maven legacy for the last millennium. The name reflects much of their core beliefs, because they believe that they have the last connections to the Domain. Some say it's in their bloodline, some possess relics, and some are just scholars who know copious amount about the ancients. But many, like Remus and Septem, were essentially born into the Order."

I let his explanation marinate for a moment. Septem was right, they had been around for longer than I could imagine. But if they were indeed as large as Abrax says, how come people aren't more aware of them?

"Sounds like they're fanatics, in some sense of the word." I say, rubbing my chin. My facial hair is growing thick, but it's far from a full beard. "They're just regular people who happen to possess relics of the Domain. But with a bit more guidance than most."

"Like yourself, for instance?" Sarina comments with a smirk. She twirls her collapsed spear like a baton.

I grin at her. "Yes, like myself."

Abrax snorts with mild amusement as he takes another drag from his pipe.

"In some sense, yes that's what it is," Abrax says, smoke coming out from his nose. "But there is some credibility to their claims. There is a way to trace back a bloodline to the ancient times to its direct source. And many in the Remnant have done such. However, those bloodlines are very rare. But for the most part, the Centum is tasked with committing their reign to locating Providence while training a successor. I was once known as such.

"If there's one thing you should take away about the Remnant, Tálir, it's that they believe themselves to be the true heirs of the Domain civilization. That belief gives birth to dangerous individuals who care for nothing except for their own ascension. They will kill innocents, burn cities, and betray one another for more power."

I look at him in horror. The code of a Maven Knight revolves around prosperity, equality, and order. Anger and fear both whirl within me like a cyclone. Many in the Remnant are tainting the ways of the Knights of old, and it makes me physically ill. They don't deserve to be called heirs to the Domain.

"That's not the Maven way. How could anyone tolerate such depravity?" I ask Abrax, my face turning red with anger.

The old man looks at me with some measure of defeat. "Because their current Centum fell from the true Maven path," he says. "Centum was given poor instruction by the previous First Master."

Wait a minute. In the catacombs, Abrax had mentioned a se'bau that failed him. It wasn't Septem. But now, the pieces fall into place.

"Centum was your se'bau," I declare as the old man eyes me. There's a sharp hint of darkness in his expression. "The one that failed you."

Abrax looks away from me and a solemn expression is on his face. He says nothing and takes another drag from his pipe. He closes his eyes in sadness.

"There's nothing more devastating than a pupil overthrowing their teacher," Abrax says quietly. "Not only did Centum challenge my rule, but my entire life's work was undone by that monster. The Remnant itself turned on me, and only a handful showed enough mercy to let me escape. Your father was one such person."

I gulp in unease. That's why Abrax had been so reluctant to teach me. He was afraid another student would fail and turn on him. I snort at the thought. I could never betray him like that.

I find his answers satisfying. I have a better grasp on what I'm up against. Septem is nothing more than a glorified fanatic. But there's one more question burning in my head.

"What is Centum like?" I ask with a grave expression.

Abrax looks at me; his face remains neutral to my question. He snorts smoke before saying, "A story for another time, lad. All you need to know is that Centum has delved into the deeper parts of our magic. You saw a glimpse of that when we faced Septem. Therefore, it's my job to prepare you as best I can for the day we face Centum. For it won't be an easy battle."

I battle the fear that begins to grow within me, like a gull battling through a storm. The task before me is much greater than I ever imagined. Abrax plans for us to confront Centum, likely to liberate the Remnant from a corrupt rule. The task is daunting, but I retain my focus as best I can. The Itinerant Mind mustn't cloud the path before me. The path of saving the world. Saving the Mavens.

CHAPTER 37

Sarina

Revelations

NIGHT HAS FALLEN around our campsite, and only the moon and fire give us light. Despite the darkness, there's liveliness to the camp that has sprung up over the last few hours. Abrax had allowed us to take a break from travelling for the entire day. We all rejoiced at the opportunity to rest from nearly three weeks of travel. So after a relaxing day of recuperation, we all decided to celebrate.

The Tomes have been a noteworthy guide for our journey. The discovery of the singular willow tree and then subsequently following the path to the Marün Canyons had been a good sign. While I'm still faintly skeptical of the devices' map, I'm nonetheless content with our current path. I have a feeling that we're heading in the right direction. With what seems to be the Imperials still a day behind us and no imminent sign of danger, there's even more cause to celebrate.

Upon scouting around our camp, Vyck and Devin said there was no sign of the Crimsons. We've been lucky. The Crimsons are likely far north of us, and separated by a vast network of canyons. It's relieving.

After a successful afternoon hunt, Vivían brought us a spotted antelope for supper. She and Abrax skillfully prepared the carcass for roasting, and their expertise is met with unwavering gratitude. Now that the roast is ready, my stomach growls in anticipation. As everyone gets their share of the meal, we pass around several skins full of wine. The air smells like mesquite meat and charcoal, and laughter echoes within the canyon.

"So I said to Vyck: 'There's no way you can carry her all by yourself.' Mind you, Vyck was several pounds lighter at this point in time," Devin recounts rather jubilantly, a side of him I thought I'd never see. "But he insists: 'Look who you're talking to. I'm Vyck, Stallion of the West!'"

Though his injuries have healed, the scars around his right eye are still fresh. His iris seems faded, and it's evident he may never see clearly out of it again. But it doesn't damper his mood tonight.

"Stallion of the West?" Vivían laughs heartily, taking a swig of wine. She nudges Vyck playfully with her foot.

"You'd be surprised at my endurance," Vyck sputters in defense of himself.

"So what happened to the courtesan?" I ask, taking a bite from the roast. "Vyck takes her from the warlord and then?"

"He throws her over his shoulder in the most romantic way possible, and runs across the catwalk as the fortress explodes behind him," Devin laughs hysterically. "Normally it would've been an epic rescue, but the execution was the opposite. I'm on the other side with the bikes just giggling at the sight of it. That courtesan was taller than six foot, and Vyck is straining to run across."

We all roar with laughter, even Abrax adopts an amused grin as he smokes some greenweed.

"Did he drop her?" Aida asks as she huddles next to Remus.

"Epically," Devin snorts, patting Vyck on the shoulder. "She drops and rolls right off the catwalk into the moat below. The water was cold enough to wake her out of unconsciousness."

"Vyck, you didn't dive in after her?" I ask in melodramatic anguish. "She was your maiden in distress!"

"I can't swim very well," Vyck replies, his cheeks turning red. "But she made it."

"She wasn't too happy with you when we fished her out of there," Devin chuckles. "But long story short, Vyck's first love ended very, very jubilantly."

"Not for me," Vyck mutters. "Nátalia, you are still missed."

Vivían huddles closer to him as the story concludes. I arch an eyebrow at her and she winks back at me. Devin sits across the fire while Tálir sits right next to me. Our legs press together, but neither of us backs away. I can see a tinge of enviousness flash over Devin's face.

The night has been filled with eating, drinking, and storytelling as comfortability grows amongst us. It's a drastic improvement from where we'd started off weeks ago. Devin has rekindled his comfortability with me, and I with him. Wounds have healed, and so have our friendships.

"Ey, how are we looking, old timer?" Devin changes the subject to address Abrax.

"Intoxicated," he grunts, puffing on his pipe.

"I think he meant journey-wise, Abrax," Tálir comments. Both men are still in their suits of armor, but have ejected their crystals as per nightly tradition.

"I never would've guessed, lad," Abrax snorts derisively. "We've still got a few days before we get out on the eastern side of here. Maybe a month before we will be anywhere near Providence. Hope there's some settlements between here and there for us to resupply."

"Good, because we might be out of wine after tonight!" Vivían cheers, taking another swig.

"We'll need more medical ointments for Remus as well," Aida adds. "We're down to one last wineskin of sedatives."

All of a sudden, enhanced by slight intoxication, my curiosity takes hold. It has been nearly a month since I'd first met Remus, and I'm still ignorant to what exactly is wrong with him. His condition is slowly becoming worse, and he requires near-constant care. I have to ask.

"Aida, you never told us what Remus has been stricken with," I ask somberly, drawing everyone's attention. "Would it be an appropriate time to tell us what happened?"

No one says anything for a moment, their expressions range from apprehensive to concern. Remus gives me the most genuine look of everyone, for his eyes reflect both pity and understanding. Aida looks from me to Remus, clearly seeking his permission.

Letting out a protracted exhalation, Remus nods solemnly.

"It happened the night of the riots," Aida begins to recount, the group starts listening in closely. "With our invitations, we thought we were looking for an Insurgent contact when the chaos erupted. We fled to the streets, but were pursued by violence and pandemonium. In the midst of our escape, Centum found us and captured us. The Imperials believed we were instrumental in starting the riots, thanks to Centum's input."

Remus adopts a grave expression as he stares into the firelight.

"However, Centum was also aware of Remus' defection and attempted search for Providence," Aida says bitterly. "If there's one thing you all should know, it's that Centum is ruthless when it comes to the all-beloved Providence. Centum will destroy anything and anyone who obstructs the path to that place. To Centum, Remus committed the worst heresy of all by trying to find Providence. So, the Remnant developed a punishment for such heretics."

An ominous feeling of dread wells up within me as I look at Remus—his expression almost on the verge of tears.

"Centum has stores of a Nanite virus that they save for the worst dissenters within the Remnant," Aida continues, her voice turning weak. "Their Order has somehow been able to harvest samples of the Nanites within a Roil. I think they're residual swarms, like rain showers after a hurricane. If injected into a specific part of the body, the limited Nanites will slowly eat away at any tissue it comes into contact with. So Centum thought it would serve poetic justice if an *outspoken* heretic no longer held the ability to speak. Remus was given the virus in the left hemisphere of his brain, leaving him barely able to speak."

She lowers her bald head gravely. "That's part of the reason we set out on this. To bring Centum to justice and help cure Remus."

A single tear rolls down her cheek as she looks at Remus, who in turn places his hand atop of hers. I feel a warm sense of adoration as I see their fingers intertwine, and I smile. It's utterly horrific what happened to Remus; his life is ticking away as he fights an unwinnable battle. I don't know much about the virus, but I can only assume it won't be long before the Nanites kill him. It's a slow and painful way to die, and I feel the utmost pity for Remus.

But despite this, he seems just as loyal and caring as he would've been without the virus. He doesn't let it hinder who he is, and it touches me.

"So, do the Nanites have little voices in your head?" Vyck asks all of a sudden.

Vivian smacks his leg. Everyone regards him with disdain.

"You ruined the mood," Devin says, putting his palm to his

head.

Remus doesn't take offense to it, however. Surprisingly, he snorts in merriment. "No— Voices—" he says with levity. "Sometimes—"

"Bone me! I knew it!"

While the mood is beginning to retake its former merriness, I can't help but feel sorry for Remus. He has spent his life serving the Remnant only for them to betray him and spoil his chance at a normal life. I know his relationship with Aida makes it even more painful—for he has to watch someone he loves experience his decline. I hold the utmost respect for the pair, and I'm more determined than ever to bring Centum to justice. To help Remus.

Hope is still present; we only have a bit more left in our journey. Saving the world is one thing, but now this quest feels more personal. There's a new motivation. If fate or the Sage God are on our side, we'll reach Providence in time to save Remus. We have to.

Once the ruckus calms and the bleariness of intoxication take hold, everyone prepares for a good night's sleep. Vivían is quick to set up her cot next to Vyck, and I almost laugh at her obvious ploy. Tálir and Abrax are preparing to undress their suits of armor. Remus and Aida lay next to each other, his hand upon her face. Devin remains alert and on watch. The fire is still lit and cackling.

I smile at the tranquility. Everyone is peaceful, content, and full of new prospects. Compassion fills the air. And it's a soothing thought as I prepare my cot for sleep.

A sound rouses me. Footsteps echo from further in the canyon.

Everyone hears it. Soft pattering of boots against the gravel, and the quiet huffing of breaths. Someone is in the canyon with us. The noise of movement reverberates from atop the canyon walls. I blink in confusion. *They're all around us?*

Imperceptibly, everyone slowly begins to move towards their weapons. Trying to avoid the mistake in the Flames, I cautiously begin reaching for my bowpistol. Abrax tries to shuffle through one of his munition packs for their gems.

There's a quiet stillness for a moment. Then chaos erupts.

Four blue stunbolts whiz through the night and impact both Tálir and Abrax. Both men are stunned even before they can load their energy crystals. They slump sideways, unconscious.

More stunbolts fly through the air, lighting up the area with an azure hue. Devin is suddenly struck by one. I start to panic. They've taken out our best fighters. The rest of us scramble for our weapons. Vivían snaps open the plasma bow and immediately fires a few energy arrows. I hear a body fall into the canyon from above. Vyck and Aida find their bowpistols and start firing back blindly.

A stunbolt hits next to my foot just as I make it to my weapons. But shouting erupts from all around us.

"O'rah tah!"

Oh shit! I think to myself as I unholster my bowpistol.

A dozen Crimsons enter the firelight of the camp brandishing stunpikes. The bowrifle fire ceases as they charge towards us. Vivían shoots two with her bow before succumbing to a stunpike. Another down. Remus is smacked upside the head with one and passes out. My limbs start to turn cold with fear. Aida releases an enraged war cry as she fires her weapon at the assailants. Vyck and I follow suite, firing our bowpistols in all directions. Six have been slain, but more charge in.

We're overwhelmed. My heart starts racing with trepidation as I toss the pistol aside and extend my spear. Aida and Vyck are swarmed and stunned by the pikes, leaving me alone. Four Crimsons charge at me with their pikes ready to strike. I try to breathe and remember how to move when attacking with *Silverlight*.

With a quick jab, the spear punctures the gut of the first assailant and drives him back. I flourish the weapon and block a hit from another. I jab again and skewer the Crimson through his left breast. I'm not fast enough, however.

In the midst of a pivot, three charge simultaneously and strike at me in three separate locations. I can't block them all, and the stunpikes unleash torrents of electricity into my body. I spasm and drop my spear before falling to the ground. The Crimsons immediately start cheering and whooping with victory. Some begin tending to the wounded. Others start binding us with shackles. The rest start gathering our equipment for travel.

They're taking us prisoners! I think to myself. Through the haze of numb pain, I feel apprehension. Crimsons start gathering us all into one location as some others begin riding our repulsorbikes. They've claimed prisoners and salvage. Now, they plan to present their spoils.

CHAPTER 38

Tálir

Retribution

MY FACE HITS THE DIRT, filling my nostrils and mouth with dust and filaments. Incomprehensible shouts make it difficult to focus even as I try to stand up. I can taste the tang of blood. Gloved hands grab my arms and yank me to my feet and start pressing me forward.

The Crimsons herd us like livestock through the empty canyons, brandishing their weapons and calling out in their tongue. They spare no punches with anyone in the group; all of us are being shoved or kicked in varying degrees. Even Abrax is being roughed up as we trek into the canyon.

We should've known better than to assume there were no

Crimsons around last night. Hells, they know these canyons better than we do, and we walked right into it. *How could we be so foolish?*

We've been herded as prisoners all through the night and into the following day. The sun is orange in the sky above the maroon canyon walls. The repulsorbikes are being ridden by Crimsons, the engines kick up torrents of dirt next to us. Exhaustion tugs at my features. But my heart pounds with adrenaline spurred by being beaten.

Stripped of our kryo ammunition and shackled together by chains, they keep me and Abrax secluded from the others as we march. Initially they tried to strip us of our armor as well, but the suits remained tightly snug on us. Only Abrax and I can undress our own armor. The Crimsons seem to be aware of our capabilities, and have placed us in the care of more broad captors. I can feel a trickle of blood seeping down the side of my face. Abrax is in a much worse state: blood runs from his nose and he cradles his right side after the Crimsons beat him. His eyes reflect horrible pain, and his breathing becomes rapid. They've likely reopened the wounds in his chest.

"Can you assholes take it easy on him?" I shout at the Crimsons. "He's already hurt."

Immediately, the end of a stunpike strikes the side of my face and I taste more blood. I stumble to the side and spots appear in my vision for a few seconds. Spitting out some blood, I'm again shoved forwards in an effort to keep moving.

They herd us through the rocky ravines that twist through the gorges, spanning several kilometers. Generally barren, specs of tan

grass and puddles of muddy water dot the landscape for variety. Piles
of rocks and boulders also span the ravines. Clouds above are
gathering, and I feel that a rainstorm is coming.

"Abrax," I whisper as I march alongside him. "What do we
do?"

He looks at me through bruised eyes. "Nothing," he replies
weakly. "We bide our time and see what they want. They took us as
prisoners for a reason."

"I hope you're right," I say hesitantly.

It takes almost until the afternoon for us to reach the
destination the Crimsons intend, and they make a conscious effort to
rough us up. After being led into a short cave at the end of the
ravine, we enter a large open canyon nearly a kilometer in diameter.
Rain falls heavily from the cloudy sky, muddying the ground. Dotting
the maroon colored expanse are tents, huts, and large pavilions that
look freshly set up. Vivían was right when she said the Outlanders
practice nomadic behaviors. Dozens of campfires have been lit under
makeshift gazebos, and racks of fresh meats are situated near each
one.

As we enter the area, I see the bustling crowd of several
dozen people, dressed similarly to the Crimsons but less militaristic.
The universal goggles and shaggy hair can be seen on each adult
whether male or female. The children are the only exceptions, but
they still sport similar russet leather-hide outfits as the adults. All stop
to stare at us as we enter the village, their faces seem emotionless
with the goggles over their eyes. Rainwater glistens off the leather.

"Kysh me'a!" some of the children start chanting. "Kysh me'a!"

"Vivían," I say, looking over to her. "What are they saying?"

She looks at me unsettlingly. "Fresh meat," she replies warily. "I should've mentioned that Crimsons occasionally practice cannibalism."

"Ey ya think?" Devin calls sarcastically. "The Hells do you mean by occasionally?"

"If they're out of livestock, then we're next on the menu," Vivían replies almost aloofly, but her expression darkens. "I know a way to get us out of this. So don't say anything stupid. I'll handle this."

"Silon!" barks one of the captors, hitting Vivían with the butt-end of a bowrifle. "Silon, avah'ky."

The other captors start to snicker before repeating the word *avah'ky*. While I hold no knowledge of their language, it's evident that the word is meant as an insult. Particularly towards Vivían—her expression reflects a repressed hatred.

I remain silent to avoid any more unnecessary abuse, and walk slowly into their village. I hear Abrax's breathing becoming ragged as he limps next to me. We lock glances for a moment, and he gives me a nod of reassurance.

Weaving through the tents and huts, the Crimsons lead us towards one of the larger pavilions near the center of the village. Nearly sixty meters in diameter, the pavilion is draped with newer flaps of tan leather. Rings of ornaments gyrate around the crest of the roof, and esoteric beads drape over the opening.

A pair of Crimsons walk ahead and part the draping beads as they force us all into the hut. Inside, the dirt ground is sporadically covered by animal pelts and fine rugs. A fine cot is situated on the far right of the chamber while a horde of salvage and treasures line the left wall. Among the cache are exotic swords, bowrifles, chests, eccentric clothes, and various exoskeleton armor sets.

A distinctive pair of armor sets catches my notice. To my astonishment, two complete suits of Maven armor are placed atop wooden mannequins for display. The bronze metal seems new, polished, and almost museum worthy. One seems larger than the other, and I deduce that perhaps the smaller is meant for a female.

My awe is interrupted by the shoving of a Crimson, who forces us further into the hut. Near the far end is an elongated table flanked by a few torches. The table is laden with a few mugs of ale, half-eaten food, and a map that drapes over the edge. A few cheap holoprojectors show static displays of fortresses and villages. Other Outland clans, perhaps. Standing behind the table with arms firmly planted is a woman of middle age.

Unlike the other Crimsons, she's dressed in finer, fitted leather hides that drape over her like a dress. She also sports metal pauldrons, leather greaves, and dark boots. Her brunette hair is wild but pulled back into a ponytail. Blackheads coat her long nose while dry skin stretches around her gaunt face. A serpentine scar slithers over her left eye.

She barely acknowledges us, and seems intent on the map and

holoprojections before her. Without glancing up, she cycles through more images in the holoprojectors. One shows a figure garbed in Maven armor. But the static obscures the person's face.

"Detas, Leir'tah," one of the escorts grunts, shoving me to my knees. "Y avah'ky."

The woman finally looks up at us, her grey eyes glint with cool contempt as she studies us. She stares coldly at us for a long moment before saying, "Bim tus."

The guards bow and leave the tent, but I can hear them stop directly outside. There is a silence in the air, as well as the stench of spoiling food and stale beer. Discomfort grips me as I meet the eyes of the Crimson woman.

"What are they saying, Vivían?" Sarina asks quietly.

"The guards presented Leir'tah, the Shepherd of Cross, with prisoners," Vivían responds in a hush. "She's ordered them to leave, though."

The woman's eyes snap to Vivían. I immediately grow apprehensive about the present danger. Vivían had deserted the Crimsons and dyed her hair in defiance of her clan's traditions. There's no way she'd be welcomed back with open arms, and I grow more fearful.

"Welcome to home, Vi' Avah," the woman says in coarse Trade to Vivían. "You travel with new group?"

"A hunter always travels in a pack," Vivían replies distantly.

I turn to see Vyck's expression of distress as he eyes Vivían. "What did she just refer to you as?" he asks.

"Vi' was my name," she replies glancing at him. "Avah was my clan title for huntress. They raised me as their finest huntress. And every huntress serves the pack leader. Leir'tah was the one I served."

While Vivían had revealed her past association with the Crimsons, it's still shocking to see it come to the forefront. She's so different from them that it's impossible to see how she could've ever been associated with them. Perhaps, at its core, that's the sole reason why she'd departed in the first place.

"Not only you desert clan, you invading our home. You bring demons to home, Vi' Avah," Leir'tah says, her tone icy enough to chill the room.

"They are not demons, Leir'tah," Vivían retorts with a plea. "They are Maven Knights, those whom the clan has vowed to protect. Isn't that the Cross Way?"

Leir'tah's grey eyes reflect a burning disgust. "Mavens extinct," Leir'tah sneers, regarding me and Abrax with scrutiny. "Only left be pretenders and liars. False wizardry is all they be. You is disgraceful for being with Remnant."

"They're not false, Leir'tah!" Vivían retorts angrily, leaning forward. "And we do not serve the Remnant! They are our enemies just as much as yours."

She paces around the table and starts to approach us. All of us are kneeling before her like subjects genuflecting for a queen. Leir'tah fidgets with some of the rings on her fingers.

"I disagree," she says mirthlessly. "You travel with wizardry false Mavens, attack mine scouts, and invade home land. Remnant want nothing but clan blood and weapons. They come with men in false armor, like these two."

She gestures to me and Abrax, and my face flushes in anger. *We are not false Mavens! How dare she.*

A noise rouses me. One of the guards enters the pavilion with one of our packs and presents it to Leir'tah. It's Sarina's satchel. I gulp in nervousness. After a few seconds of rummaging, she extracts the holoprojector and the parchment. I turn to see Sarina's face lose color, and her eyes widen with fear. Like she's staring her own judgment in the face.

The holoprojector activates and plays a message for Leir'tah. A shadowy figure expresses his waning patience with the Crimson's lack of cooperation. But more, I consider the circumstances. We've just been captured with this message in our possession and wearing Maven armor. With the addition of trespassing in Crimson territory, it very well is starting to seem like we're messengers.

"*Rest assured, if you continue to resist us, we will destroy your clan,*" the holoprojection says with finality. "*This is your last chance to join us.*"

The transmission ends and Leir'tah gives us all a cold look of abhorrence. "If you no serve Remnant, why you has message for me?" Leir'tah asks; a sneer grows on her face.

"We don't serve the Remnant," Sarina says desperately. "I took that message off the body of one of your warriors who attacked us."

I lower my head. *Why did she say that?* "You take trophy from mine warriors?" Leir'tah snarls, her eyes narrowing.

"No!" Sarina pleads. "The Remnant is our enemy, and I thought those messages could help us learn more about them—"

"SILENT!" Leir'tah barks, slapping Sarina across the face. "First, you bring false wizardry into mine home. Then, you admit to stealing message from mine warriors. You may not serve Remnant, but you have crimes committed."

A pit starts to form in my stomach as I watch Leir'tah pace before all of us. She stares at each of us with her cold grey eyes. It doesn't matter what we say now, we've dug ourselves too deep into a hole. And she's too bloodthirsty to care even if we are innocent.

"If we have committed crimes against the Crimsons, then a Crimson should take the blame," Vivían chimes in, looking at Leir'tah. "I know the law of the Cross Way. I offer the rite of sacrifice to spare them from your punishment, Leir'tah."

There's something in Vivían's eyes. Something that's both frightened and determined. Leir'tah regards Vivían stonily as she paces—her hands behind her back. The various jewels and necklaces clank together in an almost tribal sense. A meter from Vivían's face, she stops and stares blankly at her. It's just as ominous as if her face was expressing anger, but her cold detachment seems more dangerous.

"Then you be punished as *avah'kal*," Leir'tah says in a resounding voice. "You take punishment for friends, they live. We see about false wizardry."

Leir'tah traces a finger over Vivían's face. It's both tender and unsettling at the same time. Vivían doesn't flinch, but I see her nostrils flare with anxiety. Her lip starts to tremble.

"Li sey o'rah yen!" she barks as the guards rush in.

Roughly handling us, they drag each of us out of the pavilion. All of us are panicking as to what's going to happen. All except for Vivían, who has a calm expression on her face. And yet, her eyes are watery and filled with stress. A faint sense of dread wells within me. What has she done? What did Vivían bargain for to save us from Leir'tah's wrath?

CHAPTER 39

Sarina

Sacrifice

CLUMPS OF MUD SMACK against my face. A knee rams into my side. A voice shouts in my ear.

I've been a prisoner more times in the last month than I'd ever anticipated. But this is different. The shoving, the beating, the harassing; it's much more frightening than before. The Crimsons are unfeeling and uncompromising in their efforts to subdue and herd us into the pens.

With the shackles painfully digging into my wrists, the Crimsons pull me and a few of the others through the village as rain falls from the sky. Commoners shout and jeer in their language while throwing fistfuls of mud at us. Bruises start to form along my body as mud cakes the rest. My pride is struggling to remain intact. While the others are being similarly beaten, Vivían is by far receiving the worst of it.

Crimsons rush to tear at her clothes while mud is smacked against her face. Coughing up muck and blood, she tries to remain collected as a guard knees her in the stomach. The savage Outlanders laugh as she whimpers in pain.

We are led towards the center of the village where a large, ritual pit has been dug into the dirt. It's a fresh dig, since the Crimsons have recently settled this area. Nearly twenty meters in diameter and with a large wooden post at the center, the pit seems eerily sacrificial. Making our way around the circular ritual pit, we are ushered into some laserpens. Taking off our manacles, the Crimsons shove Remus, Aida, Devin, Vyck, and me into the larger pen. Abrax and Tálir are isolated from us in a laserpen a few meters away.

The Crimsons activate the energy grid, and violet beams web between the four metal conduit posts. Rain water evaporates with a *hiss* as it impacts the individual beams. Vivían isn't taken to a cage, but instead she's tied to the wooden post at the center of the pit. Her hands are bound above her head. Vivían's body seems to sag on the post as she gives into her fear.

"What do you plan on doing with her?" I cough; my breaths are shallow from being kicked in the gut.

"You see soon," one of the guards grunts in Trade. "Punishment be *avah'kal*."

The commotion finally dies down as the Crimson guards

shuffle back into the village. Commoners still stare and leer, but they don't approach the pit. They almost seem apprehensive to go near it. I get the feeling that something ominous is about to happen.

I try to steady my breathing and relax my muscles. Devin and Vyck both flop to the ground with a grunt while Aida helps Remus sit down. He's in the early phase of one of his spasms, and Aida doesn't have the sedatives on her. All we can do is hope for Remus to fight it on his own. I can only imagine what it's like having microscopic Nanites turning one's mind to mush. My brain aches as I think about it, and my stomach feels nauseous.

"Hush it's going to be alright, Remus," Aida says soothingly, rubbing his back and pressing her head to his.

Despite the horrid situation, I find some comfort in seeing one person so dedicated to another. Remus certainly reciprocates her devotion, but I'm touched by how deeply she cares for him despite his affliction. She knows his days are numbered, and yet, she sticks by and supports him. If that isn't love, I'm not sure what is.

"I get the feeling they don't like us very much," Vyck comments in a strained voice, rubbing his head.

"Isn't this just a customary friendly hazing?" Devin retorts sarcastically. His arms are splayed out in the mud. "Next is the drinking gambit."

I can't help but chuckle lightly. He's maddening as all Hells, but I'm learning to accept it. I'd never have thought I would grow fond of him and his partner.

I look over at the other pen where Tálir and Abrax are

imprisoned. The old man is on all fours, wheezing and gasping for breath. His injuries must be severe since the Crimsons held no punches around his recently healed wounds. Tálir has a bloody nose and a bruised eye.

"Tálir!" I call, eliciting his attention. His gaze is piercing, like he's trying to memorize my face. I can see the true passion in his eyes. "Are you alright?"

He gives a light smirk. "I'll live. You?"

I cough in pain, but I laugh underneath the exhalation. "I'll live longer."

He nods his head, and I can see blood and mud smeared in his long hair. He says nothing more, and focuses on helping Abrax.

"So what's our plan?" I ask the others, wiping some mud off my face. "I'm feeling the urge to send all of these barbarians to meet their retribution in the Hells."

"You're going to take them all on from in here, m'lady?" Devin comments with raised eyebrows. "I admire that fighting spirit, but we're stuck here for the moment."

"Why?" I protest bitterly. "These cages can't be that complicated to escape from. There's got to be a way to fool with the emitters, or disable a power outlet."

"It's not that simple, Sarina," Vyck says, pointing to the laser grid. "These pens are capable of deflecting military missiles and energy bolts. The only way we could shut them down is if we boned up the power couplings."

I look outside and see the metal boxes that generated energy for the laserpens. Both are situated several meters away near one of the huts on our right. A Crimson guard is stationed next to the couplings—bowrifle in hand.

Damnit! I swear to myself. We don't have anything that can reach that range. If only Tálir and Abrax had energy in their armor. They could blast the damn things to bits.

But as it currently stands, we have no means of escape.

Night has fallen upon us as we desperately try to plot an escape. The rain has stopped. Fires burn bright throughout the village and roasting meat fills the air with salty smells. No matter how hard we try, none of us are able to formulate a plan to escape. Scenario after scenario, we can't figure out an escape plan. Even Abrax and Tálir cannot seem to focus a strategy. Abrax is already barely able to stay conscious, let alone formulate strategy. Tálir does his best to tend to the old man, but his breaths are ragged and his eyes flutter.

He can't die! I won't let him!

Vivían sees our distraught, and speaks from the center of the pit. She calls, "Sarina. Don't worry about escaping. They'll set you free once they have what they want."

I look at her in apprehension. "What do you mean? What do they want?"

Even at our distance, I can see tears welling up in her eyes. "They want me. To punish me for heresy. To give me the mark of *avah'kal,* the hunter sacrifice. If there's one thing you should know about our culture, it's that sacrifice is viewed as salvation."

Vyck stands suddenly and rushes to the edge of the pen, nearly frying himself against the beams. I can see it in his eyes. The terror, the concern, and the desperate protest.

"Vivían..." Vyck's voice falters. "No. No you can't!"

I feel cold dread grasping my heart with icy fingers. I see Vivían give a weak smile, despite her terror. "If I submit to their punishment as a hunting sacrifice, they'll let the rest of you go when it is concluded. I'm not sure about Tálir and Abrax, but the rest of you will be freed."

"NO!" Vyck yells, his voice pleading. "No! We can find another way!"

She shakes her head. "Leir'tah is their Shepherd, and she leads by showing both strength and mercy. The Cross Way says that a sacrifice must be treated with honor. Even if it's with an enemy."

Vyck looks heartbroken. I don't know what fate awaits Vivían, but a pit in my stomach saps hope from me. She won't make it out alive.

No! I can't let her die!

Even as I struggle to formulate a plan, commotions come from within the village. Torches are lit, and a drumbeat punctuates the air. It's tribal and portentous. Crowds start to gather around the pit and near the pens. The power couplings aren't blocked, but now hundreds of eyes are on us.

A throne the size of a small hut is hauled by Crimson guards from the center street. Repulsor disks keep the structure floating off the ground and easier to pull via chains. It's a crude thing. Rigid, austere, and painted with signature red, gold, and silver paints. Metal crosses are bolted into the slopes, piked with skulls. Four torches are holstered on each slope. Stone steps are smooth as marble, and the chair itself wraps around the figure in the center.

Leir'tah sits with one leg over the other, a scepter clenched in her hands. She wears a more ceremonial robe, but her appearance hasn't changed. She looks at us with cold menace as her throne is dragged towards the pit. Shamans wrapped with maroon leather cloaks enter the pit near Vivían. Using a metal drum, the guards pour oil around the perimeter of the ritual circle. When finished, they place the seemingly half-empty oil drum a few meters from us. Fires are started and they circle the pit in a blazing ring. Leir'tah's throne hovers barely a meter outside the flames.

As the night wears down on us, I see the barbaric ritual preparation. My chest feels like an icy cavern, devoid of warmth or comfort. A hellish fire surrounds the pit as shamans begin to move towards Vivían. Though she wears a brave expression, I can see her watery eyes widen. Vivían's judgement awaits.

CHAPTER 40

Tálir

Hells Break Loose

"MERCY!"

Her terrified screams reverberate throughout the village, bloodcurdling and agonizing. The wind seems to carry it, and the cackling fires make shadows seem almost demonic. It's as if we've journeyed to the many Hells for our final, painful judgement.

Everyone knows of the Arc, the religious beliefs of the three nations. So I'm equally familiar with the various Hells in scripture, one for every crime or sin. Killers are sent to the eternal flame, where you are to relive the exact pain you caused the one you killed. In a twisted sense, Vivían is seemingly being judged in that part of the Hells.

Vivían is chained to the post outside of our laserpens, and dozens of Crimsons encircle the fire pit as if partaking in some dark ritual. In a sense, it is. The shamans have stripped her shirt, leaving her chest bare in a humiliating fashion. A ring of fire keeps the commoners at bay while two Crimson shamans stand inside the ring with heated iron pokers.

"Please," I hear her plea. "Please don't!"

"You sacrifice for this. Brand of *avah'kal*, of hunter sacrifice, be inescapable, Vi' Avah," Leir'tah commands coldly from her throne. "Why you try to back out?"

"She's just scared! Let her go, you bitch!" Sarina shouts from the pen several meters from me.

"Vivían!" Vyck calls desperately, his hands stressfully grabbing his blonde hair "It'll be alright. Focus on us. We'll get you out of there!"

Her eyes lock with Vyck and my heart wells with unfathomable pity, for she looks defeated. She gazes at Vyck with a passion I thought I'd never see in her. Her lighthearted and boisterous attitude has been so uplifting on our journey. Now to see her shamed, humiliated, and frightened it's unbearable.

There's a pause, and then she releases a bloodcurdling cry of pain.

The shamans craftily start tracing esoteric lines with the irons across Vivían's chest. The sizzle of burning skin can be heard underneath her screams. My stomach convulses, and I feel like vomiting. Raw hatred stains my heart at watching a friend suffer this torment. For a minute they trace some kind of symbol from her right breast across to her stomach. The symbol follows the shape of an A, but with small tendrils sprouting from it. Her screams reach a fevered pitch before halting, and she blacks out from the pain.

"YOU FRAGGING ANIMALS!" Vyck roars, nearly slamming his hand into the laser gate.

"Let her go!" I shout, my anger rising.

"Tálir, keep calm," Abrax manages to wheeze, cradling his right side.

"We can't just sit here while they torture her!" I protest angrily, facing him. "We've got to get out of here and help her."

Abrax's dark eyes shine with determinism. "We need to be smart and patient about this," he says weakly. "Mavens don't act brashly. Keep your thoughts precise."

"To all the Hells with that!" I growl, turning back to face the crowd. "I'm going to make every last one of them pay for this!"

Morning light is only a couple hours away. Even if we escape, we still have to find our repulsorbikes if we're to flee. Our weapons and supplies have been stored in a tent a few yards away from the ritual center. But without the kryos, I'm unsure how I'll be able to defend the others if we escape the cages.

It seems hopeless. We can't escape.

A beeping noise suddenly emanates from my right bracer, a repetitive pinging.

My eyes widen with both hopeful excitement and hollow dread. The shouting of the crowd prevents notice, and I gingerly lift the plate to reveal the terminal.

7% Charge it reads.

A similar noise emanates from Abrax's gauntlet, and his pained expression vanishes. Looking from his gauntlet to me, he says quietly, "We have fresh kryo residue in the armor! If we're patient, we can harness that sliver of power. Wait until they reach twenty percent. That should be enough to escape and defend ourselves."

"Maybe ten minutes' worth of energy," I whisper with determination. My eyes dart and see the oil drum resting meters from our cage. Right next to the power couplings. "I know what to do. What about the Roil?"

"It seems to be moving slowly," the old man grunts, looking at the sky. "But we'll deal with that when it comes."

The Crimsons begin chanting as the shamans halt their branding—the contusions on her chest look almost like lightning bolts. Leir'tah stands from her pedestal and started walking down the steps of the makeshift throne.

14% Charge.

"Ita vod wek hara kompi *avah'kal,*" Leir'tah says with an icy aura. "Awake for ritual sacrifice, disgraceful Vi' Avah."

Vivían remains motionless, her breathing seems faint. The last hours of moonlight and surrounding fire make her skin glow. The brand marks almost seem like torrents of fire.

"Stop this!" Aida cries desperately.

"Let her go!" Sarina screams again. "Or you'll pay in blood!"

"We'll appease your sense of sacrifice!" Vyck growls, his fists clenched in rage. "How about a village of sacrifices? Will that do?"

My blood boils. Not with hatred, but with determinism. For once, we are all united for the same cause: to free Vivían and seek retribution. Caught up in the moment, all I can think about is the thrill of our unification.

20% Charge.

Now, it's time to save my friends.

Minding my usage, I direct a Stream towards the oil drum several meters away. Emerald energy soars from my fingers and arcs towards the open container. Sparks erupt and ignite the oil. A small explosion results, and the laserpens immediately deactivate.

Chaos follows. The crowd disperses in fear as the warriors attempt to scramble their way through the throng. Those guarding the cages are so disoriented that they barely move as Abrax fires two Streams into their chests—stunning them in seconds. As the pandemonium grows, I see the others start overtaking some of the confused warriors. Armed with bowrifles, Sarina and Devin begin firing at the remaining guards.

Vyck immediately rushes to the pit, fearlessly leaping through the ring of fire. Time slows as I watch in captivated astonishment at his heroic determinism. When the time came, he was ready to jump into action. I grin with respect.

As Vyck crosses the flames, Devin fires a bolt right at the chains binding her. The bonds fall away, and Vivían is about to topple over when Vyck catches her and cradles her unconscious body.

Jumping into the pit after Vyck, Sarina rushes to cover the two from the Crimsons. Sarina's eyes find mine, and we both nod to each other.

"Abrax!" I call, wheeling around as he sends a Stream into the chest of a warrior. "Get the others to our equipment stores, I'll hold them off."

The old man regards me with a concerned expression. "Don't do anything I wouldn't do, Tálir!" he says in agreement, limping towards the others.

Quickly activating the helmet, I incapacitate more guards as I move towards the fiery pit. My HUD reads *Armor Integrity: 91%, Output Charge: 16%*, and *Kryo Charge: 17%*. Similarly leaping through the flames, I stand defensively next to Sarina as Vyck prepares to move Vivían. Upon seeing Sarina firing at Crimsons in defense of Vivían, I feel a sudden rush of emotions. Excitement, admiration, determinism, and apprehension. In the heat of the moment, I want to say something to her. But my mind falters, and I reorient to the battle taking place.

With a primal grin on my face, I turn to see Leir'tah and a dozen of her warriors converging on the pit. Armed with bowrifles and stunpikes, they seem eager to engage the wielder of demon magic. It's a euphoric sensation, the thrill of retribution. Finally, we aren't the ones at the Crimsons' mercy, and we can properly defend ourselves from them. Deep inside me burns a hatred for their craven tactics and barbaric rituals. It's time for me to unleash my power of justice for what they've done to Vivían.

Adopting a protective stance, I stand between them and Vivían as my fingers spark with kryo energy.

"Prepare yourself!" I call to Leir'tah, "because all the Hells are waiting impatiently for you."

◆ ◆ ◆

Leir'tah's grey eyes shine with a primal hatred as she paces behind her warriors. I can tell she loathes everything about the armor and its demon magic. The Remnant is full of people who use the power of the armor for nefarious and selfish reasons. So I understand her disdain. But I'm not using the magic for despicable purposes. I'm using it to protect my friends.

"You is outnumbered, false wizardry!" she says in as much Trade as she can. "You burn for interrupting ritual."

I allow my movements to flow, letting the kryo energy course through the armor and into my palms. Emerald magic sparks between my fingers, and the Crimsons flinch warily.

"Correction," I say darkly, a primeval grin still etched on my face. "You will burn for hurting my friends."

Anger and malice start to boil within my chest. I can feel it clouding my focus with red hate. I know I should heed Abrax's lesson about maintaining the balanced focus, but I choose not to. My anger and sense of retribution have taken root, and I want to use that for my focus. All of my rage, fear, and lust for vengeance fuel my focus.

With only a few minutes' worth of power, I send two blistering Streams towards the Crimsons. While only at *16%*, the energy is intense enough to cause sparks to explode out as they are flung backwards. The other warriors aim their bowrifles and fire. My energy struggles to reach *25%*. Generating a Shield, I'm able to deflect their incoming projectiles as I cover Sarina while Vyck tries to drag Vivian. She is still unconscious, but her chest is covered by a light cloth.

From behind my Shield, Sarina begins firing off rounds from her bowrifle. The red bolts find another three targets, and they drop dead to the ground. As we both retreat slowly, the Crimsons advance through the ring of fire. Like the torturers from the Hells, they purposefully approach us with cruel intent. And through the fires, Leir'tah stands with her scepter.

Her dark silhouette ripples in the fire, and her shaggy hair looks like a wolf's mane. It is here that she resembles the one who rules the pits of Hells. A near perfect parallel. The lord of Hells. His name is Inuban, and he is the bringer of death.

CHAPTER 41

Sarina

A Departing Arrival

IT HAS BEEN A LONG TIME since I've felt true solidarity.

The idea of caring for an individual like they're a member of my family has been absent from my mind for years. I've had friends, and close ones at that—but I've never thought of them as a brother or sister. And I've only known Vivían, Tálir, and the others for a shorter time than those past friends.

Yet, seeing the abuse and torture of any of them stirs feelings of wrath. I feel protective, as if I'm defending my own family.

Vyck carefully drags Vivían towards the edge of the pit. Projectiles pound against the energy barrier generated by Tálir's armor. I duck in and out of cover to fire the bowrifle clenched in my hands. Tálir holds a look of fiery protectiveness on his face as he guards us. His defensive nature is admirable. He shows passion for those he cares about, and he's determined to seek justice. Part of me finds him enthralling—the way he fights, his sense of loyalty, and the way he looked at me early on.

In the midst of the chaos, I'm perplexed as to why this feeling bubbled up. Is it because of the heat of battle? The rush of emotions after watching Vivían's torture?

I'm not entirely sure, but I do know that it's immensely satisfying to see him in the heated frenzy.

Currently still surrounded by Leir'tah and her warriors, the Outlanders advance through the fires surrounding us. The heat doesn't bother them at all. Crimsons with stunpikes and swords start rushing in as the ranged ones continue to fire from afar. From deeper in the village, I see more warriors scuttling around the ritual pit to reinforce the battle.

A feeling of anxiety wells within me as I realize that we've placed ourselves into a trap. Vyck can't risk moving Vivían through the fires without help, and we can't fight them off at the same time. As the other Crimsons start to encircle the pit, Tálir blasts another two—but only for them to be replaced by more. I fire another volley of energy bolts from the bowrifle, killing two more. It's not enough.

"You is outnumbered, false wizardry!" Leir'tah says, planting her scepter into the dirt. "You burn with others, for kysh me'a!"

"I don't plan on becoming someone's dinner today," Tálir sneers, using the shield to deflect another blast.

His armor fails though, and the barrier shatters in a mass of emerald sparks. Under his breath, I can almost hear him say, "Oh shit."

"O'rah tah!" the warriors shout triumphantly.

The Crimsons start advancing into the pit, raising their weapons above their heads and chanting. Leir'tah holds up a hand and the riflemen cease fire. The stunpike-wielding Crimsons closest to Tálir rush forward and strike. Electricity sparks as they hit him with their weapons. Tálir fights them off briefly, but succumbs to the numbing pain. I fire at them. Three fall, but my weapon overheats. It's a thirty second cooldown. *Shit!*

I attempt to back away, but I can almost feel the flames licking my back. We have nowhere to go.

"O'RAH TAH!"

There's a flash of emerald light. All of the Crimsons stop chanting and start looking for the source. Suddenly, the Crimsons closest to us are felled by multiple magic blasts as the rest begin to retreat several steps.

Looking to my left and towards Leir'tah's pavilion, I can see Remus and Aida through the flames. While a few yards away, I see the distinct bronze Maven armor fitted to his body. Within his palms swirls fiery tendrils of sage energy, and his pale face reflects powerful determination. Aida's blades are drawn, and her body is tensed with fury.

In a blur of motion, Devin rushes from the right side behind the Crimsons. Wielding his shortsword, the blade flashes through the air as he cuts down the surprised warriors. The crowd of Crimsons starts to falter in their formation, and a few more streams of energy soar from my right. Abrax walks gingerly towards the pit, his left arm extended and sending kryo energy. His right hand is clenched around a cartridge of kryo ammunition.

"Tálir!" he calls out, just a few meters from us. "Catch!"

He tosses the cartridge over the flames towards Tálir, who scrambles up to one knee and catches the metal case. Faster than I'd ever thought possible; he reloads his gauntlets and tucks the cartridge under his breastplate.

I hear the hissing of steam and my head snaps around to see Aida dumping water over a portion of the flames. As the fire dies away in the section behind me, Vyck pulls Vivían out of the pit. With Aida's help, they manage to secure Vivían further from the conflict that erupts.

"Sarina! You might need this!" Aida calls as she tosses *Silverlight* to me. "Are you ready to fight off an entire Outlander clan?"

"Are you?" I say with a sardonic snort, catching the spear. "Let's do this together then!"

She gives me an enthusiastic nod of approval before we turn to face the conflict around us. I extend *Silverlight* to its full length, and the battle begins.

◆ ◆ ◆

A certain thrill creeps up my spine as I move through the midst of the conflict. Blades flash, energy soars, blood spurts, and shouts reverberate. Yet, within all of that, there's a focus I've achieved as adrenaline rushes through me.

Back in the Flames of Z'hart, I'd been captivated by fear and survival instincts. I was unsure how to see myself in a battle, and that was something that had prevented me from effectively fighting.

But after experience, training, and possessing a will to fight, I'm a different entity entirely. I'm precise and effective, and my body turns numb to avoid any sense of fear.

In a way, I almost find it as a symbolic reversal from where I had been weeks ago. Early on, my heart had been perpetually fearful and solitude. But here I am, with the group I now call friends, not afraid of anything.

The Crimson militia, still four dozen strong, forms up along the opposite side of the pit between us and Leir'tah. A dozen huts line a diameter of fifty meters around us. The common Crimsons rush away from the fighting and into their homes. The first rays of morning barely peek over the mountains, but a faint shadow can be seen in the sky. The Roil is approaching slowly from the north.

"I'm not sure how long I can fight," Abrax wheezes, as he hunches over.

I hurriedly pat him on the shoulder. "We've got this, old man. You get Vivían into one of those tents for cover." Then to the others, I command, "Everyone, form up!"

Abrax does as instructed. Our group enters a formation naturally as Tálir and Remus generate Shields with their armor in front of us. With their positioning, the two Mavens are able to expand the reach of their Shields into an almost crescent-shaped wall. The magic barriers deflect an incoming volley of bowrifle bolts from the Crimsons. Their rifles overheat after a moment of constant firing, and there's a pause as they attempt to reload. We use it. Remus and Tálir shrink their Shields low enough to allow Devin and Vyck to fire their scavenged bowrifles.

With precision, they target and eliminate all the Crimsons with ranged weapons before reloading. The Shields expand once again as the Crimsons charge at us. With swords and staffs, they batter against the energy barriers trying to get to us. But the Shields hold. Devin discards his rifle and draws his sword in preparation while Vyck keeps his rifle ready. *Silverlight* is steady in my hands and Aida flourishes her daggers. Tálir and Remus look back at us, awaiting the order. Beyond the emerald energy, I see the remaining three dozen Crimsons crowding before the barrier.

"Tálir! Remus!" I call, drawing their attention. "Shrink the Shield again!"

I glance at Devin and he recognizes what I want to do. We move into position. As the Crimsons enter a frenzy trying to batter their Shields, Tálir and Remus decrease the energy slightly. Their Shields no longer touch the ground, and it's just enough room for this to work.

Devin and I roll out from under the Shields and hack at the

legs of the Crimsons around us. *Silverlight* has an added benefit of being easily able to sweep out my opponents' legs. Blood spurts from sliced limbs as three Crimsons topple over on my side while another four fall on Devin's. The other Crimsons notice us and relinquish their barrage on the Shields. Tálir and Remus use the distraction.

Diminishing their Shields to cover only one arm, they use their free hands to hurl orbs of green fire into the mass of Crimsons. Magic explodes into the chests of two warriors, seriously burning their flesh and sending them flailing backwards. Dispersing due to the magic fire, the Crimsons start attacking sparsely instead of as a single mass. Easier for us to pick them off.

Training with *Silverlight* has helped my movements. My stance is wide and my motions are steady and precise. The others are fluid as well, blocking and counterattacking with deadly efficiency. Our group fights as if of a single mind. Tálir and Remus provide shielding and dispersing attacks, Vyck fires from a distance and the rest of us pick off the Crimsons as they scramble. None have gotten near Abrax and Vivían's tent.

Tálir deflects a sword from a Crimson as I duck underneath the Shield and skewer the warrior from below. Remus throws Aida into the air using his Shield as a makeshift springboard. Twisting, she flings her daggers into a few Crimsons while using her legs to grapple around another's head. Devin is in the midst of fending off two simultaneously until a bowrifle bolt from Vyck blasts off a chunk of one's head. Slicing off the other's arm, Devin claims his opponent's sword and in a scissor-like motion, beheads his foe.

Barely a dozen Crimson warriors remain as we press forward into the pit and towards Leir'tah. A concentrated beam erupts from Remus' open palm and strikes the ground near three Crimsons. Like a grenade going off, the ground explodes into a mass of dirt, green fire, and flailing bodies. Tálir throws an energy disk towards a Crimson but misses. In a flash of motion, I see Remus fire a stream of energy at the disk and deflect it back into the Outlander's head. Torrents of emerald flames envelop the Crimson's face as he yells in pain. Forming a Shield, Tálir bashes the Crimson away with the hardened energy. More disks fly from Remus' hands, blasting away three more Crimson warriors.

A wooden spear is flung towards me and my heart jolts. Tálir immediately deflects the projectile, shattering the spear to splinters. Focusing my aim, I ready *Silverlight* and toss the spear over Tálir's head towards my target. *Silverlight* flies several meters and hits true, impaling the Crimson spear-thrower. Rushing forward, I wrench the spear from my opponent's body and skewer a Crimson in the midst of attacking Aida. Blood mists the air as she slices his throat for good measure.

Smoke from the fires gyrate around us as the last of the Crimson warriors falls. The sky is illuminated by an orange light while smoke billows into the stars above. Black and blue mixes as the morning rises slowly.

I see Leir'tah through the haze of smoke and death. I smile in satisfaction, for she looks afraid. Her eyes are wide, and the scepter in her hands seems to be trembling.

We have won, and Leir'tah begins retreating up the stairs of her throne. The air reeks of smoke, bowrifle coolant, and blood. We begin to advance on the repulsor throne; Leir'tah bears a look of frightened disgust.

"Demons!" she hisses dangerously as she points her scepter at us. "False wizardry! You all be rabble! Skavah!"

"We may be rabble," I say coldly as I approach the throne. "But we hold more unity and discipline than your warriors. You've lost, Leir'tah."

"Prepare to face the judgment you so willingly gave to Vivían," Tálir growls.

Even under the helmet, I can sense the dark glower present upon his face. Hate radiates from his armor like the magic energy itself. He generates an orb of fire in his right palm. Behind us, I hear someone exit the tent. Abrax limps into my view with caution in his eyes.

"Tálir," Abrax warns as he walks forward. "No. We've won our battle. We don't need to become killers of clan leaders too. Itinerant Mind!"

Tálir's helmet folds into his pauldrons and reveals the conflicted expression on his face.

"She'll hunt us for the rest of our lives if we let her live!" he protests. "A Maven Knight ensures protection and order. She'll bring chaos with her if she ever finds us again! I have to protect you all!"

Both of them make sense. I feel conflicted. Tálir is right because Leir'tah will inevitably pursue us if we let her live. But Abrax is also right because we mustn't cause anymore needless death. Leir'tah is outmatched and in retreat, and there's no honor in killing someone like that. Even after what she did to Vivían.

I step forward and place a hand on Tálir's armored shoulder. "Tálir," I say gently as he looks at me. "We've beaten her. Let's just go."

Conflict is in his eyes for a brief moment. But as my eyes lock with his, a warm sense of tranquility emanates between us. His anger and his wrath begin to slowly fade. Sincerity radiates from me as if to say, *our friends are safe.* Tálir knows what he has to do.

"I once thought that fighting the right fight was the only way to protect my friends," he says quietly. "But I see now that walking away from the wrong fight can protect them all the same."

I smile at him. *He* has *learned something on this journey of ours.*

Leir'tah's shriek breaks me from my thoughts. "You all burn for this in future! We hunt you if you steal *avah'kah!* We—"

Her words are cut short.

There's a blur. A ruby orb of blistering energy strikes the side of the throne. An explosion erupts and practically vaporizes the throne. Leir'tah gives an inaudible scream before she too is swallowed by red flames.

A concussive wave blasts all of us backwards. I hit the dirt and see spots as *Silverlight* falls from my hand. I hear nothing except a high pitch ringing as I see a bloody fireball where the throne had been. As the cloud of fire dissipates, I weakly look around for the orb's source.

My heart nearly stops. From atop the canyon wall to our left by almost a hundred meters is a repulsor convoy. Hovering in position momentarily, the behemoth begins to fly through the canyon. It soon hovers five meters over the northern part of the village near a clearing.

From an open blast door in the side of the hull, a figure stands in preparation for a combat drop. The distinctive shine of the bronze Maven armor can be seen. There's a faint tinge of ruby energy sparking from his hand.

I strain to see his face as I rise from the ground. Cold fingers grasp around my chest cavity, and my breath almost feels short. Septem's cold, pale face watches us as he brings the swift vengeance of the Remnant down on us.

CHAPTER 42

Tálir

Inspiration

"ALRIGHT, GAME PLAN!" Vyck says in a panicked voice. His eyes are wide with anxiety as he stares at the convoy.

More Remnant warriors begin dropping into the village from the convoy. I can hear magic blasts and the screams from Crimsons in the northern section. I gulp as my heart beats faster. *We cannot fight that!* The Crimsons were one thing, but the Remnant is something else entirely.

Vivían lies unconscious on a makeshift cot while Aida checks her vitals. With no medical supplies on hand, the best she can do is bandage the contusions. Vyck eyes Vivían with grave concern.

"The bikes and repulsorcart are likely being stored in that

makeshift garage along the eastern side of the village," Devin says resolutely, twirling the shortsword in one hand.

"What's to stop them from pursuing us?" Sarina asks as she collapses her spear. "We don't have a day's ride on them anymore. Their convoy can keep speed with us."

My emotions have started to subside and I can clearly think of strategy. I noted at least a dozen Remnant warriors dropping from the convoy. With the packed and panicked village between us, they'll be slowed for a few minutes. But that won't be enough.

A thought springs into my mind. I consider the chess game I played so long ago. A king gambit. Use two pawns for bait to lure the opponent into a diversion. The only difference is, the pawns will be facing a queen and knights. Even with my new experience, I know I cannot match Septem's power. But it's our only option.

I inhale deeply before stepping forward. "We need a diversion," I say pointing towards the convoy. "I can hold them off for a few minutes and give you all a head start. It won't be much, but you all can get some distance before…"

"Before what?" Sarina jumps in, a worried expression is on her face. "Tálir there's no way Septem will just let you run away from something like that! He will kill you!"

Her blue eyes seem to shine with a storm of emotions. Sarina knows that I stand little chance against Septem. Her lips purse with anger, yet her expression reflects deep compassion.

Abrax steps forward weakly, cradling his right side. "She's right, lad," he coughs. "You are not ready to face him alone. Rushing in head-on will lead to failure. We'll have to think of something else."

A ruby ball of energy destroys a hut nearly a hundred meters from us. I hear the ring of a sword slicing through flesh. Screams echo. The Remnant is massacring this village. They're closing in. We don't have enough time to formulate another plan.

"There's no time, Abrax!" I say firmly. My voice reflects both fear and resolve. "They're coming right now and we need to get out of here! I can do this. I can protect you!"

No one says anything for a long moment. Abrax looks at me with his dark eyes. I see the misgiving etched in his features. Sarina's eyes seem watery and she shakes her head in a plea. But I have to stand firm. I won't let my friends suffer anymore. Holdin back in Erron's Ville, Abrax and Devin in Z'hart City, and now Vivían. *I'm putting a stop to this.*

It's at this point that Remus steps forward and places an armored hand on my shoulder. "I— Fight— Too— " he strains to say. "Better— Chance—"

There's a beat of hope. I grin at him as he gives me a nod of solidarity. Remus has already demonstrated mastery of the armor, so I feel an overwhelming surge of inspiration. *We can do this!*

"Eyyeah!" Devin says in encouragement. "After seeing Remus kick some ass, they should have a chance."

"Leave one of the bikes for us," I say. "We'll try to hold them for fifteen minutes. That should be enough time to get to the bikes and get out of here. We'll follow as soon as we can."

The others nod reluctantly as Abrax says, "Tálir, do not

underestimate him. The powers at his disposal are far beyond anything you and Remus currently have."

Despite his concern, Abrax's eyes reflect a solemn acceptance as he limps towards me. His left hand squeezes my right pauldron before I push it aside and embrace him. It's not a goodbye, but I do it out of fear that I may not survive. Abrax pats my back, sensing my trepidation. It's almost fatherly the way he tries to calm my nerves. We let go of each other quickly.

"Remus," Aida says softly as she approaches him. "Be careful. I want both of us to be there when we take down Centum."

Remus smiles and gently caresses her chin, suppressing the pain evident on his face. Aida's dark eyes close as his touch soothes her. Devin and Vyck say nothing but they both clasp us on our armored forearms in an old gesture of respect.

Everyone starts to head in the direction of the eastern garage of the village. Everyone except Sarina.

She puts a hand on her hip and regards me angrily. "You're too stubborn for your own good, Tálir," she says. Her nose wrinkles and her lips purse.

I smirk. "I was going to say the same thing about you. Take care of the others, will you? They listen to you more than me sometimes."

Gently, I catch her right hand and very quickly place something in her palm; closing her fingers tightly around it. Something I've wanted her to have, but it's also something she deserves. Glimpsing it, Sarina opens her mouth to say something, but stops. I know what she wants to say, but I also know why she doesn't. It's like if she says it it'll spell permanent doom upon me. It'll be my final knell for failure. So she says nothing, and turns away from me.

"Sarina," I say quietly as she pauses.

With my hand still wrapped around hers, I pull her towards me. The instincts in my heart take over. I kiss her.

Her lips are soft and sweet in spite of everything, and her skin smells of charcoal. I place an armored hand softly against the back of her head. Sarina's fingers trace down my jaw as if to pull my face closer. Time seems to stop as we're rooted in each other's arms, all noise dies away. I want to stay frozen here.

Sarina pulls away with an arched eyebrow. I give her a thin smile as I let her go. She punches me lightly on my breastplate before saying, "There's your inspiration, Maven Knight."

Before I can say another word, she runs off in the direction of the village outskirts. I still feel rooted on the spot, my heart pounding in my chest. I feel ready, determined to win. I turn and see Remus raising his eyebrow at me in surprise.

"Shut up," I chuckle lightly.

Remus shrugs but says nothing as we both turn to face the incoming massacre. In the malicious darkness that approaches us, the light is present. I have Remus at my side. I have my friends waiting for me when I return. So I prepare to win.

CHAPTER 43

Tálir

Remnant Rematch

AN AURA OF POWER is present in the air, thicker than the heat of the fires around us. It bears down upon me like crushing water, making me shrink in size and significance.

Remus and I remain stationed in the ritual pit as the Remnant approaches us. It's an optimal arena. Fires are lit, the ground is uneven, the diameter is large, and we're fenced in by huts and shacks. We both load fresh kryos into our suits in preparation. The warmth of the magic flows through my legs, chest, and arms.

The morning sun peeks faintly over the mountains. But an indistinct cloud of darkness seems to be growing even as the sun rises. Our battlefield is set and our timer begins counting down. The

Roil is coming and the group needs as much time as we can give them.

There's movement from within the village. The screams have died down. A haze of smoke obscures the street leading into the pit. Someone moves ethereally from the dark cloud. He walks towards us; his steps are emphasized by undeniable swagger. Clearing the smog, I can see the cold arrogance etched on his face.

Septem walks into the pit followed by four other members of the Remnant. His sword is sheathed on his back, but I can see tendrils of ruby energy spark from his fingers. Septem's long hair is pulled back into a topknot, and his gaunt face is smeared with blood and soot.

The others wear similar outfits. Long, leather jackets atop Maven pauldrons, breastplates, and gauntlets. Pride grows in me, for at least Remus and I possess *full* suits of armor. Though he brought only four with him, I assume the other warriors of the Remnant are scouring the northern section.

They walk into the pit cautiously, but Septem remains unsurprised to see us. "It seems like I always find you at the right time, Tálir," Septem comments as he stops twenty meters from us. "Still, I have to commend you for wanting to face me again. After last time, I'm surprised you didn't crawl away like a little worm and let Abrax fight me instead."

The Remnant warriors start taking positions to try and surround us. There is a flash of light, and one of the warriors is blasted backwards—his armor singed and his body unmoving. I see

Remus' armored palm sizzling with steam. I snort in surprise. He wasn't kidding when he said he'd provide support.

"No— Sneaking—" Remus grunts, his eyes reflecting intense focus. "You— And— Us—"

"It's about time we settled our score, Septem," I add with a tinge of eagerness. "I feel like I owe you an ass kicking after our skirmish in the catacombs."

"I wouldn't call that a skirmish, Tálir," Septem derides taciturnly. His green eyes reflect impatience. "You are a child playing dress up compared to me. You think a few weeks of training make you a Maven? Romulus was just as naïve. And just as stupid."

My anger bubbles up inside my chest, and I feel a similar sense of humiliation. Like before, my singular desire is to fully disprove his allegations and make him eat his own words. I feel defiant of everything he said, and I know just how to prove him wrong.

Septem revels in his status, and therefore will be bound to defend his honor if challenged. His entitled sense of self makes him just as susceptible to goading. All I need to do is find the right words. Catching him off guard is my only solution to defeating him.

"The last time I saw you, your ass was kicked just as bad as mine," I say slyly, giving him a grin. "Abrax showed me just how insignificant *you* are."

His expression remains nonchalant as I speak to him, but I can see his body beginning to tense up. *He's competitive.* I see that now. He wants to be better than Abrax. Better than my father. Perhaps even better than Centum. But right now, all he wants to do is prove that he's better than me.

"Abrax merely had the element of surprise," Septem says, folding his arms across his chest. "I underestimated him, but I've learned my lesson. There won't be any mistakes when I face him this time."

"And what makes you think we'll just let you get to him?" I retort, cocking my head.

There's a chilling pause. The pandemonium has all but died away. Shadows start spreading more rapidly over the horizon far beyond the mountains. We have maybe ten more minutes before the Roil hits. I have to defeat Septem in that time.

I take in my surroundings for any advantage I might have over him—or he over me. Septem is unfamiliar with the terrain, but I doubt that'll be enough. Remus and I will have to use raw power to beat him.

"You don't seem to understand the situation, Tálir," Septem says with a snort. "You may have us occupied, but the others are scouring this place for your companions. You can't run from us this time."

The three other Remnant warriors start to converge on us. Two males and one female. Ruby magic forms in their hands as they advance.

"I only have one more question, Septem," I say, stalling for one more moment. "Why us? Why try to kill us in the Pyrack and in Z'hart City?"

For the first time, I see a faint sense of emotion on his face. He's surprised as he replies coldly, "It was never about you, Tálir. It was about Sarina. Centum wanted her for some elaborate plan, and I decided to not waste resources. The rest of you were just collateral."

I look at him in confusion. "So you disobeyed Centum?"

"No," Septem says. "I just… trimmed the excess. We all have our agendas. And mine currently is to recover the Tome. Which I'll take from your corpse."

The three warriors suddenly unleash Streams of ruby energy. I'm too slow to react, but Remus responds instead. A massive Shield envelops us like a barrier as the crimson magic smashes against it. My helmet slithers over my face, but Remus remains helmetless. I waste no time and roll from underneath it, sending a Blaze to catch one of the males in the chest. In a shower of sparks he's blasted backwards and his body slumps meters from Septem's feet.

The female launches a fiery Discus at me as I stand defensively. A Shield generates on my arm to block it, but I underestimate the power yet again. Her energy smashes mine apart and I stumble backwards. She advances, but I recover quickly. Channeling *80%*, I hurl a Discus at her but she sidesteps and sends one in return. She's fast. I have to be faster.

Rolling to the side to avoid her magic, I stay rooted on one knee and raise both hands. Two Streams fly towards her. My kryo charge is now at *85%*. I'm getting better at managing the usage. She blocks with a ruby Shield and keeps advancing. In quick succession, I release four separate Streams. As I suspected, she's fast enough to dodge each of them. But I'm ready and taking a play from Remus' book.

With an *88%* charge, I fire a Blaze from my palm at the ground where her feet will land. Like stepping on a mine, the soil beneath her left foot explodes in sage flames. A shriek of pain escapes her as she's hurled several yards away and into a shack. Her body smashes into it as the shack practically caves in on her. After a moment, she moves no longer.

I turn to see Remus similarly defeating his attacker with a Blaze, burning a hole through the man's stomach. Chills run down my spine at the aloofness in his eyes. He's barely wasted any energy. Remus gives me a nod as we both turn to face Septem.

Meters from us, he walks forward with a hint of swagger as a helmet folds over his face. Drawing his sword, I can almost feel the surge of energy as the ruby flames ignite across the blade. My heart pounds with fear. But I mustn't let it obscure my focus. We can do this.

Focusing my energy, I generate two orbs within my palms. I stare at him intensely. Even under his helm I can sense a measure of malice. I hurl the Discuses at him as Remus unleashes a Stream.

Twirling his blade, he parries and absorbs our magic before unleashing his own energy towards me. The wave of ruby magic flies towards my face, and instinctively I duck underneath it. Moving towards him, I extend my fingers and send a Stream at his torso.

On the defensive, Septem starts weaving and slashing his sword to deflect my attacks. Even Remus' assaults can't pierce his defense. His speed is astounding; it's as if he knows the exact spot where each Stream will hit. Part of me is both impressed and envious of his mastery.

"Come now," Septem calls through his helmet as he parries another Stream. "I expected this pathetic power from Tálir, but not you Remus. Impress me!"

A Blaze soars from Remus' left hand in response, only to be blocked by a combination of Shield and sword. I can see Remus getting just as frustrated as I. We keep pushing, hitting him from different sides. Improvising our attacks. But Septem stands firm.

However, he begins to go on the offensive. Faster than I anticipated, he unleashes several Discuses that hurl towards me. Trepidation slows my movements. Using both arms, I use a Shield to block the ruby orbs but it fails. After two hit, the Shield crumbles and another Discus hits me in the chest.

Flying backwards, I crash into several crates stacked along the perimeter of the pit. Pain wells all throughout my body despite the armor amplifying my physical prowess. My ears are ringing and my chest burns. The armor starts to feel sluggish and the HUD reads: *Armor Integrity: 27%*. Dazed, I struggle to stand up as I catch a glimpse of the duel.

Remus and Septem charge at one another like bulls. The fiery sword in Septem's hand prepares to swing down on Remus. He sidesteps and uses a Stream to blast Septem backwards. Remus hits him again with another Stream before blocking Septem's counter. My dark-haired companion even manages to deflect a sword swing with a

Shield. Remus has him on the ropes.

Even through everything, I can see a hint of unease etched in Septem's features. Remus blocks another sword swing before blasting him backwards again. Still on his feet, Septem remains aloof but flourishes his sword cautiously.

I stand and prepare to enter the fray. Now on the defensive, Septem will be more vulnerable when facing the pair of us. He's underestimated us, and I feel my confidence growing. We can beat him. *I* can beat him.

With a *46%* charge, I send a Stream at Septem as Remus rushes forward. Something ominous creeps up my spine though. At the height of his charge, Remus hurls a Discus at Septem who bats it aside casually before sidestepping. My heart skips a beat. Upon sidestepping, Septem pushes Remus into the path of my Stream. Energy strikes armor.

Caught wholly unprepared, Remus is flung a meter back into the ground. Septem wastes no time. With Remus on the ground, he stabs his sword directly into Remus' stomach. The flaming blade sinks through the armor and into his gut.

"REMUS!" I shout, rushing towards them. Remus spits up blood.

Rage and fear take hold of me. I can't fight it, for that's who I am. Who I'll always be. Passionate about those I care about. I think about the Itinerant Mind lesson, but it seems like a long forgotten memory. All I can think about is killing Septem.

Blinding anger fuels me as I direct two Streams at Septem as I charge. He bats them aside with ease. Faster than I anticipated, he swings his sword like a club and sends several waves of energy at me. Panicked by his ferocity, I place my forearms together and form a large Shield in front of me. The magic smashes into my Shield, sending sparks and causing me to slide backwards. My Shield crumbles, but I generate another to replace it. I focus my rage into the barrier, and I feel it draining more energy to stay intact. But then I realize something.

My HUD indicates a *26% Kryo Charge* and dropping. Dread clutches my chest. Septem has been forcing me to use more energy than he. Here I am, barely holding on with the last of my reserves. In the back of my head I can almost hear Abrax scolding me.

You were supposed to be serene and smart, not brash and stupid.

Before I can bolster my Shield, Septem closes the final meters between us and stabs his sword into my energy barrier. There's a screeching ring in my ears, and my arms feel like they're about to catch aflame.

Time slows as I look through the transparent energy. Remus is on one knee and his armor is burned and bloody. He tries but fails to harness his magic. We look at each other.

"GO REMUS!" I yell through the clash of energy. "I'LL HOLD HIM OFF! RUN!"

Deep in his eyes, he doesn't want to. He wants to stay by my side until the end. But in his condition, I know he wants to see Aida one last time. Just like I want to see Sarina one more time before the end. But it's no longer about what I want. It's about what I *need* to do.

Septem continues to press into my energy, and it allows Remus to escape. The Shield shatters like a pane of glass, and I can feel the last of my energy fade.

Abrax, I say to myself solemnly. *I failed you.*

Septem's flaming sword continues towards me—cutting between my bracers and piercing into my breastplate. There's a flash of light, a deafening ring, and I feel as if I've been hit by a cannonball. Burning pain wells within my chest, and I let out a scream of agony as it engulfs my entire body.

Then it stops. Septem pulls the blade from my chest and steps back. My body goes numb and I fall to the side. Something warm seeps from my chest as my vision begins to grow dark. I look up.

Septem stands above me. His helmet retracts to reveal his face, emotionless but clearly unsure of what to do next. His gaze turns to the sky and I see it. The Roil. A dark cloud of Nanites billows over the mountains and approaches us. A few minutes away at most.

There's indecisiveness in Septem's green eyes. He wants to pursue Remus to the others. But he's also aware of the Roil on his heels. I feel cold as I watch the man I loathe, helpless in the proverbial shadow.

My vision fades. In the coldness that takes me, there's one warmth that comforts me. I think of Sarina. For the first time in a long while, my mind is at peace.

CHAPTER 44

Sarina

At Our Parting

"LET'S GET THESE THINGS STARTED!" I call out as we finish packing the rest of our equipment into the repulsorcart.

The garage is a crude thing, not even completely walled in. We reached the bikes after a few minutes, but it's taken some time to load everything. Vyck and Devin work quickly to prep the bikes while Abrax tends to Vivían. She's still unconscious, but stable.

Aida and I hook up the cart to the back of a bike as Devin preps all of the engines. Anxiety builds within me. Amidst the screams and explosions, the faint *hiss* of the Roil can be heard in the distance. I reckon it's perhaps five minutes away from engulfing the canyon. My heart pounds in my chest, and I can feel my body starting to stress.

There's been no sign of Remus and Tálir, and I'm starting to fear for the worst. They should be here by now.

"Come on!" Vyck says in a hurried voice. "Everyone get on a bike. We need to get out of here!"

We push the hovering bikes out of the garage and into the open space. We're at the edge of the village, and we have a clear shot to flee through the winding paths of the canyon.

Propping Vivían in front of him on the bike, Vyck situates himself and revs the engine. The hissing grows louder, and I glance over my shoulder to see the Nanite storm creeping over the mountain. The Roil has arrived.

"What about Tálir and Remus?" I ask, my voice noting trepidation. "They should be here by now!"

"We're leaving them a bike!" Devin says desperately. "That's all we can do now. Come on, Sarina. Hop on."

I hesitate for a moment. A noise rouses me. I turn to look again and see the Remnant transport taking off and fleeing towards the western part of the canyon—away from the Roil. After a moment, it's gone. They chose to flee rather than pursue us.

For some strange reason, I feel an ominous sense of dread at seeing the transport flee. But I don't have time to dwell on it, and I turn my attention back to the group. I prepare to clamber unto Devin's bike.

"Aida—" someone calls weakly from behind us.

Everyone turns suddenly to see Remus limping from within

the village—his hand pressed against his armored stomach. I feel a wave of horror as I see the puncture mark of a sword—blood seeps from under his hand. Aida immediately rushes towards him, taking his arm over her shoulder as he almost collapses. Something portentous is in Remus' eyes. It's a look of surrender.

"Where's Tálir?" I ask desperately, nearly running towards him.

He gives me a defeated glance. "Don't— Know—" Remus sputters weakly. "Septem— Beat— Him—"

I feel a mixture of emotions upon hearing that news. Apprehension, anger, and confusion swirl within me like a typhoon. My eyes sting and I fight back the tears. *No! He can't be dead!* But deep in my heart, I know something terrible has happened. Tálir would've been here along with Remus. Septem defeated him. And Remus fled.

"Why did you leave him?!" I nearly scream. Aida makes a calming gesture to me.

"He— Told— Me—" Remus replies weakly. His breaths are ragged. "Told— Me— To—"

I bite my lip bitterly. *You noble idiot, Tálir!* He'd chosen to sacrifice himself to let Remus see Aida one last time. I admire and hate him at the same time. Hollowness eats at me. The morning sun has been entirely eclipsed by the Roil, and the world takes a shade of gray.

"Remus," Aida says weakly, her eyes glinting with tears. "You'll be alright. We just need to get you to shelter and we can—"

"No—" he coughs; traces of blood can be seen in his mouth.

"I'm— Done—"

"Don't talk like that," Aida says, her voice cracking. "I can stop the bleeding."

"No— Time—" he mutters as his legs give way and Aida lowers him to a kneeling position. "Roil— Too— Fast—"

Devin gets off the bike and starts to move towards him. "Shut up, you damn fool. You're coming with us."

Remus' bloody left hand generates a faint cackle of energy, stopping Devin mid-stride. The wind is starting to pick up, causing the makeshift tents to flap. The Roil has completely swallowed the mountain as it starts to seep into the canyon. I estimate we have a minute before it's upon us.

At its current speed, I don't think we can outrun it. My body tenses with apprehension. Unless there's a way to slow the Roil.

"I— Cover— Escape—" Remus strains to say. A grimace forms on his pale face. "Can— Hold— Off— Roil —"

"Remus, please!" Aida pleads, putting her hand to his bearded face. "Don't do this, I can still save you!"

Remus gives her a genuine smile, and I can see tears welling in his eyes. "You— Already— Did—"

I feel my heart sink in my chest, and I can detect everyone else's sense of dread. Time seems to slow as Remus gazes at Aida, as if trying to memorize her face. He then presses his forehead to hers and closes his eyes, his matted black hair falling into both their faces.

It's hard to hold back the welling emotion watching Remus say a farewell to the woman he loves. Upon seeing Aida cry as he kisses her, I can't hold my tears any further. They run down my cheeks as someone approaches me from behind. Devin's hand gently grips my shoulder. I look at him, and his expression is sincere. From the corner of my eye, I see Vyck bow his head.

There's emptiness in my heart. Tálir is gone, and now Remus is spelling his own death. Our world seems so dark at this moment. Like all hope has been sapped away. The man I care about is gone, and another one prepares to take those steps.

"We'll— Meet— Again—" Remus says quietly, opening his eyes. "Aida—"

Aida says nothing, but she cups his bearded face in her hands and kisses him one last time.

"You have the true heart of a Maven Knight, lad," Abrax says as strongly as he can. "You are more worthy of that title than most."

Remus looks at the old man with an honored glance before nodding with respect. His eyes find mine, and a story can be summarized by the look he gives. A look of warning, respect, and a deep remorse. Remus' eyes tell me how sorry he is about Tálir's choice.

Before I can respond, Remus stands up and starts to back away from us. A look of calm determination is etched on his face, and he removes the kryos from each gauntlet. The marble-sized crystals shine faintly in the shade of the storm. He holds a kryo in each hand as he turns towards the incoming Roil.

"Go—" he grunts, looking over his shoulder. "GO!"

Aida gives one last look at him before turning to flee as the rest of us follow suite. We all board the repulsorbikes as the engines whine. I board Devin's bike and tuck *Silverlight* into my belt. Sand kicks up underneath the vehicles as they take off. As the bikes speed away from the village, I look over my shoulder and see a heroic sight.

Remus smacks his palms together, seemingly crushing the kryos and unleashing a massive flash of emerald light. *He's using them without the conduits!* I can see every inch of armor glow the same shade as the magic stones. Sage bolts of electricity erupt from the suit, arcing into the air and striking the ground. He looks almost like an ethereal being; the glowing deity in the darkness. As if the Sage God himself stands to protect us.

There's a loud *bang*, and a wall of energy erupts in front of him as he splays his arms. The wall stretches to barricade the entire width of the canyon and raises high into the air. The sage energy is almost the size of a tower in Z'hart City. It's a magnificent sight.

As the Roil slams into the energy barrier… it holds, miraculously. The bikes gain nearly a kilometer before I see it start to falter. Even at our distance, the canyon echoes everything. There is a prolonged yell, an electrical *hiss*, and then the thunder of an explosion. Emerald fire subsumes Remus, and he vanishes.

CHAPTER 45

Sarina

Light in the Darkness

STILLNESS IS IN THE AIR despite the wind blowing into my face. Everything seems quiet—I can barely hear the whine of the bike's engines. No one speaks. I can feel the hollowness return to my chest, but it's no longer spurred by guilt or regret. It's filled with sadness.

I'm on the rear of the repulsorbike as Devin currently steers the vehicle through the canyon. He says nothing; his focus is on guiding the bike through the veering paths. I look back and see the blistering cloud of emerald energy form into a mushroom. Expanding over the canyon walls, the fire looks like it's expanding as a flower blooms in spring. A howl echoes through the canyon. It gradually dissipates as the Nanite swarm blows through it. And although the Roil is pursuing us, Remus' sacrifice delayed it long enough for us to escape its reach.

The morning sun climbs into the cloudless blue sky, untouched by the Roil, as we exit the crags. The maroon stone blends seamlessly with the blazing light from the sun. As if it's upon a canvass, the crags smear into the blue skyline like acrylic paints.

We're safe from the storm, the Crimsons, and the Remnant because of Remus. Although I feel immense gratitude, I also feel the emptiness of loss. He gave his life to save us. To save Aida. I can still feel the tears in my eyes, and they continue to run down my cheeks. The wind blows them away.

As the emerald fireball vanishes and the Roil grows distant, I reflect on the cost of our journey.

Vivían's torture, Abrax's wounds, Tálir and Remus' sacrifice… I realize that none of us will make it through without loss, without hardship. We are mortal individuals after all, and there can be no success without hardship. They have all taught me that throughout this journey. I can feel their pain and their loss, for they are more than just friends.

Our struggles are shared. Our successes are shared. And our destinies are shared. In my mind, that makes us stronger than friends. It makes us family. I never would've thought it possible, forming such bonds with people I've known for a short time. But life changing experiences let people grow together, not just individually.

I should've realized this long ago, when I chose to fight my battles on my own. They share that battle with me, just as I share theirs. In this moment of darkness, when all hope seems lost, they are the light. To defeat that darkness, I must cling to the light no matter what.

In the midst of the emptiness, I feel a sudden surge of determination. I won't abandon hope. The hope that we can bring Septem, Centum, and the entire damned Remnant to justice for the pain they've caused. Not just for us, but for the world.

But for now, we must flee to safety from the Roil, regroup, and recover. Traumas will need to be healed, and wounds will be mended. But then we will fight back. We'll fight back with the ferocity of a pride of lions—a pack of wolves. I will lead the others to defeat Centum, find Providence, and save this world. We won't cower next time.

The bikes finally break through the crags and we enter an expansive valley within the Marün Canyons. Opening my palm slightly, I glance at the parting gift Tálir gave to me.

A single kryo shard. His legacy passed to me.

I close my eyes as tears streak down my cheeks. My palm closes tightly around the kryo and I bring it to my mouth—kissing it as a type of promise.

The quest for Providence is still present in my mind. As it is in everyone else's. But I suspect that our journey there has just begun. We will have to battle the Remnant harder and more frequently in the future to come. Alliances will need to be made if we're to fight them, and all of us will need to grow as the journey continues. But a spark of faith ignites within me.

So, I make a solemn promise. Rescue Sahari and all of Z'hart. Defend my friends. Defeat the Remnant. Save those who need me. Save the world. Protect as a Maven Knight would do.

END BOOK 1

INDEX

The Arc: the common religion worshiped by the three nations. Belief revolves around the benevolent and life giving Sage God and avoiding punishment in the various eternal Hells.

Asi: a massive country of land exclusively inhabited by Outlanders thousands of kilometers east of the three nations.

Avah: meaning "hunter" in Outspeak.

Avah'kal: meaning "hunting dog" in Outspeak.

Bim: meaning "leave" in Outspeak.

Blaze: Form IV of the kryo magic system. Output must be 75% to 100% for this Form. Blaze is the first lethal kryo Form and appears as a bright flash followed by a large burst of energy. It cannot be blocked by any other Form.

Centum (title): the Maven title that means "First Master" and is bestowed upon the leader of the Remnant Order.

Confit: meaning "harm" in Outspeak.

The Crimson Cross: a clan of Outlanders who worship the religion of the Way of the Cross. Cannibals and pyromaniacs, the Crimsons are a brutal and aggressive clan who venture into the three nations.

Cycle: the name for a hundred year timespan after the Ending.

Det: meaning "prison" in Outspeak.

Deta: meaning "prisoner" in Outspeak.

Discus: Form III of the kryo magic system. 50% to 75% output for this. Discus can only be deflected by Stream and other Discuses. This kryo form cannot be shattered or destroyed once thrown, it must hit or dissipate.

The Domain: the universal governance of the Old World. Made up of hundreds of different races, cultures, and religions, the Domain thrived for centuries. The Maven Knights were born of this governance as their marshals of order.

The Ending: a worldwide catastrophe that ruined all civilization and nearly exterminated humanity. A sizeable population survived and started to rebuild the New World in the Cycles after the Ending.

Erron's Ville: a small town in the middle of the Pyrack desert. Serving as a salvage market and a supply stop for convoys, this simple town is the home of Tálir.

First Rule: the kryo gem has a finite amount of energy.

Frítolö (Free-toh-lo): an Insurgent code word that means "brother". This is issued along with a hand gesture to symbolize Insurgent solidarity.

Hara: meaning "in order to" in Outspeak.

Imperials: the royal military guild within the nation of Z'hart. Garbed in silver armor and violet capes, these soldiers police the nation and answer only to the ruler of Z'hart.

Insurgents: a band of underworld rebels based in Z'hart City who were spawned to fight against corruption. Spreading to all nations, their overall goal is to stop the corruption of the Remnant.

Iri: meaning "man" in Outspeak.

Iri'tah: meaning "man of Cross" in Outspeak.

Ita: meaning "woman" in Outspeak.

Kompi: meaning "to complete" or "to finish" in Outspeak.

Kryo (Cry-oh): the Maven title for the magic gems that power their armor and weapons. A finite source of magic, the gems grow from mounds in the earth. They also come in different colors and power capabilities.

Ky: meaning "dog" in Outspeak.

Kysh: meaning "fresh" in Outspeak.

Leir'tah (title): the Crimson title that means "Shepherd of the Cross".

Li: meaning "take" in Outspeak.

The Marün Canyons: an expansive range of interconnecting canyons and valleys in the far eastern Outlands. The new home of the roaming Crimson Cross clan.

Maven Knight (May-ven): the legendary marshals of the Domain and masters of the kryo magic. Despite nearly being wiped out a millennium ago, their technology, powers, and culture have survived in the form of the Remnant.

Me'a: meaning "meat" in Outspeak.

Na: meaning "no" in Outspeak.

The Night Sea: a large body of water in the Outlands near the Marün Canyons. Polluted and full of bio luminescent algae, the Night Sea is a wondrous landmark but lethal to humans.

Numeron: an ancient dialect referring to one's title in the Maven Order. This is used when giving titles to various "masters" in Maven culture.

Ones of Aster: a sub-sect of Maven Knights who seek to bring chaos and destruction to Pan'gea.

O'rah: meaning "to the" in Outspeak.

O'ran (Oh-rahn): one of the three nations located in the far north of Pan'gea. Known for their abundance of crops and fruit. O'ran and Z'hart are in the midst of a tense trade war since heavy tariffs were imposed both on ore and crops.

Oreing: the economic standard coin of Pan'gea.

Outspeak: the common language of the Outlanders.

Pan'gea: the massive continent of the New World that is home to the three nations and the land of Asi.

Pin: meaning "mean" in Outspeak.

Pits: a sinkhole-like area where excess salvage and junk are taken to be melted down. With the work being grueling and dangerous, pits are normally where slaves or prisoners are sent to serve their sentences.

Providence: a mythical location said to be the last fortress of the ancient Domain governance. It is unknown whether or not this place is a bastion of treasure, an armory, or a weapon.

The Pyrack: an expansive desert that expands from Z'hart's eastern and southern regions. Sparsely populated with small towns and salvage pits, the Pyrack is a place where most choose to live far from the concerns of the three nations.

The Remnant: an order dedicated to following the teachings and training of the Maven Order. Formed after the Ending, the Remnant trains new Maven Knights to reestablish them as the marshals of the New World.

Se'bau (Sey-bow): a Maven title for "apprentice".

Second Rule: magic energy can only be safely harnessed by Maven armor or weapons.

Sey: meaning "them" in Outspeak.

Shield: Form II of the kryo magic system. 25% to 50% kryo output is required for this Form. Shield can deflect Stream but Discus and Blaze will shatter the Shield due to concentrated kryo energy.

Silon: meaning "be quiet" in Outspeak.

Stream: Form I of the kryo magic system. Kryo output needs to be between 1% and 25%. Stream cannot break Shield, but if one is fast enough they can deflect or intercept Discus. All other Forms are unaffected by Stream.

Suzerain (Sue-zeh-rain): a Maven title that refers to a "master". In some Outlander dialects, the title translates roughly to "overlord".

Tah: meaning "Cross" in Outspeak.

Third Rule: never use a kryo without a conduit.

Tulock (Too-lock): one of the three nations in the southern regions of Pan'gea. With vast rolling plains and an overabundance of animals, the populations of Tulock are known for their industry in selling livestock. Constantly defending against Outlanders, Tulock is a much more aggressive nation than the other two.

Tus: meaning "us" in Outspeak.

Usta: meaning "we" in Outspeak.

Vapor Bay: a colony of thievery, piracy, and debauchery just outside Z'hart's northeastern border. A lakeside colony and outside the three nations, Vapor Bay serves as an ideal neutral ground for all people.

Vod: meaning "must be" in Outspeak.

Wave: Form VI of the kryo magic system.

Wek: meaning "awake" in Outspeak.

Y: meaning "and" in Outspeak.

Yen: meaning "pen" or "cage" in Outspeak.

Z'hart (Z-art): one of the three nations based in the central region of Pan'gea. Dozens of underground caverns and vast mountains provide Z'hart with an ore industry. Due to seasons of constant rain, the soil is left too muddy and weak to produce crops.

ACKNOWLEDGMENTS

I'M TRULY ASTONISHED. I've been writing stories for next to ten years, but I never actually thought I'd get one out beyond my desktop. Apprehension has been the biggest writer's block for the past three years since I drafted this story. But here it is and it's been quite the journey to get here.

So first and foremost, I would like to thank you, the reader, for giving me this chance. Thank you for your time, patience, and attention through this first tale of *The Maven Knight Trilogy*. Hope you're curious enough to see where this story goes.

Next, I'd like to thank Amazon and Kindle for providing me the tools necessary to self-publish.

But now, for the big shout outs.

Thank you to my parents as well as my brother Zachary. You're always being supportive and always giving me a spiritual reality check. I hope you found this tale better than that of "Roy" back in '10. Also, sorry that chapter about Marco didn't make it in to the final draft. Additional thanks to my extensive family all along the East Coast.

Thank you to my best buddy, and true king of the Brocean, Matthew Wyman. My partner in crime, my sparring pal, and my fandom brother. May Uthal the Barbarian and Argos the Swashbuckler forever dance to the music of sword fighting. My creativity is always fueled by our discussions and theories, hence why I bug you most days.

Thanks to my good friends Eddie, Will, and John for their wicked senses of humor as well as their sound tastes in literature. Thanks to my friend Cody, for you expanded my boundaries when it came to finding inspiration for story and characters through our many, many venting sessions. To my friend Jen, thanks for all the feedback, brainstorming, and theorizing regarding what makes or breaks a great female character. For my friend and coworker Linda, thank you for pushing me to publish on Amazon, it's something I'd never thought to do until you said something. Some shout outs to my pals Nick, Katie, Tanya, Wirth, Miles, and Charlotte. Our role-playing years back helped inspire me to hone character quirks, so I truly thank you.

Finally, I'd like to thank Megan Farley for giving me the final kick-in-the-rear to get this published. My artist and pseudo public relations handler, you've driven me to act on my passion. You had faith in this story before we even scratched the surface of our relationship, which showed me how willing you were to trust me. I'll never stop poking your brain for critiques. Love you mostest.

Blessings to all and hope to see you again for Book 2.

ABOUT THE AUTHOR

Matthew Romeo is the self-published author of *The Maven Knight*. He graduated from Randolph-Macon College in 2014 with a B/A in Communications. As vice president of the Broadcasting Club, he ran a podcast for science fiction and fantasy topics. His hobbies include: writing (obviously), drawing, martial arts, video games, tabletop role-playing games, and copiously editing his work. He lives in Richmond where he runs on coffee and pizza while writing the next novel.

Instagram: @housemontegue

To MY GREAT COWORKER
LINDA !

Matthew Murray

Made in the USA
Middletown, DE
23 December 2018